D0049386

NO LONGER PROPERTY OF
ANYTHINK LIBRARIES/
RANGEVIEW LIBRARY DISTRICT

Amira & Hamza

The War to Save the Worlds

Amira & Hamza

The War to Save the Worlds

SAMIRA AHMED

LITTLE, BROWN AND COMPANY
New York Boston

This book is a work of fiction. Names, characters, places, and incidents are the product of the author's imagination or are used fictitiously. Any resemblance to actual events, locales, or persons, living or dead, is coincidental.

Copyright © 2021 by Samira Ahmed
Illustrations © 2021 by Kim Ekdahl
Map illustration © 2021 by Kathleen Jennings

Cover art copyright © 2021 by Kim Ekdahl. Cover design by Karina Granda. Cover copyright © 2021 by Hachette Book Group, Inc.

Hachette Book Group supports the right to free expression and the value of copyright. The purpose of copyright is to encourage writers and artists to produce the creative works that enrich our culture.

The scanning, uploading, and distribution of this book without permission is a theft of the author's intellectual property. If you would like permission to use material from the book (other than for review purposes), please contact permissions@hbgusa.com. Thank you for your support of the author's rights.

Little, Brown and Company
Hachette Book Group
1290 Avenue of the Americas, New York, NY 10104
Visit us at LBYR.com

First Edition: September 2021

Little, Brown and Company is a division of Hachette Book Group, Inc. The Little, Brown name and logo are trademarks of Hachette Book Group, Inc.

The publisher is not responsible for websites (or their content) that are not owned by the publisher.

Library of Congress Cataloging-in-Publication Data
Names: Ahmed, Samira (Fiction writer), author.
Title: Amira & Hamza : the war to save the worlds / Samira Ahmed.
Other titles: Amira and Hamza
Description: First edition. | New York : Little, Brown and Company, 2021. |
Audience: Ages 8–12. | Summary: A genie informs twelve-year-old Amira and her younger brother Hamza that they are the chosen ones who must defeat a monstrous demon of Islamic folklore to save the Earth and a parallel dimension.
Identifiers: LCCN 2020043341 | ISBN 9780316540469 (hardcover) | ISBN 9780316540490 (ebook) | ISBN 9780316540476 (ebook other)
Subjects: CYAC: Brothers and sisters—Fiction. | Muslims—United States—Fiction. | Supernatural—Fiction. | Fate and fatalism—Fiction. | Good and evil—Fiction. | Chicago (Ill.)—Fiction.
Classification: LCC PZ7.1.A345 Am 2021 | DDC [Fic]—dc23
LC record available at https://lccn.loc.gov/2020043341

ISBNs: 978-0-316-54046-9 (hardcover), 978-0-316-54049-0 (ebook), 978-0-316-41661-0 (OwlCrate Jr.)

Printed in the United States of America

LSC-C

Printing 1, 2021

For Lena & Noah.
You are the magic that brought this story to life.

(You still can't have ice cream before bed, though.)

Contents

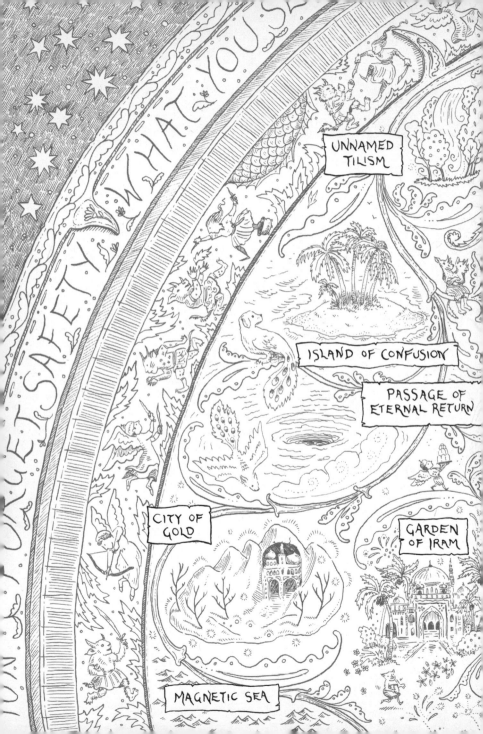

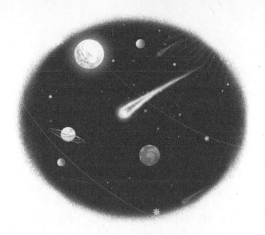

CHAPTER 1

When You Wish upon a Star

I DON'T BELIEVE IN WISHES.

Not anymore.

Wishes are for little kids and old-timey cartoon princesses and people who think a star in the night sky is actually a twinkly, enchanted jewel and not just a hot, glowing ball of gas.

I wasn't always like this. I used to make wishes when I blew out my birthday candles. And, maaaaybe, I still throw pennies into fountains (but I swear it's only for very special occasions). And if I ever see an actual shooting star and not a bright speck of light that turns out to be an airplane in Chicago's night sky, I might make a wish on it, because—hello!— seeing a shooting star in a city full of light pollution would basically be a miracle. But otherwise, I'm declaring that in this, my twelfth year of being alive, I am giving up on hoping and dreaming too hard for impossible things. Officially, precisely, this new life plan began yesterday afternoon at three PM, when I failed my karate test. *Again.*

This is the slow-motion rewind that's been looping through my brain every minute since then:

I tighten my yellow belt before stepping onto the mat. A mustache of salty sweat paints my upper lip. Sensei approaches, towering above me, eyebrows furrowed. "Focus, Amira. You got this. Third time's the charm."

I cringe. I've been trying to forget my other two failures to advance to orange belt. Ignoring my wobbly knees, I walk to the center of the mat and come eye to eye with my opponent. Or rather, eye to hairline, since I'm almost a full head taller than the little nine-year-old in front of me. Her hair is pulled back into a tight ponytail wrapped with a pink glittery bow. I got this. I smile. She scowls back. I swear she almost snarls.

It's the longest three minutes of my life.

"You hesitate, Amira. You make it too easy for your opponents to block you," Sensei told me after my humiliating defeat. "Attack. Imagine yourself defeating them."

"But how? How can I imagine something I can't do?" I asked.

Sensei gave me one of his enigmatic smiles. "Stop being scared of your own power. You have the tools, but you need to believe *here* and *here*." He pointed to his chest, then tapped his head.

It's the same old, out-of-tune song every adult sings: *Believe in yourself.* Fine. Okay. I do. My life is a believe-a-palooza. So why isn't it enough?

So, no more wishes on pretend stars. Technically, real stars are blazing spheres of plasma held together by gravity, which is not that different from us, really. I'm not giving up on *those* actual stars. Or the planets. Or the endless mysteries of the universe that I want to solve. Science is real. And failing is built into it. The scientific method expects failure. And failure is something I can succeed at.

Every evening this summer, I've hauled my telescope onto our roof-deck, taking notes on whatever celestial bodies I could find. Chicago's night skies are not the best for spotting constellations. But I did spy Mars once—a glowing red dot above the roofs in our Hyde Park neighborhood. Mostly, though, I study the moon—its craters, its bumps and bruises, its phases, how sometimes it looks like a wink and other times a sad, old face, full and hazy, low on the horizon over Lake Michigan. The moon is Earth's BFF. A friend we can count on to always be there.

All this lunar prep has been in anticipation of tonight. My single chance to experience a once-in-a-century, once-in-a-lifetime phenomenon: a supermoon, a blue moon, and a blood moon. All in one night. A celestial trifecta of awesomeness. An eclipse on the second full moon of the month *while* the moon is closer to us than at any other time in its orbit. It even looks red, hence the blood part. Personally, I think *blood moon* sounds a little gross, but it's not like I named it. Anyway, some ancients thought this rare event predicted the end of the world; some of them thought it gave people indigestion. Whatever it brings on, I am beyond excited. I may be full-on skeptical about the magical idea of believing in wishes, but the magic of science is real.

CHAPTER 2

Please Do Not Touch (I Mean It!)

"I WILL ANNIHILATE YOU!" I SCREAM AS A VOLLEY OF SMALL foam darts bounce off the back of my head. "Why did you bring that stupid gun to an eclipse-viewing party?" I growl at my younger brother, Hamza.

Hamza shoves his neon-green plastic toy into his backpack. "It's not a gun. Duh. It's a zombie bow-caster, and I hacked two different weapons to build it. It's genius."

"You're not going to be battling zombies for a telescope," I say.

"No," he says, "I'll be battling nerds, like, I dunno? My sister? Who dragged me away from a critical point in my Lego Millennium Falcon build to come see a bunch of used tools that belonged to dead Muslim astrologers."

I elbow him. "Dude, it's astronomy, not astrology. You know the difference, right?"

Hamza scoffs. "I totally know the difference."

"Oh yeah, what is it?"

He pauses for a second before answering. "One is about the study of the stars and planets, and the other is about...well...it's the study of the stars and planets but with zodiac symbols." One thing I *sometimes* kind of admire about my little brother—he never lets not knowing something prevent him from acting like he does. (But other times, it can be super annoying.)

"Ugh. Read a book, Hamz."

"That's enough, you two." Ummi whips her head around to deliver her Death Stare™. We had parked the car, and Ummi and Papa were walking ahead of us on the sidewalk, their arms linked, so they didn't catch Hamza's foam-dart assault. Since kindergarten, that look of hers has always stopped me cold, made me apologize for things I hadn't even done. But for some reason, it never works on Hamza. My dad once joked that my brother was made of Teflon, because everything slides right off him, especially rules and consequences. I kinda wish I was that way, too. But then again, my mom won't cook anything on a non-stick Teflon frying pan because she says it's toxic. So I guess there's that, at least.

"You know, there's this old desi legend Nani used to tell me and your auntie." My mom lowers her voice, making us hurry to catch up. "Bickering siblings must resolve their feuds or disputes before an eclipse passes. Or else."

"Or else what?" we respond in unison.

Ummi shrugs and exchanges one of *those* smiles with Papa—a parent-know-it-all grin annoying to kids across the world. Papa bends down and kisses her on the cheek. He's a foot taller and towers over our mom, but somehow she never seems small.

Papa turns, raises an eyebrow at Hamza. "I

wouldn't pick on your sister if I were you; she could knock you out with a couple of well-timed karate blows." I wince a little when Papa mentions karate.

"The Dojo Koan says she can use her karate only for the greater good," Hamza says, as if I need reminding about the oath I take every class.

"Trust me, little brother, kicking your butt *would* be for the greater good," I say, while my parents try to hide their laughter.

Hamza is, well, Hamza. He has been since birth, so I'm not going to let his Hamza-ness ruin tonight. I've been counting down the days since the Islamic Society of Ancient Astronomy announced this exhibit to coincide with its eclipse-viewing party. There's this medieval astrolabe made by al-Zarqali of Andalusia that is traveling to the United States for the first time. *Ever.* In, like, a thousand years. And I get to see it tonight. On the same night as the super blue blood moon. My nerd brain is ready to explode with excitement.

We stop in front of the Medinah Temple—a squat, ornate building crowned by two domes that supposedly look Middle Eastern, I guess? Every time I pass it, it always feels out of place amid the towering glass downtown skyscrapers. Papa once explained that it was constructed over a hundred years ago in a mash-up of different Islamic architectural styles— lots of intricate, floral-patterned grilles and geometric shapes. And even though Arabic script frames the giant entrance, it wasn't built by Arabs, North Africans, *or* Muslims, but by white Shriners. Or, as Ummi calls them, "people who freely appropriated other cultures and were probably wildly racist." The building was actually going to be demolished, but a year ago an interfaith nonprofit bought it to try to build something diverse and inclusive in a space that was once anything but.

As we enter the building, Hamza cranes his neck to glance upward at the calligraphy framing the doors. "What does the Arabic say again?"

I know the answer, but I'm distracted by the moon, which seems unusually luminescent in the not-quite-night sky. I check my watch. The time seems off. We shouldn't be able to see it like this, not yet.

"There is no God but God," our mom replies. "The start of the Shahadah? I can see those years of Islamic Sunday school have really paid off." Can a voice sound like a raised eyebrow? If so, that's what my mom's voice is right now.

I turn my attention away from the moon and to my family. "Can you imagine if actual Muslims wanted to build a building with the declaration of faith carved into it anywhere in America right now? People would totally say it was, like, terrorist headquarters."

My dad puts an arm around my shoulder and squeezes. "You're probably, right, kiddo. I wish it weren't true. I wish I could snap the racism out of this world. But you know you are loved, and you are enough, and the bigots of the world don't get to define us."

"Snapping away racists would have been an awesome use of the Infinity Stones!" Hamza says.

I shake my head a little, then look up at my dad and give him a small smile.

As we step through the entrance and into a grand

hall with an enormous rotunda, we are greeted by a life-size wooden statue of a brown-skinned man in painted robes and a turban holding a flute close to his mouth. Hamza reaches out and pulls a lever next to the machine before any of us can stop him—if there is a button to be pushed or a lever to be pulled, count on Hamza to do it. The statue's arm jerks upward, bringing the flute to its lips. Hamza and I both hop back in surprise. A hissing steam sound comes from inside, and a bright note soars out of the flute. The statue proceeds to play a short tune before stopping.

Our mom claps her hands. "How delightful." Then she reads out loud from the plaque at the foot of the automaton. "It's based on a design from the Banu Musa's *Book of Ingenious Devices*. They were brothers who were inventors and astronomers from the ninth century. It's likely the first programmable machine."

"Whoa. That is actually really cool," Hamza says, his mouth hanging open.

"Dude, shut your mouth. I can see bits of candy bar stuck in your molars. Gross."

Hamza play-punches me in the arm, and I retaliate, perhaps a little stronger than necessary. "Ow!" Hamza yelps. "Mom, did you see that?"

"Shhhh. You two. What did I tell you about the omen of bickering siblings? Don't make me unretire the get-along T-shirt." I can't believe she's threatening us with the consequence-of-last-resort so soon in the night. The get-along T-shirt is one of her proudest creations—a sewing machine Frankenstein's monster of two XXL white undershirts with two heads but also only two armholes. In first and third grades, Hamza and I would fight all the time, so Ummi would make us wear the joint shirt until we at least pretended to like each other.

We separate, and I head toward a display called Bayt al-Hikmah, or House of Wisdom. The placard says it was an institute for scholars and inventors in the eighth century in Baghdad. I scan the ancient, yellowed documents, and my eyes stop on a page of Arabic writing and what seem to be some calculations—*Kitab al-Jabr*—the book of al-Jabr, the father of algebra. "Al-Ja-br," I sound out the name.

"Al-ge-bra. No. Wait. Whoa! I could totally use this guy's help in math next year," I say aloud, and snort to myself.

I look up to make sure no one—especially not Hamza—heard me say that. God, I *am* a nerd. But Hamza's attention is absorbed by a spherical astrolabe—a brass globe with metal bands around it. I hear him mutter something about Magneto and reversing Earth's polarity. I shake my head. The kid is superpower obsessed.

I see my parents and some other adults heading for the roof, and I quickly join them. There's a tutorial on the use of the telescopes, and I don't want to miss anything. The telescopes we are using tonight are way more sophisticated than what I have at home. I practically float up the stairs. I wonder if this is what it feels like when adults say things like they're *giddy with excitement*. People are going to write about this night in astronomy books. Everywhere, in every country, millions, maybe billions, of people are talking about tonight's moon. And I get a front-row seat from the best viewing spot in this hemisphere.

The rooftop is packed with people, and we're all crowding toward the stage, where a round-faced, smiling auntie in a dark blue hijab decorated with constellations is welcoming us. My mom leans over and whispers in my ear, "Where's your brother?"

I shrug.

My dad tilts his head toward the door and raises an eyebrow. A sign for me to go find Hamza. Ugh. "I don't want to miss anything," I protest.

"It's okay, beta," my mom says, squeezing my hand. "The director is going to say a few words before they start the tutorial. You'll have time if you hurry."

I groan, loud enough for both of my parents to hear. I did not sign up to be my brother's babysitter. Especially for free.

I dash down the stairs back to the exhibit hall, which is pretty much empty now. I spy Hamza, bent over a small display case that is pushed up against the far wall as if a busy curator didn't know what to do with it.

I trudge over but stop short. Hamza has his back to me, so he hasn't seen me yet, but he's glancing around suspiciously. And then he opens the case and reaches in to pluck something out.

"What are you doing?" I yell.

Hamza doesn't react, gazing at the artifact in his hand.

I hurry to my brother's side, ready to lecture him, but when I look at the small object in his hands, I'm transfixed, too. Drawn to it. It's beautiful. "What is that?" I gasp.

"Al-Biruni's Box of the Moon," Hamza whispers back without taking his eyes off it. It's round and shiny—like a polished, circular jewel box. Unlike everything else in this exhibit, it's untarnished. It fits perfectly in Hamza's cupped palm.

I quickly read the museum note attached to its case:

> Built in approximately 1000 CE, al-Biruni's Box
> of the Moon was a wonder of its time. Its golden
> gears replicate the positions of the sun, moon,
> and Earth. The Box of the Moon is considered an
> early analog computer. Recovered from an ancient

shipwreck found in the Caspian Sea, the nature of the Box has baffled modern-day scientists because it was unaffected by the ravages of time or the corrosive effects of salt water. The alloys and materials used to make this miniature computer cannot be identified as any currently known to humans.

"They can't figure out how to make it work," Hamza says. "Serious bummer. Look at the tiny 3D moon, Earth, and sun—I bet they revolved around one another at some point. So awesome." It's weird, because I know he's excited about it, but his voice sounds automatic, like he's talking in his sleep.

I lean in to look closer. Hamza's right. On top of the gears lies a flat disc with etchings around the perimeter—almost like a platform for the tiny spheres. The largest globe—the one in the center of the disc and about the size of a mini-Gobstopper— is the sun. Earth, an M&M, is about halfway between the sun and the edge. The moon, a micro-Altoid, is in Earth's orbit.

It's mesmerizing.

I blink. Try to take my eyes off the Box, remembering why I came down here. We're going to miss the telescope tutorial. "Hamz, you need to put that back now. Ummi says you have to come upstairs."

"You go upstairs. I want to see if I can figure out how this works." Hamza takes a half step away from me.

I move closer to him. I can't explain why, but I want the Box. It *feels* like it's mine. "You're not supposed to take artifacts out of cases. I'm surprised alarms haven't gone off." I put my hand out.

Hamza shrinks back. I reach out. I know I shouldn't grab it. My brain is screaming at me to be careful, that it's a delicate artifact. But my hands act like they have a mind of their own and latch onto the Box of the Moon to snatch it away from Hamza.

"Let go!" Hamza yells.

"Give it! It's not yours."

We start a tug-of-war. *What am I doing? I need to stop. Why can't I stop myself?* Hamza pulls in one direction, and despite knowing I shouldn't, I jerk it in the opposite. I can feel my palms getting sweaty, and my face starts to flush. But I have to have it. I yank really hard but lose my footing, which throws Hamza off balance. Both of us fall down as the Box of the Moon—this ancient, invaluable object—arcs through the air and falls to the ground with a loud clatter as it skids across the floor.

The world screeches to a halt. My heart pounds in my ears. I shake myself out of my brain fuzziness, realizing what we've done. Even Hamza has to know how badly we've screwed up. I force myself to scramble across the floor and pick up the fragile, beautiful box with trembling fingers. I can't tell if Hamza is breathing. I can't even tell if I'm breathing. I turn it over, terrified that all the gears and the tiny celestial objects will fall out or that they've been shattered. I'm too afraid to look, but there's no other choice. We can't exactly pretend this didn't happen. There are probably security cameras in here.

But not only is everything intact, the gears are *moving.* The mini-Altoid moon is orbiting the M&M Earth.

Holy Newton's first law.

This thing hasn't worked for centuries, and now it's moving? I remember the stories Nani used to tell us—about how things would move around the veranda of their house in Hyderabad. How her mom thought it was jinn playing funny tricks. Goose bumps pop up all over my skin.

All the color drains from Hamza's face. He has to be thinking of the same story. He scooches closer to me and grabs the Box from my hands. "Maybe...we fixed it?" he says. "I'll put it back in the case. It's fine."

"What is wrong with you? You can't put it back without telling an adult what happened! We dropped an ancient artifact and probably wrecked it. I'm going to tell Ummi and Papa." I jump up and run for the stairs.

"Wait! Stop!" Hamza chases after me, but I have too big a lead and longer legs and can take the stairs two steps at a time.

I shove open the door and am blinded by a flash of crimson light. As I stop at the threshold and raise a hand to shield my eyes, Hamza charges into me. We both stumble onto the rooftop.

I open my eyes. It's dark as midnight.

All the adults are staring up at the sky, and none of them are moving.

The world around me slows down, like a scene in a movie when you know something terrible is about to happen but you can't stop it. I hear the muffled thud of my heart in my ears. I see my mom and try to get to her, but my limbs don't respond to my screams telling them to move. I call her name, but I can't even tell if any sound comes out of my mouth.

My mom turns her head toward me, her mouth open and her eyes wide. She smiles, but there's no comfort in it. Before I can scramble up, her knees buckle, and every single person standing there faints. But instead of collapsing like sacks of potatoes, they all gently fall to the floor of the roof like feathers wafting through the air.

The world jerks back to full speed. "Ummi! Papa!" I scream. I run and kneel by my mom's side, grabbing her wrist with my panicky fingers, feeling for a pulse like we learned in health class. Letting out a breath when I find one. "Ummi! Ummi! Wake up." Tears fill my eyes as I shake my mom's shoulder, then my dad's.

Is this a dream? This must be a dream. Because it can't be real.

"Amira—" Hamza pulls on my arm. "Amira."

"Hamza, run inside and find help. No. Wait. Grab Papa's phone and call 911."

"Amira, you—"

"Stop talking and do what I say!" I yell at my little brother.

But as I look up at him, I notice what he's staring at.

I tilt my head up toward the dark sky. A feeling like ice spreading under my skin makes me shiver. I stand up, and Hamza steps up next to me. A vise squeezes my heart.

A piece of the moon has cracked and is drifting away. It looks like it's moving at a snail's pace, but I know being able to see it move like that at all means it's hurtling through the sky, growing bigger. God, it's heading toward us. My eyes lock on the jagged puzzle piece of lunar rock, its edges slashing the night and making it bleed stars.

CHAPTER 3

That's No Moon!

WE NEED TO FIND SOME ADULT, SOME AWAKE ADULT, WHO
can tell us what's happening or…or…what we should
do. But how can anyone possibly know what to do
when the moon starts to break? I jerk Hamza's hand
and pull him past our parents, who are still unconscious with all the other sleeping people on the
rooftop.

My brain whirs with a million terrified thoughts,
but they all lead to this one: I have to get Hamza
somewhere safe. And suddenly, I can focus. I drag
him through the rooftop door, and we race down the
stairs, bursting into the empty exhibit hall. Panting,

heart racing, I pause for a second to look at Hamza, whose dark brown eyes are as wide as saucers. He's clutching the Box of the Moon to his chest with one hand like it's his favorite stuffie.

"Sis, what...what—"

"I don't know," I say. "But we have to find someone who does. C'mon." I don't want us to get separated, so I tighten my death grip around Hamza's wrist and drag us outside to see if there's, like, a cop or museum security. I'll take a crossing guard if they could help us. But help us...what?

The small side street is empty. Of the conscious, anyway. People are everywhere, but it's the same as on the roof, their bodies crumpled on the sidewalk in weird positions, like they're action figures that got caught in a playtime tornado of nursery school kids.

The sudden dark is quiet. Too quiet. I look down the block toward the normally busy avenue, and every car is stopped. There's no honking. No metal clank of wheels driving over uneven manhole covers. I don't feel the rumble of the El train. And why are there no planes? Oh my God. What…happened to all the planes? I think for a second that this must be a dream—a nightmare—one that feels so real you can't tell if you're really awake when you wake up or if you're waking up in the dream itself. But that broken piece of the moon, plunging through the blackness of space, looks like it's getting bigger, which means it's getting closer. Which means it's on a collision course with Earth.

"Oh God. We're going to die. This is how the dinosaurs went extinct," Hamza whispers. "A massive meteorite smashing into the planet. Da—"

"Don't you dare!" I turn to Hamza, my mouth agape. "You're going to have to put a dollar in the swear jar when we get home."

He rolls his eyes. "How was that a swear? I was about to say *dang* it, but you cut me off!"

I scoff. "You were so about to swear. I could tell."

"Only you would care about swearing during the end-time. Even Cap swore in *Endgame*."

"It's not the end of anything. No one is dying,

and…and…this…" I pause, searching for anything that sounds remotely possible. "This is probably from eating too many parathas."

"You're blaming Mom's parathas for the apocalypse? When she wakes up, she's totally sending you to boarding school in India."

I shake my head. "When I was studying the super blue blood moon, I read about an Indian superstition that chandra grahan—an eclipse—can cause indigestion. Maybe it's real, and this could be like a hallucination from that. That's the most logical explanation." I'm a big believer in logical explanations. Once, when I was stuck on a mapping problem in a geography unit, my teacher explained Occam's razor to me. When you're faced with a problem that could have multiple solutions, the simplest one is usually the right one. And in this case, a delusion based on overeating or food poisoning seems way more likely than…uh…the earth-shattering alternative. I guess?

Hamza has been looking up the whole time I've been talking. I don't think he's listening at all. But then he points one shaky finger at a bright object in the night sky while pulling at his *Star Wars* Death Star T-shirt. "That's no moon! The moon is breaking, and there's *also* a UFO. You still think this is indigestion? Indigestion makes you burp and can be cured by sticky pink medicine. I don't think *that—*" Now he waves at the thing with both hands, the thing that is not the moon but is speeding toward us. "*That* isn't a figment of my upset stomach!"

I fix my eyes on the shiny object that is much closer and much faster than the runaway chunk of moon. I blink. It looks like…a golden sofa? No, maybe a throne? What? Maybe Hamza's random, nonstop theory-spewing about the Marvel possibilities of branch realities, time-travel loops, and portals to other dimensions is…actually…real? Please, please let this be a bad dream, because a world created by Hamza's imagination would be terrifying.

We don't have time to debate reality right now. Because dream or not, I have to get us somewhere safe. Safer.

The flying golden throne (whoa, did I really say

that?) is getting closer, and I must be hallucinating, because I swear I see shadowy wisps that look like creatures sitting on it. But I blink again, and they're gone.

I spy a dumpster in front of the construction site across the street. I point it out to Hamza, who solemnly nods. For the first time in probably ever, neither of us has anything to say. We can't outrun that...that thing. But we have to at least try to hide.

We dash across the street and pull the large metal dumpster closer to the brick wall of the building behind it. The wheels squeak and screech. So much for stealth. We have no other choice, so I dive behind it, crouching low. Hamza shrugs off his backpack, dragging it behind him, so he can fit in the cramped space we've created.

"Did you see something sitting on that throne?" I ask Hamza.

"I thought I did—shimmery waves, like when you look at pavement on a super-hot summer day? But, like, only for a second?"

"Same. Weird, right?"

"Weird?" Hamza whisper-shouts. "Weird is Walter Paxson eating glue in second grade. Weird is people thinking salmon roe tastes good. This is way more than weird; it's…it's…"

"Freeze-your-blood terrifying." My voice is a scratch, barely a whisper.

Hamza inches closer to me until our shoulders touch. "I might have gone with 'nightmarish,' but blood-freezing terror is good, too." He looks at me with a small twinkle in his eye.

Then there's a piercing screech. Like a train coming to an emergency stop on metal tracks, making sparks fly.

I suck in my breath.

I peer around the dumpster and watch, mouth open, as the golden throne skids to a stop on the street. The throne is empty. Not even a glimmer of the creatures I glimpsed earlier. It's a bit hard to make out in the dark, but a bunch of black cauldron-looking pots are also behind it.

Then we hear indecipherable voices all talking over one another. And a thundering herd of footsteps.

Loud enough to wake the dead. Except everyone is still asleep.

Everyone but us.

A loud word I don't know the meaning of echoes through the still night: *Eest!*

It feels like hundreds of feet stomp to attention. Then silence.

I turn to Hamza, whose face is starting to resemble the yellow-green insides of a ripe avocado. Oh God. Please, please, don't let Hamza puke on me. If I'm about to die, I don't want to be vomited on, too. I give him a somewhat reassuring smile while also leaning out of hurling range. It might be the end of the world, but it doesn't mean I have to stop being practical. I want to whisper some encouraging words to Hamza, but all my words stick in my throat like a dry bone. Then we hear footsteps again.

Not the herd this time, only a couple. And they're getting closer. I still can't see any bodies, but the footfalls ring in my ears.

Hamza flattens himself on the ground to look

under the dumpster and then glances up at me. "It's ghosts?" he whispers. "Ghosts with loud feet?"

"Sssshhhh. They probably also have ears."

"No. No. No!" A booming, disembodied voice shouts into the dark. "Of course it was necessary to bring the army to meet them. This is the way it is done. This is how it was written."

A calmer voice answers. A voice like a frustrated kindergarten teacher trying to answer twenty questions all at once, but lower and more gravelly. "Yes, my Vizier. Yet it is merely two humans we are tasked to collect. Surely we don't need a hundred jinn brandishing swords to do that?"

Hamza grabs my knee, and I clamp my jaw shut to choke back a yelp.

"Did he say 'jinn'?" Hamza mouths.

I nod.

"With swords?" Hamza slashes an imaginary blade through the air.

I roll my eyes but nod again.

The louder, bossy voice roars again, "The Box of

the Moon has awakened. War is upon us. The Box is an instrument that must be protected at all costs. I will not chance it falling into the hands of our enemies."

I narrow my eyes at Hamza when he gives me a sheepish smile.

"I told you not to touch that thing," I snarl.

"Well, you shouldn't have grabbed it!" Hamza growls back.

I clap my hand over his mouth.

"Where'd you put it, anyway?" I ask my brother, and he silently points to his backpack.

We're doomed.

The footsteps move closer. Closer still. Then stop. Right in front of our dumpster.

I don't hear anything but a whoosh of air in my ears and the slow rise and fall of my chest.

I need to do something.

I have to do something.

Maybe a mawashi geri or an uraken sayu uchi? But my limbs are jelly, and how do I hit a ghost, anyway? I can barely hit a live human standing in front of me. I squeeze my eyes shut and remember Sensei's words. I have to believe in my power. I have power? I *have* power.

I hear a soft rustling and then the backpack being unzipped.

I open my eyes and whip my head around, but it's too late. Hamza is crouched like a spring, brandishing his zombie bowcaster. Before I can stop him, he pushes the dumpster forward and pops up, yelling, "Back off, foul ghost jinn!"

The words have barely left his mouth when he's lifted in the air and over the dumpster by an invisible force.

"Hamza!" I scream, pushing past the dumpster to see him floating vertically about ten feet above the ground.

"Let go of me," he shouts before unleashing a volley of foam darts into the empty space in front of him.

"Ow. Ow. Ow!" a voice howls as the darts bounce off the air.

Two...uh...things that look kind of like silver skewers appear in the air in front of Hamza.

"Don't make me a human kebab!" Hamza screams, dropping the bowcaster to shield his face.

I run toward Hamza, jumping in the air, trying to grab his foot, but something snatches me by the collar and pulls me up and away.

"Hold still, small, rambunctious human. This is for your own good," the annoyed kindergarten teacher voice says as the silver skewers shoot straight for Hamza's eyes.

CHAPTER 4

Bleary Eyes, Scared Hearts, Probably Gonna Lose

I SCREAM AND TWIST AND KICK AT THE DARKNESS. MY form is terrible, but Sensei never taught us katas while being *suspended in midair*. Still, I manage to kick some...thing, because the toe of my sneaker jerks back when I hit it. Which—ow!—this thing is muscly and obviously really tall if I hit it from this high up.

"Enough!" I can practically feel a gust of wind on my face as a loud voice booms in front of me.

I turn toward Hamza, who is wriggling and flailing in the air next to me, shouting Urdu swears.

"Hamza!" I yell. "Watch it."

"Cursing in Urdu doesn't count," Hamza snaps back. "Besides... a little busy over here trying not to get skewered."

"I didn't mean the swearing! I meant watch out for the pointy-stick thingy aiming for your eye."

"Shush, both of you," the louder voice booms again. "Or I *will* instruct the army to subdue you."

Hamza and I shut our mouths and stop moving. I do not want to be impaled by levitating skewers wielded by invisible creatures. And, wait, did the voice say *army*?

"My Vizier, perhaps a gentler approach?" the kindergarten teacher voice asks.

There's a harrumph, and I'm dropped to the ground.

"Ow!" I yell, standing up and rubbing my backside. "He said gentler."

Hamza is placed, standing up, on the ground next to me. He looks at me and grins like getting let down easier means he won the make-the-nightmare-voices-be-nicer-to-us game.

I open my mouth to speak, but before any words can come out, I see a flash of silver and feel something like a cool gel pen streaking my eyelid. I flinch, my eyelids trying to bat away the, uh, ink? What the...

"Hey," Hamza says, "stop with the eyeliner. Wait. Is this poison makeup?" Hamza squeezes his eyes shut and starts rubbing them.

My own eyes get watery, and as I blink away the tears, blurry shapes slowly come into view.

"Now, was that so bad?" the kindergarten-voiced, uh...person or whatever, who happens to be holding the silver skewers, asks.

My jaw drops, like, to the floor, exposing my tonsils to the world. My voice catches in my throat. I blink, then blink again. "Hamza. Hamza," I whisper, "open your eyes."

A creature—twice as big as the tallest person

I've ever met—is standing in front of the immense, ornate gold throne. He's dressed similarly to the men in the paintings in the exhibit—a fancy variation on the kurta pajamas we usually wear to Eid. A long navy-blue tunic of raw silk with a pattern of paisleys in gold embroidery, a white silken sash tied at his waist, fitted gold pants ending in maroon velvet khussa slippers with bronze-tipped ends that curl toward his ankles. The entire outfit is topped by a violet cloak with a band collar that reaches to his jaw.

He has a large face: wide nose and lips drawn into a forced smile. Oh, and he is blue. Bright, royal blue and semitransparent.

Hamza and I uncharacteristically grab for each other. So either this *is* an indigestion-fueled Aladdin genie nightmare or we're dead.

A hundred or more creatures flank his throne— all of them with skin, if you can call it skin, of varying shades of vivid blues, reds, oranges, and yellows. They're all ghostlike, their edges bleeding into the air in waves emanating from their bodies, like when you apply too much watercolor to a bumpy canvas.

This is not how I imagined death. I imagined it all light at the end of the tunnel and light as a feather and less Chicago street at night facing multi-colored...umm...creatures. No. I should call them what they are, even if the word scares me. They're jinn. The loud, bossy voice threatened us with an actual *jinn army*. So we have a lot more than words to be scared of.

We're all staring at one another. Not saying a word. *Awkward*. Finally, a goose-necked, long-armed, nearly translucent orange jinn—the one holding the silver skewers—steps toward us. Now that I can see them more clearly—they're not exactly like barbecue skewers—one end is shaped like a leaf and has an engraving on it. It makes me think of the old, tarnished silver kohl pot my nani used to keep on her dresser. She would dip a silver stick into the pot of black eyeliner to spread it across her lids.

The orange long-necked jinn is also wearing glasses. Thick black plastic, nerdy dad glasses. Hamza and I both lean back at the same time. The orange jinn clears his throat and raises his eyebrows (jinn have eyebrows, I guess?) at the Hulk-large blue jinn, who also clears his throat. I didn't realize that coming face-to-face with actual, real, live jinn involved this much mucus clearing.

"Oh...yes. Yes. Introductions. I am Abdul Rahman, jinn Vizier to the Emperor of Qaf, King of Kings, Ruler of the Eighteen Realms, Holder of the Peacock Throne, Protector of the World Between Worlds, the mighty Shahpal bin Shahrukh. I command battalions of his jinn army, some of whom you see before you. Fear not. We do not come to harm you, but to implore you for help." Simultaneously, the jinn around him take a knee and bow their heads when he speaks the emperor's name.

My eyebrows shoot up. WHAT? I mean, I know what jinn are—beings of smokeless fire. Besides Nani's tales of mysterious moving objects, my great uncle in India told me stories about jinn hauntings. How they shape-shift and can possess people and animals and even trees. After giving me a long grammar lesson about how the word *jinn* could be both singular and plural, a great aunt told me about an entire jinn city built in an abandoned well of her childhood home in Hyderabad. I was so freaked out I couldn't sleep the rest of the trip. I was only eight. Then, one of my cousins tried to make me feel better by telling me a story about a protector jinn that took the shape of a snake and slept under his bed. Did. Not. Work.

But an entire army of jinn? Shape-shifting fire demons with weapons? Not in stories, but in real, actual life? No. No. No. Hard pass. This has to be a nightmare. I can feel my brain circuitry overloading, because there is absolutely no logical explanation for this. None. Zero. Giant neon words flash across my mind: DANGER, AMIRA MAJID. DANGER.

Out of the corner of my eye, I see Hamza. He's pulled away from me and is now bent over, shoulders shaking. I step closer to him without taking my eyes off the blue and orange jinn, who, in turn, can't seem to take their fiery eyes off Hamza.

"Hamz. Hamz," I whisper, placing my hand on

his back. Oh God. He's totally losing it. AND SO AM I! But I'm trying to stay calm, using my karate breathing.

Hamza slowly unfolds himself to standing, and when I look at his tear-streaked face, I realize...he's laughing. *Laughing.*

"I'm sorry....I'm sorry, but did you say he's the Emperor of Cough? Cough! Is he also the King of Sneeze?"

I...I...he's bananas. The world is probably going to end, and Hamza is cracking jokes and cackling in front of an army of multicolored, flaming-eyed jinn. The only upside to this turn of events is that now I know this is actually real. Reality is something I can deal with. Besides, my brother is never this annoying in my dreams, only in real life. Fear and confusion pulse through me. I eye an alley not far from us. Maybe we can make a dash for it. We have to run, get away. But where would we even go? Who could we run to for help? I try to clear my mind, assess our surroundings and our enemy. (Opponent? Jinn? Army? People?)

Then I hear soft laughter. It's not Hamza. His laughter is both infectious and loud. It's the jinn. The smaller orangey one, the one with glasses, is chuckling. He makes eye contact with Hamza, and suddenly they're both howling. Oh my God. What is happening? My brother's soul mate is an orange jinn?

I elbow Hamza and whisper, "Cut it out."

Abdul Rahman turns his enormous head toward the orange jinn and raises his squished-caterpillar eyebrows.

"My Vizier, the human is making a joke. A joke! How delicious. We simply don't have enough jokey wordplay in Qaf. So serious. So much drama." The orange jinn grins wide, and his black plastic half-moon glasses begin to slip from his nose; he pushes them back.

"Wearing glasses is such a pain," Hamza says to the orange jinn after their laughter fades away. My brother doesn't even wear real glasses! Only, like, when he's cosplaying Clark Kent or something.

Abdul Rahman and I exchange looks, our eyes wide in disbelief as my brother and the other jinn discuss keeping glasses in place. I think this is what my parents feel like when one of us does something so ridiculous or dangerous that they're too shocked to speak. (To be clear, it is almost never me who's risking injury to life and limb.)

Hamza continues, ignoring my Death Stare™, "Why don't you get contacts? Or why don't you use magic to improve your eyesight? You do have... magic? Or powers? Or something, right?"

The orange jinn sighs. Looks almost wistful. "Would that we could. Unfortunately, since we're beings of smokeless fire, we would need flameproof contacts, which no one has invented yet. However, the polymers used for our glasses are highly heat resistant! And, sadly, we don't have any magic that works against old age. We do age, like humans, but much, much slower. Speaking of elderly ailments, I think my sciatica is acting up." He rubs his backside.

"Bummer." Hamza shrugs. "You should try Tiger Balm. Our nani swore by that stuff. Totally reeks, though."

"My deep gratitude for the pain-relief tip. I'm

Maqbool, by the way, aide-de-camp to the vizier and eternal servant to the King of Kings." He bows deeply before us. "It is my honor to meet you." Then, turning to Abdul Rahman, he adds, "Perhaps my Vizier should also consider wearing *his* glasses? I find mine quite helpful. You know, for reading things, like recipes, or, perhaps, ancient scrolls with important prophecies."

"Glasses are absolutely unnecessary. I have perfect forty-forty vision," Abdul Rahman scoffs, folding his arms across his barrel chest and sticking out his lower lip like a toddler who'd been denied a second helping of ice cream (or, maaaybe like me, but only when my mom tells me I have to get the kid-size shake, *as if*).

Who knew old jinn could be so dramatic?

Hamza looks at me and mouths, "Forty-forty vision?"

"Vanity is the enemy of dignity," Maqbool whispers under his breath as he steps behind Abdul Rahman. "These kids *should have* seen us immediately," Maqbool mutters and shakes his head. "They shouldn't have needed *more* of the collyrium of Suleiman. The Chosen One was marked at birth. Once in a life is meant to be enough."

"What's collyrium? Who's Suleiman?" Hamza asks.

Abdul Rahman whips his head around, like a literal 360 degrees, his nostrils flaring and actual fire in his eyes, clearly about to chastise *someone*. My mom gets that same nostril flare (flames not included). "Do humans know nothing? Suleiman the Wise, he who could command jinn? His collyrium is a type of ointment for the eyes that expands mortal vision, allowing humans to see jinn and—"

I shake my head to wake myself up, to get myself into the now, to find my voice, which is apparently hiding in the depths of my belly. I need a bravery falsetto. A bralsetto. *Fake it till you make it, Amira.* "Stop! Everyone. Now. If this is real...if we're really not dead, then someone needs to explain themselves. Right. Now. And when I say someone, I'm looking at you, Abdul Rahman. Vizier...Sahib? Sir Jinn?" I'm trying to channel my mom when she is in one of her righteous-anger moods—usually when she's watching the news and swearing at the TV when she doesn't think we're listening to her. But my mom has way more fire than I do, and my flame starts to flicker.

Hamza jumps in to help. "Yeah. If you really aren't here to hurt us, then why do you have an army and flames in your eyes? And that jeweled dagger in your belt, uh, sash thingy?" Hamza points to an ivory hilt swirled with pearls and emeralds that hangs at the vizier's side. "You're basically a cartoon villain right now." Hamza has always been drawn to weapons. Even as a kid, somehow every stick he picked up looked suspiciously like a blaster.

"And why are our parents unconscious on the roof? What did you do to them?" I quickly add.

Abdul Rahman's blue face turns a reddish hue, making him look almost purple. Is he…flustered? Are feelings a thing for shape-shifting beings of smokeless fire? As I'm watching his face change shades, I also notice that he and the other jinn seem to be taking on more shape, their edges and lines becoming more defined. They're still sort of translucent but seem more solid. Real. Earthly. Maybe it's the effects of our atmosphere or maybe this collyrium thing actually works and I'm finally starting to focus.

Maqbool turns to Abdul Rahman and then kicks him in the shin.

"Ow!" the blue jinn yells at his aide-de-camp. (Note to self: Jinn can feel pain.)

"Oops! A thousand pardons, my Vizier. My foot slipped. This planet's gravitational pull disrupts my reflex control," Maqbool says, clearing his throat. "Perhaps we should tell Amira and Hamza the entire story?"

"You know our names?" I ask. "How?"

Abdul Rahman takes a deep breath. Do jinn breathe? Oxygen? Fire needs oxygen to burn, so... I guess physics works for supernatural beings, too? "You are the children of Adam and Eve, who will save the land of Qaf—"

Hamza giggles when he hears the name Qaf, again. I'm really starting to think he can't help himself. Like it's a unique humor disorder that only he has. I take a cue from Maqbool and gently kick Hamza in the foot. Maqbool laughs and shakes his head. I have a feeling humans really amuse him. Especially my brother.

Abdul Rahman continues, "Centuries ago, a prophecy was written in the Everlasting Scroll of a great war that would divide the Eighteen Realms and could very well end life on Earth."

"Holy—" Hamza begins.

"Whoa!" I interject. "Go back. Do you even know how to tell a story? You went from the beginning to the end with literally zero details."

"Perhaps my Vizier would permit me to continue?" Maqbool asks as he brings his right hand to his heart. Or heart area, at least? Abdul Rahman nods. Maqbool gazes at us, smiles warmly, and begins. "Forgive my Vizier. He has not interacted with humans for many centuries. And because the land of Qaf is a place where time is not linear, where neither past nor present exist in the ways humans understand them, his storytelling skills are a bit lacking."

"You're hardly a spry young jinn yourself," bellows Abdul Rahman.

"With respect, I am still two centuries younger than you and visited with humans but a hundred Earth years ago," Maqbool continues, winking at us. "Think of Qaf as a parallel dimension—the universe of jinn, peris, devs, ghuls—eighteen realms united under a single king—the great Shahpal bin Shahrukh, who rules with a firm but fair hand that has allowed Qaf to exist in peace. And so, too, the land of mortals."

We step closer together. Hamza seems to be shivering, and my fingers feel like ice despite the warmth that grows around us, coming in waves off the jinn.

"Do I even want to know what all those other things are?" Hamza blurts out.

"We are all creatures of fire, but with different traits and abilities. Some use the word *jinn* to encompass all such beings," Maqbool explains.

"Oooh! Chaos cousins," Hamza shouts, then tries for a deep, narrator voice: "A world on fire...a family ablaze."

I ignore Hamza's movie-trailer voice-over attempt. "A peri is kind of like a fairy. Do you seriously not remember any of the Urdu lullabies Mom sang us?" I ask. "Like the sleep fairy one?"

"Yes. Yes. The Neend Peri!" Abdul Rahman cheers. "She is the one who put your parents and the rest of the world to sleep."

"The whole world is asleep?" I gulp. "Every single human? Is that why all the cars are stopped and..." I pause. Oh no. "What about the airplanes? Did they all crash?" I suddenly feel very light-headed.

"I think I'm going to throw up," Hamza says, clutching his stomach.

"Do not puke on me, bro." I jump back.

"My Vizier, you're scaring them," Maqbool quickly chimes in. "Children, no one has been hurt. It is as if the world is in suspended animation—nothing has fallen from the sky. All that was in the air is cloaked, if you will. Neend Peri put all earthly beings under a sleep enchantment—consider it a type of pause—so they will *seem* dead when the ghuls and devs—demons—break through the moon and try to overrun Earth."

I think my blood just stopped circulating. "Umm...
is this you trying to *not* totally freak us out? Because
it is one hundred percent not working."

Abdul Rahman sighs, and the earth beneath us
quakes a little. He seems a little exasperated. "The
moon is a stopper—a plug between worlds. The
Emperor of Qaf is the guardian of that stopper. He
placed it there many millennia ago after the Great
Celestial War between the beings of Qaf that ripped
the fabric between our worlds. But now Ifrit, a terrible
and cruel dev, is leading a rebellion against our king.
He has promised each realm a piece of the moon—
their own portal to Earth—if they join him. Many
have already fallen under his maleficent influence.
One portion has already broken asunder. If Ifrit tears
the moon apart, devs and ghuls will stream through
the membrane between our worlds and wreak havoc
on Earth. The emperor is already in retreat. The two
of you must face Ifrit in battle and defeat him."

What the... I fall to my knees and bury my face
in my hands. Hamza plops down beside me and

leans his shoulder into mine. I hear him sniffle. This can't be real. But it is real. It can't be. It shouldn't be. My body feels like it's on fire but also freezing. My brain can't form a single thought, but also fireworks are going off in my mind. And not the pretty red heart-shaped kind that get set off over Navy Pier every summer weekend, the kind that can malfunction and blow your hand off. I squeeze my eyes shut. I want my mom and dad here so bad right now.

I hear Hamza choke back a sob. When I open my eyes, it's still just us. And an army of jinn on an otherwise lifeless street in front of us.

Maqbool leans over us. "I am deeply sorry, children." His voice is soft, and he looks into my eyes like he knows exactly what I'm thinking about. Correction—who I'm thinking about. "You'll have to say goodbye to your parents. Only you can defeat Ifrit and end the war in Qaf. You are the last, best hope for your people and ours."

"But...I'm not a warrior....I'm twelve." My voice breaks. "All I want is for Ummi and Papa to wake up.

Find someone else to help you. Someone more qual-ified for the position. Maybe someone who actually *wants* it."

"Yeah, like adults. Or, you know, heroes who've been strengthened by gamma rays or that have vibra-nium weapons or are mythical demigods. Not kids." Hamza stands and takes a deep, shuddery breath, then reaches for my hand and pulls me up. Together we turn to face the hulking jinn—or, rather, his belly.

Abdul Rahman exchanges a look with Maqbool, who merely nods as a shadow passes over the blue jinn's face. He bends forward slightly and places his overly large palms gently on our heads. An electric shiver runs through me. "In this last millennium, I have learned something about the capacity of mortals—God's greatest creation. Your true heroes aren't the ones who are fearless. They're the ones who are scared but fight anyway. This is your strength," the jinn whispers. "This is who you are. This is your destiny."

This Is Our What Now?

"UHHH...EXCUSE ME?" I MUTTER AS MAQBOOL LOOKS SOL-emnly at me, his smile erased. Meanwhile, Abdul Rahman is grinning and nodding madly. This bad jinn, good jinn routine is a little whiplash-y. I'm about to launch into my understanding of Qadr, or fate, the way I learned it—which is that we all have freedom of choice.

"Wait. Wait." Hamza jumps in before I can get another word in. "Are you saying this is our one true destiny? That we are being called to go on a celestial journey to save our world and yours? We. Are. The. Chosen. Ones?" Hamza's voice cracks a little, like he can't believe what he's hearing. I give him a gentle nudge, an understanding smile. Even if he's annoying, he's still my little brother, who is bravely trying not to cry.

Abdul Rahman keeps nodding. Maqbool allows a small grin to cross his face.

"YES! This means...this means we're going to get powers, right? Interstellar weapons? Mind-control abilities? Epic! The Majid siblings, ready to kick butt and take names!" Hamza practically levitates with glee. A minute ago he was holding back sobs, and now this? Meanwhile, I feel like I'm sinking into wet cement and the ground is going to swallow me whole.

"Well, we did think you'd be, perhaps, older. And it's technically Chosen *One*, not Ones." Maqbool raises an eyebrow at Abdul Rahman.

The blue jinn raises his palm to Maqbool's face. "One? Ones? We have no time for these Earth semantics. What's the difference, anyway?"

"Singular versus plural," mutters Maqbool. "Which you would know if you only wore your reading glasses and honed your English language skills."

"Pishposh! Enough arguing. You sound like those cantankerous brother inventors.... What were their names? The Banu Musa! Yes, that's it! See, I am still sharp as a celestial steel blade."

"We saw their stuff in the exhibit!" Hamza adds. "They seemed super smart."

"Indeed, they were geniuses," Maqbool says to Hamza, then turns back to Abdul Rahman. "Perhaps they didn't take well to your sharp, jinn-splaining criticism, my Vizier."

"Humph. I was trying to be helpful! But none of this is the point. Adhere to the point!" the jinn vizier booms, clearly irritated at his sidekick. "These children *are* the ones. That is all."

Maqbool rolls his eyes. "That's debatable."

"Take note." Abdul Rahman raises both of his giant, blue, heat-emanating hands and points at the moles that Hamza and I have around our right temples. When we were little, our relatives thought it was so cute we had the same mole in the same spot. They all called it the Majid Mark. "They bear the signs. The mole, the curly tresses."

"I would describe mine more as wavy, but, hey, no need to split hairs. Get it?" Hamza laughs. Maqbool joins him. He actually slaps his knee. I mean, the joke isn't even funny. *Save me.* I'm caught between destiny-imposing jinn and a bad-punning brother. I'm doomed either way.

"My Vizier, sometimes a mole is merely a mole, not a marker of sacred duty."

"Yeah, what he said," I add.

"And what of the Box of the Moon? Al-Biruni clearly states it is made for The One. When it comes to life, our hero will rise. And so it has passed."

"Or heroine," Maqbool says, nodding at me. At least he's a feminist.

While we're talking—or more like when Maqbool and Abdul Rahman are bickering—Hamza drops to the ground and digs through his backpack. He stands back up with the Box of the Moon in his hand. He's beaming.

I glare at him. Anger fills me. Hamza's fiddling with that thing—our fighting over it—is what set this entire disaster off. We're not heroes. We're agents of catastrophe. I ball my hands into fists at my side. Trying so hard not to pummel my brother right now or scream bloody murder into the night where the entire world is asleep, except us. And if we're heroes, if these jinn have magic, why aren't we on the roof waking up our parents?

Hamza opens the lid, and Maqbool and Abdul Rahman draw closer. The gears move slowly. And so does the tiny moon.

Maqbool gasps. Abdul Rahman straightens to his full height, which seems even taller than before. "There is no time to waste. We must leave. Now. Or this will be the end of everything you know. It is written."

I didn't have a smart-alecky reply for the *this is the end of it all, you have to do this, the pen of destiny commands you* speech from a giant blue jinn. And the seriousness in his voice kind of, at least temporarily, knocked the wind out of Hamza's do-I-get-to-have-a-mythological-hammer-because-I-alone-am-worthy clamoring.

We slowly trudge up the stairs to the roof. I don't want to leave without saying goodbye, even if our parents are asleep. I have no idea what to expect or what's ahead or where we're going or when, or if, we'll be back. And it's like the only reason I'm walking forward is because my body is doing it automatically. This must be what the lamb feels like when it's going to the slaughter. I know it's only a metaphor, but at some point, there was a real lamb. An innocent lamb that was walked to its death and asked no questions. Dumb lamb.

Maqbool follows us in. For our protection, he said, in case any of the ghuls slipped through. Ghuls. *Ghouls!* Maybe those old, scary fire-spirit stories Nani used to tell weren't tall tales.

My feet are like lead, and each step up feels impossibly hard to make. A tiny part of me wants to believe that I'll walk through that door, onto the roof, and everything will be normal. And my parents will give Hamza the classic disappointed-but-kind-of-amused look they've perfected. I make that wish. I hold it in a tiny place in my heart. But with each step closer to the roof, I remind myself I don't believe in fairy tales. I don't believe in wishes. I don't believe in magic. So how can I possibly explain everything that's happened in the last…I dunno…ten minutes? Hour? Hours? I have no idea how much time has passed. Or has it stopped since the jinn said they exist outside of time? My brain is about to explode. It's too much stuff to fit inside my head. For now, all I need to do is wrap my hands around this doorknob and push.

I gasp.

They're all still here. Lying on the ground in the same position. Like dolls. I walk over and kneel next to my parents. Hamza does the same. They look… calm. Like they're having sweet dreams. My dad even has a slight smile on his face. No furrowed brows. No tense muscles. Whatever that sleep fairy—the Neend Peri—did, it must be working. I bend over to hug my mom, but for the first time ever, she doesn't hug me back. She can't. I choke back a sob and kiss her on the cheek and do the same to my dad. I see Hamza whisper something in their ears. I don't know what words to say. All my words are stuck. But something floats through my brain, and I grasp the small silver capsule-shaped locket at my throat, strung around my neck by my DIY paper clip necklace. In that capsule is a tiny rolled-up scroll with writing on it. The Ayatul Kursi. The throne verse. The protection prayer. Before she died, Nani would always tell us to recite this prayer before bed so angel guardians would watch over us. I always thought of it as a metaphor, but now I hope it's real. We need all the help and protection we can get.

I hear sniffles over my shoulder. It's not Hamza, because he's next to me. I turn and see Maqbool wiping his glasses with the ends of his kurta. Little smears of ash dot his cheeks. When he sees me staring at him, he quickly puts his glasses back on and wipes the soot off his face with the back of his hand. He clears his throat, "Sometimes we…uh… our eyes, I mean…drip…ash. You know, downside of being made of smokeless fire."

I knit my eyebrows together, a little confused. But I'm a carbon-based life-form, not flame-based. What do I know?

Wait…jinn must be carbon-based, too, though! They're made of fire, which is mostly carbon dioxide, oxygen, nitrogen, some water vapor, like us. He was…crying? Maqbool was crying ash. Whoa. Jinn have feelings. Like people.

I stand up. Since I don't seem to be asleep—or at least not waking up anytime soon—I guess we're going to do this. I guess we don't have any other choice. It doesn't feel brave, but the chain reaction started, and I can't do anything to stop it at this point. My choice is either to be swept along into it, trying to fight an immovable object, or to figure out how to make myself the unstoppable force.

I rub my silver pendant between my thumb and forefinger, then tap Hamza's shoulder so he'll stand up next to me.

"Are you ready?" I ask him.

A wave of fear crosses his face. Hamza rarely shows when he's scared—he doesn't like to, anyway. But he's only ten. Of course he's scared. I'm twelve and terrified out of my mind.

"Yes," he says, straightening himself as if he heard

my dad utter the command, *posture*! "We got this, sis."

I nod. "But first, we have to use the bathroom. I have no idea if there are rest stops along the way or what the plumbing situation is in Qaf. And you know if you hold your pee too long, you can get a bladder infection."

"Amira. Oh my God. You're not our doctor!"

"What? We're Indian, dude, we were basically born half doctor."

After our necessary pit stop, I sneak into the employee break room and get some snacks from the vending machine and stuff them into my tiny cross-body purse. I'm really regretting not bringing a bigger bag that could hold more than hand sanitizer, lip balm, and a few treats. Like the status of bathrooms, I have no idea what food is like in Qaf. Do smokeless-fire beings eat? (Note to self: Ask how fire without smoke works—could be a possible science fair project.) Is their food good or even consumable by humans?

I mean, our digestive tracks are probably very different. And you can never be too prepared. Before heading back out, I down a giant handful of M&Ms, because if two kids are all that stand between now and the end of the world, I think eating too much candy and not flossing tonight are the least of my worries. Still wish I had a flosser, though.

When I step out onto the street again, I see a figure of giant flame standing in front of Hamza. I scream, and the flame immediately disappears. In its place is Maqbool.

"Relax, sis. Maqbool was showing me some tricks."

"These are no mere tricks, young hero," Abdul Rahman bellows. "The flame is the essence of who we are. And as such, should not be used as entertainment." He looks down at Maqbool with a raised eyebrow.

Maqbool shrugs and winks at me. I shake my head.

"Please, children. Take a seat," Maqbool says, and gestures toward the enormous…uh…golden throne.

It's the shiniest yellow gold, its arms bejeweled with rubies and pearls like my mom's guluband—the thick choker necklace she wore at her wedding.

A line of jinn soldiers—there must be over a hundred of them—kneels in front of the throne. They were kind of hanging back before, and in all the chaos and my terror earlier, I didn't get a good look at them. So I give myself the moment now. They're all wearing brightly colored outfits that resemble a pishwaaz— basically a dress with a twirly, pleated skirt worn over tight pants. Each of them has long silver braids draped over their left shoulders and daggers glinting in sashes at their waists. Their bright, jewel-toned skin shimmers with flecks of silver. They're magnificent. And they're all girls. Women. At least, I think they are. Have no idea how gender works in the jinn world. One who kneels directly in front of the throne looks up and catches my eye. She stands and raises a cupped palm to her forehead in greeting, like I've seen people do in the old seventies Bollywood movies my parents watch. "Adab," she says. *Respect.* Her voice is like music. "I am Razia. We are the Khawla ki Supahi—the Khawla Warriors. It is our sacred duty to protect you on your journey to the land of Qaf."

Hamza snickers when she says "Qaf." I elbow him. "Uhh, sorry," he says sheepishly. "You're girl soldiers. There's girl jinn?"

"Really, Hamz?" I ask, and elbow him again, this time a little stronger.

"Ow. That actually hurt."

A mysterious smile spreads across Razia's face. "Jinn are ever-changing. We are not bound by human understandings of boy and girl, of gender as fixed. We are shape-shifters. We are fluid. Some, as those of us who swear allegiance to the memory of the magnificent warrior Khawla, commander of the Rashidun Army in the Seventh Conquest, choose this female form to honor one of the greatest military leaders in history—human or otherwise. Others shift to be in harmony with themselves."

Razia steps aside and gestures for us to sit on the golden throne. It's really like a couch, if couches made of gold existed. Hamza and I take a couple of hesitant steps forward. I stop and turn to Maqbool and Abdul Rahman; I crane my neck to look up at them. Abdul Rahman seems to grow taller every time I speak to him. "Can you please share, like, a travel plan? Itinerary? Do we need ID? Does our TSA precheck work? Obviously, no way to get a signed permission slip right now. I mean, how do we get where we're supposed to go?"

"Yeah, where exactly is this Qaf place?" Hamza fake-coughs for effect.

Abdul Rahman scrunches his eyebrows at Hamz and opens his mouth to speak, but Maqbool jumps in with directions. "First, we fly to the Himalayas and then walk through a door in a giant wall."

"We what now? Fly on that thing? With you? There's no walls, no engine...and I'm...I'm..." Hamza can't finish his sentence, but I know what he's going to say. He's scared of heights. He tries to play it off like it doesn't bother him—he even joined a rock-climbing gym to try to get over it—but I see his hands tremble. I know how scared he is.

"Have faith. There's simply not enough time in the world to explain every detail to you. For now, understand that we, the jinn, and our constant combustion act as an engine. We must make haste. Look!" Maqbool points at the piece of the moon that is floating in the sky and seems to be getting bigger. That means closer. In the absolute chaos since we hid behind the dumpster, I was distracted from the absolutely wild situation of the moon breaking apart.

"But I...I..." Hamza begins.

"It's okay," Maqbool says as he shrinks to our size. "It's impossible to fall out. A force field surrounds the throne. It is impenetrable to all forms of human weapons. Nothing will hurt you. If you get really scared, let me know; I might have something to help you."

Hamza nods. He seems okay with this explanation. I guess I don't have much choice but to be okay with it, too. Still, I'm dragging my heels until large hands lift us up and deposit us on the sofa-size seat of the throne. It's Abdul Rahman; his head is maybe two stories off the ground now.

Before I can protest being rudely jinn-handled, he

quickly shrinks to human size. It's so fast and disconcerting, it makes me a little dizzy and nauseated. Hamza is getting that yellow-green inside-of-an-avocado look again.

Maqbool and Abdul Rahman arrange themselves on either side of us—like we're sitting down to family movie night—and the golden throne seats us all comfortably. Surprisingly, it doesn't even hurt my butt to sit on it. Then the Khawla ki Supahi get in formation behind the throne. I crane my neck and see them step into their black cauldrons. I do a cartoon double take. But even on second look, it doesn't change: Ethereal jinn warriors are still standing in black iron pots that almost blend into the surroundings. This story gets weirder and weirder. Maybe we're going to teleport to Qaf, and that's what the jinn call flying, because I don't see how any of this apparatus can fly, even though we saw the throne approach us in the air. Maybe it was all an illusion? What did Maqbool mean when he said the jinn were basically the engines? How does a giant golden throne have any lift? There are no wings on a cauldron. How does the air circulate above and below? If these things do manage to break the bonds of gravity, how is the weight and shape not going to send us plummeting down? I mean, the jinn can survive it, I guess? But Hamza and I are flesh and bone, not smokeless fire.

"Ud jao!" Abdul Rahman stomps his foot and commands. He might be human-size now, but his voice is still giant. Also, it sounded like he was speaking Urdu. Ud jao. *Fly!* Or . . . whoa. Maybe I speak jinn now? Jinni? Jinnglish? Janglais? (Note to self: Does osmosis work with languages? Could be an independent study for science.)

We lurch forward, then the throne is propelled down the street like it's a runway. One that's way too short! We're going to bite it on the Eataly building. We were supposed to get gelato there tonight. Their mango ice cream is the best. Seriously, so smooth and creamy. And . . . oh my God! We're on a collision course! I close my eyes. I can't look. It doesn't matter if we're in the care of magical creatures. This is not normal. Humans are not supposed to do any of this. We're not even supposed to see jinn unless we're like…possessed. I don't know why I didn't think of it before. We're possessed. That's the only logical explanation, and by logical, I mean illogical and…

Ahhhhhhhhhhhh!

We're in the air. My stomach has dropped. I really have to pee again. I should've peed twice before leaving. Oh no. I can feel actual wind on my face. I thought this invisible shield was impenetrable. Why is there wind? Can birds hit us? Are all the birds asleep, too? Why is it winddddyyyy?

Keep your eyes closed, Amira.

Don't look down.

Don't look down.

I looked down. Big mistake.

I let my left eyelid hover half open to sneak a peek at Hamza. Poor kid must be terrified. I have to be brave. For him. I turn my head ever so slightly and see Hamza, totally zonked out on Maqbool's shoulder.

"Hamza!" I scream. "Wake up. Are you okay?" I look at Maqbool, both eyes open, trying to ignore how every muscle in my body is freaking out. "What happened?"

"Huh? Oh, him. Nothing. The Neend Peri gave me a temporary sleep potion for the trip. And Hamza mentioned to me that he was scared of heights. Sometimes I have trouble sleeping, too, what with turbulence or unexpected bird strikes into the protection shield."

"Why didn't you give some to me so I could sleep, too?"

Maqbool's mouth falls open. "I only had a drop left in the vial—more than enough for a solid nap for a human child, but only a single one. Sorry. Besides, look around. Would you really want to miss this?" He gestures widely. "You're okay. You can't fall out. Even if an evil jinn could disrupt the shield with a well-timed volley of a poisoned arrow *and* you fell out, one of the Supahi would fly down and grab you up in her pot! No worries at all."

Yeah. Sure. No worries, except that an evil jinn might shoot me with POISONED ARROWS. Hahahaha. I'm totally calm. I take a deep breath. Try to remember the breathing Sensei taught us. Breathe in. Hold at the top of the breath for three seconds.

Exhale for five seconds. And repeat. I keep breathing as I glance at Abdul Rahman, whose head is resting against the side of the throne, his eyes closed. What? Does everyone else get to sleep on throne rides?

Since I don't have much choice, and who knows when I might possibly fly in a throne again, I find a drop of courage and glance down. Chicago has fallen away and is now nothing but twinkling lights in the dark night sky. As we rise higher and higher, Earth, my home, falls into shadow. And as we pass the bright, broken moon, I see the deep cracks in its surface, ready to shatter my world.

CHAPTER 6

I'm on Top of the World!

WE HIT THE GROUND WITH A SOFT THUMP. I'D CLOSED MY eyes when one of the Supahi told us to get ready for landing. Now, as I open them, they're shocked with the brightest green that's ever blasted its way onto the cones of my eyeballs. I step off the throne while Maqbool rouses Hamza, and Abdul Rahman starts talking to the Supahi in a language I don't understand. We're in a valley of green grass surrounded by sky-high, skinny pines growing on slopes that eventually rise up to rocky, snow-tipped peaks, some of them hidden by clouds.

It's pin-drop silent. I stuff my eyes with the wonder

of the Himalayas. My dad saw them when he was a kid, but none of his descriptions can compare with the real thing. It's like I've been photoshopped into the perfect postcard.

"Epic!" yells Hamza as he spins around to take a look. So much for that quiet. "Sis, we flew on a throne to the Himalayas. Flew!" he says, then turns to Maqbool. "Can we ride it up Mount Everest? I bet I'd set a world record for youngest to climb it." He points at the high peak in front of us.

"Ahem," says Maqbool, turning him around and directing his finger to a mountaintop completely covered in clouds. "First, save Qaf, then we can discuss it. But I must say, I hardly think flying on a throne powered by mystical beings counts as climbing. Though it might not be that different from the Sherpa guides who do all the work and get very little credit and next to no money for risking their lives." Maqbool harrumphs, and small flames shoot out his nostrils.

Hamza and I jump back.

"Sorry. Sorry. Not to worry. It's okay," Maqbool

says, trying to soothe us. "Those flames don't burn. Maybe singe, the tiniest bit."

Wow. No third-degree burns, only minor singeing. I feel perfectly safe. (Not.)

Razia, the Supahi who spoke with us earlier, approaches with two bowls of some kind of soup and a round flatbread that looks like the rotis our mom makes. Razia hands us the food. "Eat now. The journey is long. The Himalayan nettle and fern shoots gathered in the foothills will give you strength."

"You don't have to ask me twice," Hamza says. "I'm pretty much always hungry."

We sit cross-legged on the ground while Razia and Maqbool join Abdul Rahman out of our earshot.

I grab hand sanitizer from my bag and rub it into my palms and fingers—tips and nails included— but Hamza dives right into the soup. Ugh. Who knows what germs jinn have and who has sat on that throne.

Ripping off a piece of the roti, I'm reminded of how Ummi makes it on her tawa, a kind of shallow, round cast-iron skillet with sloping sides and no handle. It belonged to her nani. And it's one of her most prized possessions. She pours a thin stream of oil in a spiral on the pan and then adds the dough that she flattened by hand into a thick pancake shape. My chest tightens thinking about her and Papa and everyone else we've left behind. I look at Hamza's face. He's staring deeply into his bowl, his eyes a little shiny. I can guess what he's thinking.

"Do jinn eat?" he asks, blinking as he looks up at me. "Like, do they have stomachs? Intestines?"

Okay, I guess I didn't know what he was thinking.

"I don't know, dude. The jinn digestive system hasn't exactly been the first thing on my mind. But since they're not eating the soup…um, maybe they don't eat human food? Or only one meal a day? A week?"

"Did you notice that none of them had to use the bathroom before we left? Isn't that weird? I mean, I know I always complain when Mom tells us to pee before we go anywhere in the car, but I almost always have to go. She's always right about my bladder."

"Why are you so strange?" I chuckle. "The moon

is breaking, the world is asleep, and we're supposed to be some kind of superhero warriors—and your most insightful observation is about how jinn toilet habits are different from yours?"

"My brain can have lots of thoughts at the same time. You should try it," he snips. Then adds, "Burn!"

"Whatever. It's not like you're special. Everyone's brains think about more than one thing at the same time. That's just... brains!"

"Children, please come," Maqbool calls as we sop up our last drops of broth with our rotis.

We walk over and hand our bowls to Razia, who takes them and pushes them into the dirt; they move right through it like the mud is a thin layer of not-yet-firm Jell-O. When she sees our surprised faces, she says, "Those bowls are made from earth, and to the earth they shall return."

"So... zero-waste recycling," I say. "Awesome." She smiles.

"Enough talk! No time to discuss recycling. That's something you humans should've been thinking about for the last several hundred years. Too much dillydallying," Abdul Rahman scolds. I get it. We've wrecked the entire Earth by polluting the ocean, skies, and land.

"Is dillydally a technical jinn term, or…" Hamza giggles. Maqbool joins him. He's basically the perfect audience for Hamza. He laughs at all his jokes, even when they're not funny. And weirdly, Maqbool seems to have matched Hamza's high-pitched chuckles. My brother's laugh is literally infectious.

Abdul Rahman clears his throat. "Beyond those trees lies the village of Kalap." He points to the tall pines ahead of us. "There, cloaked in the hills, is the Arena of Suleiman. Under the dome are gifts he left for you, three millennia before your birth."

"Gifts? Yes! What are we talking about here? Like a Lego birthday-gift situation? Or like something more in the hero category, like a Lasso of Truth, maybe, huh? No. Wait. Wait. Don't tell me. I prefer a surprise."

"And surprised you certainly shall be, my young Hamza." Maqbool places a hand on my brother's shoulder.

I have a feeling it's not going to be the surprise he's hoping for. And Hamza missed the most important point. Left for *us* like three thousand years ago? By Suleiman? How could that even be possible?

We set off through the pines with the Supahi surrounding us, protecting us. But it doesn't make me feel safer when I look up into the daylight and still see a hunk of the moon, floating anchorless in the blue sky, like it's ready to drop at any moment. I know that technically, it's still really far from us. On a normal day, the moon is over two hundred thousand miles away. But nothing about this day is normal, so who knows if regular laws of physics work anymore.

"We are still in the land of men," Abdul Rahman explains as we reach the tree line and step into the dense woods. I feel the temperature drop immediately.

"Excuse me," I say. "I think you mean the land of *humans*." He might be an all-powerful creature made of fire, but that doesn't mean Abdul Rahman can't be called out for being sexist. I'm teaching an old jinn new tricks!

"Humans," he corrects, and nods at me. "Once you have retrieved your necessary objects, we shall proceed with haste to Qaf."

"They're superhero weapons, aren't they?" Hamza asks, his voice full of glee. "This is how we get our powers, I bet. I want a hammer only I can wield, and, let's see . . . a shield. Of course. Vibranium. Top of the line. Also, Black Panther gloves with claws and—"

Hamza stops mid wish list. We've stepped out of the woods and into a clearing where the sun shines like a spotlight on an immense domed structure. It's round and looks like it's made of some kind of rough deep brownish-black stone that glimmers in the sun. Its dome looks like it's ten times bigger than the Taj Mahal's. And it feels ancient. I don't know how else to put it. But it's like this building has an energy, a spirit, that is waking up from a very, very long, longer-than-Rip-Van-Winkle, nap. Goose bumps pop up all over my skin.

Abdul Rahman assumes his double-human-size stature again and pushes open the giant iron doors—they must be two stories high—then shrinks back.

As we step through the doorway, every jinn grimaces a little, like it hurts to walk in. The outline of their bodies blur and waver, a flicker of flame, like when we first glimpsed them. The inside of the building is dark, but the black walls sparkle here and there with little flecks of light. Looking up into the dome, it feels almost like night. Torches circle the wall, and as the Supahi take position around the circular building, they light them with flames that leap from their fingertips.

With the torches ablaze, I walk toward the center of the massive room, spinning around, in awe of the size of this place, and when I look straight above me, I see what looks like a very large treasure chest floating above us—it must be three stories high.

I yelp and dash to the side, terrified it will fall and crush me.

"How...how...is that thing in the air and why?" I say aloud to anyone listening.

"That is a question that has gone unanswered for millennia. And that's where your necessary objects are—your gifts," Abdul Rahman says.

Hamza, who has been walking around the room and probably only half paying attention, approaches the center, turns to the jinn, and says, "Can you make yourself tall again and grab it? I'm dying to see what we got. Let's goooo!" Hamza's eyes sparkle with the possibilities, but I get that queasy feeling in my stomach. The kind I get right before a test when I know I can't study for it anymore and have to hope I've done enough. Except I never got a chance to prepare for this...test.

"We are unable to assist you in that exact manner," Abdul Rahman says. "This structure is a strange place, existing in the world of men—"

I clear my throat, really loudly.

"Pardon. Existing in the world of *mortals* yet imbued with some magic we have not been able to ascertain or conquer." He shakes his head.

"Okay, but can you say it in simple English words that actually make sense?" Hamza asks the same question I'm thinking.

Maqbool steps in. "What my Vizier means is that

our powers under the dome are limited. We cannot shift. We cannot rise. In here, we are constrained to the essence of our most elemental self—fire. Our energy is nearly fully consumed to hold our countenance and shape as you see before you."

"So basically you're no help?" I ask. "All you can do is stand around, without powers, and try not to torch us?"

"I would say that, in his infinite wisdom, Suleiman the Wise created this challenge for the champion alone," Abdul Rahman says with a raised, bushy eyebrow.

"You mean, champions," Maqbool adds, emphasizing the plural.

Abdul Rahman ignores him. "Suleiman the Wise, the last human warrior to enter the gates of Qaf, knew what was written in the Everlasting Scroll, of the saviors to come. Of you. To ward off false heroes—those loyal to Ifrit who might act as spies—he set challenges forth that only the Chosen One... er...Ones...can figure out. You must collect the chest and its contents to continue. To gain the tools you will need to battle Ifrit and the obstacles he has set in your path."

"Besides, no jinn has figured out how Suleiman was able to levitate the chest for these many years," Maqbool says.

We have to solve a problem that thousand-year-old shape-shifters can't figure out. Excellent. We're really off to a great start. *Help.*

"Hold up now. We have to meet challenges from the good guys to overcome the obstacles from the bad guy?" I shake my head. "You don't have any idea how to help us, and Suleiman thought this would be a great way to give us what we need? If he was so wise, why couldn't he have made this more straight-forward or, you know, easy? And what the heck happens if we can't get this magically levitating chest down from up there?" I point. "Do we go back home? Is there a reset? A time-turner type situation?" I tuck my hands into my pockets as I say this; I don't want Hamza or anyone else to see them trembling, but I'm sure everyone can hear it in my voice.

"Yeah!" Hamza adds for emphasis. "Plus, no one should have to work for a gift. It should be given freely or else it's not a gift.... It's a...penalty."

No one responds immediately, but I think I already know the answers to my questions. Abdul Rahman looks up toward the ceiling and the floating chest. Maqbool looks down at the ground. I want to scream, *Answer me!* But I don't. Why bother? Even if there was an answer, it wouldn't make any of this better. Maqbool and Abdul Rahman start bickering in their jinn language, and I chew my lip, imagining how much worse everything could get.

"I got this, sis!" Hamza shouts. When I turn to the sound of his voice, he's thrown his backpack onto the floor and is starting to climb the roughly hewn walls of stone. The toes of his sneakers wedge into little grooves, and his fingers grasp some corners jutting out of the stone. Oh God. No. He's not going to make it. It's way higher than the walls he climbs at the gym, and he never makes it more than ten or twelve feet up a wall before he falls. And he's not wearing a harness or helmet, and there's no cushy mat beneath him.

"Hamza," I whisper-shout, because I don't want to startle him. I rush over to the wall he's climbing—his ankle is a little beyond my reach. "Climb down right now," I order. "You know I'm in charge when Ummi and Papa aren't around."

Hamza pauses and turns his head ever so slightly. "It's okay! I mean, I flew through the air on a golden throne, and I didn't even puke. I think part of my new powers is being over my fear of heights."

"You don't have to prove anything," I say without reminding him he was snoozing while we were flying because of a sleep potion. "Climb down so you don't get hurt."

"Sis, I'm fine." His voice wobbles a little when he says this.

"What are you going to do if you manage to get level with the treasure chest thingy? It's still floating in the middle of the room. Did you also magically get Spidey web shooters?"

"No, but that would've been so cool. I'll figure it out when I get there. Stop distracting me."

I shut up and step away from the wall. I don't want him to fall because of me. And maybe he's right. Maybe he didn't need the sleep potion. Maybe he's over his fear of heights. He has been going to a therapist about it. She gave him a mantra to say when he climbs. I hope he's saying the words now.

My hands tingle from fear for my brother. If he falls…no. No. Don't think about that. Don't think about Ummi and Papa. Don't think about Hamza smashing his head against this stone floor ten thousand miles away from our parents. Dang it. Every time I tell myself not to think about the worst possible scenario, it's the only thing I *can* think about. My fingers are ice-cold. My blood must've rushed to my head, because now *I* feel dizzy watching him.

He's pretty high up. Definitely higher than fifteen feet. Higher than he's ever climbed at the gym. He's doing it! I watch as he finds one toehold after another. One little edge to grip. I don't take my eyes off him. He looks up, reaching for a corner that I can barely even see. But he stops, pulls his hand back, hesitates. Oh no. No. He's panicking. I can feel it. His free hand is struggling to find a gap in the stone or grasp any little point. It slips from one edge.

I hear a gasp, which isn't my own. It's Maqbool. Staring at Hamza, everyone else simply fell away. "Help him," I whisper to Maqbool.

"I don't...I cannot increase my size to reach him. The cauldrons don't fly in here. I am at a loss." Maqbool hangs his head.

"So if he...if we...are not the Chosen Ones...or even if we are, he could fall to his death? Even without your powers, there has to be some—"

Hamza screams.

The world stops. Everything stops, except for the sound of Hamza's voice that echoes off these dark, cold walls and the sight of my brother's hands slipping from the rocks. Him falling backward through the air like a leaf, so small and fragile. While I'm standing here, helpless.

Before I can move my feet, before I can even scream, the Supahi slide across the floor below Hamza and form a tight circle, joining hands in the center so they look like the spokes of a giant wheel. They break Hamza's fall, but a few of their arms flicker in and out from corporeal to phantomlike as he drops the final few feet to the floor with a thud.

"Ow!" he yelps as he lands on his butt. He's going to be sore, but it could have been so, so much worse.

I race forward and pull Hamza up off the floor and give him a big hug for a second. My parents would love to see this. The hugging part, not the Hamza-almost-falling-to-his-death part. His knees buckle, but I hold him up. I hear the blood rushing in my ears and the thumping of my heart.

I pull back, allowing Hamza to bend over, his hands on his knees, taking deep gulps of air.

I punch him in the arm. (Lightly! I swear.)

"Hey! That actually almost hurt," Hamza says. "What's your deal?"

"Well…I'm…I'm sorry. But no more you-might-die stunts. Mom and Dad will kill me if I let you crack open your skull. Besides, what were you think-ing?" Since my parents aren't here, I have to be in charge, imagine what they would do or say. They definitely would've given him a stern talking-to, but they would definitely not have sucker punched him. (Lightly!) That part was all me.

"Obviously, that I could do it." Hamza pulls himself up to standing. "I dunno....I thought maybe I could conquer my fear of heights. I believed in myself. Why couldn't you believe in me, too?"

Hamza looks dejected. There's probably only been a few times in his life I've seen such a crushed look on his face. He's usually the upbeat, always-sees-the-glass-half-full sibling. "Hamz, I do believe in you. I believe in you being alive. Even if you annoy me once in a while." I'm trying to be jokey, but it kind of falls flat. He nods and heads toward Razia, who is holding out a canteen of water.

I glance over and see the worried looks on the faces of all the jinn. I don't think they're so much worried about Hamza's near death/serious injury experience as they are about what the heck happens next. I'm guessing *this* wasn't written on the Everlasting Scroll. (Note to self: Ask who wrote the scroll and how old it is. This would be a cool project for history class.) I watch as Hamza takes the water and slinks down by a wall where he's hidden in shadow.

I sigh. Sitting sounds good. Pretending this whole thing isn't happening sounds better. But there's no chance of that. I step closer to the wall, but as I near it, I feel my paper clip necklace and the silver-colored Ayatul Kursi pendant slightly lift from my collarbone in the direction of the wall. I move closer still, and I can feel a little tug at the back of my neck. I look around and see the Supahi standing at attention while Abdul Rahman, Razia, and Maqbool appear in deep conversation. No doubt finally realizing that we're not the Chosen Ones. No one is even looking at me. This isn't a jinn trick. I pull the necklace off, letting it dangle from my fingertips, and inch nearer to the black stone walls. As I approach, a force yanks the necklace out of my hand, and it flies the last several inches between my fingertips and the wall, and sticks.

My necklace sticks to the wall.

I put my hand on the dark stone. Those little bits

of sparkle shine in the light of the torches. I rub my hand across the metallic sheen. My brain whirs. This looks so familiar. Paper clips sticking to stone...

I suck in my breath. Every year we take a field trip to the Field Museum of Natural History. Usually it's for the dinosaurs. But in fourth grade, we did a unit on magnetism, and Ms. Maley took us to the Hall of Gems & Minerals. There were all these rubies and diamonds and emeralds and really fancy necklaces. But in a corner was a small case with a hunk of nondescript black rock with a bit of a sheen to it, a line of paper clips stuck out of it like they were trying to stab through the surface of the stone. Our teacher told us that without this rock, the magnetic compass would never have been invented during the Han dynasty in China.

Oh my God. It's lodestone. This entire structure is made of lodestone.

I know exactly what to do. (At least, I think I do.)

CHAPTER 7

It's Getting Hot in Here

"I DON'T GET IT. WHY ARE YOU SO EXCITED ABOUT A LOAD of stone?" Hamza sidles up to me as I wave my hands around, all excited as I figure out how to explain what I need to Abdul Rahman, Maqbool, and Razia. The properties of lodestone may limit jinn powers— Maqbool said they could only be their essential selves in here—and that's exactly what I'm counting on.

"Lodestone. It's a type of stone that is magnetized. It's pretty rare. I bet museums would go bananas if they saw a whole structure of it."

Hamza shrugs.

I roll my eyes. "Pay attention in science class. The

treasure chest"—I point to the domed ceiling—"is probably held up by magnetism. To free it of its maglev bonds, we need to demagnetize the walls." I'm so excited that my words spill out of my mouth, banging and smashing against one another.

But I'm met with blank stares. Aargh. No one is getting it. I wonder if I've made a miscalculation. Forgotten basic principles of magnetism? I sigh. Sensei's words come back to me: *You need to believe here and here.* He said that while pointing to his head and heart. We don't have a lot of other options. Might as well try this one. The worst thing I could do is fail. And be humiliated. But the world might end anyway, so at least my cringeworthy moment wouldn't last long.

I take a deep breath, put on my best explain-y teacher voice. "Lodestone is a permanent magnet, except it's not technically permanent."

"So an impermanent permanent magnet. That makes no sense." Hamza knits his eyebrows together.

"It means that the magnet retains its, uh, magnetism without help from an outside source, unlike other magnets, which eventually lose their power. But...anyway, a permanent magnet actually *can* be demagnetized. With heat. Since the entire building is lodestone, we need to heat the walls up a lot. Like, to one thousand degrees or more."

"But how would..." Hamza trails off, a grin spreading across his face. "Like maybe with fire?"

I nod. "Like maybe with fire."

Maqbool's eyes light up, literally. Razia smiles.

"Would someone please explain in terms a jinn can understand?" Abdul Rahman furrows his very wide brow.

"Wow, jinn really don't know how forces on Earth work, do you?" I'm maybe being a bit bratty about this, but after all of Abdul Rahman's raised eyebrows and exasperated tones, he kind of deserves it.

Abdul Rahman scoffs. "I know the important things!"

"I understand," I say as I spy Maqbool and Hamza trade looks and try to stifle their giggles. "What I need is for all of you jinn types to unleash your inner fire so we can heat these walls up to one thousand degrees."

"Yeah, let your flame flag fly!" Hamza yells.

I nod. "Stop using your energy to keep this shape. Be your true jinn essence."

"This is a most unorthodox request from a champion," Abdul Rahman says. "I'm certain Suleiman the Wise meant for you to get this chest down yourselves."

"That's exactly what we are trying to do," Hamza says.

"Yes," I say. "With science. Brain muscle, not muscle muscle. And with a little help from our friends." I smile.

"Very well, then." Abdul Rahman nods. "Children, shelter yourselves in the entryway." He hands us the cloak from around his neck. "Wrap this around yourselves. It will protect you. Flame cannot penetrate it."

We hurry toward the building's entry—as far as we can get from the jinn. No time to lose. We've lost so much already.

Hamza and I crouch down, and I throw the violet

robe over us. It's featherlight, and we can see through the fibers. How can it protect us from anything?

We huddle closer. Neither of us say it, but I can feel our shared thoughts in the air between us: *Please, please let this work.* My hands get all clammy. I shiver.

Then the room is on fire.

Through the weave of the cloak, we see orange-blue flames leap from the skin of all the jinn. They touch the walls with their hands, and their bodies transform into infernos. Even with the cloak protecting us, the heat hits us like a wave, like when you step too close to a raging bonfire. The lodestone glows, its metal sheen ablaze. Sweat pours down my back.

Right before we melt into human goo, I hear a crackle, a pop, and see the large iron chest careening toward the floor. It's going to shatter. It's going to split open the ground. But inches before it touches, I see Razia and two dozen or so other Supahi whip out their daggers and slide them across the floor, taking up a rectangular formation, catching the chest on the hilts right before it crashes to the ground. The jinn return to their people-like form, and the room immediately cools.

"Did you see that?" Hamza yells, jumping up from behind the cloak. "How fast they moved? The blades catching the light? Total slo-mo movie sequence except, you know, not in actual slow motion. The Supahi should meet up with the Dora Milaje. They'd be unstoppable."

Hamza doesn't seem to be freaking out that much about this whole Chosen One, Earth-ending scenario because I think half the time his imagination is planted in an alternate superhero reality anyway. He's living the ultimate fan fiction. I wish I could feel the same. Maybe it would give me immunity from the terror ripping at my insides even though I'm thrilled that I was right about the maglev bonds holding up the chest.

Hamza races toward the iron chest, and I follow close behind.

"Use the robe! Don't touch it with your hands!" yells Maqbool. "You'll burn yourself!"

The deep gray iron chest is unadorned. There are no latches. I guess Suleiman the Wise figured if someone got it down, they were owed whatever was inside. There's a handle jutting out from the top. I wrap Abdul Rahman's cloak around it as he nods with approval. Then, together, Hamza and I heave open the lid.

The inside looks like the night sky—black velvet illuminated with tiny stars spreading across the fabric. They look like they're embroidered with threads of silvery moonlight. We reach in to take the gifts awaiting us: a dagger with an ivory hilt bejeweled with bright blue lapis lazuli. Hamza's eyes widen with excitement as he holds it in his hand.

"Celestial steel," whispers Maqbool. "It can cut through anything."

I touch a smooth leather quiver filled with emerald-tipped arrows. Next to it is a black bow that has the same metallic sheen as the walls. It feels good when I pick it up. Solid. I pull the straps across my chest and settle the quiver and bow against my back. They're impossibly light. Lighter than when I lifted them out of the chest. Not sure how the physics of that works, but like I said, all the regular rules feel a little bent right now. I mean, yes, I figured out that the walls were lodestone and could be demagnetized, but also, there is no place in the world with this much lodestone. And I had to use a jinn furnace. Though, if I believe the whole *it was written* line that Abdul Rahman keeps quoting, then Suleiman the Wise would have known everything would happen as it did because he read it in the Everlasting Scroll. Still don't really believe the destiny angle, because every single moment up to now feels like some weird combination of being in the wrong place at the right time, luck, and random lessons from science class.

Hamza reaches in one more time and pulls out a silver-gray—"Uh...is this a ribbon?"

I rub the fabric between my fingers. It feels like... silk? But more elastic-y. Rubbery silk. It's too wide to be a ribbon. I grab one end and let it unfurl toward the floor, scrutinizing every inch to see if I can figure out what it's for.

Hamza sniffs it.

"How is smelling this thing helpful?"

"It's about as helpful as what you're doing."

"I'm sizing it up," I say, trying to sound convincing. "So I can figure out its, uh, purpose." I take the loose end in my free hand and flip the sash from vertical to horizontal, holding it out at arm's length in front of me. Its long, wide pleats fold smoothly one over the other.

"You know what this looks like? Remember when Ummi and Papa went to that hospital fundraiser?"

Hamza nods.

"Papa wore a tux. This looks like the sash he wore around his waist. Ummi said it had an Urdu name.... a cummerbund!" Kamar. *Waist.* Band. *Strap.*

"Does battling the Ifrit mean wearing a magical tuxedo? It's not my first choice, but I'm in." Hamza seems totally serious as he says this.

"I think Ummi said the original meaning of the Urdu word—kamarband—was for what soldiers in the Indian Army used to tie around their waists to hold weapons. So maybe that's what it's for."

"Not exactly blown away by this, er, gift? But I guess I can't exactly stick a dagger in my pocket," Hamza says, and starts wrapping it around his waist.

Maqbool clears his throat. "Is there only one cummerbund?" He catches Abdul Rahman's eye. "Seems odd seeing that there are two Chosen Ones. Don't you agree, my Vizier?"

"It's obviously meant to be shared," he responds.

I get why Maqbool is suspicious. We're not exactly hero material. I mean, who could possibly think that a girl who can't pass the test for her next karate belt and her younger brother, a rock climber afraid of heights, would be the ones chosen to save the world? I wish Maqbool believed—or at least could fake it. It would make me feel a lot, lot, lot better if he seemed as sure as Abdul Rahman is. But the tiny part of me that isn't completely and totally freaking out is kind of psyched that I solved this challenge using my knowledge of magnets! (Note to self: Figure out if there's any way I can get extra credit in science class for this.)

"Hang on," Hamza says. There's an envelope, too. He picks up a brittle yellow paper between his fingers—it looks like it could crumble into dust any second—and turns it to the back, where there's a dark red wax seal. It looks like a star and there are some words, Arabic letters maybe? They look a little like Urdu, but I can't make them out.

"Khatam Suleiman," Razia whispers.

"The what now?" Hamza asks.

"The Seal of Suleiman, made by his Ring of Power," Maqbool answers. "He has left this for you."

"Let me open it," I say, carefully prying the envelope from Hamza's hands.

I break the seal. I keep waiting for, like, a concealed trap to set off flying poison darts, but nothing happens. My dad says I shouldn't always expect the worst. But so far, everything has kind of been worse than anything I imagined. Dropping the envelope back into the chest, I carefully unfold the letter and read aloud:

To the champion of Qaf,

You have met the first challenge with aplomb. I have arranged these for your wits only to solve so that no impostor may claim the mantle of champion. Beware that more dangerous obstacles await you. Set by the offspring of the one who rebelled, the dev who tore a hole in the fabric of the universe.

It is written that you alone stand between man and his ultimate destruction—

Uh, record scratch. "What's up with the sexism. It's constantly the world of men or the destruction of man." I roll my eyes.

"Who cares," Hamza says. "Keep reading. Or give it to me, I'll—"

"Get your mitts off of it."

"Look." Hamza points to the bottom of the letter. "There's something in different color ink, like a special message." Hamza moves closer and reads over my shoulder. *"What you seek is seeking you.* Well, that's not creepy. And what does the next paragraph say? The writing is so tiny."

He shoves in to get a better look, bumping me and pushing me forward. I stumble and throw out a hand to balance myself. Hamza reaches for my elbow to pull me back so I don't fall into the chest.

"Children, careful! That paper is very—"

But Maqbool doesn't get a chance to finish because a small tremor shakes the floor, making Hamza fall into me, and instead of helping me straighten up, Hamza tries to grab my arm to pull us both back, but he misses and grabs the letter. Before he can move his hand, the floor shakes again, pulling us apart. And the paper along with us. Hamz and I each have a piece in our hands. The two halves spark and turn to ash immediately.

Uh oh.

This is bad.

A much stronger tremor shakes the room. This time, even the jinn stagger forward.

This is worse.

"The Box of the Moon. Check it!" shouts Abdul Rahman.

Hamza's backpack is by the wall where he was sulking. We race over to it. He grabs it and opens it. The gears are in motion, and the tiny moon is closer to Earth.

Nope. I was wrong earlier. *This* is worse. The worst. Like moon-shatteringly bad. Literally.

Abdul Rahman joins us to take a look at the moving moon in the Box and turns an even deeper blue than he already is. I can feel heat pulsing off him. Like he's holding back his fire. Abdul Rahman claps his hands, and the sound explodes across the dome. "That's it. We can't wait any longer. We make for the Obsidian Wall. Now. No more arguing and no more destroying ancient documents, or I'll turn you both to ash."

We hurry back to the golden throne, feeling occasional shocks beneath our feet as the treetops sway above. We're mostly silent. Personally, I'm keeping my mouth shut because I'm afraid I'll puke. Hamza hasn't said a word, either, which is a rare occurrence. Wish my parents were here to see this. Wish my parents were here, period. Not sure what is more terrifying: Seeing that piece of the moon growing larger in the sky and noticing the cracks on the lunar surface getting deeper, or having a jinn threaten to turn us to ash like Suleiman's letter.

I can tell Abdul Rahman feels bad about what he said. He's been hanging back with Maqbool, who is moving his hands around wildly while he speaks in a language I don't understand. And Abdul Rahman's face actually looks...sad?

We all take our places on the throne again. Heading for the Obsidian Wall. Whatever that is. I don't even bother to ask the question, because I'm guessing we'll get yelled at again. Not really sure how this Chosen One thing is supposed to work, but it sure does involve a lot of shouting.

Once we're seated, Maqbool clears his throat and raises an eyebrow at Abdul Rahman, who slowly nods, then speaks, "Ahh, yes, children, I must explain something to you." Clearly, someone got a talking to.

"We will now begin a short journey to the Obsidian Wall." Hamza opens his mouth to speak, but Abdul Rahman cuts him off. "We will traverse close to the ground, merely feet above, as we ascend up the mountain. This is simply faster than walking at human speed and will prevent unnecessary trips and falls." Hamza looks relieved.

"Maqbool informs me that normal human children are of a curious nature, and so I shall share with you a tale. Of Suleiman the Wise. Of his defeats of Ahriman, the mighty rebel dev. Of how Suleiman helped Shahpal bin Shahrukh unify the Eighteen Realms in peace these many centuries."

On the Schism of Qaf

Some three thousand human years ago, a powerful, wise, and just malik ruled—

"Wait. What's a malik?" Hamza interjects, and immediately gets side eye from Abdul Rahman.

"In Urdu, it's like king or master, maybe?" I say, then shush him.

"Ahem. As I was saying…" Abdul Rahman clears his throat.

> *A wise king who reigned over a time*
> *of peace and prosperity for his people on*
> *Earth, Suleiman, son of Dawood, was*
> *bestowed by God with many gifts. Among*
> *these were the ability to speak with animals,*
> *to control the winds, and to rule jinn with a*
> *Ring of Power: the Seal of Suleiman.*

"Woah. Hold up," Hamza interrupts again. "There were rings of power before *Lord of the Rings*?"

"Yes! There are many rings of power in your history and ours. You would think that Suleiman the Wise would at least garner a footnote. Tolkien could have shown some respect," Maqbool scoffs.

"Excuse me, am I interrupting? Are you two about to settle the age-old problem of cultural appropriation in the next instant or may I be allowed to continue?" Abdul Rahman asks, not even trying to hide his sarcasm.

We all nod guiltily.

It is written that many jinn willingly served in Suleiman's grand army and pledged fealty to him, for his wisdom and fair treatment of all beings were renowned. It is written that those jinn who openly defied him, who menaced his people and kidnapped children—

I gulp. "Uhhh...did you say *kidnap children?*" Hamza pokes me in the ribs with his elbow.

Maqbool immediately jumps in. "We are not *those* types of jinn. Like humans, jinn have free will to do good or evil or anything in between. Fear not. With my life, I swear to protect you from any miscreant jinn, dev, or ghul."

This is supposed to make me feel better, but it kind of doesn't.

"Interruption!" bellows Abdul Rahman. He is so testy. He hasn't eaten a thing; I wonder if he's hangry.

"Humble apologies, please continue, my Vizier." Maqbool grins.

> *It is known that Suleiman the Wise had the ability to magically bind mischievous jinn, dev, ghul, or peri. To trap them within brass vessels, perhaps for eternity. It is said his favorite prisons were small oil lamps that were so cramped—*

"What!" Hamza nearly jumps up from the throne seat. We're only a few feet off the ground, angled as we ascend the mountain, but Maqbool catches my brother before he can test the strength of the invisible force field. "Are you talking Aladdin and his magic lamp and genie...a genie that is...oh my God...blue! A blue genie...jinn...genie. Heck, yes! You're the blue singing genie, aren't you?"

"Insolent child. How dare you insult me so. I am the Vizier to the King of Kings, Emperor of Qaf. I am not some disreputable jinn cast out from society and bound to a lamp for my misdeeds." Abdul Rahman's face turns fuchsia. That's new.

"You're also very pitchy when you sing." Maqbool giggles.

Hamza and I look at each other and laugh. Abdul Rahman narrows his eyes at us, but I swear it almost looks like he's holding back his own laughter. He continues:

Long story, short. Believe me, this is a true epic that could be told over many nights by our gifted storytellers. Our beloved emperor believed the Eighteen Realms of Qaf—each inhabited by different tribes of creations—ought to be unified, and so he did this after the Great Celestial War. After all, we are a singular creation—all fashioned from fire—even if physical traits and elements of our culture vary. The emperor brought peace, a golden age of Qaf, where there was a renaissance of art and music and literature, where

*we built our great cities and created
beautiful gardens. But one sought the
throne and threatened to tear our world
asunder. The rebel dev, Ahriman, father
of Ifrit, whom you will now face. The
rebel stole the Peerless Dagger from the
emperor's armory—the blade that once
cut the fabric between worlds, that can
sever the stars with the mere thought of
its wielder. On the night of an eclipse,
Ahriman began to carve out a piece of the
moon—each of eighteen portions linked
to one of the Eighteen Realms. Even the
dagger's first slash unsettled the heavens,
causing tremors on Earth that cracked the
Himalayas, swallowing some settlements
whole, sending small meteorites crashing
into your oceans. Shahpal bin Shahrukh
beckoned Suleiman the Wise, binder of
jinn, demon-slayer, to Qaf that he could
quell the violence and bring the rebel dev
to his knees. Commanding him with his*

*ring, with his seal, Suleiman bound the
dev into a small brass lamp, soldering it
with the fire of the sun and burying it in
the depths of the moon. With Suleiman's
help, the emperor reshaped the moon,
the stopper between our worlds, and he
has been its sole guardian all these many
ages. Time passed, and the only trace
of Ahriman's rebellion lay on the face
of the moon—humans call it the Sea of
Storms.*

*His son, Ifrit, who now controls the
Peerless Dagger, wants to avenge his
father. To set him free. So they can seek
the Ring of Power, which has been lost
over time, clues of its existence scattered,
mislaid. Some say it is buried in a secret
location. Others say it was lost to the
ocean depths. And Ifrit will break the
moon and scar both our worlds forever
to find it.*

My knuckles are white, and my fingers ice-cold at this new information. That makes this all even worse. "Uh, excuse me. You didn't explain back in Chicago that Ifrit's equally evil dad is buried in the moon. So we could possibly have to fight two super-villains? Excellent."

"Time was too short to convey all the details!" Abdul Rahman shouts. "The Chosen Ones must face this, that is all. It is written."

"So, basically, this is a prison break and a revenge tale," Hamza says. "Dang. That's kind of epic."

I catch Maqbool's eyes as he looks away. I don't think Hamza quite gets it. But I bet Maqbool knows what I'm thinking: *How can we possibly win?*

The golden throne passes through a veil of mist, and the Supahi softly descend in their black flying pots, bringing us to the ground as well. We are so high—above the cloud line—I can't even see the bottom of the mountain. I shift Hamza away from the slope—his forehead is beading up with sweat. We turn to face a wall so high and wide I can't see the top, and it seems to go on forever. The Obsidian Wall. It's smooth and shiny, glass-like black rock. Whirly, swirly patterns in the surface are almost mesmerizing, drawing me closer. I reach my fingers out to touch it, and the Wall oozes around them; my fingers melt knuckle-deep.

"Gross!" I yelp.

"Cool!" Hamza yells at the same time.

Before I can pull my fingers out, Maqbool shouts at me to do it slowly. I listen and ease them out of the Wall with a squelch. "Ick. Disgusting," I say as I try to wipe the black sticky substance onto my jeans.

"Sorry, should've warned you about that," Maqbool says. "The Obsidian Wall is an optical illusion. It's not made of rock. It's a substance that is both liquid and solid at the same time. It's—"

"Oobleck?" Hamza and I interrupt together.

"The portal to the other world is oobleck?" I ask.

"I have no idea what oobleck is besides an odd-sounding human word," Abdul Rahman harrumphs. "But then again, many of your words sound odd to my ears."

"Old ears," Maqbool mouths to us.

"I saw that!" Abdul Rahman bellows.

Razia and some of the Supahi around her choke back their giggles.

"It's a mixture of cornstarch and water," I say. "But it's so much more than the sum of its parts. It acts like a liquid, but it's not a liquid. It acts like a solid, but it's not a solid. It's a suspension because the cornstarch grains don't actually dissolve in the water and react differently to different amounts of pressure. It's a non-Newtonian fluid." A satisfied smile spreads across my face.

"Nerd," whispers Hamza.

"Nerds get the job done," I whisper back.

Maqbool claps his hands. "Did I not tell you, my Vizier, how wonderfully odd humans are? Oobleck! What a delightful word."

"Oobleck! Poobleck! Call it what you will, strange human children, but my only concern now is where has the portal to Qaf gone?" Abdul Rahman pokes at the Wall with a series of quick jabs with his finger, which meets a solid surface and doesn't get sucked in. I freaking love science.

"Gone? Do you mean you cannot find the door?" Maqbool asks.

"It should be right here. According to my JPS." Abdul Rahman removes what looks like a brass pocket watch from inside his vest.

"GPS, you mean," Hamza says.

"No, I mean what I say and say what I mean. JPS. Jinn Positioning System." He shows us the watch, which looks more like a compass. When he turns it to the wall, a red arrow points at a Q where north would be. "This is definitely it."

"Isn't there another way around?" I ask.

Maqbool shakes his head. "This portal was built by the emperor for Suleiman the Wise and the other anointed so that only those humans with true business in Qaf could pass. He alone commands it so that no ill-intentioned can pass from our world to yours. The door *should* appear for the Chosen Ones." Maqbool tries to make eye contact with Abdul Rahman, who clearly is avoiding it. "Perhaps put on your reading glasses, my Vizier, to see if you've read the settings correctly." He walks back and forth in front of the Wall as another tremor, the strongest one we've felt, makes me grab for Hamza to steady myself. This can't be right. None of this is right.

"Maybe it's hidden, like we need to say a secret password or something," Hamza suggests, then sits down in front of the Wall. He quickly jumps up. "I got it! Mellon," he shouts.

"Melon? Are you still hungry? We just ate," I say.

"Not melon. Mel-lon. The Elvish word for 'friend.' You know, that riddle from *Lord of the Rings*? A sign above a door says something like, 'Speak, friend, to enter.' And the magic word is actually just 'friend.'"

"Oh my God. It could be the end of the world and you think the answer is going to come from Hobbits?"

"First of all, it's Gandalf who says that. An actual wizard. And it was worth a shot. Besides, that book is about the end of the earth, too. . . . Middle Earth, anyway. And small people who go on a quest to defeat a great evil. Sound familiar?"

I sigh and am about to make a smart-alecky remark, but my eyes are drawn to the darkening sky. No. No. No. Hamza gazes up and sees the same thing I do: a burst of fire, an explosion on the moon's surface. I see it so clearly now. Another piece of the moon is about to break off. And we're still here. On the wrong side.

Suddenly I hear Hamza exclaim, "Excelsior!" And then I see him take a running start. He wants to smash through the goop wall, apparently. But before I can yell at him to stop, that it's useless, he bounces off the Wall with a loud thwack and falls to the ground, clutching his shoulder.

"I thought I had a chance," he groans as he stands up.

"You know how oobleck works. The faster you run at it, the harder it's going to get."

"I know, but I figured maybe…I dunno…jinn oobleck would be different?" He points at the sky. "Desperate times."

The ground beneath our feet rumbles again. This time even more violently. I grab Hamza's backpack and reach for the Box of the Moon. *Oh no.* One of the gears is spinning fast, too fast, and as the tiny moon moves…it could mean…

We all look up to see another chunk of the moon float away and into the sky. The trees around us bend at unnatural angles. In the distance we hear cracks and the tops of some trees falling. There's a second of silence. Then a deafeningly loud WHUMP.

"By Suleiman's beard, NO!" Maqbool yells, pointing to the top of the mountain range as we see a peak crumble, setting off an avalanche.

CHAPTER 8

The Element of No Surprise at All

I SCREAM. I THINK IT'S ME, ANYWAY. I CAN'T TELL IF THE screams I'm hearing are my own. I'm staring up at a mountain that is rumbling down toward us. We are going to be crushed under rock. Stupid, stupid portal. How can we be the Chosen Ones if we can't even get past a wall of oobleck? My brain feels like oobleck, like impossible-to-understand, mysterious goo. Now it's in an oobleck loop. God, I'm going to die thinking about oobleck. Vijay Kumar did a science fair project testing the strength of oobleck. It was actually pretty cool; he did all these experiments with it, cutting it with a hot knife, stabbing it, aiming a high-velocity force...

My eyes fall on the dagger Hamza tucked into the cummerbund around his waist. Before I even realize it, I'm reaching for it, and I'm watching myself like I'm outside my body. I grab the bejeweled hilt of the blade, pull it out of the sheath, turn to Razia and the Supahi, and scream, "All together, PUNCH IT!" In unison, the warriors punch the Wall full force, and I plunge the dagger into the substance at the same time it hardens, pulling down with all my strength until the surface cracks. Razia kicks at the break, and a chunk wide enough for us to fit through breaks off. We have only seconds before it becomes liquid again; I grab Hamza and our bags and shove him through the seam. The jinn morph into something like an orangey mist, follow us through, and recorporealize on the other side as the Wall shifts and shivers and a liquid curtain covers the rip we tumbled through.

Hamza and I are both on our knees in sweet-smelling grass, blobs of oobleck stuck to our clothes and hair.

"Sis! You did it!" Hamza jumps up, pulling an elastic-y, rubbery bit of oobleck off his nose.

I look up at him and smile, then fall totally backward onto the grass, closing my eyes. I can hear Hamza high-fiving the jinn and Maqbool letting out a little victory yelp. I'm glad they're happy, but I feel like I just ran the hundred-yard dash at full speed—heart pounding, a little light-headed. I can't believe that worked. And I also can't believe we are still at the beginning; it's not even the hard part yet. But we made it through. We're here now. And this is the only real there is.

I gulp some air, then open my eyes and look around.

"What is this place?" Hamza walks away from the Wall. Pushing myself off the ground and out of my disbelief, I join him.

We're in a garden, but it's unlike any garden I've ever seen. A carpet of emerald-green grass rolls out from our feet in gentle waves. Enormous palm trees line the perimeter alongside red, purple, and orange flowers. Trees the shape of weeping willows, their branches heavy with fruit, dot the garden. It smells like night-blooming jasmine—I know because it's my mom's favorite flower. She says that in India there are stories of how the scent could make people act drunk and go wild. Maybe that's why I feel a bit woozy. I sit down on a sloping bank beneath what I think is an apple tree, but the fruit shines like rubies.

The Supahi seem to be checking their flying pots for damage. Jinn transportation needs the occasional tune-up, I guess? Meanwhile, Hamza is wandering around and yells back, "This place smells like chocolate!"

"What are you talking about? It's jasmine!"

"No. It's that chocolaty smell that hits you when you're walking in the West Loop. You know, the smell of magic."

He's right. About the magic. Not about how the garden actually smells right now, because it's 100 percent jasmine. But when you're in downtown Chicago on certain days, especially in late summer, the streets smell like chocolate. It's because of a chocolate factory, but for a long time, I thought it was because all the chocolate fairies lived in Chicago. Hold up, if peris are real, I wonder if there are chocolate fairies here. That would be awesome.

"The garden smells as you wish it to. Generally linked to a strong memory or an affiliation to what is most on your mind," Maqbool says as he approaches me under the tree.

Hamza walks over. "Wow. That's cool. But I'm really glad I wasn't thinking of, like, a sewer. That would really stink." Hamza snort-laughs. "Get it? Stink?"

I roll my eyes. Apparently, no matter what he faces, Hamza is always his Hamza-est. I don't bother to ask him why he'd be thinking about sewers. It would probably involve some convoluted explanation about Ninja Turtles. If you ask me, it looks like the Turtles live in storm drains and not the sewer, because they're not surrounded by bodily waste, which...ugh. Gross. Why does my brain do this?

"Yes, indeed. It is quite cool, as you indicate," Maqbool says. "But sometimes, in Qaf, things are not always as they seem. Perceptions may vary. And it would be smart of you to be wary of that."

Hamza nods, only half paying attention, and wanders off. I stand up to ask Abdul Rahman and Maqbool what the next steps are. The sooner we get to it, the better. I watch Hamza walk oddly, slowly, toward a silver gazebo almost like I'm watching him through waves of a mirage. Through the boughs of the leaves in the path between us, I see an older man with a pointy grayish-black beard praying. Hamza greets the uncle, who turns to him. I can't hear what they're saying, but I see them both smiling and nodding. Hamza is good at making friends anywhere we go, always ready to chat people up. It's not quite so easy for me. A tree near Hamza and the old man bows and bends; its branches are filled with gleaming garnet fruit, pomegranates, I think. Hamza throws his head back and laughs at something the man says and then reaches for a fruit.

Maqbool, who's been talking to Abdul Rahman, glances up and yells, "Stop!"

Why is Maqbool getting so worked up about fruit? Are we supposed to be on some special diet here? Hamza's always hungry. I'm starving, too. Even though we ate that nettle broth and bread only an hour or two ago. Though, maybe, it could've been longer? I don't have any idea what time it is or if Earth time even works here.

As Hamza wraps his fingers around the fruit, the bright, sunny daylight turns bloodred. Invisible alarms blare. Hamza jumps back, and I race toward him. As I reach him, the kindly old uncle transforms into an orange-skinned, pointy-toothed monster— body like a person but with a face that looks like a wolf. I'm guessing he's a ghul like Maqbool explained—like a dev but with much sharper teeth. Great.

We scream, and Razia and the Supahi surround us immediately, daggers drawn.

The monster opens his jaw so wide I think he

could swallow us whole. He laughs and says, "Our master, Ifrit, was correct. The prophecy is engaged. So be it. We stand at the ready." Razia hurls a dagger toward him, but he disappears into a mist and the dagger falls to the ground.

"We have to go back," I whip around and yell at Abdul Rahman. "Take us home, now. This is stupid. That was...he...it was—"

"A ghul. One of Ifrit's spies, I'm afraid," Abdul Rahman speaks in a voice that for him must feel like a whisper. For once, I wish I hadn't been right. "The emperor dispatched us to return with you undetected. In this endeavor, we have failed. For this, I am sorry, but we cannot return. The way is closed. The way is sealed. Until we save Qaf, no being may enter. Or leave. This is for the safety of both of our worlds."

Hamza gulps so loud I can hear him. "But are we safe?" His voice sounds so little, like when you watch old videos of yourself when you were in kindergarten and can't believe how tiny your voice sounds. That's what he sounds like. That's what I *feel* like.

Maqbool puts a hand on his shoulder. We both

know what that means. The only way back home is through this place. Through Ifrit.

"The fruit was a trap, alerting all of Qaf to the entry of a mortal into our realm." Maqbool shakes his head. "The element of surprise has been taken from us. But we will persist." I watch as Hamza looks down. I feel like I should yell at him because he always, always touches everything, but it's not like he could've known that the fruit was a five-alarm human alert for Ifrit.

Abdul Rahman walks through the garden. The rest of us follow. What other choice is there? Stay here and be eaten by wolf-faced ghuls with sharp teeth or...continue on our journey to meet a possibly even scarier monster who could also probably eat us? Ugh. Sometimes I wish my brain wouldn't ask so many terrifying rhetorical questions. One of my friends told me that sometimes her brain is quiet, like she doesn't constantly think about stuff, and I had no idea that was even possible, because mine pretty much has a running monologue all the time.

We walk only a few minutes and pass through a

curtain of fragrant purple and blue hanging flowers when a series of drumbeats greets us, starting slow but then getting faster and faster. To the right, I see small, rose-colored jinn pounding out beats on what look like dhols—oval-shaped Indian drums—strapped across their chests. They look young. Are there jinn kids? Do they go to school? Do they switch to virtual school during a pandemic? How do their immune systems even work if they're beings of smokeless fire? So many questions are banging around my head, but I have a feeling I might not get all the answers I want.

As we step toward a vast stone courtyard, there are pillars circled with white jasmine garlands (I was right about the jasmine smell!) and orange-gold gauzy fabric is draped from pillar to pillar, creating a tented roof. In the center is a large throne mosaicked with jewels, and next to it, a smaller silver throne. Almost like a whisper of wind, creatures step out from the trees. They're jinn of every size and every color from even the biggest box of Crayola crayons. Through the bushes emerge beautiful winged creatures. The shades of brown of their skin glow like they're lit from the inside; they all have shiny black hair coiled on their heads. Vibrant silks are draped around their bodies like saris. And from their backs unfurl scalloped, emerald-colored wings. They are the most gorgeous things I've ever seen.

"The woodland peris," Maqbool whispers in my ear about the fairylike creatures. But they're not like any fairies I've ever seen in books or movies. I mean, they're brown, like me!

The jinn and peris gather in front of the throne, murmuring, staring at us. One of them, about my height and wearing a sparkly diamond tiara, steps to the smaller throne as she folds her beautiful, dandelion-colored wings. She looks directly at me and tilts her chin, literally turning her nose up. She does not seem impressed. I gulp. I look down at my jeans, red Chucks, and white T-shirt with the Bill Nye quote, *We are the stuff of exploded stars.* I glance at Hamza, wearing his *That's No Moon* Death Star tee. They seemed funny to wear to an eclipse-viewing party. But it all feels kind of babyish and not very warrior-like now. I feel the weight of hundreds of eyes staring at us. I don't think Hamza and I are the heroes they expected.

Everyone hushes and falls to one knee. Hamza and I look at each other and shrug. We are about to join in, but Maqbool shakes his head at us and whispers, "Human beings bow to no other creations." We stay standing but have to shield our eyes when a blaze of light enters the courtyard.

"Your flame, Abba. Dim it. Weak human eyes cannot handle your brilliance," the stuck-up fairy sitting next to the throne says and throws a squinty fake smile our way. Whatever.

"Welcome, visitors. I am Shahpal bin Shahrukh, King of Kings, Emperor of Qaf. And I humbly offer my gratitude for your presence." He slightly bows his head to us. *To us.* In unison, the jinn and peris pivot toward us and do the same. They are really formal about their intros.

As the emperor weakens his flame and sits down, he takes shape for us. He's tall, with a face that seems a bit longer than it should be, like he's out of proportion. His skin is the color of sandalwood, and I swear, I almost get a whiff of it as he sits down. (The sandalwood soap we get from India is my favorite.) He's wearing a long, two-toned golden-green kurta and skinny pants underneath, but what catches my eye is his burgundy robe, embroidered with silver and gold threads. It looks like it's trimmed with real stars because of the way they glow like the velvet lining of Suleiman's iron trunk.

"Rise, all! Come forth, heroes."

"That's us," Hamza says, dragging me toward the throne, Abdul Rahman and Maqbool close on our heels.

"My king, it is my deep honor to introduce you to Amira and Hamza, of the clan of Majid, from the realm of Chicago along the shores of the greatest of lakes." Abdul Rahman waves a big blue hand over each of our heads as he says our names.

"Two? Heroes?" The king extends each word.

"They bear the marks. They have passed the challenges of the iron chest and...uh...passed through the Obsidian Wall, which I also knew was a challenge!"

Hamza whips out his dagger to show the court and nudges me, so I pull out one of the emerald-tipped arrows from the quiver on my back. Then he plucks a glob of oobleck from my hair and raises it into the air. A wave of ahhhs and ohhhs moves through the court, so I don't tattle that Abdul Rahman didn't seem to know that getting through the Wall was one of the challenges.

"Two heroes for the price of one!" quips Maqbool. Abdul Rahman does not look amused.

The emperor rubs his chin, then claps his hands. "Excellent. Two human champions of Qaf! We are twice blessed. You may be very small, but I have seen small humans accomplish many things."

"Yes, like learning to walk and use the toilet by themselves," says the fairy with a crooked smile. "Incredible feats! They probably receive trophies for such victories."

I try not to look too irritated, but I'm not always

good at hiding my feelings. I narrow my eyes at the peri. A silence falls over the court. The king smiles, then laughs, then throws his head back like he's having a raucous old time...at our expense.

"Forgive my daughter," the king says. "Aasman Peri has quite a wicked sense of humor and has kept me in stitches these many years."

"Charmed to meet you," she says in a sticky, sweet voice. "I am the First Peri of Qaf. Our greatest scholar on human habits and culture. Passing the first two challenges is one thing, but you must pass all three to prove your worth."

"Wait. What? You're Cough's greatest scholar?" Hamza says. "You're like my age. Ten. Eleven, tops."

"That's eleven in *fairy* years. We're much more mature and learn at a faster pace. And it's Qaf, not cough, silly human. I'm completely fluent in your language, but you can't even get one name right. Or perhaps that is what you consider humor?" Aasman Peri scoffs.

"Umm, can we get back to the more important

point? What is the next challenge?" I ask, shaking my head. Hamza almost busted open his head trying to get to the iron chest, and we barely made it through the oobleck before an avalanche nearly crushed us. I'm not sure how long our luck will hold out.

"The Insurmountable Challenges should hardly be of consequence to the Chosen One...Ones. As if swatting a fly." The emperor grins.

"*Insurmountable* Challenges?" Hamza blurts out, and then turns to Abdul Rahman, who conveniently forgot to mention their name. "That's what they're actually called? And can we go back to how unfair it is that we have to, like, *earn* the privilege of fighting for our lives? That's—"

"False advertising and...and bait and switch," I sputter.

"And seriously uncool," Hamza adds.

"Don't get your human underwear in a bundle," Aasman Peri says. "They're only insurmountable for impostors."

I gulp.

Hamza leans over and whispers, "Do they think underwear is made of actual humans?" I nudge him to stop his giggles.

Abdul Rahman puts his head down in shame. "Forgive me, my king, but we had little time as a second piece of the moon broke away before we could pass through the Wall."

Gasps and cries go up from around the crowd.

"Only sixteen left!"

"We're doomed!"

"How can a couple of kids save us?"

"Ifrit will make us exsanguinate all of Earth's humans!"

Suck the blood out of people? No wonder some of them have such sharp teeth! My mouth drops open. This is so much worse than even my worst imagining. And I'm a total catastrophizer!

The emperor raises an illuminated hand, and the crowd quiets down. "Dastangoi!" he bellows.

A small, wizened old peri who looks a little like baby Yoda with smaller ears and wings slowly makes her way to the throne.

"We don't have all day, Lalla Fouzia," some jinn shouts.

"Shut it, Asim," another jinn yells back. "Show some respect to the storyteller. She's older than everyone here and will probably outlive you."

"Or put a curse on you!" another voice from the back adds.

The ancient dastangoi takes her place in front of us. Unlike everyone else, she's wearing simple white clothes and an unadorned deep red robe. She takes a seat on a small wooden chair that two jinn guards bring out for her. She clears her throat and raises her gnarled hands. Black smoke whirls in front of her, and she begins to write in it with her bent fingers.

On Suleiman the Wise and the Mortal Prophecy

You know of Suleiman the Wise and the defeat of the rebel dev. Banished forever into the Realm of Nothingness. In the very center of what you humans know only as the moon.

As the dastangoi speaks, figures appear in the smoke, first a man with a sword in one hand, raising a fist with a giant ring on it in the direction of a dev who swirls into a minitornado and gets trapped in a brass oil lamp. Then the lamp being buried deep into the moon's core. Our moon. Our beautiful moon, a whiff of white smoke in the gray clouds surrounding it. She continues:

> *Suleiman the Wise warned us that the son of the rebel dev would seek to avenge his father. That the Peerless Dagger would pass from father to son, that Ifrit might rip the moon apart and tear Qaf asunder, for each realm is inextricably linked to a piece of the moon. We searched for him high and low through all the realms, but his mother created a tilism from his infant tears and her sorcery. A slice of a magical world, hidden between realms. A pocket universe. And there she concealed*

*him, fearing for his life, beyond the reach
and sight of the great king. She, too, knew
the prophecy of her son. Of Ifrit's rise to
greatness, of his strength unparalleled.
And of his sudden, swift fall at the
anointed hands of a son of Adam and Eve.*

Here the dastangoi stops, her smoke figures disappearing into the air. She scrunches her face at us.

*Err, the children of Adam and Eve,
I mean. For only by the will and deeds
of the chosen can a creature of Qaf
be defeated and sent to the Realm of
Nothingness until the end of time. So it is
written. So this tale ends.*

With that, the mysterious dastangoi stands and steps through the branches of trees that make way for her and then bend down to cover her path.

Aasman Peri rises from her small throne with a

thick leather roll in hand. To her left is a stone table, and she unfurls the roll, placing four swords on the surface.

She turns to us. "These are the swords of Suleiman: Sam Sam, Qam Qam, the Scorpion, and the Spine-Cleaver. You must choose one. And you must choose wisely."

"How come we get only one?" Hamza asks. "Are we supposed to share? Or?"

The peri shrugs. "It was a very ancient prophecy, and they weren't exactly good on the details back in the day. All I know is you get to choose one. You decide which is right. It is said that only one can cut down the evil of Ifrit."

Out of the corner of my eye, I see Maqbool nudge Abdul Rahman, who turns his shoulder to him.

"I'll do it!" Hamza says, his right hand shooting up in the air like he's the teacher's pet.

"Hang on a second. You already have a knife thingy."

"You have a bow and arrow!"

"Which I don't know how to use. I'll get the sword.

That way we'll both have, uhh, sharp, pointy objects with which to defend ourselves." I try to sound confident, like I know what I'm doing, but really, I don't think I'm fooling anyone, especially myself.

"Fine. But I don't think the older-sibling rule should always apply. It's not my fault I was born second." Hamza concedes and steps back, gesturing me toward the table.

My hands shake. I clench them into fists at my side to try to calm myself down and to not seem like I'm scared, even though fear ripples through me. I stand before the table, staring at the shining swords. They all seem...I don't know. Dangerous? Extremely sharp? Do you need a license to carry a sword? I can't imagine walking around Michigan Avenue with a giant sword in your hand. Especially if you're Muslim. It would definitely not fly at TSA. Can't imagine trying to explain that. *Oh, hello, airport security person, it's little ole me and my trusty sword I've nicknamed Spine-Cleaver. Nothing to see here.* Have I mentioned that I'm really good at procrastinating?

"Choose, already," the peri hisses in my ear. "It's

not like the fate of the entire universe depends on it or anything."

"Chill. You're not making it any easier," I snarl back. "I need to make the right choice."

"The Chosen One is supposed to know which sword belongs to them."

I let my hand hover above each sword, praying for a sign. I don't know, a tingle, an eerie whisper coming from the hilt of one of the swords. Hoping maybe the right blade will choose me. I close my eyes. Try to breathe in the essence of each sword. And...

Nada. Zippo. Zilch.

I don't feel a thing. Not a shock of electricity. Not a surge of knowingness. Not even goose bumps.

I open my eyes. Everyone is staring at me, waiting. A hesitant smile crosses my lips. *Choose, Amira. Make a decision.* I look down. One of the sword handles is wrapped in leather that seems slightly worn. Comfier than the others, if a hilt can be described as comfy. It's as good a reason as any, I guess? I've got a one-in-four chance of being right. Eeek. I wrap my fingers around it and lift it into the air above my head.

"For the honor of Grayskull!" Hamza's lone voice resounds in the courtyard.

Nothing happens. Not a single thing. The sword doesn't light up. I don't suddenly grow taller or get muscles. Or have a costume change. Sigh.

But as I step away, turning to the court, I hear a loud, slow clap behind me. I swivel my head around. It's the emperor.

"You have chosen the Scorpion. The most favored of all of Suleiman's swords. This is the one with which he battled and conquered the rebel dev Ahriman. In you...uhh...both of you, we place our faith." Thunderous applause fills the courtyard, and the emperor rises to join a standing ovation.

Hamza bounces up to high-five me. I have to admit it feels good to have done something right for once, on the first try. This challenge wasn't exactly insurmountable, though. They really should reconsider how they name stuff around here. Mostly this was my picking comfort over flashy style, which is my default anyway. "We got this, sis," Hamza whispers to me. I wish I had his confidence. For now, I'll have to pretend, and maybe one day it will be real.

"They have met and bested the challenges! Let the heroes be trained in the use of their new weapons. Let the royal gifts be given. Let us feast. Our heroes set out at dawn," the emperor commands. Everyone scurries away, and tables of food and drink are brought out. Torches are lit as evening descends on the garden.

Two of the Supahi take Hamza to a small clearing by some trees, where they show him how to throw his dagger and practice sword fighting. I can tell by the smile on his face that he's having a great time. Of course he is. Since he was, like, five years old, he and his friends have been having backyard sword fights with random sticks and branches, and now he gets to practice with the real thing. I can hear my mom's voice: *It's all fun and games until someone loses an eye.* Like, literally.

I watch everyone get to work. Maqbool finds me up by the table, staring at the other swords, wondering what would have happened if I'd chosen the wrong one. "Shouldn't we be hurrying to find Ifrit?" I ask. "This feast is awesome, but it also seems like a waste of time."

Maqbool nods. "Battles wage in the other realms. Even now, the emperor's guards are ferrying messages back and forth, conveying his stratagems and plans. But the Garden of Iram is protected—by enchantment and design. For now. It will be the last place to fall should Ifrit succeed in defeating the emperor's forces in the other realms and convert all to his cause. But time moves differently for us here in Qaf than it does for you. As we are not bound by the binary form, neither are we bound by linear progression. You likely have only a few days in Qaf to defeat Ifrit before he manages to break through the final defenses and enchantments of the Garden. And when you do—"

"If we do."

"No. *When* you do, you will return to your own world right before you left. Time will be our gift to you. Tonight, I will train you with your sword and your bow and arrow. Then you will take food and rest. Tomorrow we depart in search of Ifrit."

"You're coming with us?"

"I swore to you that I would protect you from jinn, dev, or ghul, with my life if necessary. I intend to honor that promise."

I smile at Maqbool. When he smiles back, his face gets all wrinkly. He's like the favorite uncle at every Eid party. The one no one can beat in a game of H-O-R-S-E and who always warns you when one of the aunties makes sheep-brain cutlets and tries to pass them off as mashed potatoes.

Maqbool asks me to join him by a tree where a crowd of jinn have gathered after setting up a target. I guess this is archery training. I grab my bag and see Hamza's backpack by the throne. He never remembers to put his backpack in the right place at home, either. When I reach down to grab it, I pause and unzip the main compartment, pulling out the Box of the Moon and opening the lid. The gears are moving again, and the tiny moon seems totally out of orbit, hurtling toward Earth. This can't be good.

CHAPTER 9

Magical Horses Can't Talk, Duh

I WAKE UP NESTLED IN A COCOON OF SOFT, VELVETY FAB-rics. I have no idea when I fell asleep or how long I slept. All I know is my right shoulder is sore from pulling the bow back to shoot a gazillion arrows into a tree trunk. Or to try, anyway. I hit the target three times. None of them in the center. Maqbool pretended not to seem worried, but I could tell by how soft and gentle his voice got that he was super worried but hoping really hard I would figure it out, eventually. So was I. I don't even want to discuss my sword fighting skills—or lack thereof. The movies make it look a lot easier than it is. At one point, I had to use two hands and choke up on the hilt. One of the peris with purple ombré hair is a master swordsperson, and they tried to instruct me but eventually walked away shaking their head.

I rub the sleep out of my eyes and notice the writing on my palm. Maqbool was telling me about the differences between the creatures of Qaf. I didn't have a notebook, so I took notes on my hand:

TAXONOMY OF FIRE SPIRITS
Jinn: can possess anything, flaming eyes
Peris: wings, fly, bossy?
Ghuls: Super-pointy teeth, smelly feet
Devs: Mean, polka dots or stripes, drool a lot

That's all I can make out since some of it sweated off while I slept, I guess? Honestly, I stopped paying attention at some point when Maqbool started explaining about devs being known to rip creatures' limbs off. I stand up and run my fingers through my hair. Going to find some food and avoid thinking about the purpose of all those sharp teeth.

The morning light in the Garden of Iram is an orange-gold, and the air smells of my panic and desperation with a subtle hint of jasmine. Even knowing I won't be able to see it, my eyes still search the sky for the moon. But the emperor used an enchantment to cloak it in an attempt to confuse Ifrit's troops. I get why he did that, but it was a reminder of home, and not seeing the moon—the real moon—scares me. I make my way into the courtyard and find Hamza there already, eating a fruit that looks like a bright amethyst banana and chatting with Aasman Peri, who sports a dagger on one side of her belt and a scimitar on the other.

"Sis, Aasman Peri is going to help us find Ifrit. Isn't that awesome?"

Fantastic. A stuck-up fairy who thinks I'm totally stupid is joining us.

"Oh…great. Thank you."

Aasman Peri gives me the once-over. "You're definitely going to need my help."

"And we will be there as well," Maqbool says as he and Abdul Rahman join us, holding their flying pots in hand. (Note to self: Figure out if there is a formula for the jinn combustion powering these things. Does $F=MA$ even apply here?)

The jinn have their one-person black cauldrons; Aasman Peri has wings. I thought this was going to be more of a hike-type quest. Apparently, I was wrong, but how exactly are Hamza and I going to fly along? I am not going to be carried by Aasman Peri. She'd probably drop me. On purpose.

Maqbool takes Hamza aside and hands him what looks like a small vial of silver pellets. "Ayurvedic medicine, for the fear of heights," I overhear him say. "But the effect is temporary. Use them judiciously."

As I eavesdrop, the rose-colored jinn with the dhols march into the square, beating on their drums. They are followed by the emperor, who is surrounded by his Guard and trailed by a...a...Pegasus? The emperor takes the winged horse by the reins and leads it to us. It's not a Pegasus...not exactly.

The horse's coat is a deep, shiny ebony, and as it

approaches us, it unfurls its velvety blue-black wings. It has wide nostrils and three eyes. Ummm... *three eyes?*

The emperor smiles. "I see you are in awe of the stunning steed before you. She will serve you well. Her three eyes allow her to see beyond time and space, beyond what seems and what is. She may well be able to see what you cannot. I have bid her serve you loyally, and she will abide my wishes and your commands."

Hamza sidles up to the horse and lets her sniff his hand. He strokes her nose. "Can she speak, too?"

"Speak? It's a horse. Horses don't speak." Aasman Peri rolls her eyes. "Do I have to teach you humans everything?"

"A winged horse." I jump to Hamza's defense, even though *he* can speak for himself. "The moon is breaking apart; we flew on a golden throne to get here; we burst through an oobleck wall after demagnetizing a levitating iron chest to get a magical cummerbund. And somehow thinking a three-eyed, flying horse could talk is a wild idea?"

"Human brains are so narrow." Aasman Peri steps back but makes a pouty face toward the emperor, who raises an eyebrow at her.

"I also present to you these two other gifts to aid you on your journey," the emperor says, and one of his Guard hands him a slim jade tablet, about the size of an iPad mini, and an engraved silver canteen. "This tablet is imbued with the wisdom of Suleiman. And may serve as both map and consultant. You may ask it questions along your journey, should any arise...."

"Should any arise?" Hamza whispers in my ear while the emperor continues to speak. "I still have a billion unanswered questions about the flying golden throne."

"This tablet is your key to journeying through the realms," the emperor says. "The realms of Qaf are interconnected but not bound by earthly limitations of time and space. After the Great Celestial War, the realms were separated, but to unite us, I had links, two-way passages, built so that the realms could be joined both symbolically and literally. But now we have closed all portals to the Garden. You may exit, but there is only one path to return. The only way through is forward. Once you leave a realm, you cannot go back. Like this, we are able to hold Ifrit's forces in abeyance. You must remember this."

Hamza and I nod, and the emperor hands the tablet to Hamza, who immediately begins looking for a Home button and an on/off toggle. Then the emperor gives me the small silver canteen. "This is the Flask of Endless Water engraved with the protection prayer. You must fill it at your first stop, the Garden of Eternal Spring, with the healing waters of the Zam Zam pool. But take care in doing so. Should you succeed, from then on, you will never be thirsty.

"Maqbool, Abdul Rahman, and my beloved daughter shall be your companions and be of much assistance to you as you navigate our world. But remember, Ifrit will only fall at your hands. Alas, I wish I could spare Razia and the Supahi, that they may join you in your quest, but they are needed to battle Ifrit's dev and ghul forces in the Realms of the Cow Heads and Carpet Ears."

Maqbool puts a finger to his lips when he sees

me scrunch my eyebrows and part my lips to speak. I elbow Hamz, who claps his hand over his own mouth. We can save the Cow Heads and Carpet Ears questions for another time, I guess? But seriously, *Carpet Ears*? Are they, like, fuzzy shag or are they shaped like rectangles hanging off their heads?

"We will battle Ifrit's armies, distract him, that you may fall upon him, defeat him, and banish him from these lands forever. Securing our peace. And yours. The fate of billions lies in your heroic hands."

Gee, no pressure.

The emperor places a hand over his heart and bows his head. "Peace be with you on your journey, our champions. Children of Adam and Eve. Heroes of Qaf."

"Peace be with you, also," Hamza and I respond.

Aasman Peri goes to hug her dad while I check our bags and make sure everything is secure. Hamza is still fiddling around with the tablet.

"I think you can ask it questions directly, but I don't think there's a Home screen."

"Like Siri, but it can pronounce our names right."

I nod.

Hamza gives the tablet a shake. Totally unnecessary. But he will do anything for dramatic effect. He positions his mouth close to the jade tablet and asks, "Will we defeat Ifrit?"

The jade begins to darken, and inky rainbow swirls move across the blank screen, like when you see oil on hot pavement. Words begin to emerge in the center: *Look for the answer inside your question.*

"That makes no sense! Is this thing busted?" Hamza shakes the tablet again. The words fade, but new ones appear: *Ask again later.* Hamza groans. "I get the Google Maps part, but the weird Magic 8 Ball messages are not helpful." He slips the tablet into his backpack, which he shrugs over his shoulders.

"Children, it is time," Abdul Rahman says. He and Maqbool help us onto the back of our horse, which is conveniently fitted with a surprisingly cushy brown leather two-person saddle. Still, my butt is probably going to be sore after this. I've been on a horse only twice. I had a sore butt both times, but neither horse had wings.

We wave, and our horse unfurls her strong wings in front of us and kicks off into the sky. The emperor, along with the other jinn and peris, waves to us until they're nothing but tiny dots below. Those silver pellets seem to help Hamza's fear of heights—we need, like, a lifetime supply; it will make family vacations so much easier. He seems so...unbothered. His obsession with superheroes has paid off, because he's really into this whole Chosen One thing. He hasn't brought up our parents at all, and I can't stop thinking about them lying on that rooftop in Chicago. Waiting for us. I don't care if time moves differently here.

I. AM. FREAKING. OUT.

The weird thing is, I seem to be the only one. I get that my little brother is excited by all the weapons and magical-creature stuff, but I can't understand why he doesn't seem more nervous. How can he be so...so...together? Maybe he's the real Chosen One and I'm tagging along for the ride. Like he's Frodo in *Lord of the Rings.* I don't think I'd be Sam, though. More like Pippin. But all I can really remember about him from the movies is that he sang well, always seemed to mess up, and was hungry a lot. I can't hold a tune, but the other two things fit.

"First stop, the Garden of Eternal Spring to fill your flask with Zam Zam water," Aasman Peri says as she flies alongside our horse with Maqbool and Abdul Rahman slightly behind, flanking us.

"Question," Hamza says. "Why are you called Aasman Peri? Isn't that just what you are? Aasman fairy? It would kind of be like me being called Hamza Most Amazing Kid in the Universe. Which actually kind of has a nice ring to it." Hamza grins.

The peri shakes her head. "I'm the First Peri of Qaf, so it's a title, too, silly human. Besides, don't humans have the Tooth Fairy? Do you call her Tooth? I don't think so."

Hamza frowns. "I guess you have a point. Sorry."

"You humans! Let's just get to the Garden of Eternal Spring. I really hope none of the trees eat us," she smirks, and floats ahead of us after dropping that bomb.

"Did she say the trees could *eat* us?" Hamza gulps.

"Maybe we misheard," I speak my wish out loud.

"Maybe she said, feet us? Seat us? Beat us? That makes more sense. I mean, trees don't have teeth or digestive systems, and photosynthesis must still be a thing—"

"How is *beating* us better than *eating* us?" Hamza yelps.

"We could live?" I squeak. God. What have we gotten ourselves into?

"Easy, Zendaya," Hamza says, patting our horse as we descend toward the Garden of Eternal Spring.

"Zendaya? You named our winged horse after your celebrity crush?"

Hamza's mouth drops open like he's shocked: *Shocked! I tell you!* Then a small smile emerges on his face, and his cheeks get a tiny bit pink. "Oh... uhhh...well...y'know. It's a super-awesome name. And we can't exactly keep calling her 'Horse,' can we? Is she technically a horse anyway? Does the third-eye thing officially make her not a Pegasus?" Hamza pauses and gets this dreamy look in his eye. "She's so smart and has a cool vibe, and Spidey can totally trust her...uh...we! I mean, we can totally trust her—"

"Are you talking about the horse or the actress?"

"What? The horse. Duh." That bit of pink on his cheeks is now a full-on blush—as much as a desi can blush, anyway.

"Zendaya it is." I decide to save him from any further embarrassment. Sister of the year, here I come. Besides, we need to focus, put our heads down, and get this thing done. If, in fact, we can get it done, because I have no idea how to defeat a powerful evil being who lives in a different universe.

We land in a clearing. Maqbool and Abdul Rahman immediately leap out of their flying pots, swords drawn—against the trees that might eat us, I guess? But I can see why they're on guard. Goose bumps popped up all over my skin the second I swiveled my head to take a look around. I closed my eyes when Zendaya landed. I mean, we're on a flying horse, which does not seem to work with any kind of animal evolution or biology that I can understand. And Zendaya was flapping her wings so slowly I have no idea how she generated enough thrust for lift, so I'm dealing with all this by closing my eyes. It's like when we learned about suspending disbelief when we read books, so we can believe in the Force or time-controlling wizards or invisible jets or whatever, but this time it's real life. I'd stick my fingers in my ears, too, if I wouldn't look like a three-year-old having a tantrum. Hamza would never let me live that down.

But the reason I feel like ice is coursing through my veins is that the Garden of Eternal Spring looks exactly like a beautiful forest in a Disney movie. Lush trees and shockingly bright green grass that feels like a soft carpet under our feet. Sunlight glints off the leaves, making them sparkle. I'm surprised cartoon birds aren't singing while they fly around our heads. It looks like a dream. But the air *feels* like a nightmare. Dense. Thick. Like there are bad things in it. I shiver. I look over at Hamza, who is telling Maqbool how hungry he is. I pull my cross-body bag around to the front and start digging around for something for Hamza to eat; a bag of M&Ms drops out. Bending down to pick it up, my eye catches a tree in the distance. There's a halo of light around it. I stand up, squinting, and step forward. Hanging from its branches are...orange belts. Orange karate belts. Like the one I failed to earn three times in a row. Like the one I can't stop brooding about because I want it so badly it actually stings my eyes to think about the nine-year-old who kicked my butt. It's not just embarrassing....I mean...it is, totally. But it's also kind of carving out a hole in me and leaving an empty space in my middle.

I blink my eyes and give my head a good shake. It must be low blood sugar. Mom is always worrying about low blood sugar because I fainted one time in gym after I skipped my lunch to study for a test. So now I'm paranoid about that, too. Aasman Peri walks up to me and asks what I'm staring at, so the orange belts are definitely in my head, then she points through the trees down a path where I see sparkling blue glimpses of pond—maybe a hundred yards away.

"Only you and Hamza can fulfill the challenges," she says.

"Filling the flask is a challenge? How hard can it be?"

She shrugs, then turns to call Hamza's name, but I grab her arm, stopping her. "I got this. Can you please give Hamz this granola bar? I can tell he's getting hungry, and he gets slaphappy when starvation kicks in. It's so much worse than hangry."

With my palm wrapped around the hilt of my—well, Suleiman's—sword and the other clutching the flask, I head down the path. My hand shakes a bit, so I hurry. It's sunny and bright, but it's almost too much. Like I've oversaturated the colors on a filter; it actually makes me feel a little nauseated. But the Zam Zam pool is stunning. So clear, so bright. I bend down and quickly dip the canteen in the water, filling it to the brim. Then I sip from it. The water feels cool, almost soft against my throat. True to its name, the Flask of Endless Water fills right back up. I literally cannot understand at all how science works in Qaf, but it is awesome. I keep thinking about something Mr. Clarke suggested to us in fifth-grade science, when we were debating alchemy: Maybe magic is only science we don't understand yet. That basically sums up this whole place.

I stand back up and fasten the lid onto the flask when I hear a scream. *Hamza.*

Running toward the sound of his voice, I trip and stumble across the vines and branches that crowd the path and seem to be grabbing at my arms and feet. I swear it wasn't this overgrown when I walked here earlier.

Where is everyone else? More screams draw me deeper into the woods. I pull out my sword, chopping at the branches as I go. Running even faster, I start to pant and can feel the sweat along my hairline.

After machete-chopping some giant weeds, I come to a screeching halt. Hamza is pinned to a tree trunk by its branches. He's writhing and trying to pull them off him, reaching for the dagger in his belt. But that's not even the real problem. The real problem is standing with its back to me—a giant purple-spotted, two-headed dev. A monster with a gray rhino-horn sprouting from each of its foreheads. I freeze, a sour taste rising in my throat. The dev draws a sword and begins to lift it.

Do something, Amira.

I step forward with my sword, but a branch reaches

out and wraps itself around the blade and lets out an awful screech. A branch? Screeching? A screeching branch! Then all the other trees start shrieking, and the sound doesn't only ring in my ears, it echoes inside my brain, making me dizzy.

I release the hilt of the sword, and the screaming branch flings it behind me down the path. Without thinking, without realizing what I'm doing, I grab my bow and an emerald-tipped arrow from my quiver. I hurry to pull and load my arrow, trying to get my elbow aligned properly, the way Maqbool showed me. Shifting my body so I'm perpendicular to the terrifying, sword-wielding purple dev, I imagine a straight line from the tip of my arrow to its heart. I shout, "Hey! Purple-horned thingy!"

It twists its right head and sees me. It shouts or grunts something. I can't quite make it out, because when I'm scared, sounds muffle in my ears.

Hold on, one more second.

The dev is so huge it has to shift its feet awkwardly to fully swing around to face me. It raises its sword above its heads.

Now!

I let the arrow fly, and it hits the dev squarely in the solar plexus.

Its mouths drop in shock. So does mine. I actually hit my target!

The dev's feet start turning to ash, and it twists and coils into a tiny tornado. Right before its faces become dust and whirl away, it shouts, "Why are there two of you?"

I run to grab my sword from where the tree threw it. (The tree threw it?!) Then I race back to Hamza, who is struggling against the branches. They don't seem to be moving anymore or tightening around him, but they're not loosening, either.

"Get me out of here!" Hamza yells.

"Stop squirming. I don't want to cut you." I carefully begin hacking at the branches that have pinned Hamza's arms. He has cuts all over his skin and a lash on his face that's bleeding.

Shouts come from behind me, and I whip around as I see trees being hacked at. I suck in my breath. Maqbool emerges from the thick woods, followed by

Abdul Rahman and Aasman Peri. They hurry to our side, Maqbool freeing one of Hamza's legs and Abdul Rahman the other.

Hamza stumbles forward into my arms. There are small cuts and scrapes on his ankles as well. I ease him to the ground and crouch next to him to inspect his wounds.

"Pour the water on them," Aasman Peri says.

"Water? No, we need a disinfectant or antibiotic cream; water could have bacteria in it and—"

"The Zam Zam water. Didn't you fill the flask? These wounds aren't that bad. It should work."

"Oh!" I grab the flask and pour out some water on the deepest cuts on Hamza's arms and then cup some in my hand and let it drip onto the gash on his forehead. The water starts to bubble and fizz, like when you put baking soda in vinegar.

"Hey, what the—" Hamza begins to speak, but before he can finish his sentence, the bubbles dissipate and the wounds close, leaving shiny new skin in their place. Dang, this flask *is* handy. One day, I hope I can analyze it—its properties and materials. *This* would be the best science fair project ever. I can see my trifold poster board now: The Magic of Science or The Science of Magic, or something like that.

"Took you long enough to get here!" Hamza laughs a little before grabbing his side. "Ouch. I thought that branch was going to make me puke up my guts."

"Ew," Aasman Peri says. "I know you had a near-death experience, but no need to be so graphic. Humans are very dramatic."

I give her the stink eye. "Where were all of you anyway?"

"We were caught up by the trees as well. Hamza wandered off before I could stop him, and when we tried to search for him, roots and branches kept preventing our passage. They were blocking us in faster than we could cut ourselves free," Maqbool says.

"You wandered off?" I use my mom's I-can't-believe-you-pulled-this tone as I glare at my brother.

"Look, I was starving. I smelled s'mores. Then I *saw* them. I swear. Hanging from this tree."

"The one that captured you?" I ask.

Hamza nods. "I reached for a s'more, but when

I did, the s'more disappeared and one of the tree-tentacles grabbed me. I guess I was so hungry I was hallucinating."

Abdul Rahman shakes his head. "No. Some of the tree-jinn have aligned with Ifrit. One of them, who is still loyal to Shahpal bin Shahrukh, tried to warn me, but its warning came too late. The jinn simply made you see your heart's desire and—"

"Dude, your heart's desire was s'mores?" I ask. "Not, say, getting out of here or having a superpower like flying?"

"What? S'mores are ooey-gooey deliciousness. What did you see? A chemistry lab set?"

"I...I...did you say the trees were jinn?" I ask, turning to Abdul Rahman. I absolutely do not want to bring up the orange belts I saw earlier. It's too embarrassing.

"Duh. How do you think they move and stuff?" Aasman Peri asks, like this is knowledge we should have been born with.

"But that's not the worst news," Abdul Rahman continues. I clench my fists to keep my hands from shaking. "We've learned that Ifrit has placed a large bounty on your heads. And if he has recruited some of the tree-jinn in this place to his side, he has more allies than we had anticipated and his forces are closer to Iram than we had thought. I must leave you now to warn the emperor. Iram's borders must be reinforced. Iram cannot fall."

We begin walking with our heads down toward Zendaya so we can depart. Hamza and I pull out the jade tablet. "Where do we go next?"

The words *Crystal Palace* appear on the face, then disappear into a swirling pool on the tablet as other words emerge: *Forget safety. Live where you fear to live.*

"Worst advice ever," I say.

"No. It rocks. Conquer your fears, sis. We're heroes," Hamza says, then hurries to the clearing, where he spots Zendaya waiting for us.

Maqbool walks up next to me. "He's right. You are a hero. What you did back there. That was extraordinary." He smiles, then walks over to Abdul Rahman as he steps into his pot, readying himself to fly back to the Garden of Iram. Maqbool hands him a pair of eyeglasses. Abdul Rahman rolls his fiery eyeballs but takes the glasses and tucks them into an inner pocket of his robe. They give each other a slight bow with their right hands raised to their hearts. Then Abdul Rahman kicks up and into the blue sky.

I feel a tiny pang of sadness when he flies off. Not sure why—he's not exactly easy to warm up to—but, I dunno, I think his leaving…with there being only the four of us left, it feels…lonely. Lonelier. We're so far away from home. Far from everything we love. And if something happens to us, no one will know.

"Oh no." Aasman Peri's voice shakes me out of my worry. "My bag, our provisions, they're all gone. One of Ifrit's allies must have stolen it. How are we going to keep you alive now?"

"What provisions?" Hamza asks, then pauses for a second. "Hold up. Hold up. Do you mean you had food? I've been starving since we left Iram, and you had food?"

"My father put me in charge of feeding you, and I had to make sure to ration it out. You need food for the entire journey, and I didn't want to run out too soon. You can't defeat Ifrit if you starve to death first."

Welp. "But I thought this trip was going to be two, three days tops. We don't even have enough food for that? And we're still going to return home right before everything went all upside down, right?" I'm starting to feel like there's more to the story.

"If you're successful," she responds.

"When you're successful." Maqbool jumps in. "You will return to the Before. Time *is* different here, but to human bodies, even a single day could *feel* much longer. We don't have enough data to know for certain. We only know that we don't experience time in the same way as you. And we are trying to prepare for all possibilities."

"So we are on Qaf time, but our stomachs are still on Earth time?" Hamza asks. "Like jet lag, but worse...dimension lag."

Maqbool nods.

"Can we gather some of the fruit from any of the good tree-jinns around here?" I ask.

"Too risky." Maqbool shakes his head. "We don't know which trees were inhabited by Ifrit's jinn. Such a possession could turn the fruit to poison."

I gulp. I guess I'm going to be rationing our granola bars and M&Ms. I wish I had some Oreos, too. And salt-and-vinegar potato chips. I've never really faced death before, and I guess I'm meeting it head-on, fueled by dreams of junk food.

Aasman Peri flies twenty feet into the air, her wings flapping wildly. "I know the perfect place we can stop. It's only a slight detour. The Azure Palace tilism, where a beautiful fairy queen reigns and employs the greatest chefs in all of Qaf."

"I thought we couldn't skip around realms. They're interconnected like a coil, right?"

"Yes. Yes. But this tilism is carved out between realms. Created by Queen Peri. She is loyal to my father, but she rules this small kingdom, a place of peace and refuge for the peris who want to inhabit neither Earth nor the realms of Qaf. It's a lot of retirees, basically."

"Retired fairies?" I ask.

"Why do you look so shocked? You can't expect us to work all our lives. Besides, the United Peri Workers would never allow it."

I tilt my head at her. "A union? You have a union?"

"Not me. Since my dad is an emperor, I'm technically management. But," she whispers, "I totally have sympathy for the cause of the common peri."

Really, what else is there to say after learning that fairies have a union to ensure their rights? At least Aasman Peri believes in social justice, I guess?

We mount Zendaya, and with Maqbool flying behind us as a lookout, we take off for the Azure Palace. Aasman Peri describes the feasts that will await us, and Hamza seems particularly interested in the fairy dessert offerings. I tune out, occasionally hearing things like "rosewater ice cream" and "orange blossom cream ladoos" and "pomegranate chocolate pot de crème." I look down at the jade tablet, which is still in my hands, and whisper the same question we asked when we left Iram: "Will we defeat Ifrit and return home safely?"

The screen goes black, and an answer floats up from the depths of the tablet: *Ask all...only from yourself.* Ugh. I'm too afraid to ask myself anything because part of me doesn't want to know the answers.

CHAPTER 10

This Illusion Is Real

WHAT'S THE OPPOSITE OF A PEP TALK? A DISCOURAGING downer? A daunting demoralizer? A dampening diatribe? Is a sign of the apocalypse that I'm doomed to alliterate only with *D*?

I zip the jade tablet into Hamza's backpack. He barely even notices because we're descending and he and Aasman Peri have been talking about food for nearly the entire ride. Maqbool has mostly been quiet, keeping an eye out for anyone or anything that might be following us. Apparently, Maqbool can also do a complete 360-degree head turn. It is as stomach-gurgling and nausea-inducing to watch as when I first saw Abdul Rahman do it. But since it's for our protection, it's also kind of cool.

As we plunge through thick gray clouds, I realize they're actually plumes of smoke. As in, smoke from a fire. In the distance, sapphire-colored minarets are burning. I'm guessing that's the Azure Palace? Also guessing it's not supposed to be on fire.

Aasman Peri gasps and flies ahead of us. Zendaya follows, and Maqbool is right on our heels. By the time we land, Aasman Peri is already running toward the palace. Everywhere around us, the grass, the trees, the shrubs are all burned. There's a sickly sweet smell to the smoke, like rotting bananas.

Hamza's bag buzzes. If our phones are working here—in another universe—Ummi and Papa are going to ground us for life when they see the data charges. If the world doesn't end, that is. Maybe even if it does. Hamza opens his backpack, and it's not his phone at all. Of course not. He pulls out the Box of the Moon. We don't have to lift the lid to know what's happening—the gears are grinding. They never made that loud of a noise before, and the little moon is shifting closer and closer to Earth. A red flash lights up the interior of the backpack, and when I reach for the jade tablet, I catch a sentence right before it fades away: *Be suspicious of what you want.*

What does that even—

"Help!" screams Aasman Peri.

We take off running, Maqbool in the lead, and as we sprint under the half-burnt leaves of what I think might've been a mango tree, we find Aasman Peri on a bridge with her back to us and a giant mint-green ghul—he's nearly two stories tall—towering over her. She has her scimitar out, and it drips with lime-yellow goo. It's blood, I think? Gooey ghul blood? She's backing off the bridge, and when she practically bumps into us, we see why she wants to run—aside from the towering green ghul. Mini minty-green ghuls are forming from the goo and clambering down the big ghul's shins. They make a splooshing sound that might be the grossest thing I've ever heard aside from Hamza's airsick puking. They plop to the ground, and bits of the ooze slip out of them and then are slurped back up into their bodies.

For a second, we're all frozen in shock. The tablet lights up in my hand, but I don't have time to look at it. Maqbool jumps between us and the advancing mini minty ghuls and shouts, "Run!" as he brandishes his sword at them.

We start scrambling away, but I slip over a smoldering tree root and almost drop the jade tablet, finally glancing at it as big bold letters flash: *The outward is a reflection of the inward. Show him his face.*

"What does that mean?" yelps Hamza.

"Maybe he turns to stone if he sees himself," I say, "because he's a monster, like Medusa?"

"Who is Medusa?" Aasman Peri asks.

"A woman from Greek mythology with snake hair who turns people to stone with her stare," I say. I don't make a snarky comment about the peri's so-called in-depth knowledge of human culture because, well, I can imagine my mom frowning at my rudeness.

Aasman Peri gasps. "European monsters are scary."

"No time to discuss that. We need to find a mirror. Now!" I glance back at Maqbool, who is holding off the ghuls by felling some of the dead trees. He's moving in and out of his body, from physical form to mist to physical again so he can quickly cut down trees and set the dead wood on fire. But there are too many mini minty ghuls, and the big ghul is raging, advancing, emitting terrible roars.

"Do you have a compact? You know, for, like, when you reapply lip gloss?" I ask Aasman Peri.

"What is a compact?"

"I don't think they wear makeup in this dimension," adds Hamza. "I mean, they're all weird colors and stuff—"

"Excuse me!" Aasman Peri swats at Hamza with one of her wings. "Who are you calling weird? We might not use human paint to color our faces, but that doesn't mean we don't take care of our appearance and adornments. Besides, we can make humans see us how we want....wait!" she shouts. "That's it! The Lake of Illusion. It's like a mirror, but the fairy queen warns that we should not disturb its surface lest we awake the monster that makes its home in the poison. It's said a single drop on your lips can make you lose sight of everything."

"Not like we have a lot of other options since the tablet only talks in code. Lake of Illusion it is. But we're going to need bait to draw the big ghul there."

Aasman Peri and I both turn our eyes to Hamza.

"Why do I have to be the bait? It's always the youngest!" Hamza moans before shrugging and throwing up his hands. "Whatever. What should I do?"

Aasman Peri flies into the air right above our heads. "Maqbool is holding off the little ghuls, so we only need to get the attention of the big one. He's mostly yelling and waving his colossal arms in the air." Aasman Peri flies closer and yells something in the jinn language to Maqbool.

Hamza takes off toward the bridge.

"What are you doing?"

"What I do best. Causing a distraction," Hamza says. "You and Aasman Peri need to take the lead, and once the ghul sees me, I'll run after you. Hopefully, he'll follow me."

I nod. "Be careful," I whisper.

"Yeah, right. Me, careful?" Hamza smirks, and runs to the bridge, screaming and waving his arms.

Aasman Peri flies back toward me and tells me where we're heading. We watch as Hamza starts throwing rocks at the giant ghul. Who is clearly not amused. He takes one giant leap over the bridge, over Maqbool's burning dam, over Maqbool, who has increased in size. The ground thunders with each of the ghul's steps.

Hamza starts running in our direction, screaming as the ghul follows. My heart is pounding in my ears, and there's a tingling in my chest. Aasman Peri flies low to the ground, and we dodge branches and crumbling trees along a dirt path until we come to a silver-blue pond. The surface is absolutely still. It's like a mirror melted onto the ground.

"Remember: Don't touch it. Don't go near it," whispers Aasman Peri. "Have your weapons ready. I'm going to fly Hamza behind there." She points to a wide trunk of a tree, which is only partially blackened. I nod.

Whipping out my bow and arrow, I take position behind an outcropping of boulders. Pretty sure that my tiny arrows will feel like a pinprick to this ghul, but if this whole *show him his face* mysterious instruction from the tablet doesn't work, we're not going to have a lot of time to figure out another plan.

My breath is raggedy, and I try to calm myself down. I try to remember Sensei's words, but I don't have time for a pep talk. The flutter of Aasman Peri's wings pulls my eyes upward, and I see her arms locked around Hamza's chest, his legs flailing. The earth rumbles as the ghul approaches with his lumbering steps. Aasman Peri drops Hamza behind the trunk, and he falls right on his butt. She shushes him when he tries to complain and motions to him to grab his dagger while she flies up into the treetop, her scimitar at the ready.

The giant mint-green ghul plods into the clearing. His jinn skin color reminds me of mint chocolate chip ice cream. (Now all I can think about is ghul-skin-toned ice cream. Gross.) My heart races. My fingers holding the bow and arrow are damp with sweat, and I'm using all my energy to try to keep them still. All he needs to do is see himself in this pool. And then, hopefully, he'll turn to stone or ash or be killed by poison fumes. *Stay still, Amira. You got this. All you have to do is do nothing.*

Maybe it was better when I wasn't trying to give myself a pep talk, because as I whisper the words to myself, my fingers slip. I watch helplessly as one of my emerald-tipped arrows flies through the air, arcing itself right into the ghul's thigh and then bouncing off like I hit him with a balloon. Excellent.

He turns his enormous minty-green face toward the rocks I'm hiding behind and roars. Teeth! Sharp, vampire-y teeth. Giant ones. Able-to-eat-humans-in-a-single-bite ones. Oh no. This was not the plan. *Think, Amira.* Think of anything besides becoming a ghul snack!

"Hey! Over here, you nuclear puke—colored oaf!" Hamza yells, stepping out from behind the tree trunk.

My voice catches in my throat. I try to take a breath, but my lungs feel like stone. The ghul turns toward Hamza, raises a leg, and begins to pivot in his direction.

I dart out from behind the rocks and scramble to the very edge of the pool, the thick silvery liquid licking at my heels. I grab another arrow, secure it into my bowstring, aim toward the sky, and let it fly. This time it hits the ghul square in the chest and sticks! Before he pulls it out and flicks it away like a tiny twig. *Sigh.*

He's mad. Not that he was calm before. But now that I'm staring at his face, I can see his bloodshot eyes and a tiny tiara of horns that protrude at what would be a hairline, if he had hair. Flames burst from his wide nostrils, and as he steps closer to me, I close my eyes. If this is going to be it, at least I went down fighting. Sort of fighting. Kind of cowering.

One more step and he's towering above me— massive tree-trunk legs and smelly, hobbity feet inches away from me. I turn to look at the pond behind me. It's as smooth and silvery as a mirror. It doesn't seem possible that it's liquid. Out of the corner of my eye, I swear I catch a glimpse of our backyard back home.

"Don't fall in!" Aasman Peri yells.

I turn around as the ghul leans over; I can feel the heat from his nose flames. He pulls a hairy fist back while I squeeze my eyes shut and hold my breath.

And then...nothing. I open one eyelid, then the other. The ghul is leaning all the way over me and gazing at his face in the pond. He doesn't seem to remember I'm there at all, even though his huge chin is hovering terrifyingly close to the top of my head.

"Move," Hamza whisper-shouts. I scramble on all fours between the ghul's legs toward Aasman Peri and Hamza.

The ghul doesn't notice us at all; it's like we've vanished. I look down at my hands to make sure I'm still corporeal and not a ghost—it wouldn't surprise me if I've been scared to death, literally. The ghul leans farther over, staring at himself in the silvery, mirrored surface. He raises a hand to his face and cradles it tenderly, like he's touching a baby. The ghul leans farther still, until his face is almost touching the surface, and then one of his massive feet slip, then the other. We watch, with our mouths open, as the ghul somersaults into the pool. It ripples, gurgles, and swallows him without a sound.

"That's it?" Hamza asks.

"Did you want fireworks? Let's get—" I don't get to finish my thought because the ghul lurches out of the lake, beads of liquid silver running down his arms. He screams and writhes around as a humongous purply iridescent serpent rises from the silver surface, wrapping its tail around the struggling ghul. The serpent opens its mouth wide—its jaw as big as a house—and swallows the ghul whole. We see the outline of the ghul slide down the gullet of the serpent, exactly like when our pet snake in science class swallows a once-frozen mouse. We all shudder. The snake tilts its purple head, turning its fiery eyes toward us. Without saying a word, we run into the forest of burned trees.

Straggling back to the clearing where we landed, we find Maqbool brushing leaves and ash from Zendaya's wings. A toothy smile erupts across his face when he sees us. How have I not noticed how big and how crowded in their mouths jinn's teeth are? Guess I was afraid the response would be *all the better to eat you with, my child*. If only I'd known trees could eat us here, too, I maybe would've asked more questions.

Hamza runs over to Zendaya and whispers in her ear. She bats all three of her eyelids in response.

"Weren't you worried something had happened to us?" I ask Maqbool, a bit out of breath.

"Of course." He nods. "But while I was beating back the mini ghuls, they vanished into puffs of smoke, and I knew that you must have defeated their creator."

I raise an eyebrow, not quite understanding. Maqbool continues, "They were part of the large ghul. They weren't independent beings. He had to tear a piece of himself apart to create each one."

"Kind of like when you pull apart a worm and both halves keep moving?" Hamza suggests while he pets Zendaya.

"So many gross facts I'll never be able to unsee or unhear," I say.

"Why would you want to unsee anything?" Aasman Peri asks. "The more you see, the more the knowledge can empower you. That's what Abba says, anyway."

"Speaking of the emperor," Maqbool says as he refastens his sword at his side. "We must press on. Abdul Rahman has not sent a status report. We must assume the emperor's forces are falling. No time to lose. And no more detours," he says, staring at Aasman Peri with his eyebrows raised sky-high. "We're supposed to be helping them, not getting them eaten!"

Aasman Peri crosses her arms in front of her, allowing her wings to enfold her. "Well, you went along with it." She pouts. "Maybe you should've been a better guide. You are the oldest one here, after all. By...a lot."

"I can brook no opposition. On that account, you are correct." Maqbool steps to Hamza and asks to see the Box of the Moon. When Hamza hands it to him, we all lean in and see the thing we fear most, the gears whirring, the moon moving. Even though it's a tiny little mechanism in our hands, the weight of what it means isn't lost on me.

The moon is breaking. Broken.

Soon our home will be overrun with the kinds of ghuls we just fought. Sure, the world's armies could handle one, dozens, maybe even hundreds of monsters? But what if there are thousands or more? What about when it's an army of towering ghuls with powers and mini ghuls erupting from their wounds? What happens then? Earth doesn't have Lakes of Illusion and ghul-gulping sea monsters. Not to mention that I have no idea what it would really mean for Ifrit to free his dad and have two super evil, super evilest villains running around. Two kids can't beat them all. I don't care if we're the so-called Chosen Ones or not. We've barely scraped along so far, and we haven't even met Ifrit. We would've been lost without Maqbool and Abdul Rahman, and, yes, even Aasman Peri. Though, if you think about it, she's the entire reason we had to take on that minty ghul in the first place. Her mouth and Hamza's bottomless pit of a stomach.

We can't be this stupid again. Stay on target.

That's the only thing we can do. What we have to do. Move on. See this through till the end—whatever that is. It's like the emperor said, the only way through is forward. We can't turn back.

The tablet shows us a sketch of a beautiful, gleaming castle. The words *Crystal Palace* appear over a squiggly map that looks like you need 3D glasses to see it. That's the whole point of Zendaya's three eyes—according to the emperor. She can see in and through multiple dimensions at once. I show Zendaya the tablet, and she snorts and nods. Aasman Peri bites her lip, her eyes super wide and round. She's scared. I can almost smell the fear coming off her. Could be fairy sweat, but I'll stick with fear for now, even though she'd never admit it. I know what that's like because I don't want to admit I'm scared, too.

CHAPTER 11

Crystal Dragon Breath Really Stabs

QAF FEELS LESS SUNNY. NOT LIKE THE DAY IS ENDING AND the sun is going to set, but literally like the power of the sun is fading and the dark is taking over. Like the blanket of gray clouds that moves into Chicago in winter and pushes the cold into your bones.

Hamza shivers as we get stuck in a cloud bank. I blow onto my hands, hoping to warm them, but as we descend, a bright burst of color rips the clouds away. Below us is all jagged colorful crystal and sharp edges. No wonder Aasman Peri didn't want to stop here. There's no place to even land without getting pierced, it seems. And I definitely do not want to die getting impaled by rainbow glass. As he unsheathes his sword, Maqbool flies down before us, signaling to Zendaya to hover in the air. Her wings beat faster.

Flying over the stabby crystals, Maqbool cuts through them with his sword, creating a flat place for us to land. I can imagine my dad yelling at us to stop because landing on cut crystal or glass doesn't exactly seem safe. But it's not like we have a choice. We can't go back, only forward, until we find where Ifrit is hiding and crash into our supposed destiny.

Zendaya doesn't land, though, and we watch as Maqbool turns his flame on high, fusing the shards together, smoothing all the edges so we don't get sliced up while walking. Traveling with beings made of fire definitely comes in handy. He beckons us and flies onward, continuing to cut a path through the glass prisms and melting them down to smooth the way.

"Dude, it's like the Fortress of Solitude," whispers Hamza, awe in his soft voice. Before I can ask, he turns to me, guessing what I'm about to say. "It's in the comics and the movies. Superman's secret head-quarters in the Arctic? Filled with his parents' memories from Krypton. It's where he goes for—"

"Wild guess. Solitude?" I say.

"When he needs to figure things out," Hamza snaps back.

"Are you saying some human stole our idea, pretended it was theirs, and made money off it? The Crystal Palace is tens of thousands of human years old!" Aasman Peri's jaw drops. "How rude."

Hamza and I glance at each other. "Hey," he says, "remember when Mom yelled at that coffee shop dude when he tried to tell her—"

"That sprinkling cocoa powder on a *chai tea* latte really brought out the authentic Indian flavors." I use air quotes the way Ummi does every time she hears chai tea. *That means tea tea!* she always says.

"She was so mad." Hamza grins.

"As she should have been. That drink sounds like an insult!" Aasman Peri screws up her face, like she's eaten an entire lemon. "Humans are a highly dissatisfying creation."

"Hey, not all humans, okay? Besides, weren't we, like, basically forced to come here to save your world because of the bad jinn and devs and ghuls?" Hamza jumps in.

"It's saving your world, too! We may have some evil creations, but humans are even evil-er."

"According to?" Hamza asks.

"Me. Plus our historians. You humans hate people because of skin color and who they love. And you throw garbage into your seas and leave junk in space. You pollute the stars. *The stars!* You're the only creation that destroys your own environment and kills other species and mounts their heads on walls for sport, which is very strange and highly gruesome!"

Hamza opens his mouth, but I grab his arm and shake my head. We're all on edge right now. The air feels weighted down, and we're only getting by the obstacles by dumb luck. No reason to get into an argument. Besides, Aasman Peri has a point. Several of them.

I take Zendaya's reins in my hand, and the four of us march ahead, silently, on the smoothed path of broken shards that Maqbool created. We watch our steps and take care not to slip or trip in this forest of crystal spears. It's still overcast, but rainbows reflect in all the prisms, which doesn't make sense. The triangular glass needs a light source to create the rainbow—dividing the clear light spectrum into different colors. But the rainbows aren't refracted here. They're not cast onto other surfaces. Looking around, I realize that everything is clear, cold crystal. The crystals have trapped all the color on the inside.

"This realm is ancient. It's existed since before our time. There are no written records of its history. No one's lived here in who knows how long. Maybe ever," Aasman Peri whispers as we crunch forward, her breathing slow, almost thready. "Light doesn't penetrate to the ground. There's no source of water or food. It's only an abandoned relic, used as a link between realms."

"And the Crystal Palace?" I ask.

"Balances in the mouth of a massive dormant dragon," she squeaks, then points. "And it doesn't seem to be sleeping anymore."

We stop short. We spy Maqbool beyond the human-size angled crystals that block our path. In front of him is the beautiful, multidomed Crystal Palace. Clear minarets spiral high into the air. Arched windows are etched with flowers and leaves. Interlocking geometric patterns rise and meet above a giant open doorway.

The entire palace rests in the mouth of an emerald-scaled dragon whose closed bejeweled eyelids lift slowly, one, then the other. It's beautiful and terrifying. And the dragon lets out a tremendous roar, sending flames shooting past the castle straight toward us.

"Shield your faces!" yells Maqbool.

A jeweled dragon is attacking us?!

I grab Hamza, pulling him down into a duck-and-cover tornado squat we learned during safety drills at school. We huddle next to Zendaya, readying to be burnt to a crisp by the enormous flames coming from the dragon's mouth. Instead, I feel an icy droplet nick my arm. I peek at it as a tiny bead of blood pops to the surface of my skin, then pluck a mini crystal spike from my arm. What? How? We have freezing rain in Chicago, and hail and sleet, but this is different. And it hurts. Turning my neck to find where it came from, I see the dragon flame expand above us, but it doesn't rain down in embers or brimstone. Instead, I see thousands—no, millions—of crystal shards arc into the air and pause for a millisecond, then lash down on us. I scream as pellets hit my neck. I fall over Hamza. Zendaya whinnies, turns, and brings her blue-black wings together over our heads like palm fronds, protecting us from the miniature crystal daggers.

Even with Zendaya's wings shielding us, I'm too chicken to look up to see if Maqbool and Aasman Peri are okay. Scared of the *plink-plink-plink* sound the crystal rain makes as it clatters to the ground. Terrified of the dragon's fiery snarl. Some Chosen One I turned out to be.

Hamza's back trembles, and I inch closer to him. A small bird the color of the inside of a blood orange lands on my sneaker. Aasman Peri moves nearer to us, using her bright yellow wings as a shield. Hamza spies the bird and then looks up at me and says, "I guess this little guy is scared. Same, buddy. Same." The orange bird hops into Hamza's palm, and he strokes its tiny head with his thumb.

"What is happening?" I ask as the rain crystals pile up around us, ankle-deep and rising.

"Rain of the Fire Crystal Dragon," she says. "We need to move. Or else we'll be buried for eternity. Like them."

"Them? Who's them?" Hamza asks what we're both thinking. Though I kind of don't want to know the answer.

Aasman Peri frowns and sweeps the shards away from around our feet. "Them," she says, pointing.

We peer into the glassy surface, and deep below, we see the faces. Blue, orange, green, red, yellow. Winged. Horned. Wide-eyed looks of terror frozen on their faces. Devs. Ghuls. Peris. Jinn. Captured beneath the crystal.

All the color drains from my face. The blood

in my veins feels like ice. Hamza chews his lip and trains his eyes on the bird in his hand. It chirps. Then chirps again, louder.

"What is it, little guy? Sorry, I can't speak bird." Hamza's voice is soft, and there's a quiver in it. I think we're both trying to ignore the plinking around us and the shards piling up and the likelihood that we're about to become Lucite trophies.

"That's not a bird," Aasman Peri says as it hops from Hamza's hand onto his backpack. "It's Maqbool."

"Shape-shifted into a bird to escape the shards. Smart," Hamza says, and the bird chirps again and again, pecking the bag.

"The tablet. Duh. He's telling us to read the tablet!" I grab it from the bag and ask the jade surface what to do. Words appear: *Everyone sees the unseen in proportion to the clarity of his heart.*

"Ahhhhh!" I scream at the screen. "For once, use words that tell us something useful. That mean anything!" I bury my face in my hands. My eyes sting with tears. This is stupid and useless. *I'm* useless.

"Hey, look," Hamza says.

I blink away a tear and turn back to the tablet: *Fine. Just get on the horse.*

"Wow. The tablet can be snarky. I wonder how they coded that into its program?"

"Hamza! Get on Zendaya," I shout, and grab him by his sleeve, hauling him up. We all clamber onto Zendaya's back. She immediately gallops forward.

Ow! Ow! Ow!

We try to protect our faces from the crystal rain, but one nicks me right above my right eyebrow and really stings.

"Hey! Wait," I yell at Zendaya. "Halt. Heel. Stop! She's heading right for the gates of the Crystal Palace. Inside the dragon's mouth!"

"We'll be fried! Roasted! Toasted! Human s'mores! I don't want to die being eaten by a dragon," Hamza yells.

Even Aasman Peri screams as we near the wide entrance of the palace.

The flames engulf us.

I don't feel the thousand little gashes in my skin anymore. Don't feel the crystal daggers falling. Don't hear the plink. I squeeze my eyes tight and feel Hamza's forehead buried in my back. There is no sound and nothing to see but the darkness behind my eyelids. In that quiet dark, the moon appears. Broken, drifting away. Some chunks hurtling toward Earth. In the cracks of the moon, in the broken parts, I see Ifrit's forces, clambering, fangs bared, toward our home. A swarm of ghuls blots out all the light, and Earth falls into darkness.

"Open your eyes, silly human." Aasman Peri's voice is shrill in my ear. But it must mean...I raise one eyelid, then another, as Zendaya whinnies and comes to a stop near a sparkling stream, where clear water runs over smooth gray stones. We're alive! Quickly, I check my clothes, my arms, my hair. Nothing singed. I don't smell like burnt toast. And I don't have a scratch on me—not a single nick or cut on my arms. I look down at the tablet that I'd been clutching in my arms: *Everyone sees the unseen in proportion to the clarity of his heart.* Now that I have a moment to think and am not panic-dodging tiny crystal rain daggers, I realize there's something familiar about those words that have reappeared on the smooth jade surface.

Hamza jumps down from Zendaya. "Are we dead? Is this Jannah? Where are the fat baby angels with harps and stuff?"

Aasman Peri play-punches him in the arm. "There's no such thing as baby angels with wings. Babies can't do anything. They're so high maintenance. What would be the point?"

"Uhhh, old-timey Valentine cards?" Hamza shrugs.

Aasman Peri ignores him. Probably for the best. "You're alive. We're all alive. Zendaya drove us through fire—"

"But the fire wasn't real. Oh my God. That's it, isn't it? *Everyone sees the unseen in proportion to the clarity of his heart.* That's what the tablet meant. That's what Zendaya could see." Maybe I'm finally figuring out how to decode the tablet's funny messages.

The little bird zooms out of Hamza's backpack and whirls and twirls into a spiral. Before it touches the ground, it transforms into Maqbool.

"Please give me the power to do that," pleads Hamza. "I could be famous."

Maqbool laughs. "Humans have many powers that we do not. And you get to eat delightful foods like Flamin' Hot Cheetos. Flaming foods! Even we jinn haven't created such wonders. No need to envy us. And you are right, Amira. It appears the flames and the crystal rain were the dragon's illusions."

"But how? I felt the pain. I saw my blood! How can all that be an illusion?" I ask.

"The mind is a powerful tool that can be used as a weapon against all—humans and jinn alike. As you saw from all those buried in the crystal—trapped, in a way, by their own minds. Zendaya could see through the illusion with her three eyes. We were able to pass through, thanks to the clarity and goodness of your hearts. And our faith in each other." He sweeps a hand to his chest and bends his head down in a half bow. I get a little choked up when he does this.

When we first came through the Obsidian Wall, Maqbool warned us that things in Qaf are not always what they seem. Our senses have been tricked in so many ways. I have to remember that, but how are we supposed to know when we *can* trust our own eyes and ears? I dismount and take a look around. We're in beautiful woods of thick trees, their boughs crowded with tiny orange blooms. The air smells like chamomile tea and wet moss. What a perfect place for a nap. If only. "So where are we?" I ask. I stare down at the tablet, but it's gone blank. Perfect. Still being temperamental, I guess?

Aasman Peri shrugs. Maqbool rubs his stubbly chin. "That, I do not know. This tilism—remember, these are worlds created from inanimate objects—is not one I've ever heard of. It seems to be embedded in the Realm of the Crystal Palace. Most intriguing."

"We're in the dragon's belly, aren't we? We have to get out of here. This is like when the Millennium Falcon was swallowed by a giant space slug." Hamza hops from one foot to the other. His entire body hums and vibrates. This is how he gets when he's nervous. Like right before rock-climbing competitions. I don't blame him. Nothing makes sense to me here. I can't figure out the science. And, hello!

Enchanted emerald-scaled dragons that breathe fake flames are real?

"You're not in the dragon's belly. We are in an uncharted tilism, a hidden pocket in this realm," a voice booms through the dense trees. "This place is not on any map and cannot be detected by JPS." Abdul Rahman emerges from behind the branches, and from the look on his face, he doesn't have good news.

CHAPTER 12

Hindsight Is 40/40

"AS-SALAM-ALE-KUM, MY VIZIER," MAQBOOL SAYS, GREET-
ing Abdul Rahman as they clasp arms, not in a
handshake, but, like, an armshake? Fingers wrapped
around each other's right forearms. They exchange a
meaningful look. "What news from Iram?"

Abdul Rahman takes a seat, cross-legged on the
soft, mossy grass. We join him. He unties a sack he's
been carrying and settles a blanket on the ground;
we help him unpack the food he brought. He and
Maqbool whisper, but I'm too hungry to pay attention. Hamza and I tear into the food, eating Indian-
style with our fingers, but not before I squirt some

antibacterial gel onto our hands. The world may be ending, but I'm not about to eat food with dirty hands. I shovel delicious saffron rice into my mouth. It's studded with golden raisins and pine nuts and candied carrots, kind of like a sweet biryani. We also gulp down mango juices; some of the syrupy liquid dribbles down my chin. I wipe it away with the back of my hand and use my clothes as a towel to dry off. Hamza stares at me, mouth open.

"What?"

"You used your T-shirt as a napkin." He shakes his head. "This journey has really changed you."

I almost throw a little shade Hamza's way, but I stop myself. Having him here means that I'm worried about him every second because of, well, the whole big-sister thing, which runs deep in desi culture. The oldest is always The Oldest. But it also means that I'm not alone. I'd never tell him this, obviously, but his dorky remarks make this whole bizarre situation a little less horrible because it reminds me that no matter what happens, we're still ourselves. I pass him one of the doughnut holes covered in sugary syrup, and he pops the whole thing into his mouth, wipes his face with his shirtsleeve, and smiles.

"Ahem." Abdul Rahman clears his throat. "We are in a bit of a bind."

"Really. Tell us something we don't know," Hamza says.

"Why would I do that? The list would be nearly endless; we'd be stuck here for eternity."

"Never mind," I say. "What's worse than, oh, the moon breaking apart and Earth possibly being overrun by evil ghuls and devs?"

"That the leader of those evil ghuls and devs has created this tilism as a trap," Maqbool says.

"I knew it!" Aasman Peri pipes up. "I've never heard of this place. It's not one of the Eighteen Realms. And it's not a rest stop, oasis, or uninhabited island, either."

"You have rest stops?" Hamza says.

"How else would—"

"Children. Enough. The problem is not merely that this tilism is unmapped. It's that we don't know where or when it is," Abdul Rahman says.

"Well, how did you get here then?" I ask.

"I arrived at the Crystal Palace and walked through the dragon's mouth, just like you did. For with age comes deep wisdom."

A grin spreads across Hamza's face. "By any chance did that wisdom come from watching us gallop through and then following us?"

Abdul Rahman raises an enormous eyebrow at him. "It is perhaps true that I saw you from a very, very far distance. I cannot be certain it even was you. Anyway, what is done is done! No need to dwell on the how or why."

Hamza mouths, "You're welcome."

But Abdul Rahman pretends not to notice and continues talking. "Besides, entering is not the problem. It's getting out. That's why your jade tablet is not working. Ifrit has created some kind of cloaking system over this place. He's blocked the entrance, and the only way we can get out is if he chooses to create a portal. Or if we can escape as his minions enter."

"What? No. That can't be it. Hoping we can sneak

around his horde of goons when they arrive is not a plan," I say.

Maqbool stands up and walks away from us, looking around the woods, peering down the path, rubbing his orange chin. When he turns back toward us, he has one of those *aha!* smiles on his face. "The scroll. We should consult the Everlasting Scroll. You did return with it, did you not, my Vizier?"

"Yes, of course. Of course!" Abdul Rahman unties his outer cloak and begins rummaging through his pockets, pulling out all sorts of odds and ends and dropping them onto the blanket. A brass spyglass, a silver teacup, a pack of Big Red gum (obviously an Earth souvenir), a small conch shell, and a pair of red plastic reading glasses. His robe is way bigger on the inside than it looks like on the outside. Then he pulls out a scroll, tightly rolled and tied with a red ribbon.

Maqbool picks up the red glasses and hands them to Abdul Rahman. "Please, my Vizier. Indulge me and use your reading glasses."

Abdul Rahman harrumphs and plucks them from

Maqbool's hand and pushes them up on his face. The red glasses on his giant blue head are actually kind of hilarious. Aasman Peri giggles, and he stares at her over the tops of the lenses, his eyeballs especially fiery. She bites her lip. Maqbool tries to hide his sly smile.

Abdul Rahman mumbles something under his breath, and I catch only a few words: *absolutely unnecessary, eye exam two hundred years ago, perfect 40/40 vision.*

He unfurls the long scroll across the blanket. The paper is thick and vanilla-colored. You can see the fibers in it, and the writing goes nearly to the rough edges. The script looks like Urdu, sort of? A flowery calligraphy script that's similar to Persian. I feel a pang of guilt because I never really learned to read Urdu well. I can make out a few letters and words, but that's it—the vowel marks are sometimes optional, and I had trouble figuring out which letters connected to which. The letters are a dull, tarnished gold, but as Abdul Rahman moves his finger beneath each word, the letters illuminate and shine like the twenty-four-karat gold jewelry in the Indian stores on Devon Avenue in Chicago. Once he completes the sentence, the light of that line blinks off, and it returns to a faded gilt.

Each of us stare at Abdul Rahman as he reads— a bit slowly, muttering words here and there. Every time he looks like he's about to say something, we lean forward, like we're waiting for the answer to a cliff-hanger.

His mouth drops open all the way from the jaw joint, like he's an alligator. All his sharp teeth visible in his very, very large mouth. His tongue is a blueish pink, like he's been sucking on a blueberry Dum Dum. His already ginormous eyes bulge from his head.

"My Vizier?" Maqbool leans in and peers over Abdul Rahman's shoulder. He shoves his own glasses over his nose, and I watch, my breath held, as he scans the scroll. His orange face turns papaya, then cantaloupe, then yellow, then lighter. I think he's literally turning white from shock, like he's seen a ghost. But I can't imagine that jinn would be afraid of ghosts, so this must be super bad.

My palms get all clammy, and I try wiping the sweat off on my jeans. After what feels like an eternity but is likely only a few seconds, I finally blurt out, "What is it? Tell us. Do they eat us? Turn us blue? How bad can it be?"

"I told you to wear your reading glasses!" Maqbool ignores me and speaks directly to Abdul Rahman as his face climbs back up to a deep orange, almost red.

"I...I...don't...my vanity. I have failed these children. I have failed the emperor, brought all of Qaf to the brink of destruction...." Abdul Rahman drops the scroll, and all the light goes out of it.

"Will someone talk to us? We're right here. How have you failed us? What's happening?" I'm yelling now, and I don't care if the jinn can turn me into a burnt tween twig.

Maqbool raises his eyes toward us, bits of ash rimming his lower lids. "I am so sorry, children. The prophecy. The Chosen One. It's...it's not as we thought."

"Use words that actually make sense!" Hamza yells, his hands curled in fists at his side.

Abdul Rahman rises to his full height, towering

over us. He places a heavy hand on each of our shoulders. "I misread the prophecy." His voice trembles as he speaks.

"You what!" My head might explode. Right. Now.

"There is a Chosen One. But my classical Urdu was off, and some words were unclear, I fear.... My vision...some numbers blurred. The Box of the Moon awoke, but... Maqbool was right; I should have been wearing my reading glasses." Abdul Rahman looks right into my eyes. "The prophecy states that I, Abdul Rahman, Vizier to the Emperor of Qaf, King of Kings, Ruler of the Eighteen Realms, Holder of the Peacock Throne, Protector of the World Between Worlds, the mighty Shahpal bin Shahrukh...I was to travel to Earth when Ifrit rose to return with the savior. The mighty warrior to protect our world and yours. The one who, in infancy, was anointed heir of Suleiman the Wise, taken and nursed in Qaf by Queen Peri herself, who daubed his eyelids with collyrium and assigned him the spot of destiny with the blessed ink of Qaf." Hamza and I both touch our Majid Marks—the identical moles on our faces.

"Get to the point!" I scream.

"I was to return with the true Chosen One, the famed warrior, Amir A. Hamza, from Earth year 1022. I have utterly failed." Abdul Rahman bows his head and falls to his knees before us.

I stagger backward. Hamza turns to look at me, his eyebrows scrunched, a confused expression on his face. This can't be right. This can't be happening.

I take a deep, shuddery breath. Then another. "So…wait…you're saying…you brought us…two kids from Chicago in 2022…here…by…by mistake? Because you were too vain to put on your stupid reading glasses? You're a bajillion years old! You lead a jinn army and you…you got this wrong?" I fall to the ground and start crying. I don't care. I can't stop myself. I was right. We should never have been here. This was never our job. We weren't chosen for anything, except bad luck.

"So we're not the Chosen Ones?" Hamza's voice breaks as he plops down next to me. "We're nothing but…but…regular kids?"

Aasman Peri doesn't say anything. She silently scooches over and envelops us in her wings.

"Children. We do not ask your forgiveness, for this mistake is beyond mercy. We are aggrieved at our deep error," Maqbool says.

I look up at him, my face streaked with tears, my eyes burning. "Fix it. You're jinn. You have powers. Figure it out!"

"Take us back. Return us and then go get that other dude. Easy peasy," Hamza says. "How could you be a thousand years off? Did the moon break in his time, too?"

Abdul Rahman finally glances up. I don't make eye contact with him. I can't. I'm a giant ball of rage. And when I'm this mad, it comes out as furious bursts of tears.

"This is what we tried to explain when we said time doesn't work in the same way here. Human time is not our constant. The moon is rupturing in your world, in the year 2022. But the Chosen One exists in 1022—your past. I would merely have had to enter the portal in his time, but I didn't. I entered it in yours. He would have battled Ifrit here, in Qaf, setting the world right for you. And in defeating Ifrit, would right our world for us."

I kneel and close my eyes like we do in the dojo during mokuso—a kneeling meditation—breathing in and out. It's about calming our minds, clearing them, but it's more than that. It's about preparation. About being present. Right now, I have to be here. I have no other choice, because wishing I was back in Chicago with my parents isn't going to change anything. I open my eyes. "Hamza's right," I say.

"I am?"

I nod. "We're kids. You should return us to where we belong and get the right Chosen One, the only one—Amir A. Hamza—and have *him* battle Ifrit. You said time works differently here. So reverse it. Go back." I pause. Catch my breath. "Help us," I plead.

Maqbool wipes his hand over his face. When he removes it, he looks like he's added a hundred years of wrinkles to his forehead. "We can't," he whispers. "It has begun. The way back is sealed. To return home,

Ifrit must be defeated. If he's not, you will have no home to return to."

Hamza pulls the collar of his T-shirt between his teeth. It was a nervous habit he had when he was little. He mostly grew out of it by second grade. I can hardly blame him for reverting to it now. Aasman Peri's eyes blaze at Abdul Rahman, but she stays with her wing around Hamza's shoulder and walks him over to Zendaya to get a swig of water from the flask.

I step closer to Abdul Rahman, wrap my arms around my middle, like I'm holding myself together. A wave of queasiness sweeps through me. I hate puking, but if I projectile vomit in Abdul Rahman's face right now, it might be worth it. I swallow hard, tasting the bile in my throat. I open my mouth to scream. But someone else screams before I do. A voice in the woods that sounds like a little girl. A familiar voice. "Help! Mommy!" It's a voice that sounds a lot like mine.

CHAPTER 13

Who Do You Think You Are?

HAMZA TAKES OFF RUNNING THROUGH THE WOODS toward the voice. We chase after him. I wriggle my finger in my ear as we run. That voice. The one that sounds like me? I swear I can hear it inside my head.

We pass a small waterfall, and even with the crash of water in the pond below, the voice grows stronger. But we don't see anyone. Hamza points directly at the cascade of rushing water. He's right. The voice is coming through the veil of water. Without saying anything, without even pausing to think, Hamza pumps his arms back and leaps into the water like he's jumping into the ocean depths and lands...on his feet in the ankle-deep pond. I shake my head. He turns to me, a huge grin spreading across his face. This is so Hamza. If we weren't possibly about to die, I would laugh. Hamza pushes forward toward the waterfall.

"Hamza, hang on. Wait," I say, but he either doesn't hear me or doesn't want to listen and steps through the cascading water.

"What the...guys! Get in here!" We hear Hamza yell back at us. We rush through the waterfall and into a damp cave.

The walls are smooth black stone, and above us, a hole in the rock allows a ray of brilliant sunlight to pool on the cave floor. In the very center of that circle of sun is a bright gold cage. Big enough for a lion. But there's not a lion in the cage. There's a girl, cowering, crying in the corner. She's thin, and her skinny brown arms are wrapped around her legs. A thick black braid runs down her back, tied with a worn red ribbon. The braid...the ribbon...they're so familiar.

Too familiar. Goose bumps spring up all over my wet skin. It looks like...but how?

"Are you okay?" Hamza asks, approaching the golden bars.

I stay behind, frozen in place, as the others step forward into the dank cavern. For a moment, they block my view, and I can't see the girl anymore. But I hear her grunt and rise. Then Hamza gasps. "Help me," the voice says.

The others move aside, each turning to look at me, their eyes wide with shock. I step closer to the cage, the voice, the girl. And it's...me. I mean...it...she looks like me but with slightly distorted features— eyes too far apart, nose narrower. Like a Silly Putty face impression. And she—it?—looks younger than I am, maybe seven or eight years old. It can't be. How can it possibly be? I shake my head, blink, try to make myself see correctly. But the image doesn't change. The girl doesn't go away. She approaches the bars, and Hamza presses himself closer. She's speaking. *In my voice.* Or sort of a higher-pitched imitation of my voice. "My father sold me to Ifrit. I can help you find and defeat him! That will release me. Please," she begs, pointing to a rusty lever Excalibured into the rock.

It's a trap! I want to scream, but my voice sticks. My whole body sticks. Like I'm trapped in a giant glob of Jell-O. Some *thing* is blocking me. Every hair on my arms stands up, my breathing loud in my ears. Why isn't anyone doing anything? Saying anything? Their eyes look glazed over like some *thing* is affecting them, too. I watch as Hamza leaps to the lever and pulls it down. The entire front of the cage rises in the air like it's being lifted by invisible puppet strings.

The little girl falls into Hamza's arms, thanking him. The others crowd around her. The force holding me back releases me, and I wonder if it was something mystical or just me, freezing up, caught in the headlights, not sure what to do. It wouldn't be the first time. Still, I stay back. Maqbool offers her some water. When she drinks, she stretches her neck so far back it doesn't seem...normal, natural. When she returns the bottle to Maqbool, she holds my gaze; I swear the color of her eyes blinks from brown to red for a second.

"How come you're here? How can—" I finally manage to pluck words out of my throat.

"I told you." She giggles. "My father sold me to Ifrit."

"But you're human. There's no humans in Qaf. And why do you look like me but younger? How is that even possible?"

Hamza looks at me and then back at the girl, whose features begin to shift. He starts to back away from her. "You said you could take us to Ifrit."

The girl turns her head away and, in a flash, short, crimson-colored wings erupt from her shoulder blades. She whips back around, crooked fang-like teeth bared in a face that has more wrinkles than a Shar-Pei. Small blue horns sprout from her forehead. "And I shall, with pleasure," she says, her voice a shriek.

"Whoa. She even got your squeaky voice right!" Hamza blurts. Before I can even roll my eyes at him, the terrifying imposter-me flies at him, her hands reaching for his throat.

I scream.

Maqbool pushes her back with his arm. She falls to the ground. Laughing, she raises two fingers to her mouth and whistles. It's an awful, screeching sound and so loud they probably heard it all the way back in the Garden of Iram.

"She ensnared us with an enchantment!" Abdul Rahman bellows, then turns to the fake-me. "Your life will be forfeited for your deception!"

"I...I...don't understand. Who are you? Why did you look like...me?"

The impostor-me laughs. "The ghul you encountered when you first set foot in the Garden replicated your likenesses for Ifrit's troops that we would know you from all jinn."

"What, like wanted posters in old movies?" Hamza asks. "He's a pretty bad sketch artist if you ask me; Amira's nose doesn't—"

"Enough!" Abdul Rahman yells.

Maqbool grabs the crimson-winged peri by the arm while Abdul Rahman yells at us to run out of the cave. There's no time to argue or think. Aasman Peri extends her wings and flaps them, creating a wind at our backs, pushing us forward. We emerge soaking wet and slog to the bank of the pond. A blast of hot air from Abdul Rahman's flame dries us off.

That's when I hear it. A drumbeat. A sound like a million hooves thudding the ground.

Maqbool hands over the imitation-me fairy to Aasman Peri. Is she really a peri? Her wings are short, not like those of the other fairies we've met in Qaf, and she has horns like some dev. "An army. She summoned an army," Maqbool spits.

Without speaking and without answering the jumble of questions and the freaked-out *What? What? What?* falling from my lips, Abdul Rahman and Maqbool begin felling trees in front of us, creating a barrier between us and whatever army the peri has summoned. The only way through to us is along a narrow pass that bottlenecks about a hundred yards from where we are, so I guess they're hoping this will give us more time. But time to what?

The thunder of the march grows louder. Hamza and I start piling smaller branches and any stones we can find onto the wall. Zendaya flies off, and Hamza yells out to her as she rises into the sky.

"She will scout the advancing army," Maqbool says without stopping his movements. "She will find if the way to leave is open and fly the two of you out of here." Now he's tying stones to the ends of the vines hanging down from the trees. Weapons, I guess?

"We can't leave you," I say.

"You can and you will. We pulled you into a battle that wasn't yours to fight," Maqbool says.

"It is now," I whisper. In my heart, I know it's true even if I secretly wish it weren't. We're here. And all my wishing isn't going to change that.

Abdul Rahman is digging a pit fifty feet in front of us at a speed too impossible to follow, covering it with brush. A booby trap. To trap some of them when they make it past the barrier. To give us time to escape. Neither of them says so, but it doesn't seem like we can fight off an entire army. Two old jinn who need reading glasses, a spunky fairy, and two kids with no powers. The odds are definitely not in our favor. Escape is our only chance.

I rush forward to help Abdul Rahman while Hamza piles up rocks we can use to throw at shape-shifting monsters made of smokeless fire. I'm guessing the message on the Magic 8 Ball jade tablet would not be reassuring right now, so I don't even bother asking it about our chances.

The sound is getting louder, and I swear I can feel my heart lodged in my throat like a sideways chicken bone.

"Hey! Ow!" I whip my head around when I hear Aasman Peri cry out.

The evil peri has wriggled her way out of Aasman Peri's grip and is wielding a small, sharp dagger that she apparently kept hidden in her boot. Aasman Peri pulls out her sword and advances, pushing the peri back toward the pond.

I drop the branches and run back to the barrier,

holding Hamza back, out of the way, as the two peris eye each other.

The evil peri jabs forward with her dagger, forcing Aasman Peri to take a few steps back as she lashes out with her sword. The peri dodges her slashes and laughs. "You are no match for me, young one. I am Arwa, a do-nasli, a half-clan. I have survived hundreds of years, cast out from the society of my mother's peri tribe and my father's dev kinfolk. Reviled by all. Alone until Ifrit gave me a home. I owe him my allegiance. I have survived it all. And today is not my end."

They circle each other almost like a dance. I scream at Maqbool and Abdul Rahman, but they keep setting the traps, assuming, I guess, that Aasman Peri can handle herself. But her worried-looking face doesn't make me feel so sure.

Hamza bends down, grabs a rock, and hurls it right at Arwa's body. The stone connects, and there's a crack as it hits her rib cage. Dang. I guess the rocks as surprise weapons are more effective than I thought. Arwa screams, and in that instant, Aasman Peri lunges forward and uses her sword to disarm her. I hurry over to grab Arwa's dagger before she can pick it back up. When Aasman Peri kicks her in the chest, the peri-dev falls to the ground, clutching her side and rolling over.

"Yes!" Hamza shouts, and gives me a fist bump. But our joy from this tiny victory doesn't last long. In the distance, we hear the screams and shouts of the devs and ghuls as they approach. They're getting closer. And I'm absolutely pee-in-my-pants, puke-up-my-guts terrified.

"Jinn! Hello! What's the plan? Wait here to be devoured by ghuls?" Aasman Peri asks, taking her eyes off Arwa, who is still on the ground. In that moment, the peri-dev rolls over, pulls a small knife from the sash at her waist, and whips it in Hamza's direction.

"Nooooooooo!" I scream, and watch as the knife somersaults through the air directly toward my little brother. I hear the roar of my voice muffled in my ears. My feet feel like they're stuck in molasses as I reach out toward Hamza, who can only stare forward, frozen with fear, as the knife hurtles toward him.

A flash of orange blazes in front of me, and when it slows, I see it's Maqbool, who has thrown himself in front of Hamza, catching the knife right in his chest as he's fully corporeal. Maqbool crumples at my brother's feet. Arwa laughs and claps her hands. Aasman Peri kicks her forward and steps on her back as Arwa curses at her. I don't see anything else as I leap toward Maqbool, who is bleeding on the ground, his hand clutching his chest. Hamza is crouched over him, shaking his head and muttering, "No, no, no, please no."

Abdul Rahman drops the branches and flies to Maqbool's side. He lifts Maqbool's head and cradles it in his lap.

"Do something!" I scream. "Use your powers. Seal the wound with your flame."

Abdul Rahman merely looks at me and gently shakes his head.

This can't be it. These jinn are like thousands of years old. Could a knife kill them? There has to be . . .

wait. The Flask of Endless Water. Yes! That's it! Pulling open the backpack, I grab the flask and dump its water all over Maqbool's chest. He coughs and sputters and opens his eyes. It's working. He's going to be okay. But when I look at his hand clutching his chest, I see the blood still flowing from his wound.

Arwa laughs, and when I twist my body to glare at her, my eyes fill with tears. Aasman Peri has bound the peri-dev's hands and feet. But not her mouth. "Your healing waters will make no difference. The tip of that knife was dipped in poison from Shaytan's well—it writhes through his body right now. No balm or blessed water will heal it." *The devil's well?*

A tidal wave of anger unlike anything I've ever felt sweeps through my body, lifts me from the ground like a balloon being filled with helium. I rise and stride toward Arwa, who is now standing, one wing half broken and drooping. Aasman Peri holds onto her with one hand, her other hand gripping her sword. Aasman Peri's teeth are clenched as she looks at Maqbool.

I punch the cruel peri-dev in the face.

"Ow!" we both yell. Yellow-green blood and snot

spurt from her nose, and I clutch my right fist. I had no idea punching someone could hurt so bad but also feel so good.

A small cough-laugh erupts behind me. It's Maqbool. "I see you've found your power. Humans never cease to surprise or amaze me," he whispers, and beckons me and Hamza to his side.

"It has been a great privilege to meet you," he says. Hamza and I both kneel, gently placing our hands on Maqbool's arms. "You are all that heroes should be."

"But—" I begin to say.

Maqbool quiets me with a little shake of his head. "Never mind what some dusty scroll says. It does not matter what the prophecy claims. I know in my heart who you are. You are *my* Chosen Ones. You *are* the champions of Qaf. The ones who will set this world and yours right. It is always the old who push our young into battles they should never have to fight. I am sorry for this. But you have risen to the challenge with aplomb. Peace be with you, children, always." Turning his eyes to Abdul Rahman, he says, "My Vizier, it has been an honor to serve with you."

"The honor has been mine, my friend. You have served with courage and much-needed humor. Your name will be written in the history of Qaf for all jinn to know, for eternity. May God light your path home."

Maqbool's eyes begin to close, then open slowly again. Tears splash down my cheeks, and I bury my head in his shuddery arm. "One last request, my Vizier," he sputters.

"Anything, my friend." Abdul Rahman kneels, bending close to Maqbool.

"Please, please, remember to wear your reading glasses." Maqbool looks to me and Hamza and turns his lips up in a small smile. He winks his left eyelid. Then both slowly close.

Abdul Rahman says something, but I don't hear any of the words. He rises and takes our hands and bends his head in prayer. We join, closing our eyes. But the moment is not silent because the thundering is getting closer. When I open my eyes, Maqbool's body has disappeared; only ash is left in its place.

A shadow passes high over us; Zendaya is returning, wings beating furiously as she descends.

"The way out is open," Abdul Rahman says, apparently understanding her neighs. "Children, you must leave at once. Aasman Peri and I will hold them off until you can escape."

"No. You'll die, too," Hamza yells.

"Don't be dumb, silly humans," Aasman Peri says as she ties Arwa to a tree and gags her. "The horde is too close, and they'll shoot us down or soar up and battle us in the sky if they catch all of us trying to escape. We'll distract them. But as soon as Zendaya touches down, jump on and fly, you fools!"

Hamza wipes away the tears at the corners of his eyes. "Did you just quote Gandalf?" he asks.

"Ha! As if! More like that J.R.R. Tolkien guy quoted me. He's always stealing my lines." She shares a small smile and unsheathes her sword as she and Abdul Rahman take up positions behind our barrier.

Hamza and I also pull out our blades but hang back. His shoulders slump, and I feel like I should say something to him; something, I don't know, big sisterly, assuring, inspiring. But no words come because all my thoughts are for Maqbool and what he gave for us. I do the only thing I can do—I put my hand on Hamza's shoulder. He knows what I want to say.

At that moment, an arrow whizzes through the air and sticks in a trunk in one of the trees in our barrier wall. Then another. Through the woods, we see them coming, screaming devs and ghuls, shoving one another down, hurtling toward us.

I look up, and Zendaya is only a few feet above us. Grabbing Hamza's hand, I drag him closer to the pond by a clearing wide enough for Zendaya to land. We move toward her, but she neighs as she approaches and shakes her head and pulls up her front hooves like she means to kick someone.

Then we're yanked from behind, lifted up by our collars, and thrown into a tremendous black pot by a terrifying yellow dev, who looks down at us, snarling. The pot levitates, then lifts us into the sky, away from our friends.

CHAPTER 14

Escape Room Rules

I SCREAM.

Not words. Not demands. Only a high-pitched cry that's part sadness, part rage and is totally ripping me in two.

The yellow dev, who I now see is covered in contrasting darker green spots, doesn't even turn to the sound. He's leaning out of his huge black cauldron as the ground falls away. It's exactly like one of the pots the Supahi flew in when we were on Earth, except much larger. I'm still slightly confused about how the aerodynamics work, even though Razia explained that the cauldrons were formed from cavorite—an antigravity substance that I thought was fictional! She also said they're controlled by the creature flying it—so the dev is his own literal internal-combustion engine. Maybe that's why the floor of the cauldron feels hot— the heat coming off this dev's ginormous feet. If I could figure out the formulas and harness all this for Earth, I'd be, like, the youngest Nobel Prize winner ever.

I pinch myself. For real. Because I realize what I'm doing—ignoring that Maqbool was killed and that we're not the Chosen Ones but are here because of some dumb Scooby-Doo case of mistaken identity. I'm pretending we weren't just kidnapped. We learned about this in S.E.L., social emotional learning discussions the school counselor leads that are cringey but also kind of real. This whole thing that I'm doing? Avoiding the problem? The counselor would say that it's denial and that I'm using dreams of my future science glory to push reality out of my mind because our reality is totally FREAKING ME OUT! I bite my lip, and when I turn to see Hamza huddled on the floor, legs pulled into his chest, forehead resting on top of his knees, every part of me grows cold. Denial is not going to get us out of this. Maybe nothing can, but I have to try. I drop down next to my brother and gently shake his shoulder. "Hamz, are you okay?"

He looks up, his eyes red and rimmed with tears.

"Okay? No. I'm not okay. Maqbool is dead. We got taken away from Aasman Peri and Abdul Rahman and Zendaya. And that thing"—he points at the distracted dev—"kidnapped us. And is, I don't know, going to make us into his servants or dinner or something. We're not the Chosen Ones. We're nothing."

I brush away my own tears. "We're not nothing," I say. "And we're not alone. We have each other." But we don't have our weapons. The dev disarmed us, and our sword, dagger, and bow and arrows lay at his big feet. The only way to get them is to go through him. He's burly and big—his upper body seems two sizes too big for his legs; I'm not even sure how they hold him up. I don't really think we're going to win a cage match...er, a cauldron match...with him. I imagine he'd rebuff my mawashi geri kick with a flick of his fingers. My mind wanders to Maqbool and to what

243

he said about us, to what he found so funny about humans. I realize we do have one thing going for us. Our big mouths.

I stand up. My legs shake, but it's not like I have any choice. We have to try something. Hamza takes my offered hand, and I pull him up next to me. I jab the yellow-green dev. "Hey. Hey, you."

He doesn't turn. He's still staring down at the landscape. Hamza and I exchange a confused look, then peek over the side of the cauldron. We're not over land anymore. We're flying over a choppy bright blue sea.

Hamza pokes the dev in his double-wide arm. "Hey, snot-nosed spot face, where are you taking us?" My brother wipes his runny nose with the back of his hand as a smile starts to emerge on his face. The world is falling apart, our friends are dead or lost, but leave it to Hamza to find something to make him smile.

"Yeah, bug breath," I goad. "We demand to know what—"

The dev snarls. Oops. Maybe insults weren't

the best tactic. He turns and looks at us and then clears his throat; it's deep and phlegmy and gurgly. Gross.

Hamza draws his hands up to his face. "Don't even think about hocking a loogie at us, dude. We're small but scrappy. We're so scrappy. The scrappiest...we're Scrappy-Doos!"

"Yeah! And...and...I do not abide spit!" I yell, channeling my mom.

The dev snorts and...smiles? I think. "There are reports that you human children are odd little creatures." He speaks like he has marbles in his mouth, which kind of counteracts the terror of his snarl. "I'm not going to eat you. I don't deign to eat humans. Blech. I'm not a rakshasa. Although to ignorant humans like you, I suppose you think we all look alike." He folds his arms over his broad chest and scowls at us like somehow *we've* wronged *him*.

"Hey, don't turn this around on us. We're not the bad guys here. You kidnapped us, remember?" I say.

"I saved you from certain death," he harrumphs.

"So what *do* you plan on doing with us?" Hamza asks.

"Deliver you to Ifrit and collect the bounty on your heads."

"What?!" I yell. "You saved us from certain death only to deliver us to...certain death?"

"Nothing is certain." He shrugs.

"You're a bounty hunter." Hamza nods like he's all wise. "Then you must have a code. It should be against your code to kill us. We're innocent children who were in the wrong place at the wrong time." Hamza tries to make puppy eyes at the dev. "You should be saving us. This is the way."

"Hamz, he's not the Mandalorian."

"Worth a shot," Hamza says with a half grin. "Bounty hunter, we will pay you twice what Ifrit promised you if you let us go."

I don't bother to remind Hamza that we don't have any money that would work in Qaf. Or that we really don't know if they even use money. Seems more likely that they would have a barter system. It's not like we've seen any stores. Anyway, Hamza trying to cosplay us out of this situation might buy me a couple of minutes to figure out a plan.

My friend Simrit had an escape room birthday party last year. It was different from this moment, because obviously no chance of death, plus we had chocolate cake after. I don't see cake happening in this scenario. But to escape, we were instructed to be logical, smart, one step ahead of our opponents. Have a plan.

Putting together an escape plan:

1. **Assess the situation.**
   Cons: We are in a black cauldron hundreds (?) of feet above a churning sea. The cauldron is shoulder-high for us, but only about knee-high to the dev who has kidnapped us. Pro: The dev shows no interest in eating us.
2. **Search the room (cauldron) thoroughly.**
   It's round, and there are no corners and no exits or door. Open top; easy chance of falling to our deaths. (Is death by falling better or worse than death by Ifrit?)

3. **Locate any and all items that could be used as weapons.**

   Our actual weapons are here literally between the dev's giant, hairy feet. Can I grab my sword and stab him before he stomps me?

4. **Work as a team.**

   Hamza is doing a baby Yoda impression and arguing with the dev about the bounty hunter code, which actually only existed a long, long time ago in a galaxy far, far away. Maybe it's preventing the dev from doing anything bad to us. Yay, team?

5. **Be quick; be calm.**

   I'm neither quick nor calm. Is it possible to fake both? (Note to self: Can "fake it till you make it" work in life-or-death situations?)

Did I mention my team did not win the escape room?

I'd tuned Hamza out while trying to hatch a brilliant plan or, more truthfully, while I hoped something would come to me like a flash of lightning. He's still going on and on, but the spotty neon dev seems distracted. He keeps glancing, leaning over the side of the cauldron with a worried look on his face, a little puke green around his neck. Could he be scared of…?

I might be formulating the dumbest idea ever, but in the absence of all other ideas, the dumbest one wins out. I pull the lilac elastic hair tie from my wrist and twist it around my hand into ammo for a finger gun. My pulse pounds, and my hands sweat. I hope the hair tie doesn't slip. Need one more second. I pause, and the next time the dev glances over the side of the cauldron, I shoot my hair tie, arcing it high over his head. He sees it out of the corner of his eye and turns his back to us and leans over the cauldron, watching as my hair tie floats down to the sea. This is our chance. I get into a before-a-race crouch, and Hamza immediately gets what I'm trying to do. Sibling telepathy for the win! I count to three with my fingers, and then we hurl our bodies against the wall right next to the dev's knees.

"Hey! What are you—"

The cauldron tilts, and the dev's feet start to slip out from under him—he's top-heavy, so we need... a...big...PUSH! Hamza and I each grab a leg, and with the dev's center of gravity already leaning over the side, we yank them up, flipping him over the side.

Oh. My. God.

The dumbest plan in the universe worked. My sneaky rubber band battles with Hamza paid off!

The cauldron tilts back now that most of the weight is gone, and as we glance over, we see the chartreuse dev trying to claw his way, hopelessly, against the air. "I can't swiiiiiimmmmm." His voice fades as he falls until we hear a splash.

I peek over the edge of the cauldron and see the dev actually doing a halfway decent doggy paddle toward a sandbar. Not an Olympian, but he'll make it. (Note to self: Do they have sports here? What would Qaf Olympics look like?)

Hamza high-fives me. "I love it when a plan comes together!"

"How was that a plan?" I ask. "The only reason I did that was because I had no actual plan."

"No plan was the best plan."

"That makes zero sense. Who told you that?"

"Uhh, you did."

"What? I never...Oh! I didn't say *no* plan is the best plan. I said the *simplest* plan is the best plan. Occam's razor. Basically, don't overthink things. The best solution is usually the easiest."

"Exactly. That's what I said."

"Aaargh. That's not what..." The cauldron jerks, then bumps. Hamza turns to me with a worried look on his face. "It's only turbulence," I say. "Turbulence in the air is like a boat going over a wave." I try to sound calm. Remember when I mentioned that whole denial thing? This cauldron might be made of antigravity matter, but it still needs an engine to fly. And we threw our one-dev engine over the side. So this is not so much turbulence as an emergency landing!

Another jerk.

Still crouching low, I grab the sides of the cauldron. Hamza does the same. I inch over till I'm opposite him, hoping our weight will balance it out. But we hit a row of invisible speed bumps, then start plummeting and—

AAAAAHHHHHHH!

We're falling fast, and the force is making my teeth rattle and my cheeks wiggle.

"We're going to crash!" Hamza yells as palm trees come into view. "Brace for impact!"

CHAPTER 15

The Jinnternet Is Loading, You'll Have to Wait

I WRAP MY ARMS AROUND MY HEAD, TORNADO DRILL–
style, and screw my eyes shut. Don't know if we're still
over water or have drifted over land. Not sure what
would be better. I don't think there are any of those
airplane emergency water-landing slides attached to
this thing.

"We're going to diiiiiiie!" Hamza bellows.

We land with a gentle thud.

Neither of us move.

"Was that it?" he asks. "It wasn't nearly as life-passing-before-my-eyes as I thought a crash would be. I barely had a chance to think about dinner."

"Thanks for bringing the drama, though." I rise slowly and do a 360-degree turn in the cauldron to check out where we are. Which apparently is the most perfect beach ever. Tall palm trees wave lightly in the breeze, and sparkling blue-green water laps onto the shore. I grab my sword, bow, and quiver and begin to jump over the side of the cauldron; the move feels cool and almost superhero-ish—until the toe of my right sneaker catches on the rim of the pot and I face-plant in fine white sand. The sand is as soft as flour. Still doesn't feel great up my nose, though.

Hamza tumbles over the side. "Where are we?"

Brushing the sand off, I stand up and reach back into the cauldron to grab the rest of our stuff. I pull the jade tablet out of the backpack, hoping it's working again. But it's blank except for a spinning wheel in the center. Apparently the jinnternet is glitchy. Excellent.

"What's it say?" asks Hamza. He's sitting and drawing lines in the sand with a twig.

I show it to him and shake my head.

"They can make pots fly, but they can't make their GPS, er, JPS, work?" He stands up and walks away, his head down.

I'm not sure what to say, but I hurry to catch up to him. He's always been the one with twice the energy of normal humans. Seeing him so deflated scares me. "Hamz, it's okay. We'll figure it out," I say, but there's not a lot of confidence in my voice.

"Really? How?" He turns to face me. "We're stuck on some island in a...a...parallel universe with a monster who has a bounty on our heads. And the icing on the cake is that we're not even the ones who are supposed to be fighting him! There's nothing special about us. We're two confused, lost kids, not the Chosen Ones. And because of us—because of me!—Maqbool is dead!"

"Hey," I put a hand on his shoulder. "Don't say that. He wouldn't want you to think that. Someone will find us." *Fake it till you make it.*

"How would you know? You're just saying that. It's like every time I fall from the climbing wall and Mom or Dad tries to cheer me up by saying, *you'll get it next time, kiddo.* Like, how could they know that? I know adults say those things to try to encourage us, but sometimes they kinda feel like lies."

I open my mouth to say something but snap it shut. He's right. I have no idea what's going to happen next or how we'll get back home. But I'm also sort of irritated at him for being...so...ten years old, I guess? I rub my forehead. I know my mom would be disappointed in me for being annoyed with Hamza because of the whole big-sister and be-kind-to-your-fam thing, but UGGGHHHH....I'm sick of always being the responsible, older sibling.

I take a deep breath. "Look, we need to figure out some way off this island. Make this pot fly again or—"

"How? You said yourself it doesn't make sense, according to science. It has no boost, right?"

"Lift," I sigh. "Razia told me it has antigravity matter in it, but it needs to work in tandem with a force. Jinn combustion is like the engine—the force that works in opposition to the weight of a plane and—"

"Aaaarghhh! It doesn't matter! We're stuck here. Don't you get that? How can you be so calm? Maqbool was killed in front of us. Ummi and Papa are unconscious a bajillion miles away, or however far Chicago is, and you don't even care!"

I ball my hands into fists at my side. I can feel my face getting hot with anger. "I care! But acting like a baby isn't going to help us get out of here. We have to be rational."

"Shut up! Having feelings doesn't mean I'm a baby. It means I'm a normal person, not a robot. And how are we going to get out of this anyway? You think you're going to defeat Ifrit and send him to the Realm of Nothingness or whatever with your wicked karate moves that can't even take down a little kid?" Hamza scoffs.

My chest heaves up and down. I can barely hear myself think because of all the feelings that are screaming in my brain right now. I grit my teeth. "What would you know about thinking? You never think! You took the Box of the Moon out of the case and now we're stuck here! It was all a ginormous accident that was your fault!"

Hamza, who had been rising on his toes, seems to deflate. "Whatever. I'm going on a walk. Don't follow me." He grabs his dagger, turns, and heads down the beach.

My first instinct is to run after him, to stop him from going, to tell him it's too dangerous, that we don't know what's out there. But I don't. I walk back toward the cauldron and sink into the sand, leaning against its curved side. I bring my knees into my chest and sob.

After about fifteen minutes, I dry my face—I'm guessing it's about that long because the time on my phone is stuck on the time we left Chicago. Crying isn't going to help us get out of this place even if it felt good to let it out. My throat is dry and raw, so I take a sip of water from the flask and wipe my lips. It's hard to know how long it's been since the dev kidnapped us. I need to find Hamza, and we need to assess the food situation and figure out how to get out of here.

I consult the tablet again. It's working! But all it shows is a tiny, round island—I'm assuming it's this one—in an endless sea. ISLAND OF CONFUSION is the only label on the map. Does that mean it's a confusing place? That it mixes you up? Does *confusion* mean something else here? Or that the mapmaker is really bad at naming stuff? Maybe it's like Accident, Maryland, or Hell, Michigan, or Pee Pee, Ohio. Hahaha. That last one totally cracks me up. In fourth grade, my friend Dimple and I did a project for a geography unit where we mapped out all the places with strange names. Pee Pee is technically named for someone with the initials P. P., but we cracked ourselves up so much when we were presenting, even our teacher couldn't help but laugh. Maybe that's what this place is—a beautiful island with a weird name. I'm guessing that Pee Pee, Ohio, is not as pretty as this, though.

"How do we get—" I start to ask for the tablet's help but am distracted by a loud cry. It's a cross between a honk and a scream. A scronk? The scronking continues, and I get up, making sure my sword is at my side and my quiver is strapped to my back. The scronking doesn't seem too far away, so I follow it. It leads me deeper into the island through some trees. I make sure to pay attention to the direction where I came from, and I slash *X*s with my sword into some tree trunks along the way to mark my path. Hopefully, I'm not damaging the trees too badly, but I need to make sure I can get back to the cauldron and the beach.

I push some low palm fronds out of the way and jump back as a creature my size scronks repeatedly and loudly at me. I raise my sword and scramble back. Nothing should surprise me in this place, but I'm looking at a peacock with lion paws and the face of a dog. It's covered in copper-colored feathers that glint in the sun. It's like a Frankenstein's monster of a bird, canine, and big cat. I feel a bit queasy looking at it. So. Not. Normal.

When it sees me back away, its scronking diminishes, and it dips its muzzle toward its right leg. And I see a deep gash near its paw. This animal—bird-dog?

pea-lion?—is injured. Maybe that's why it's scronking so much.

"Easy," I whisper, putting away my sword as I inch a bit closer. Maybe the healing water in the flask can help? I pull the flask in front of me. "I have this special water. Maybe it can heal your paw? Claw? Foot? It's okay. I won't hurt you."

The creature first steps back, trembling. Its round brown eyes look scared. I hold my free hand out so it can see I don't have any weapons. The creature makes a little yelping sound and then bows its head and wags its tongue a little. I'm taking this as a sign it won't shred me with its lion claws.

I take another step closer. Then another. When I'm right next to it, I pour a little water on the gash. The creature...coos? Is it a baby? Big baby. Its shiny brown eyes watch as the gash heals. I look up at it and nod and smile. It licks my cheek with its tongue, leaving a trail of slobber across my face, which I try to wipe away inconspicuously. This thing might like me now, but I don't want to insult it by acting like its spit is gross. (It totally is.)

It raises its nose to the sky, and above us, I see a similar creature circling as it descends. The pea-dog (note to self: this name doesn't work, at all) flaps its beautiful wings and scronks, but it sounds joyful this time. Like when a kid sees its mom.

The mom. I guess it's the mom, because her feathers are mostly one color like the baby, and usually female birds (does she qualify as a bird?) aren't as colorful as the males. Which kind of feels very rude of Mother Nature. Anyway, the mom is as big as an elephant, with the same golden retriever face, peacock plume with coppery-bronze-colored feathers, and lion paws, and she lands right in front of us. I step away as she places her paw on top of her kid's. My heart pinches. It's such a parent thing to do, trying to make your kid feel better when they're down. Can't count the number of times Ummi or Papa did that for me—put their hand on my hand or on my shoulder. Like after the third time I failed my karate-advancement test. Or after I inadvertently wrecked my life cycle of a star project for the science fair and had to pull an all-nighter to build a new one. Not sure how they did it, but somehow by placing a hand on mine they didn't only make me feel better, they made me feel like I could do it. Like it was a small mistake and not the end of the world. That's the magic people have. The real magic. I wish I could feel that way now. I wish they were here. A lump wells in my throat. I choke back tears.

The mom peacock-dog turns to me and bows her head and fans out her feathers. I don't know what else to do, so I bow back. Maybe a normal greeting for their kind?

"You have my humble gratitude for saving my baby." She's speaking. Words are coming out of a dog's mouth, and every second I'm here I keep wondering how this place is going to outweird itself. *Ta-da!* Peacock-dogs speak human languages.

I'm sure my face is twisted up in all sorts of confusion, because the creature looks at me and smiles. "I am a simurgh," she says. "To your kind, I suppose, we are a bit of an enigma. We appear to be hybrids of Earth-based animals. Yet here, we are what we are."

"Oh, I...I...I don't think it's weird at all that a dog can speak." Obviously, it's totally weird, but I'm not going to say that out loud! "I mean...also, I really like dogs. And peacocks. Also, your lion paws are probably super handy to, um, kill...uh...prey with?"

The simurgh laughs—I think it's laughter—it sounds like a very breathy inhale and exhale. "You have nothing to fear from our kind. We fight on the same side, Amira, champion of this world and yours."

"I...I'm not a champion, though." My chin drops. "Abdul Rahman made a mistake."

"You approached an injured creature and offered it compassion and love. There is no mistake. You are a champion."

A smile crosses my lips. "Thank you," I whisper.

"I must warn you: Leave this place, now. The Island of Confusion can make even creatures of Qaf lose their mind and wander the sands for years, certain it has only been moments, until time turns them to ash."

I shudder. "How? How do we get off this island?"

"Ifrit, the devil you seek, is close. Can you not feel the air thickening? Taste the foul dust on the wind? You must cross the sea; see with your unseeing eye beyond the fog to reach him. It is no small feat. For the island will want to draw you back, sink its claws into you, and thus it will have done Ifrit's bidding."

"What about you and your baby? Do you live here?"

"No. The Island of Confusion is no home but a trap. A roc—an enormous eagle-like bird—loyal to Ifrit waylaid us as I was flying my child to the safety of Iram and the court of the emperor. As I held my child in my paws, he slashed at them, hurling them toward the Island. I rushed after as soon as I clipped the roc's wings, sending him spiraling into the sea."

"Can you help my brother and me? Can you fly us off the island?"

"Would that I could. But I must carry my child to the safety of Iram and cannot lift the weight of two additional human children in my paws. Forgive me."

My heart sinks. If we don't defeat Ifrit, Iram will be the final realm to fall—that's why creatures are fleeing there in hopes of finding safety. Even if the simurgh could fly us there, it would mean we gave up. It would mean the end of everything. "I understand," I sigh.

The simurgh turns her head, plucks a copper

feather from her plume, and carries it to me in her mouth. I take it. "Though I cannot help you now, if you find yourself in dire circumstances, you need only burn this feather and I will hasten to your aid. It is the debt I owe you. Now, I take my child to join the many who are already at Iram's gates seeking safe harbor. Peace be with you."

With that, the simurgh clutches her child in her paws and flies off. I watch her rise, her coppery-bronze feathers glinting in the sun. Now we're really alone. I have to find Hamza. We have to get off this island. A red-orange mist swirls over the cool jade tablet's face when I ask it about Hamza: *Love is the bridge between you and everything.* More unhelpful, cryptic messages that sound weirdly familiar. Then a photo of the island emerges out of the swirly mist, and the tablet zooms in, like it's Google Earth. It shows Hamza on the other side of the island, lying down under the shade of a palm. Taking a nap? His timing, as always, is absurd. Not like we have an apocalypse-creating monster to stop or anything.

The photo zooms in more, closer, to Hamza's face,

his forehead. The tablet draws me in, like I'm watching a 3D movie but without the funky, germ-infested plastic glasses. Then I see what Hamza sees, but his dream is like a film being narrated by that deep-voiced dude who does the voice-overs for trailers.

Hamza's Island Adventure

The breezes on the Island of Confusion, the perfect temperature, the gentle lapping of the waves, the impossibly soft sand, all these things are meant to lull visitors to sleep, to a half-waking so they never leave. Hamza, never one to say no to a delicious nap, finds the shade of a perfect palm tree under which to lie down. Curling his body into a comma and using his bent arm as a pillow, he soon enters the world of dreams.

In his dream, he walks on the soft sands of an island, much like the island on which he sleeps. He comes upon an old man with white hair and a long white beard standing in the middle of a tranquil sea. Next to the

*man is a large wooden ship. In the ship, all
sorts of animals peek overboard. The old
man beckons Hamza, who walks on top of
the water to reach him. Of course, this is
not possible in the real world, but the world
of dreams is limited only by imagination.
As he approaches, the old man bends
low, for he is much taller than at first
he seemed, and whispers some words to
Hamza over and over.*

*"I get the message," Hamza says.
"It was burned into my brain by the
fifty-second time you said it."*

*Hamza bolts up from the sand, from
his sleep. The daylight has not changed,
and Hamza assumes he simply dozed off
for a few moments. He rises, stretches, and
looks to the choppy sea, wishing it were
like his dream. His stomach grumbles.
He reaches into his pocket to grab a
half-finished granola bar, which he
quickly devours. But he is still hungry.*

Hamza glances up at the date palm under which he drifted off to sleep and sees it is full of ripe brown dates. At first, he tries shaking the tree, but the trunk is sturdy. He barely sees any movement. Then he searches for sticks, then rocks, which he throws at the bunches of dates near the top of the tree. Again, to no avail. At this point, he really regrets not taking his backpack with him. There would at least have been some of the snacks Amira stashed in there, he thinks to himself.

His stomach grumbles again, and he clutches his belly, wrapping his arm around the cummerbund he and Amira retrieved from the iron chest. Removing it, he pauses to look at it, pulling it at either end, surprised at the elastic stretch it has. He steps closer to the rough trunk of the palm, rubbing his hands over the grooves and indentations in the tree.

"I think I can do this," he says.

*He loops the cummerbund around
the trunk, securing it behind his back,
creating a type of harness belt. He tugs at
it, pushing his back into it to make sure
it feels secure. He doesn't have a climbing
helmet or any padding, but desperate
times... or desperate hunger, anyway...
call for extreme measures.*

*Carefully, he finds a notch for his left
toe in the tree, then for his right. Using
his hands, he guides the loop higher and
takes another step up, left, right, left, right.
He eases himself up, trying hard not to
look down. About twenty feet in the air,
he glances below and gets that familiar
queasy feeling. His heart flutters; his palms
grow clammy. He closes his eyes for a
second. He thinks of how Amira taught him
to meditate like she does in karate. Taking
deep breaths, in and out, he tries again,
pushing himself, one foothold at a time. A*

sense of elation starts to overtake him, but he tamps it down. Can't celebrate too early.

When a stalk of dates is within reach, he plucks one of the brown wrinkled fruits and pops it into his mouth. The sun-warmed sweetness of the date may be the most delicious thing he's ever tasted, and it reminds him of one Ramadan when his dad got them special dates imported from Egypt for their iftars. He and Amira were both too young to fast, but they still woke with their parents for the predawn meal of suhoor and, of course, joined for every iftar. Friday iftars were his favorite because it meant hanging out with cousins and friends, and his mom almost always made his favorite kheema parathas.

He sighs as his stomach grumbles but doesn't try to push the memory out of his mind like he's been doing during the entire journey to Qaf. Instead, he imagines his parents encouraging him, as he knows they would. He takes the dagger from his side and carefully cuts down a stalk and lets it fall to the ground. "Yes, I'll wash them, Amira," he says out loud. He knows how the conversation will go with his sister. He wishes she were here to bother him about proper food handling and to see him climb this tree, higher than any wall at the gym.

Slowly, he makes his way down the trunk, and when his feet touch the soft sand, he removes the cummerbund, reties it around his waist, and yells, "Yes!" with a double fist pump. No one is there to see it, but he knows what he's done. He holds his head up; he may even be taller.

He places the dates on a palm frond. Surveying the area around him, he begins pulling some of the large leaves to the side and gathers some of the dead branches and trunks, dragging them all to the open beach.

"That dream," he says, "walking on
the water....We're not going to get off this
island by air. We're leaving by sea."

I blink, shake my head, jerking myself out of my
tablet trance. The jade surface goes blank. "A raft.
He's making a raft!" I practically scream to no one.
We're going to get out of here. I check the tablet for
directions, run through the trees, reach the shore,
then race along the lapping waves to find my brother,
the words of the tablet ringing in my head: *Love is the*
bridge between you and everything.

CHAPTER 16

We're on a Boat to Nowhere

CHOSEN ONES, CHOSEN ONES/WE'RE NOT REAL, SO WE'RE on the run/Fight a ghul, any size/Throwing devs, from the skies/Look out! Here come the fake Chosen Ones.

I hear Hamza before I see him, mumble-singing his own lyrics to the Spider-Man theme song. Even though his out-loud earworms make me want to bang my head against our fridge, I kind of admire his glass-half-full approach to life. Don't tell him I said that.

As I round the corner, I spy Hamza gathering giant palm fronds and narrow, dead tree trunks that look like bamboo except they're a rose gold color, with the stripe-y ridges running vertically and not horizontally like you'd see on normal green bamboo. "Putting survival-camp skills to good use?" I ask.

He swivels his head around, and a smile spreads across his face. "Best sleepaway camp ever. You really missed out."

"Hardly. I went to astronomy camp at the Adler Planetarium."

"Nerd camp, you mean?"

"I told you before. Nerds get the job done, little brother."

We don't apologize. We don't need to. We get each other. Sibling shorthand is sometimes unspoken.

I help Hamza gather more materials to build a raft and tell him the story of the simurgh.

"You helped a giant peeing dog with lion paws, and now its mom is in our debt?"

"Oh my God. I only said pea-dog as a description. Like peacock dog. But, yeah." I nod and show him the feather. "And we can use this to call her in case of a real emergency."

"A real emergency?" Hamza smirks. "Well, maaaaaybe one will come up."

"You never know. Our lives have been pretty boring so far." I giggle. Hamza chuckles. Soon we're both clutching our stomachs and laughing. I snort. That only makes Hamza laugh harder. Laughing while we're stuck on an island and the moon is being ripped apart as we face certain death seems like a weird choice. But it also feels like the right one. The only one. I laugh until I cry. I remember Papa saying, "I don't trust anyone who doesn't laugh." He was quoting Maya Angelou. He loves quoting poets. One of his faves is Rumi, a Persian Muslim poet from, like, hundreds of years ago. He always says Rumi's words are a kind of guide if only you listen to the heart of what they mean and don't get a whitewashed translation. You know, the usual parental wisdom that adults give with this faraway look in their eyes, like they're figuring out the key to life's mysteries. Honestly, to me, life's mysteries are like: Why does candy corn exist? Or why can't girls' clothes have pockets? I wish a dead poet could help me figure those out.

Our laughter slows, and Hamza shows me how to make a rope by twisting together palm fibers—basically like braiding hair, real tight. While I'm braiding away, Hamza reaches into his bag and pulls out a double-size pouch of Big League Chew and shoves a wad of gum into his mouth so his right cheek puffs out like a chipmunk storing food. I hate gum. I'm still traumatized by his sticking gum in my hair when I was in first grade—it was so hard to get out that Ummi had to take me to a salon to get my hair cut. I was pissed. I'd been growing out my hair because I wanted to be Rapunzel for Halloween. Which, if you read the Brothers Grimm story, is pretty creepy and weird and, as my mom later told me, was kind of a rip-off of an ancient Persian story about Rudaba, a beautiful girl who unfurled her black hair from a tower so the boy she loved could climb up and see her because their parents didn't want them to get married. I don't care who I fall in love with, I am never letting them use my hair as a ladder. *Ouch.* Love is not supposed to hurt. Physically or metaphorically.

Hamza blows a giant bubble as huge as his face,

and when it pops, the sound jars me out of the world of long-haired damsels in distress. Carefully pulling the popped gum from his face, Hamza begins sticking it between the slender trunks. "Are you using gum as—"

"Glue? Yeah. Basically," Hamza says, then shoves another wad into his mouth.

"Give me some, then."

"You? Are you going to chew gum? I thought you hated gum."

"Yeah, well, we're kind of in a pinch. Do not get any in my hair, though. Because I don't care if we're about to face some Big Bad, I will kick your butt if your sticky, spitty gum touches a single strand."

Hamza grins and hands over the Big League Chew.

After we've chewed through all the gum and Hamza cements the fallen trees as well as he can, we start to tie the ropes around the raft. It's small, barely enough room for the two of us. *Please let this float.*

We do our best to fashion oars out of the palm fronds and some fallen branches, using more of the palm fibers to fasten the leaves. Not sure how sea-worthy the raft will be, but I don't have any better ideas. I keep looking up at the sky, but no one seems to be coming to rescue us, so we have to save ourselves. Who knows if they even know where we are.

Hamza gathers some dates that he climbed the tree to get. I congratulate him, and he gives me a sheepish smile in response. I'm proud of him. But I don't tell him, because, well, I don't want to get mushy. As we finish up, Hamza gives me more details about the weird dream he had about the old dude with a white beard and a boat full of animals. It's what I saw on the tablet. But I'm only now realizing what it might mean because I didn't put all the clues together.

"You think the dream was about Noah? As in Noah's ark? God, I hope it's not a sign of a flood," I say. "That's the last thing we need."

Hamza shrugs. "I dunno. I took it more like a sign of my hunger because I usually have really weird dreams when I'm starving."

"Fair point. Let's take another look at the Box of

the Moon," I say, grabbing it from the backpack and flipping the lid. The moon is totally out of its orbit, the little Earth is spinning super fast, and the gears are whirring so quickly they're a blur. We shouldn't keep looking. It only makes everything seem hopeless. Hopeless-er, which I didn't even think was possible. Nothing we're doing is helping, probably because we're not the ones who should be here.

Hamza has the tablet in hand and asks if we're going to make it off the island: *The art of knowing is knowing what to ignore* flashes across the screen. What does that even mean? Should we ignore the moon breaking? This impossible island trying to trap us? The lack of indoor plumbing? Aaaarrrrghhh. Hamza and I lock eyes. I shake my head, then pause to take a deep breath. "One thing at a time. First, let's get off this island," I say. We'll figure out the next thing when we come to it. I hope.

Together, we drag our rickety raft to the shore's edge and then gently shove it into the water and clamber on. Using our "paddles," we actually start moving away from the shore into the gentle blue waves. Not too far in the distance is a curtain of fog—from the island, it looked like a blank canvas.

"Yes!" Hamza shouts. "It's working!"

It. Is. Working. Holy Newton's second law. Something is going right!

"The simurgh said we have to cross the sea and see through that fog and we will find Ifrit." I thought it would feel like a relief to be getting closer to what we need to face, but it's basically, completely, freeze-my-blood terrifying.

We paddle faster, and the fog thins. Glimpses of another shore come into view. But when we're halfway there, the current shifts and pushes against us, the fog screen rethickening. Even when we paddle away, the waves send us back to the Island of Confusion. "No!" I yell. "Paddle harder, Hamz."

"I'm trying, but it's not working!"

Moments later, we're back on the shore of the Island of Confusion. Maybe this is what the simurgh meant. This place *wants* to trap you.

We try again.

And get pushed back again.

Again and again, we paddle, make it about halfway to the other shore, get a brief glimpse of another island, and then get shoved back here. After what feels like the two-millionth time, we pull the raft back onto the shore and fall onto the beach, panting and totally beat. Even though every one of my muscles is screaming inside, I'm too tired to make any sounds. I feel the exhaustion in my bones. Even my face muscles are tired. I army-crawl to the backpack and pull out the tablet and start jabbing at the screen.

"Do you plan on poking it to death?" Hamza asks.

"I have to do something. Nothing else is working," I say, shaking the tablet. "Tell us how to get off this stinking island!" I yell at the smooth jade face. I get what feels like a tiny static shock in return. "It tried to electrocute me!" I toss the tablet away. "Stupid, stupid, only occasionally magical, tablet."

"Don't take this the wrong way, but you're acting like me," Hamza says. Then he sits up. "Oh my God. Do you think this island magically switched our personalities? Like I'm going to be the nerdy, responsible one now? The one who eats all my vegetables and wants to read instead of watch TV? Ugh. Fate worse than death."

I roll my eyes at him. He kind of has a point, though. I'm not acting like me. I take a deep breath. I walk over to the tablet and pick it up. There's a message. Finally. "Raise your words, not your voice," I read out loud. "What's that supposed to mean?"

"Maybe it's really mad you yelled at it. Or it could be busted. Either one!"

I shake my head, frustrated. "C'mon," I say, grabbing one end of the raft. Some of the ties are starting to loosen and look worn, and I don't think it's going to last much longer. "Might as well give it one more try. If we get stuck on this island, we'll only have dates to eat, and that is way too much fiber for anyone."

Hamza drags himself off the sand and joins me. Once more, we push the raft into the sea and begin paddling our way to the other shore. *Raise your words, not your voice. Raise your words, not your voice. Raise your words, not your voice.* What does that mean? Whisper? What words? Wait. What if—

"Hamza, tell me about your dream again. The one with Noah." My memory of what I saw on the tablet is growing hazier by the minute, and I'm hoping Hamza remembers it more clearly since it was actually his dream.

"I don't know 100 percent if it was him or maybe a very old dude in a brown robe with a boat of animals."

"He said something in the dream, right? Some words?"

"Oh, umm, yeah. Let me think. He sort of whispered it...."

We are nearing the center, and I can feel the current starting to work against us. "Hurry, Hamz."

"Do you think that saying *hurry* actually makes my brain work faster?"

"Ugh! We're getting pushed back again."

"Okay, okay. Well, there was a lot of water in the dream, and then there was that big boat of animals. And he said something like, *ibn ya dim sum*?"

"What? He said, 'son of dim sum'? I don't think that's it."

"I dunno. I'm hungry. Dumplings at MingHin

sound so good right now. Besides, you know my Arabic stinks."

"Uh, maybe because you never paid attention during Sunday school at the masjid?"

"Wow. Are you really guilt-tripping me about that? I was playing a game on my phone one time. One time! And I will never live it down."

"Hamz! Focus!"

"Okay, okay." He closes his eyes and takes a deep breath. The pause lasts forever. His eyes fly open. "Iftah ya Simsim!"

"*Raise your words, not your voice.* Whisper it to the current." I have no idea what that means or if this will be of any use, but it's better than getting pushed back to shore again.

Hamza leans over the raft. I can barely hear the words, but I know what he's saying: *Iftah ya Simsim. Iftah ya Simsim. Iftah ya Simsim.*

Ripples fan out across the water. Then the water around the raft begins to bubble and swirl into a whirlpool that grows bigger and bigger. I start paddling away from it, but we're not moving. My sweaty hands slip on our makeshift oars. I throw mine down and start using my hands in the water to push us away.

"It's a tornado in the water! It's going to suck us in!" Hamza yells as the strength of the vortex grows.

"A tornado would be above the water," I shout. "A whirlpool sucks you down; a tornado sucks you up."

"Perfect time to correct me on weather terms. Thanks, sis!"

The water around us changes shades, from turquoise to green to yellow. We're not quite getting sucked into the water, but we're not able to move away. The whirlpool grows deeper until it's like a black hole in the water. We're dead. So dead.

I squeeze my eyes shut but then force them open when I hear a whooshing sound. The whirlpool seems to be slowing, and the hole fills up with water again. Through the white foam of the rushing water, an object rises to the surface.

It looks like a shoebox made of swirly wood, and as the water calms, it drifts toward us. Before I can stop him, Hamza reaches out and grabs it and starts to pull the top open.

"Stop! That could be a bomb or booby trap or something. What if a mini ghul jumps out of it and bites your finger off?"

"What if it's a jinn that we free and that wants to grant us three wishes?"

I roll my eyes. "If jinn granted wishes, don't you think that one of the, oh, hundreds of other jinn we've met would have already done that?"

"It's called optimism. You should try it some time." Hamza pops open the lid, which is on a hinge. Luckily no tiny ghul crawls out, but neither does a lifesaving jinn. Nestled in the box is a spiral. An object tightly coiled like a snake and held together with small leather bands, begging to be released. It looks like it's made of marble, maybe? It's a translucent deep blue, nearly black, with swirls of stardust sprinkled through it.

"It's beautiful," I whisper. "The colors, the cloud of stars, it's like the Milky Way."

Hamza sucks in his breath. He's in awe, too. He should be; it's amazing. He bends in closer to get a better look. The specks of starlight twinkle. "I would kill for a Milky Way right now."

I glance up at him. "I meant the Milky Way galaxy, you goof! Not the candy bar."

"Yeah. Okay. Right...I knew that. Just saying I'm hungry, and it doesn't look like we can eat that."

"Give me your dagger," I say to Hamza.

"You better not poke me with it because I'm having a stab of hunger." He laughs. "Get it? A stab of hunger...because...the dagger and...the candy... and...okay, fine." Hamza hands me the dagger since I'm shooting darts at him with my eyes.

I unknot the leather bands holding the coil in place, and the object starts to move, to uncurl itself. Oh God, please don't let this be some ancient snake. I can't deal with any more serpents.

But it's not a snake or even alive, I don't think. In a blink, the coil unfurls into a staff.

"Whoa. That was amazeballs," Hamza says. "Sort of like a slap watch but in reverse."

Okay, clearly we haven't switched personalities. I take the staff in hand. It's smooth and cool to the touch.

Hamza runs his fingers across it, then gasps. "My dream! The old guy had a staff and was holding it in the water. That's when he said the words. Maybe if we..."

He doesn't need to finish his thought. I stick the staff into the water, and I can feel the current release us, like when you come up for air after you've been swimming. I pull it through the waves, and the raft glides easily through the water. The fog between us and the hidden shore lifts.

I'm so thankful something is going our way.

Using the staff as a kind of oar, I draw us closer to the other shore. Hamza relaxes; I can feel him breathing easier. I am, too. At least we've passed this obstacle. I'm trying not to think about the giant one that still lies ahead. The one possibly truly insurmountable task. The most deadly of all.

Hamza plucks some dates out of his bag and rinses them in the sea and hands me some. I'm so tired and hungry I don't even give him a lecture about how even if water in oceans and rivers looks clean, it's a cesspool of bacteria.

Hamza chews in silence for a while, then says, "I think the samosa was right."

"The samosa?"

"The giant peeing dog you told me about. Didn't it say it believed in us?"

"Oh my God. Stop calling it a peeing dog." I roll my eyes. "It's a simurgh. How do you get samosa from simurgh?"

"Whatever. Like I said, I'm hungry. Starving. Famished. All the *s* words are blending together! Anyway, if that creature believes we're Chosen, we might as well act like we believe it, too. Not like it could get us in deeper water. Haha. Get it? Cuz we're on a raft? I crack myself up."

I shake my head. But maybe my ridiculous little brother is onto something. Not like we have much to lose. The simurgh believes. And Hamza did have that dream. And the fog is lifting so we can glide to the other shore. The other shore where Ifrit is supposedly waiting for us. We're silent the rest of the way. The words we whispered into the water, the ones from Hamza's dream, keep coming back to me. They sound so familiar. *Iftah ya Simsim.* A light turns on in the dark corner closet of my memory. I remember where I heard those words before. During Sunday school at the masjid, we sometimes watched Arabic-language kids' shows so we could hear different accents. One day our teacher showed us the Arabic version of *Sesame Street.* It was called *Iftah ya Simsim.* She joked about how silly the name was—like a little inside joke. The name means: Open Sesame (Street). Ha! It would be awesome if Grover saved us—when I was a kid, he was the only monster at the end of the book I ever wanted to meet.

CHAPTER 17

Fool's Gold

THE FOG TOTALLY LIFTS, AND HAMZA AND I IMMEDIATELY shield our eyes from a blazing light as we pull the raft onto the gleaming shore. Blinking as my eyes adjust, I breathe and try to take it all in. I am surrounded by gold. The shiniest yellowy gold. I mean, literally everywhere I look, every structure I see, the mountains in the distance, all seem to be made of gold.

"This gives new meaning to the gold standard," Hamza smirks. "What's this place called?"

The tablet responds immediately. I guess it's working *now*. "City of Gold," I read out loud. "A little obvious." The place name disappears, and other words rise to the smooth jade surface: *What you seek is seeking you.* That's exactly what we saw in that note from Suleiman that turned to ash in our hands. We're looking for Ifrit, and he wants us to find him, which is bite-back-my-screams scary. It means we're close.

"So this is it? The tilism made from Ifrit's tears?" Hamza asks. "Does he cry gold?"

"Maybe? Or it could be like he wants all the gold. Literally. So he made this place in that image."

"That's so basic. He probably has a fake foreign accent and a villain cackle, too." Hamza flips open the Box of the Moon. The gears seem to have slowed. At first, I think that's good, but when I look closer, I see that the little moon has nearly collided with Earth. I guess it's close to completely breaking and opening the gateway between worlds so that Ifrit's hordes can run amok. This is it. Win or die. We don't even have time to be scared. Scared-er. More scared. The scared-est. Besides, I think terror has seeped into my bones and is now a permanent part of my DNA, so it's like I'm used to it? Like it's become me?

And the choices are (1) be overcome by fear or (2) use it, like Sensei says, to channel adrenaline before a karate bout. (Hopefully, one I'll win.)

"So do we, like, call for him? Here, Ifrit. C'mon, little guy." Hamza makes the kissy sounds like when you're trying to draw out a cat.

"Uh, maybe we should make a plan first before calling out the biggest evil of Qaf?"

"Maybe sneeze to get his attention? Get it, cough because of Qaf. So, sneeze. I know, I know, I keep telling that joke, but, man, it never gets old."

"Oh my God. Hamz, could you stop goofing around. We could be heading to our deaths. The world could be doomed."

"So, basically, the best time to make jokes."

"I'm serious. We're not the Chosen One. I mean, Ones. How do we fight him?"

"I'm going to say, with our weapons?"

"Duh, I mean—"

"You shoot him with the bow and arrow, and then if we have to, we go with hand-to-hand, or hand-to-claw or paw, combat. We really should've asked what he looks like so we'd know what to expect."

"Hamz. This could... this could be it." I catch his eye.

"Sis. In every book and movie where the good guys are outnumbered or outgunned, they win because they have to. Because good triumphs over evil. And sometimes superheroes we thought were dead step out of flaming portals or a Force ghost appears or a T-rex shows up to save the day." Hamza gives me a half smile. I know he wants to believe in a fictional save-the-day mash-up. I want to believe it, too.

Even if I know real life doesn't work like the movies. I lift my chin, nod, smile, and grab Hamza's elbow. "We got this, little bro."

Handing Hamza the flask, I tell him to take a drink before I take a few sips myself. Quietly, we fasten our weapons in place. Hamza tucks his dagger into the cummerbund, which is tied tight around his middle. Looks like that thing mainly only helped him climb a tree, but at least we got dates out of it. I make sure my quiver is secure across my back, the bow over my shoulder, and the sword and sheath attached to the hip holder Aasman Peri gave me.

Aasman Peri. Abdul Rahman. Maqbool. My mind strays to them for a minute, but I can't linger on everything that's already gone wrong. Or on how Maqbool's death ripped out a little piece of my heart. I have to push all that out of my head and focus on Ifrit, or things could all get so much worse. I have to be ready. I can't let Hamz down.

My brother and I walk up the beach and over golden sand dunes. We scurry down and start walking along what looks like a winding path of crushed golden gravel. Trees surround us, but they're not real trees. There are no leaves, only bright, bare yellow branches that curve up toward the sky. It's a graveyard of skeleton trees.

Passing through the fake woods, we come across a pond that looks like it's filled with liquid gold.

"That is really impractical. Like, how can you swim in melted metal?" I mutter. Then I turn to Hamza, remembering the monster in the Lake of Illusion. "Don't touch it."

"I wasn't going to," he scoffs, and crosses his arms across his chest.

"What? Like you haven't gotten us into, uh, *situations* because you have to touch everything?"

"I'm curious, okay? What's that thing Ms. Khan always says in science class?"

"Curiosity conquers fear? Fine. But it also killed the cat."

"Because it was a dumb cat!"

I roll my eyes. "Have you noticed that this place—"

"Would even make King Midas want to throw up?"

"No. I mean, yeah, good point. But it's not real gold, I don't think. Look." I dig at the ground with the toe of my sneaker, and the golden gravel crumbles into dust. I haven't tried grinding any of my mom's gold jewelry to dust, because I value my life, but I'm pretty sure gold doesn't crumble like this. I walk through the border of gilded trees and up to the face of a cliff, and when I claw at it with my hands, pieces fall away. "It's like clay." I rub some of it between my fingertips, and they come away streaked with gray, the gold instantly dimmed.

It's a fake world.

Maybe that's why the geography feels all smushed—dunes to woods to cliffs. It's all pushed together, crammed in, like my crayon drawings from nursery school, with everything I wanted in the picture—a beach with a snowman next to a giant chocolate cake. Ifrit was holing up here, in this pretend, made-up world of his weird imagination? He isn't fighting; he's hiding. Making other people do his dirty work. Maybe he's not so strong and brave after all.

The faux gold cliffs rise higher as we walk through, and the valley between them grows narrower until it's barely two people across. I'm not claustrophobic, but I feel squeezed in here, like the air is too thick to breathe. My steps feel heavier. We push through and slip out onto a desert plain. In front of us is an enormous cliff, and built into its rough face is a palace. Domes and minarets and curved windows and columns are carved into the golden cliff wall. It's a weird architecture mash-up and looks like a cross between the Taj Mahal and the Museum of Science and Industry back home in Chicago.

"It's built like Petra," I whisper as I start walking toward the building, drawn to it. Like I know this is the place we're supposed to be.

"Huh?"

"Remember during our Golden Oldies Movie Night, when Ummi and Papa made us watch that one with the archaeologist and his dad on a quest to find the Holy Grail and there was this really pale immortal knight protecting it in a castle built into a cliff?"

"I am 100 percent sure I fell asleep," Hamza says as we enter. The place is weirdly empty. All the decorations and fancy carvings are on the outside. There's no furniture. Not even a chair, only a huge, echoey, empty round room with a grand staircase that winds upward. We start climbing.

"That movie was a little boring. Anyway, Petra is a place in Jordan—an old city partially built into red cliffs. It's pretty cool," I say. "But this"—I gesture widely as we wind around another story looking down at the huge, empty hall below—"is kind of tacky."

"For real. We're totally going to kick this fake-gold, busted-monster-in-hiding's butt." Hamza laughs, and the echo bounces around the walls. Creepy. We step through an archway to the outside and come onto a large balcony that looks out onto the valley and past the barren forest of gold and onto the dunes that slope down to the sea.

"Who dares enter the City of Gold uninvited?" a loud voice bellows from the balcony of a minaret.

Gulp.

It's Ifrit.

Don't panic.

He's bigger than Abdul Rahman.

Calming thoughts. Calming thoughts. Fields of lavender. Sea. Cool breezes. Chocolate cake.

His chest must be as wide as a truck tire.

Breathe. Remember to breathe.

He is pink with gold stripes encircling his thick arms.

Am I still breath—

Actually, the pink with gold stripes isn't that scary. It's kind of fashion-forward. But his teeth—are all of them canines? Those...those are scary.

Ifrit begins descending the stairs toward us.

Hamza and I exchange terrified looks and both take a few steps back, but the balcony isn't that big. There is no place to hide.

He points an accusatory pink finger at us. "How were you able to breach the barriers before you, small humans. You are humans?"

"We are the champions of Qaf.... defenders of Earth. And we're not that small. The doctor says I'm in the sixtieth percentile for height," Hamza begins strong, but by the end, his voice is a squeak.

I step in. *Fake it till you make it. Fake it till you make it.* The simurgh believes, I might as well believe. "We are the ones you've been waiting for. I mean, we're the ones we've been waiting for. That's technically how the saying goes. But you were also waiting for us. And stuff." Wow. I'm not good at faking it. No wonder I only get cast as "silent townsperson" in school plays.

Ifrit strokes his waist-long indigo beard, then opens his mouth and roars. With laughter. He's cackling. At us. Rude! He turns his back to us and starts pacing back and forth across the width of the balcony, talking more to himself than us. "These? Children? Are the ones I feared? All these centuries. I waited. Biding my time, building my armies, to throw Qaf into chaos so that I could rip the moon apart. One piece cut away as each realm falls." Ifrit pauses and passes his fingers lightly over the diamond-crusted hilt of a blade, which I guess must be the Peerless Dagger. He looks back up, narrowing his eyes, and continues, "I made my entire life's purpose to avenge my father and destroy the human savior, Amir A. Hamza, the storied warrior. The legend. And this"— he points that pink index finger at us again—"this is who Shahpal bin Shahrukh sent to seek me? Defeat me?" He throws his head back and laughs. "Shahpal must be most desperate, indeed." He's hooting so much he has to bend over and grab his knees.

I get that this mistaken-identity thing is sort of funny, maybe ironic, but it's not bend-over, wet-your-pants, cry-your-eyes-out hilarious, which is what, apparently, Ifrit thinks.

Hamza and I exchange glances, and Sensei's words come back to me: *Imagine yourself defeating your opponent. No matter their size, surprise and focus are your friends. Believe in yourself.*

While Ifrit is bowled over with uncontrollable fits of laughter—I swear I saw orange snot squirt out of his long, skinny nose (gross!)—I assess our surroundings. The path to the turret stairs is clear, and if one of us can get up there, we'll have a strategic advantage from the tower. Higher ground gives you an advantage, Sensei says. I motion to Hamza to switch weapons. I grab his dagger and hand him my sword.

Ifrit leans over the balcony. I guess he hasn't laughed in a million years and really needs to get it out? Tears fill his eyes, making them cloud over. Golden rivulets splash down his face, and his tears plunk to the balcony floor like golden beads; from each bead, a tiny tree begins to grow. Right there, on the balcony. I guess his tears are like fool's gold. Since Ifrit's momentarily blurry-eyed, I nudge Hamza— now's his chance. He flattens himself against the cliff wall and scurries up the stairs to a balcony under a double minaret. The second of the round towers sticks out at an odd angle from the first. Like the landscape, the architecture in this place is all weird and asymmetric.

They told us Ifrit's mom created this tilism from his tears to hide him from the prophecy after Suleiman defeated his father. I wonder if he was alone here the whole time, if, as a kid, his randomly plunked tears are what made this place so bizarre and misshapen.

Focus, Amira! This might be your only chance. Surprise is your friend.

With Ifrit bent over, wiping away the golden stream of his laugh-crying, I know this is my moment. I swear my heart is going to explode out of my chest; sweat pours down my back. There is no deodorant in the world strong enough to conceal the literal smell of my fear right now. I close my eyes. For a tiny moment, I see my mom and my dad. I see myself pushing Hamza in a baby swing when he was a toddler. I hear my mom cheering as seven-year-old me rides my bike down the block for the first time. I feel my dad's arm around my shoulder as he looks at the moon through my new telescope on a cool, crisp night. I don't just see those moments. I feel them. I feel the love bursting out of every single one. I open my eyes.

I take a deep breath and charge.

And then it's like I'm watching myself outside of my body. *Am I dead? Did his golden tears kill me? Wait, have I been dead this whole time?* My body moves without my brain even telling it what to do. I feel my right hand curl into a tight fist. Energy pulses through my muscles, my legs like springs, all my rage and fear and anger flowing through my fist, and I shock Ifrit with a hard, high punch, a seiken jodan zuki to the bridge of his nose while he's still partially bent over, using his vulnerable body positioning and change in center of gravity to my advantage. When my fist connects with his face, I hear a satisfying crack, and a river of green blood bursts from his nose. He howls, and every bone in my hand stings. But I don't stop. I don't retreat. While his right hand tries to stop the blood flowing down his face, I press forward with a seiken chudan zuki punch to his solar plexus, which throws his balance off.

I can't believe this is me. I can't believe I'm doing it. *I'm* doing it. From above, I hear Hamza cheering me on. "Finish him, sis!"

With Ifrit flailing around and his nose still bleeding, I feel my adrenaline spike. My heart races, and for a moment, the scene slows. I hear everything—the squish and ooze of his green blood as it pools at his feet, and the swoosh as it flows around the tiny golden tear-trees. I hear the plink of the last of his teardrops that bead up on the balcony floor, and I feel the blood seeping through the faux-gold surface, turning it muddy, softening the structure. There's a rustle of wind blowing wisps of hair across my face, and I stretch my fingers wide, then recurl them into tight fists and send my energy into my right leg. I blow a puff of air out of my lungs and scream, delivering the one kick that always throws me off balance, the one I can never get right but that I know generates the most power. If he wasn't so huge, even bent over, I'd be aiming for his head, but I know I can't reach it. So I aim my spinning roundhouse kick—my ushiro mawashi geri—right where his floating ribs should be, if jinn even have ribs. When my foot meets his burning pink skin, we connect with so much force a shock wave runs up my leg and into my spine, throwing me backward onto my butt. Instinctively, I draw my fists up to protect my face. I don't even realize my eyes are squeezed shut until I scamper back to standing and whip them open and see that I've knocked Ifrit down. His full length takes up nearly half the balcony, but on the floor, he looks smaller, as if the blood pouring out of his nose is shrinking his body.

Ifrit roars and yells and leaps up, like he's doing a backbend in reverse. I was right; he is smaller, the size of a tall human now, but his teeth are bared. There are literal flames in his eyes. I may have hurt him, but somehow he feels even more ferocious and terrifying. When he's fully standing, he pushes his right palm against his side where I kicked him—and I hear pops and crackles like he's shoving his jinn ribs back into place. The sound makes me gag a little; I can taste bile in the back of my throat. I can't throw up. This would be a really bad time to puke.

He unsheathes his sword, which must be almost

as tall as me. I step back, the dagger in my hand looking about as effective as the knife from the Easy-Bake Oven I got for my sixth birthday. I take a deep, shuddery breath. Ifrit is standing there, his chest heaving, shoulders rising. My eyes dart toward Hamza, who is now climbing on the outside of the main turret—he's fastened the cummerbund into some kind of harness, and he's leaning precariously over the cliff's edge. I see him look down and then close his eyes for a second. I want to message him through sibling telepathy: *You got this. Don't look down, Hamz.* His stomach must be in knots. He flashes his eyes open and nods at me. When he turns the blade of his sword to the second, extended tower, I know what Hamza needs. Time.

"Hey. Hey, you," I prod Ifrit. "Do you think standing there all bloody and gross is going to, what, scare me to death?" I close my free hand into a fist so he can't see my fingers shaking.

He grunts. "You are most unwise, tiny, foolish human. Many far more powerful than you fear me and kneel before me. You are as an ant I can crush underfoot."

"I believe that. The stink from your hairy feet alone could kill most creatures." I keep an eye on Hamza as he uses Suleiman's celestial steel sword to hack and saw through the second tower, tiny bits of the faux gold crumbling as he does.

"Shahpal bin Shahrukh is truly a fool to put his faith in you. If you are the best Earth has to offer, it is hardly a place worthy of conquest," Ifrit continues.

"Then why bother? Stay here in your City of Gold and do...whatever you do. I dunno, I could maybe hook you up with a Switch or something. *Legend of Zelda* seems right up your alley. Dungeons, puzzles, paragliding. Or maybe *Animal Crossing*. You'd probably be ace at bug catching. I'm talking hours of fun to occupy your, uh, eternity."

Even though every muscle in my body screams not to, I take a step forward, trying to give him my mother's Death Stare™ to stop him in his tracks, prevent him from moving from his spot. Ifrit needs to be under that tower of gold clay that Hamza is slicing through.

"You think this is a game? It is not. The conquest

of Earth is merely one benefit. Once the moon is torn asunder, while my army runs rampant over your home, I shall free my father, who has been entombed by the treacherous Suleiman for all these centuries. Confined so that his suffering would be endless, a lesson for all. Bound in a brass vessel. Brass! How unworthy. We shall search the entirety of time and space, if need be, to find Suleiman's Ring of Power, and then we shall reign together, father and son, taking rightful dominion over all lesser creations on Earth and Qaf."

"I only understood like 50 percent of what you said. If you want to rule over Earth, you might want to bring your fancy talk down a notch. Maybe switch up your syntax, use some contractions, shorter sentences. That kind of thing."

"You mock me? Here? Now? At this time when your only assurance is death? Humans are so weak in body and spirit. So unaware when their doom is upon them."

I try to ignore him and my wobbly knees, my sweaty palms, and the puke that threatens to spew out of me. "You may also want to consider giving your beard a serious trim. You are way beyond hipster. At that length, you're beyond Santa. You've got a whole haven't-bathed-or-shaved-in-months vibe. Not a good look." I shake my head, then cautiously steal a glance up at Hamza. His sword is nearly through the clay tower. I shove my dagger back into my belt.

"You are a very frail and strange little creature." Ifrit points his finger toward my head, like he's taking aim.

"Now!" Hamza yells.

Ifrit turns his head to look, and I grab my bow, string it in a flash.

"No!" he yells. "Suleiman's Scorpion was meant only for the true Chosen One!" I release the arrow while Hamza delivers a final blow to the crumbling tower. Time slows again, and I see the confused look on Ifrit's face, his eyes bulging as my arrow arcs through the air. The top of the tower teeters and then tumbles in a million pieces toward Ifrit. My arrow hits him in the neck while hunks of clay pile down on him. He twists and tries to reach for the Peerless

Dagger before he's buried beneath the rubble, but a poof of smoke and ash is all that's left of him.

Hamza hoots and raises a fist in the air. My chest swells up, and for a second, I feel like I could fly. Like I can get my orange belt in karate and plow down any little kid who stands in my way. We did it! WE. DID. IT. It doesn't seem real even with all this fake-gold dust in my hair and up my nose. We saved Qaf and our parents and the whole world. Us. Together. Best summer vacation EVER.

But while Hamza and I are high-fiving from far away, the balcony shakes and the rail begins to give way. I look out and see the trees falling like they're being bulldozed, and the cliffs begin crumbling. There's golden dust and clay flying through the air. A crack splits the balcony and begins pulling it apart, stranding me in one corner.

"The mountain is coming down!" I scream, realizing I can't make it to the door. "Get out of there!"

Hamza refastens the cummerbund to a balcony rail on the remaining turret and wraps the other end around his hand. My heart leaps to my throat. I know what he's going to try to do. I look down as the balcony rumbles again. No way we can survive that fall. "You're not Spidey! Even if you still wear the pj's!"

"I can do this!" he yells back, and before I can say anything else, he swings down from the balcony, holding tight to the cummerbund. It is incredibly, embiggeningly flexible. And the whole time I'd been thinking Suleiman had made a fashion faux pas by leaving it for us. I guess he did know what he was doing after all.

Hamza flies from the minaret toward me. I step as close as I can toward the widening chasm on the balcony—no way I can jump to the other side—and hold my arms out. This is the most ridiculous thing we've ever done, and we've done lots of absurd stuff. Ask our parents. Luckily, I barely have time to think, because Hamza smacks right into me and grabs the strap of my quiver while I wrap my arm around his waist. We're like a two-headed, four-armed, very awkward dev. The cummerbund's elasticity only stretches so far, and it begins to pull back toward the minaret where it's tied. As soon as we make it across the chasm so we're on the door side of the balcony,

I yell, "Jump!" We drop down as the cummerbund snaps back and the turret it was attached to disintegrates, raining chunks of clay on us.

We throw ourselves through the door. The entire palace is coming down. We race down the winding stairs barely ahead of the destruction. With the walls starting to give way, we have to skip steps and leap across the giant cracks in the floor. As we fall through the arched entrance of the palace, the entire ceiling behind us caves, and the blast of debris throws us forward in clouds of gold-colored air. Hamza and I both start coughing. I try to wipe the grime off my face and blink it away from my eyes. I turn to look at the palace.... The entire structure is about to go *kaboom*. I grab Hamza's hand and yank him forward. The cliffs surrounding the palace are giving way. We have to get out now or that narrow passage that led us here will be blocked.

We race through the tight valley, shielding our heads and faces from dust and clay fragments. That's when the lightning comes, ripping through the sky, striking cliff tops and the trees ahead of us. Hamza is right behind me; I can hear his labored breathing. But we're not going fast enough. We need to move faster. This entire tilism is coming down. Maybe without its creator, the magical world can't hold together? Like the gold, it can't last because it's not real.

We make it through the valley, but when I turn back, I can't even see through to the end. Looking ahead, I stop short. The lightning is striking the ground almost every second now, and the entire forest of gold trees is ablaze as fiery stones fall from the sky.

"Hurry!" I scream. "We have to get to the raft! It's the only way off the island!"

We race through the trees, zigzagging between flames and dashing up the dunes, but when we get to the top of the dune, I realize there is no escaping. Our raft is on fire.

We slide down the dune, the City of Gold crumbling behind us, flames everywhere. Tears and dust streak my face. I fall to my knees, sinking into the soft sand. We defeated Ifrit. We saved Qaf. We saved the world. But we'll never be able to tell anyone about it. To see our parents again. Our friends. Our home. Because we weren't able to save ourselves.

"Sis, c'mon. What are we going to do? How do we get off the island? Maybe we can swim for it?"

I look up at Hamza. It hasn't hit him yet. He hasn't realized. "Sure, it's worth a shot." I sniffle, wiping away tears and snot on the back of my sleeve. I know neither of us are strong enough swimmers to make it to the other shore, which we can't even see now because of the clouds of smoke.

Hamza drops the backpack and starts to take off his shoes. Should I say something? Should I tell him it's too far? That the lightning makes it even deadlier? That there could be other monsters in the sea? That the current and waves are too strong for us? We're out of options. This entire place is burning, and soon the fire will push us into the water anyway.

I stare at the stuff that fell out the backpack when Hamza dropped it. Granola wrappers. A bunch of Nerf bullets. The flask and the jade tablet. I reach over to see if it has any final weird, cryptic words. It does: *You were born with wings; why prefer to crawl?*

Hamza glances at it as he pulls off his socks. "We could really use one of those flying pots right now." He shrugs.

I sniffle, nod. Start taking off my shoes. *Wings. Crawl.* Oh my God! It's actually being literal for once.

"Hamz, the feather! From the simurgh! She said to burn it in an emergency." I reach into the back pocket of my jeans and pull out the coppery feather. It's a bit bent and smushed, but hopefully that won't matter. I throw it onto the raft. It flares and shoots a bronze beacon high into the sky.

"It's like the Bat-Signal! Cool."

"If it works." But I barely have time for doubt, because soon I hear a deeper version of the scronking the baby simurgh was making when I found it. Through the smoke and gold-dust-filled air, I can make out the coppery-bronze wings of the simurgh. They're immense, and I watch Hamza's face as he catches his first glimpse of the simurgh's lion paws and dog face. He turns to me; his mouth drops wide open. *Iftah ya Simsim.*

The simurgh lands on the water's edge, her wings

shooting water droplets into the air when they meet the sea.

"No time to talk. Hurry, children," she says. "Climb on my back."

I grab the dagger and sword while Hamza shoves the tablet into the backpack.

"Leave the weapons. We must fly over the Magnetic Sea to reconnect with the Garden of Iram. The sea may draw your weapons—any substantial metals—downward and could sink us."

I hear the simurgh, but I'm reluctant to throw down the dagger and sword. "What if we encounter other enemies along the way? Allies of Ifrit? How will we fight them?"

"Yeah," Hamza adds. "Those weapons are the only reason we even got this far."

The simurgh bows her muzzle. "Dear ones. It was not the weapons that made you champions. It is your hearts. Your love and belief in each other and yourselves. The way will be clear. Ifrit has fallen, his troops are scattering and being taken into custody by the emperor's army. As you helped my child, so I now help you. This is how I repay my debt to you." ·

I nod and throw down the weapons—the dagger, the sword, and the bow and arrows. I gasp and put my hand to my neck. My necklace. *No.* I can't leave it. I pause for the tiniest second, then quickly pull off the silver pendant and toss the paper clip chain to the sand. The simurgh nods an okay—it's small enough. I clasp my hand tightly around it, our protection prayer.

"Climb on my back. We must make haste. This tilism will fall, and if we are here when it collapses, we will be trapped between realms forever."

She bends her neck so we can slide down it onto her back. We barely settle in when she takes off, rising up at an angle so steep I'm afraid we'll fall off. Her beautiful, immense bronze wings flap against the smoke. I turn to take one last look at the City of Gold in flames, smoke rising, and watch as it disappears in a snap, like it's been swallowed into a pocket of air.

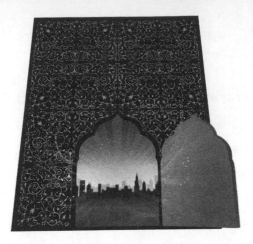

CHAPTER 18

Do You Believe in Magic?

FLYING BACK OVER THE INTERCONNECTED REALMS OF QAF, little fires dot the land, and I can see where battles were fought. There's rubble, broken trees, and what look like giant cracks in the ground. But I also hear music and see 3D fireworks over some of the realms we didn't stop in. We swoop closer, and jinn and peris look up at us and wave. Hamza hoots and hollers and shoots finger guns at the celebrations. It's finally sinking in. We did it. We weren't what they expected. We weren't what Ifrit expected. And we weren't what I expected. But I guess sometimes unexpected things can change the world.

I keep replaying those moments with Ifrit in my mind. How I was terrified but somehow didn't melt into a puddle of goo. How I kept saying I didn't have a choice. But I did. You always have a choice. And I made a choice. Lots of them—some of them were even good ones. This warm feeling wells up inside me. I guess I shouldn't have underestimated me.

Circling lower and lower, we approach the Garden of Iram. There's music—drums and horns—and cheering and clapping that grows louder as we get closer. It's for us. The simurgh lands in the stone courtyard where we took off from. It feels like a million years ago but also like we just left. Maybe that's what they meant by time working differently here. Time flies when you're trying to prevent an apocalypse.

The simurgh lowers her neck, and we slip off. Throngs of multicolored jinn—spotted and striped, horned and hairy—surround us. Then we hear a high-pitched voice through the crowd. "Took you long enough. I guess you'll be wanting a parade and, what, like, a feast in your honor, too?" Aasman Peri steps into the center of the courtyard, her wings unfurled, her arms crossed in front of her chest, and a small smirk on her face.

"Did you say feast?" Hamza asks. "Excellent, because I'm starving." He and Aasman Peri high-five and work their way through the crowd to a table filled with sweets.

I shake my head. I turn to say thank you to the simurgh. "Without you, we would've been dusted or snapped up into the void of that tilism," I say. "Thank you."

The simurgh bows her head to me, and I bow mine in response. "As you showed a kindness to my child, so I showed one to you. My debt is repaid. May your journey home be safe. Peace be with you."

"And also with you," I say. The simurgh's child scronks in the distance, and she turns her muzzle to the wind and sniffs, a smile crossing her lips as she heads off to find her baby.

I hear someone clear their throat behind me. I'd know that deep, telltale throat clearing anywhere: Abdul Rahman. "So the heroes return." He gives me a small smile as I face him. "Perhaps he had some doubts at first, but once our dear friend Maqbool really knew you and saw the courage of your hearts, he believed in you to his dying breath. I only wish he could have been here to witness your triumph." An ashy tear drips out of Abdul Rahman's right eye.

I cast my eyes down and nod, a lump welling in my throat. "I know," I whisper. "But I kind of feel like he is here."

Abdul Rahman clears his throat. "Of course...I believed, too. Perhaps you were not what the prophecy intended—"

I raise an eyebrow.

"Fine. Indeed. We may have only crossed paths because I am vain and refused to wear my reading glasses, for which my dear friend correctly chastised me. And, which, by my troth, I shall wear from this moment forward. I might have been mistaken in my reading of the prophecy, but there is no mistake that you were...you *are*...the true champions of Qaf."

Abdul Rahman meets my gaze and bends low, stretching out his arms. I step into them and hug him. He's warm—literally, because he's made of smokeless fire. And I can feel both sadness and joy in his embrace. Because I feel the exact same thing.

A whiff of sandalwood passes through the courtyard, and all eyes turn to the dais and the throne as the emperor enters, fully ablaze. I squint. Aasman Peri, who is standing next to my brother several feet away from me, makes a pinching gesture at her dad with her thumb and forefinger, and immediately the flames lessen and we can see him. A crown of emerald and ruby leaves on his head, his deep blue, gold-embroidered velvet robes sweeping the ground. All the creatures in the courtyard, except me and Hamza, bow. With his subjects' heads bent, the emperor meets our eyes and silently thanks us, placing a hand on his heart as he takes his seat on the throne.

"Rise. My family, we have waged a great war so that all creatures of Qaf may continue to dwell in peace. We have lost many beloveds to the armies of Ifrit. We shall have justice, but let us not seek vengeance on those who in our very lifetimes were not merely allies, but friends. More than friends—family.

We shall heal the rifts in the realms of Qaf. Once again, the barrier between worlds, the luminous moon, is in its rightful place. Shining on the people of Earth each night, incandescent to us even in our days."

The emperor points at a distant round object, now uncloaked, in the sky. There it is. Our tiny, far-away moon. Their moon. "We have much rebuilding to do, but on this day, we give thanks and celebrate our two warriors come from their home to save ours, and, in turn, save theirs. To you, Amira and Hamza, champions of Qaf, we are forever indebted. Songs shall be sung and tales shall be told of the storied descendants of Suleiman the Wise."

I almost speak up to correct him, to tell him we're not really the heirs of Suleiman, that we were never the true Chosen Ones. But Abdul Rahman taps my shoulder and gives me a look like, *don't even think about it.* No point now anyway, I guess?

"You two siblings, mere children of Earth, have shown us the power of bravery and the unbreakable bond of love. You shall be known forevermore in the

land of Qaf as Amira the Valiant and Hamza the Brave."
With that, Emperor Shahpal bin Shahrukh rises from
his throne, and all the jinn and all the other creatures
in the courtyard turn to face us and place their hands
on their hearts and say, *Jazāk Allāhu Khayran.* I know
this phrase. My nani used to say it to me all the time
when I would bring her tea or help her get up when she
was getting too old and too frail to do it by herself. It's
a super-nice way of saying thank you: *May God reward
you with goodness.* A little lump wells in my throat at
the memory and for this moment, too. Because, even
though I desperately want to be home right now, this
is also a goodbye. One thing I learned about goodbyes
when my nani died was that sometimes they really
hurt even when you know one's coming.

"Before Amira and Hamza depart for their world,
let us pray for all those that we have lost."

We join the others filing away to say our prayers
to the fallen, our goodbyes to Maqbool. I don't know
what we would have done without him. He died saving Hamza. And I never really got to thank him for

that, for believing in us, for giving us hope when we didn't have it. I hope he can hear me now.

Only Aasman Peri, Abdul Rahman, and Zendaya accompany us to the Obsidian Wall. The door is clearly outlined in the dark oobleck surface. When Abdul Rahman opens it, we spy a golden sand beach, an endless blue lake lapping at the shore. Far, far in the distance are the blurry, glittering outlines of... buildings...skyscrapers. "Wait, is that—"

"Chicago!" Hamza yells, pointing to the soaring skyline as it focuses into shape before our eyes. "How?"

"The emperor reigns over the portal, silly. Now that the enchantments are lifted, he can place it where he wishes," Aasman Peri smirks. "Still not quite getting the hang of this whole Qaf thing?"

Hamza shrugs. "Sorry I couldn't wrap my mind around your bizarro world geography while I was focusing on saving my butt! And the butts of all the world!"

Aasman Peri shakes her head. "Humans are really weird."

"Weird is awesome!" Hamza says, and laughs.

Abdul Rahman raises both of his bushy eyebrows. "Now that order and peace are restored, when you step through this door, you will be returned to the moment and place before we first crossed paths, before the moon broke. All will be as it was. The sleep song of the Neend Peri will have spared humanity from the horrors of watching the moon break, and the humans of Earth shall have no recollection of what transpired. There will be new fissures in the moon, evident only to you. For the rest, it will be as if they had always been there."

I grin. A time slip! Which shouldn't be possible, because time travel requires that space-time be bent, and we'd need a vacuum in space to bend time back on itself, creating a closed time loop, but the gravity required to do that would crush us and . . . science still rules, but I guess I'm starting to believe in impossible things, too. Or at least that some things can't quite be explained by the science we know, *so far.*

I want to say something, but my words all get stuck and I choke back a few tears. I don't know why I'm sad. I mean, I can't wait to be back home. To see my parents. To be normal. But I'll miss Qaf, too. I look up at Abdul Rahman and Aasman Peri. Abdul Rahman's face is crinkled as he wipes away his ash tears. Behind all the fire and raised eyebrows, he's a total softie. Even Aasman Peri looks…affected; she's making that bit-into-a-sour-lemon face again. "I don't know how to say goodbye and thank you. This place—" I begin.

"Is absolutely murderous bonker balls?" Hamza jumps in.

"Well, yes, okay. That. But also, it's a place where I made friends." I hug Abdul Rahman. I can tell Aasman Peri is not a big hugger, so we high-five. My brother does the same.

Then his backpack buzzes. We all turn to look at him. He pulls out the jade tablet. "The simurgh only said we couldn't bring weapons, so I didn't think I needed to throw it away." We lean in to read the message: *Goodbyes are only for those who love with their eyes. For those who love with their hearts, there is no such thing as separation.*

It's something my dad wrote to me once in a card. Before he had to go away for an extra long work trip. It's like the other sayings that vaguely reminded me of something...Oh. My. Poetry. "I got it!" I yell. "All the messages on the tablet. They're sayings from Rumi. Or rough translations, anyway."

"That poet Dad is always talking about?"

"Yeah! I knew they all felt familiar. Weird coincidence."

Abdul Rahman raises a bushy eyebrow. "There are no coincidences. The messages must always have been meant for you." He smiles.

"So we get to keep this thing?" Hamza asks.

I elbow him.

"What? We got to travel to an entire other universe, and I want a souvenir. I don't think there's a gift shop with snow globes." Hamza quickly stashes the tablet back in his bag.

"You will always have the memory of me. That should be souvenir enough." Aasman Peri grins.

"You're right," I say. "I definitely won't forget you. Any of you."

Aasman Peri gestures to the door, and Hamza and I step through, waving. As it closes, we hear Abul Rahman's voice booming, "Don't forget to return the Box of the Moon!"

The door closes. We watch as the wall vanishes into the night around us. And when we turn around, we find ourselves back on the doorstep of the Medinah Temple.

CHAPTER 19

A Whole New World

I GENTLY PINCH HAMZA'S ARM.

"Ouch! Why did you..." Hamza doesn't complete his sentence because he spies his zombie bowcaster lying on the ground by the dumpster right where he dropped it and rushes to grab it.

"Because I wanted to see if I was dreaming," I whisper to myself. Obviously, I'm not, because no way Hamza's bowcaster is going to ever make a cameo in my dreams. We're here. We're really here. I look up at the ornate carvings along the archway of the Medinah Temple. Listen to the honking and traffic noise as the bright lights of a plane blink in the sky. I take a deep whiff of the Chicago night air, which smells like a mix of chocolate and stale hot dog water. It's home. And it's perfect.

"Give me the Box of the Moon," I say as Hamza stuffs his bowcaster into his backpack. He hands it to me, and I flip it open. The moon and sun and Earth are all back where they should be. The gears seem totally dead again. Like they were before. "We have to put this back."

Hamza casts his eyes downward. He looks disappointed. I want to keep it, too, but it is an ancient artifact and should be in a museum. I snap the lid shut and hear a little crack. Oh no. I used too much force.

"Oh my God," Hamza says. "If *you* broke that thing, now? After yelling at me about it? That would be...epically hilarious!"

I frown at Hamza. "I didn't mean to. I swear I was trying to be gentle!" I hold up the Box to inspect it under a streetlight. It's not cracked. But the bottom seems to be popped open the tiniest sliver. Wedging my fingernail into what looks like a seam, a little drawer snaps out. "What the heck?"

Hamza edges in next to me, and I pull out a tiny scroll and unroll it.

"Please don't let it be a doomsday prophecy. I've had enough of almost being eaten by brightly colored ghuls with sharp teeth!"

"Sshhh," I hush him as I hold the tiny piece of paper open by the edges. First the letters look like Urdu. But I blink, and I swear they turn to English. Hamza and I exchange looks because...can that be real? I guess my sense of what is real has changed forever now. I read the words on the scroll:

> *To my brother,*
> *Amir A. Hamza*

"It's for him. The real Chosen One!"
I continue.

I fashioned this from the celestial alloy you bestowed upon me, its properties as mysterious as they are miraculous, bound by neither laws of Earth nor Qaf. As per your wishes, the Box will come alive only for your descendants, when hate begins to tear the moon asunder. May love prove to be the balm that heals the fractures.

"How can love be a balm? Like lip balm? Tiger Balm? You need something way stronger than that to heal the moon's fractures." Hamza steps away and begins to walk up the stairs as I continue to stare at the words.

I whisper. "It's a metaphor. And maybe it means the Box *was* meant for us. Maybe we're like the spiritual descendants of Amir A. Hamza?"

"But the scroll said he was the Chosen One. The one to defeat Ifrit."

"Right, but we knew that and defeated Ifrit anyway."

335

Hamza lifts his palms up and shrugs, confused.

I don't blame him. "Don't you see? We only thought we were the Chosen Ones because Abdul Rahman told us we were. Then we found out we weren't because of the prophecy on the Everlasting Scroll."

"Been there, done that, bought the T-shirt. I know," Hamza says.

"Well, what if it's not a jinn or a musty, yellowy parchment that decides if we're the Chosen Ones. What if we decided that for ourselves? It wasn't destiny. It was us."

"Is that supposed to be, like, deep and philosophical and stuff?"

"Oh my God. Whatever. Let's go in. I'll put the Box back, you cover me," I say as I tuck the scroll into my pocket and push the secret drawer back into place. My mind whirs and could spin on about this all night, forever. We were the Chosen Ones. Then we weren't. Even though we still kind of were. Huh?

I take a huge breath and walk in the doors. It's quiet. I panic for a second, then realize that everyone is on the roof for the viewing party like when we left. I hurry to the exhibit case where the Box of the Moon was, and Hamza walks ahead, first putting a finger to his lips and then doing that pointing, two-finger *V* at his eyes and then around the room so I know he has an eye out. As if this is the most dangerous situation we've been in all night. All night? Was it only one night? Technically, it's been no time at all. Can't quite get my brain around that, either.

With the Box back in place, Hamza and I race up the stairs to the roof. We burst through the doors. For a moment, I close my eyes and hold my breath. There's no sound but my heart beating in my ears. When I open my eyes, there are Ummi and Papa leaning over a telescope, then turning to see us as we barrel into their arms.

"What's wrong?" my mom asks as she looks down and gives me a kiss on the cheek, then tousles my brother's head, which is buried in my dad's chest.

"Nothing," I say. "I guess...thank you...for bringing us here tonight."

"Yeah," Hamza adds. "Everything's awesome. It's

not like we were swept away by a jinn army and taken through an oobleck wall to a parallel universe where we had to fight a very scary pink-and-gold creature with sharp teeth to save the world."

I give Hamza my raised eyebrow, chin jutting out, *really?* look.

My dad laughs and says, "You really have quite the imagination, Hamz. And of course, where else would we take our favorite astronomer?" He rubs the back of his index finger across my cheek.

I smile and ask my mom if I can have a turn at the telescope. I look through the eyepiece. This telescope is so much stronger and the view is so much brighter and clearer than in my telescope at home. I adjust the focus knob. Wow. There it is. The rarest of events: a super blue blood moon. The moon is huge and nearly completely reddish-orange, meaning it's blocking almost all the sun's light. It's beautiful. But when I was last here—uh, minutes ago?—a piece of the moon was floating in the sky and I thought the world was ending. Then we found out it sort of was ending. But we stopped it with a little help from new friends.

I zoom in a little closer. There's a circular crack along the bottom quarter of the moon, and it looks almost like a light is shining through it. "What's that?" I ask, letting my mom take a look. "The circle of light surrounding that shadowy spot."

When she stands back up, my brother checks it out through the telescope. "That new?"

My parents give us these quizzical looks. "Are you pulling our legs, right now?" my dad asks.

When they see our blank faces, my mom responds. "It's the Amir A. Hamza Sea. You two were named after it. Supposedly an ancient ancestor on my mom's side? You know this story."

Hamza and I exchange glances. *Holy time loops.* I want to shout, but I contain myself. I can tell Hamza is about to burst, too. I clear my throat. "Right. Duh. I guess it looked different with the whole redness-of-the-moon thing tonight," I try to cover, because who would forget what they're named after? And, if the sea has always been there in this timeline, then does that mean we were meant to save Qaf? So basically... we saved Qaf already and that's how we instinctively knew we could save it again? Wait. What? Time travel plus fate are very, very confusing.

"Your dad and I always thought it was so spectacular, like the fissure has its own inner light," Ummi says.

The moon has lots of "seas." They're not filled with water or anything, but that's what astronomers called the large dark spots that they think were formed by volcanic eruptions on the moon. Or, when, say, a terrifying dev was waging a war to break the moon apart.

"And you know what I always say when your mom says that: The wound is where the light enters you," my dad adds.

"Rumi!" My brother and I shout in unison.

My dad nods, a proud smile on his face. "Now who's hungry?"

Hamza's hand shoots up. Of course.

We walk down and find ourselves back on the street where we first met Abdul Rahman and

Maqbool, traffic noises all around us again, planes like shooting stars in the night sky. Hamz and my parents are debating between pizza and Italian beef. Hamza turns his head and sees me standing on the sidewalk looking toward the dumpster we hid behind.

He leaves my parents, who are unlocking the car, and walks up to me. "I miss him, too," he says, and puts an arm around my shoulders.

I wrap my arm around his, too, and nod. Then we quickly step back because we don't want our parents catching us in a weird sibling-affection moment. "It's strange, isn't it? Time and destiny and fear and all that stuff. Like, we were just over there, scared out of our brains. And now here we are back to our regular life, after saving the entire world."

"Well, *I* wasn't that scared," my brother says.

I glance sideways at him and grin. "Yeah, sure. Like I was the only one who was afraid I'd pee my pants when I saw the fangs on that first ghul. Anyway, I'm glad you were there with me, even if you are an annoying little brother."

"And I'm glad you were there with me, even if you are a bossy older sister." He smiles and then raises his fist to my mouth like a microphone. "Amira, you saved the world from being overrun by slobbery, toothy, green, blue, and purple devs and ghuls, some of which had very smelly, hairy feet. So what are you going to do next?"

I pause. I think about all the possibilities. About everything I've seen and done. About how wild it all was. Slowly, I turn my lips up in a smile. "I'm going to take my karate test again and kick some nine-year-old's butt!"

"Yes!" Hamza fist-pumps his microphone hand. "Totally here for kicking little kid butt!"

My parents call to us. We turn, laughing, toward the car, but I stop, turn back. There's an alley across the street, and I swear...I squint, take a step forward. I think a whiff of black smoke slithered and slipped into the alley like it was moving with a *purpose*. And for the briefest flash in the middle of that black smoke, I thought I saw a pair of bright yellow eyes. I shake my head. When I blink, it's gone. Just my imagination. Just an alley. On a quiet side street. In the city of Chicago. On the night of a super blue blood moon.

"Sis, what is it?" Hamza asks, tugging at my elbow.

I shake my head. "It was nothing. At all."

"Good. Let's go. Ummi gave in; we're getting Italian beef. Gonna get mine dipped with sweet and spicy peppers, and then I'm going to devour a slice of chocolate cake the size of my head."

I watch as Hamza hurries to the car, high-fiving my dad. My mom smiles and says something that makes Hamza laugh, their voices mingling with the sounds of the city. I grin. A part of Qaf feels almost like a dream already. Something fuzzy that doesn't seem quite real. But the scroll in my pocket, the tablet in Hamza's backpack, those things are evidence that it was.

Maybe we weren't exactly the real Chosen Ones; maybe choosing us was all a mistake of bad eyesight. Maybe I am an ordinary kid without any powers who got lucky fighting a demon. Or maybe it wasn't luck at all. Maybe it was Big League Chew, a stretchy cummerbund, random facts about oobleck, and two kids who really, really wanted to get home in time for dessert.

Author's Note

Hi, friends!

When I was a kid, there was a place in my backyard where four lilac trees grew together, their branches meeting at the top, so they formed something like a cave I could walk into. When they were in bloom and a breeze blew by, tiny pale purple leaves would rain down on me as I stared up into the slender boughs, and I'd pretend it was a portal to a magical world. I didn't know it then, but those were the very earliest seeds of *Amira & Hamza: The War to Save the Worlds.* Those seedlings were nurtured by stories passed down from family and flourished when I first came across the incredible tales in the *Hamzanama,* or *Dastan-e-Amir Hamza.* In English, the title is often translated as *The Adventures of Amir Hamza.*

My first language was Urdu, a language of the South Asian subcontinent and one that has an amazing tradition of oral storytelling. You know the bedtime stories the adults in your life sometimes tell you from memory? That's oral storytelling— tales spun and passed down by word of mouth over the years, each storyteller adding their own flourish.

That's how the stories of Amir Hamza were first related, through oral tradition, and, yes, I mean tales, as in plural, because the *Hamzanama* is a collection of stories centered around the great warrior Amir Hamza. And the history of how these stories began and were collected is almost as legendary as the tales within the book. There is no single origin story of the *Hamzanama*, no "first" author. Historians say the main character, Amir Hamza, is named after the uncle of the Prophet Muhammad (PBUH), Hamza bin Abdul Muttalib, a warrior renowned for his bravery who died in the seventh century CE. Other historians trace the origins back to another Hamza, a Persian rebel who lived in the early ninth century. Still others claim different origins.

Even though we can't pinpoint the exact inspiration for Amir Hamza, we do know that the story first appeared in Persia and passed through the Arabian peninsula to South Asia and beyond. How does a story pass from one culture and country to another and in different languages? That's the magic of oral storytelling! One person shares it with another, and so on. Yes, portions and versions of the story were written down across the centuries, in Persian and Arabic and Turkish and Georgian. There were Malay versions and Javanese and Sudanese and Balinese. Some of these versions were 1,200 pages long! And, of course, the adventures of Amir Hamza came to India and were translated into Urdu, and that's where this winding story comes back to me.

In India, the rulers of the Mughal Empire, which lasted from the sixteenth to the eighteenth centuries, often employed dastans, or court storytellers, who would narrate tales for the emperor. One emperor, Akbar, loved the various adventures of Amir Hamza so much that he commissioned a printed illustrated version of the epic for himself. It was twelve volumes long, with 1,400 paintings that captured different scenes. The scenes now show us how the stories of Amir Hamza were adapted and "modernized" to fit the times, incorporating clothes and weapons from the Mughal Empire, even though the epic was already hundreds of years old. Sadly, only two hundred of those paintings survived, and the only text from those volumes that we still have is what is printed on the backs of the paintings.

But the story of Amir Hamza didn't end with those lost volumes; different versions and translations continued to pop up and, of course, the oral storytellers—in my case, my great-great-grandmother, and so many elders like her—continued to tell bits of the legend to their grandchildren. Some bedtime stories my great-great-grandmother told my mom incorporated a mischievous peri—a fairy who loved mangoes—and shape-shifting trickster jinn. So a tiny part of my family history lives in the story you read. Of course, as a writer, I've taken artistic license in my description of the creatures of Qaf and of the devices that Amira and Hamza come across. Jinn, devs, ghuls, and peris are also in the stories of my childhood and exist across the Islamic world, in our history, culture and faith. Remember what I said about oral storytelling? Each storyteller puts a new spin, a piece of themselves, in the tales they tell.

Amira & Hamza: The War to Save the Worlds is fiction, woven strands of stories that lit up my imagination as a child and an adult. Stories connect us, even when we're apart. Even when circumstances have separated us. I hope a piece of Amira and Hamza's adventure connects with you. You're a part of the story now, too.

Creatures of Qaf

Just like the tales of Amir Hamza, the characteristics of the creatures in the *Hamzanama* are rooted in religious beliefs and influenced by a variety of cultural traditions and legends from across the globe, from Turkey to Zanzibar, from Iran to Indonesia. Stories of these creatures traveled across time and continents and became a part of my own family's lore. What I'm sharing about these creatures is by no means definitive—not the one and only way to understand them—but I hope it gives you a springboard to explore the amazing stories of these creatures yourself. A quick note on spelling: The names below are transliterated from Persian, Urdu, and Arabic. These languages are not written with the letter characters we use in English. We take the sound of the letters and "translate" them into English letters, so sometimes you'll see the words written differently because there is not one exact way to transliterate them, as it depends on how the speaker pronounces them.

Jinn: (You might also see this word written as *djinn*.) According to Islamic tradition, God created humans from clay, angels from holy light, and jinn from smokeless fire. Some jinn are thought to be shape-shifters—they can take human or animal form. They have free will and can be good or evil. They are invisible to humans but can choose to make themselves visible. Characteristics of jinn vary from culture to culture. For example, some cultures say there are different types of jinn—associated with air, water, earth. Some scholars point out pre-Islamic origins of fire spirits that are similar to jinn.

Peri: (Also written as *pari*.) Beautiful winged spirits with an origin in Persian mythology that spread across the Islamic world. Some believe that peri are a benevolent, if somewhat mischievous, form of jinn. In Urdu, my first language and the language of the Mughal court, the word *peri* is translated as "fairy."

Dev: (Also written as *div*.) A monstrous creature, often depicted with claws and long teeth and horns and sometimes with human bodies but animal heads and hooves. They are often at war with peris. The origin of the dev, an evil spirit, is said to have come from Zoroastrianism. Like peris, some cultural traditions say that devs are a category of jinn, a malicious fire spirit.

Ghul: This is a word you might recognize—it's the source of the English word *ghoul*. In fact, the idea of a ghoul was introduced in Europe with the publication of *One Thousand and One Nights*. With an origin in Middle Eastern folklore, ghuls are said by some to be able to shape-shift and love to live in desserts. They are demonlike, evil creatures that—yup, you guessed it— are sometimes considered to be another category of jinn.

Ifrit: (Also written as *afarit, efreet, afrit*.) Ifrit is the big bad guy that Amira and Hamza have to square off against. In the Mughal version of the *Hamzanama*, the hero Amir Hamza also battles a terrible demon named Ifrit. But, in reality, the term *ifrit* is often considered a category of demon—one that is very powerful, cunning, and wicked. The word *ifrit* is sometimes also used as an epithet—a derogatory word for a mean person.

351

Simurgh: This is one of my favorite creatures of Qaf! Kind, powerful mythical birds from Persian mythology, simurghs were originally defined as bird-dogs, having the face of a dog and the feathers of a peacock. Their feathers are usually colored bronze or copper, and they sometimes have the paws of a lion. Over time, the idea of a simurgh became linked with other mythical birds such as the Arabic rukh or, in English, the roc, giant eagle-like birds.

Khawla ki Supahi: The Khawla warriors are a jinn battalion that I made up but that was inspired by a real Muslim woman warrior, Khawla bint al-Azwar, who lived in Arabia during the seventh century. Said to be incredibly courageous, she disguised herself in knight armor to fight side by side with her brother, not revealing herself until after the battle was over. A skilled horsewoman and weapons master, she became a great general, eventually leading a group of Muslim women warriors into battle with the Byzantine Army.

Razia: The leader of the Khawla ki Supahi in the book is also named after a famous Muslim woman, Razia Sultana, who ruled the Delhi Sultanate, an Islamic empire based out of Delhi, India, from 1236 to 1240 CE. She was the first female Muslim ruler of South Asia. Originally appointed by her father, who believed she was more capable than all of his sons, she was later overthrown by the region's nobles, who opposed a woman sitting on the throne, even though Razia was supported by the general population.

Other Historical Notes and Figures

Al-Biruni: Abu Rayhan al-Biruni was an Iranian academic and brilliant polymath (someone renowned for their knowledge and skills in multiple areas) who lived from around 973 to 1050. He is considered a legendary inventor, mathematician, historian, scientist, philosopher, astronomer, astrologer, and author (of 150 books!) who could speak multiple languages. There really is a crater on the moon named after him, and an asteroid, too. He's thought to be the first person who divided the hour into minutes and seconds on a base 60 system. And, yes, he really did invent a device called the Box of the Moon. It was a mechanical lunisolar calendar with eight gears that showed the relative position of the earth, moon, and sun—a kind of early computer! Sadly, no actual Box of the Moon artifact has ever been found (I made that part up for the story so Hamza could get his hands on something!), but some of al-Biruni's sketches and writing still exist, and that's where I drew inspiration for Amira and Hamza's Box of the Moon.

Book of Ingenious Devices: This is a real thing! It was written and illustrated by the Banu Musa brothers around 850 CE. The brothers worked at the Bayt al-Hiqma, or House of Wisdom, in Baghdad, Iraq. The book has illustrations and descriptions of about one hundred different devices, including automatic machines, called automata. Some of the inventions were inspired by other works, while some were totally original ideas, such as automatic fountains, mechanical trick devices (like 3D puzzles), water dispensers, tools like a clamshell-shaped grabbing device, and mechanical musical machines like the automatic flute player that has a cameo in this book!

Suleiman the Wise and the Ring of Power: The prophet and king Suleiman, known in the West as Solomon, was the son of David and is an important figure in Christianity and Judaism as well as Islam. In Islam he is referred to as Suleiman the Wise for his intellectual prowess. His other gifts included the ability to speak with animals and to control jinn. According to legend, his Ring of Power, also called the Seal of Solomon, was made of iron or brass engraved with a five-pointed star. It allowed Suleiman to command jinn and also imprison them in vessels such as oil lamps! (Sound familiar?) But the jinn he put in lamps were probably not the kind that gave you three wishes when you freed them. Suleiman also used the ring to seal commands and letters such as the one found by Amira and Hamza. There are many legends about this ring and what happened to it after Suleiman's death. Some say it was thrown into the sea by a demon and swallowed by a fish. Others say it was buried in the desert along with Suleiman's many treasures. Note: Suleiman the Wise is *not* the same as Suleiman the Magnificent, who was a sixteenth-century Ottoman ruler, who is a super interesting and legendary historical figure in his own right.

Further Reading

To learn more about the *Hamzanama* and see some of the remaining Mughal illustrations, or to learn more about some of the creatures I mention, the following books and links are a good start, and I highly encourage googling to read more about the amazing histories I tapped into for *Amira & Hamza: The War to Save the Worlds.*

The Adventures of Amir Hamza. Translated by Musharraf Ali Farooqi. Modern Library, 2012.

Google Arts & Culture. "The Hamzanama." https://artsandcul ture.google.com/exhibit/rwKSxX7YjiTZJg.

The Kidnapping of Amir Hamza (illustrated). Retold by Mamta Dalal Mangaldas and Saker Mistri. Mapin Publishing, 2010.

Legends of the Fire Spirits: Jinn and Genies from Arabia to Zanzibar. Robert Lebling. Counterpoint Publishing, 2011.

Victoria & Albert Museum. "Hamzanama." http://www.vam.ac .uk/content/articles/h/hamzanama.

Acknowledgments

The story of Amira and Hamza has taken me on a wondrous adventure into storytelling. And that was possible because of you, my wonderful readers. Thank you for being a part of this journey.

Middle-grade fantasy is a new age group and genre category for me, and there were moments I wasn't sure I knew what I was doing. But the amazing thing about being an author is that even though writing often feels like a solitary venture, when you look up from your keyboard, you see all the magical helpers who are ready to cheer you on and lift you up along the way.

Love and eternal gratitude to my magical agent, Joanna Volpe, whose enthusiasm for the tale of these two goofy, determined siblings helped this story take flight. Appreciation and virtual hugs to the entire team at New Leaf Literary & Media, especially to Kate Sullivan for her eagle eyes and insight, and to Jordan Hill, Abbie Donoghue, and Jenniea Carter for their patience, support, and good humor in keeping me together. Thanks to Veronica Grijalva for all things foreign rights and to Pouya Shahbazian for shepherding this story beyond the bookshelves.

When I first got into publishing, I had a list of dream editors and imprints, and at the top of that list was Alvina Ling and Little, Brown Books for Young Readers. See why I believe dreams can come true? I'm grateful to Alvina for her brilliant editorial vision and for pushing me to tell the best story I could. My deep appreciation to the incredible team at Little, Brown Books for Young Readers who helped usher this story into the world, including Ruqayyah Daud, Emilie Polster, Bill Grace, Mara Brashem, Siena Koncsol, Victoria Stapleton, Christie Michel, Jen Graham, Nyamekye Waliyaya, Shawn Foster, and Danielle Cantarella. A million thank-yous to Karina Granda, whose cover design absolutely blew me away, and Kim Ekdahl, whose illustrations brought Amira and Hamza to life. Jackie Engel and Megan Tingley, I am so honored to have another book with Little, Brown Books for Young Readers. Thank you all for believing in my stories and in my ability to tell them.

I am grateful beyond words for friends and family, early readers and delightful cheerleaders. Shukria and merci beaucoup to Pierre and Marie France Jonas, Sayantani DasGupta, Patrice Caldwell, Dhonielle Clayton, Sona Charaipotra, Amy Adams, Rena Barron, Ronni Davis, Gloria Chao, Lizzie Cooke, Kat Cho, Anna Waggener, Sara Claus Ahmed, Nathan Small Claus, Asra Ahmed, Alia Thomas, Zayn Thomas. To the twelve-plus cousins and all my aunties—the family jinn tales are with me forever. And thanks to Ali A. Olomi and Rabia Chaudry for your fantastic Twitter threads and podcast episodes on jinn and other wondrous and terrifying creatures.

Heartfelt thanks to my parents, Hamid and Mazher Ahmed, for their eternal support and encouragement.

Thank you to all the elders whose stories sailed across time and oceans to find a place with me, in a language they never spoke, in a world they couldn't have imagined.

To Thomas, every one of my books exists because after hearing me talk endlessly about a story idea, you once said, "Why not write it down?" My story intertwines with yours, forever, my love.

And to Lena and Noah, your brilliance, curiosity, laughter, and hugs are all the reasons, the inspiration, the everything. This story is yours.

D0049422

BOOKS BY ERIC BERNE, M.D.

THE MIND IN ACTION
A LAYMAN'S GUIDE TO PSYCHIATRY AND
    PSYCHOANALYSIS
TRANSACTIONAL ANALYSIS IN PSYCHOTHERAPY
THE STRUCTURE AND DYNAMICS OF
    ORGANIZATIONS AND GROUPS
GAMES PEOPLE PLAY
PRINCIPLES OF GROUP TREATMENT
SEX IN HUMAN LOVING

SIMON
AND SCHUSTER
NEW YORK

SEX in Human Loving

ERIC BERNE, M.D.

HQ
31
.B525

TO ALL THOSE
WHO HAVE BEEN MY FRIENDS
FOR STILL THESE MANY YEARS . . . IN LOVE,
APPRECIATION, AND GRATITUDE

ALL RIGHTS RESERVED
INCLUDING THE RIGHT OF REPRODUCTION
IN WHOLE OR IN PART IN ANY FORM
COPYRIGHT © 1970 BY CITY NATIONAL BANK, BEVERLY HILLS, CALIF.
PUBLISHED BY SIMON AND SCHUSTER
ROCKEFELLER CENTER, 630 FIFTH AVENUE
NEW YORK, NEW YORK 10020

FIRST PRINTING

SBN 671-20771-7
LIBRARY OF CONGRESS CATALOG CARD NUMBER: 77-130466
DESIGNED BY CARL WEISS
MANUFACTURED IN THE UNITED STATES OF AMERICA

CONTENTS

PART I: SEX AND SEX ORGANS

1 / WHY SEX IS NECESSARY

CONCORDIA UNIVERSITY LIBRARY
2811 NE HOLMAN ST.
PORTLAND, OR 97211-6099

2 / THE SEXUAL ACT

3 / THE EXPLOITATION OF THE SEX ORGANS

PART II: SEX AND PEOPLE

4 / FORMS OF HUMAN RELATIONSHIP

5 / SEXUAL GAMES

6 / SEX AND WELL-BEING
OR PREVENTIVE INTIMACY

PART III: AFTERPLAY

7 / QUESTIONS

8 / A MAN OF THE WORLD

APPENDIX: THE CLASSIFICATION OF HUMAN RELATIONSHIPS

TABLE OF FIGURES

FOREWORD

This book is based on the Jake Gimbel Sex Psychology lectures which I was privileged to give at the University of California in April and May of 1966. Dr. Salvatore P. Lucia, Professor of Medicine and Preventive Medicine at San Francisco Medical Center, was on the selection committee, and I believe it was mainly through his influence that I was chosen for this honor. I am grateful to him and to the other members of the committee for giving me such an opportunity. About 600 people attended and overflowed into the aisles and the back of the auditorium, each from a different background and with a different way of approaching the subject. The original program read as follows:

THE 1966 JAKE GIMBEL SEX PSYCHOLOGY LECTURES UNDER THE AUSPICES OF THE COMMITTEE FOR ARTS AND LECTURES, UNIVERSITY OF CALIFORNIA, SAN FRANCISCO MEDICAL CENTER

SEX IN HUMAN LIVING

APRIL 6   Talking About Sex
APRIL 13   Forms of Human Relationship
APRIL 20   Sex and Well-Being
APRIL 27   Sexual Games

The above four lectures will be given at 8:30 P.M. in the Medical Sciences Auditorium, San Francisco Medical Center.

MAY 23   Language and Lovers

The above lecture will be given in the Field House, University of California at Santa Cruz.

All interested persons are cordially invited to attend.

§   13

Although "all interested persons" were invited to attend, the audience consisted mainly of students, faculty, professional people and their co-workers. Dr. Lucia was a most gracious and diplomatic chairman, and my assistant, Miss Pamela Blum, ably assisted in the platform arrangements. Meanwhile, Dr. Lucia's secretary, Marjorie Hunt, arranged to preserve the lectures on tape, and Miss Olga Aiello typed them out for me. Without this service, of course, the lectures would have been lost forever, since I had no text and my notes consisted only of topic headings.

But primarily I am grateful to the late Jake Gimbel for making such a series of lectures possible in the first place. When he died in 1943, he left a substantial trust for this purpose, to alternate between Stanford University and the University of California. Since then, the Lectureship has been held by a list of distinguished authorities. They have set a standard which is such a difficult challenge that it has taken me four years to attempt to meet it by placing my thoughts in writing before the public, and it is with some diffidence that I do so even now.

There has been a considerable emergence and spread of sexual knowledge since these lectures were given. In 1967 began the publication of the monthly journal *Medical Aspects of Human Sexuality*,[1] the most reasonable, reliable, and respectable periodical of its kind. It has much less of the slightly sensational and disapproving attitude of its most illustrious predecessor, the old *Zeitschrift für Sexualwissenschaft* wherein the pioneers of psychoanalysis published some of their early papers, and which was a prime source for Havelock Ellis and students of the "psychopathology" of sex of that era. During the same four-year period, the Sex Information and Education Council of the United States[2] emerged into prominence under the leadership of Dr. Mary Calderone, of New York. The impeccable qualifications and manner of Dr. Calderone have undoubtedly contributed to the wide acceptance of her work, particularly in promoting

sex education in the schoolroom. A third force in emergent sexual knowledge is the classified advertisement columns of the *Berkeley Barb* or *Tribe* and other underground papers, which reveal the prevalence and variety of departures from the official vis-à-vis position in sexual intercourse much more poignantly than Kinsey and his associates did, although less romantically perhaps than Havelock Ellis' writings. A fourth influence which has made itself felt in a significant way during the past two or three years is the legal relaxations: the acceptance of homosexual consent liaisons in England, and of pornography in Denmark, for example. Best of all is the recent conjunction of sex with healthy wit and humor (as opposed to morbid, distasteful, or derogatory jokes), as in the satirical *Official Sex Manual*,[3] and the sexy picture parodies in *Evergreen* magazine. The current advanced position is that sex is reasonably decent and is here to stay, so we had best face it. This is in distinction to the rightist position that sex is nastier than anything, and the radical position that nothing is nasty so that sex will not suffer if it is thrown into the pot with violence and garbage.

All of these influences, including the underground papers (which have to be repudiated by everyone else for reasons of "respectability"), come into fullest flower in the writings of Dr. Eugene Schoenfeld, who forthrightly enlightens the public in a weekly column under the name of Dr. Hip Pocrates.[4] (He has now retired from this activity.)

The greatest change which has taken place during this period, however, is not an educational one but a practical one. The fuller impact of "the pill" on American life is marked by the emergence or resurgence of the "emancipated woman," with her claim for full sexual equality. The manuscript of this book was combed by several of them for signs of "male chauvinism." Some of the examples they found were pretty hairy, so I made appropriate changes in the final draft. In other instances, where I felt "female chauvinism" was rearing its head, I have stood my ground, and allowed

them to have their say in footnotes, where they are represented by the initials EW, with my replies on occasion labeled EB. In fairness to EW, I should say that I have not included their many approving and enthusiastic comments.

What I have done in this book is tell it like I think it is, which entails the use of colloquialisms, imagery, and case reports. Anyone is at liberty to keep it out of the hands of their children under sixteen, or under eighteen, or under twenty-one (or under forty, for that matter), if they feel a need to. I will gladly receive the documentation of anyone who wishes to correct any error I have made in facts. As to matters of opinion, I cannot conscientiously defer to someone else unless he or she has listened to more or to more cogent sexual histories than I have during the past thirty years. I imagine that there are some pimps and prostitutes who know more about sex in general, and some scientists who know more about particular aspects of it, than an experienced and interested psychiatrist does. On the whole, I think that there is as much science as art in what I have put down, and any disputation should be supported by an appropriate body of evidence.

A lot of what is written here was not said in the lectures, or was said in a different way. For one thing, I have learned a lot since 1966, and for another, lecturing is different from writing. Thus it was necessary to edit, change, cut, rearrange, and add to the lectures, to bring them up to date and make them more readable. In order to do this most effectively, I have adopted the device of writing as though I were writing for an audience of one. In other places I have referred to a writer called Cyprian St. Cyr, who is the purported author of a work entitled *Letters to My Wife's Maid*. These letters are supposed to have been written while St. Cyr was traveling with his wife to faraway places, and are for the purpose of preparing the young lady in question to venture out into the world alone when she leaves her present employment. That is a suitable context for the present work, which is

therefore written in the spirit of St. Cyr's "Letters," while still endeavoring to maintain the tone of the original lectures as well. In line with this, the previous order of programming, as given above, has been abandoned, along with the original title of the series.*

Because of the many changes which have been made, it is only fair to say that neither the Jake Gimbel Trust nor the University of California is responsible for any of the opinions expressed. That responsibility is solely my own.

I want to thank the members of the San Francisco Transactional Analysis Seminar for spending several evenings listening while I read the manuscript to them, and for the many valuable suggestions and constructive and destructive criticisms they made, and also those who read the whole manuscript at their own leisure and did likewise. These include, emancipated or square, Bertha Joung, Al and Pam Levin, Arden Rose, Valerie Venger, Nadja and Valerio Giusi, and Rick Berne.

CARMEL, CALIFORNIA
APRIL, 1970.

NOTES AND REFERENCES

1. *Medical Aspects of Human Sexuality*, edited by Theodore Bawer, M.D., and David M. Reed, Ph.D., and a board of consulting editors. Published monthly at 18 East 48 Street, New York, N.Y. 10017.
2. SIECUS, 1855 Broadway, New York, N.Y. 10023.
3. *The Official Sex Manual,* by Gerald Sussman. G. P. Putnam's Sons, New York, 1965.
4. *Dear Doctor Hip Pocrates,* by Eugene Schoenfeld. Grove Press, New York, 1969.

*The "official" title of this book, for those who prefer to think of sex in a more academic way, is "Cerebral and Behavioral Correlates of Coupling in Higher Primate Communities."

INTRODUCTION: TALKING ABOUT SEX

A

SEX IS WET

Sex is not an easy subject to write about, mainly because it is wet. In fact it is more than wet, it is slippery. Anyone who ignores that is going to feel a little sticky talking about it. I knew a poet once who wrote about it beautifully, but without impact, and I said to her, "I think it's a mistake to use dry words to talk about wet feelings." So she started to use wet words, and then I said, "Wet words aren't good enough either. You have to use words that people's minds will slip on." She liked that, and in return told me that a pregnant woman sitting by a window thought of a black snake. I didn't understand that, not being a woman, but it sounded right. It sounded better than the pregnant woman who was very proper in her speech, and said that she was hoping to have a good flow of milk so she could raise a bust-fed baby. That one reminded me of the joke about the lady from Boston who always apologized when she talked about "chamber" music or "cocktail" parties, and who reported

one day that a friend of hers had fallen over a precipeepee.

To start off with, I think we should review our vocabulary and decide which words will most clearly and comfortably say what we are talking about.

B

SOME COLD DRY WORDS

The words that people use for sex start with *conjugation*, which is what lower organisms do, and *copulation*, which is for higher animals. *Sexual intercourse* is for people. Scientists call it co'-i-tis, although if it makes them nervous they sometimes call it co-igh'-tus, but *co'-i-tus* is what it is. *Sexual union* is something you can talk about in front of an audience, but only on Sunday. In fact you can talk about any of these except sexual intercourse. You are not supposed to talk about that; instead you must communicate. Communication may be very difficult, and it gives some people, including me, a headache, so just plain talking is better if you can get away with it. Even listening to other people communicate can give you a headache sometimes, especially if they don't know what they're communicating about or whom they're communicating with. In short, communication may cause trouble, and most people who indulge in it should learn to talk to each other sooner or later if they want to get along. The worst kind of communication is called a continuing dialogue, which may give the participants not only a headache but often chronic stomach trouble as well. Sometimes, however, people in a continuing dialogue start talking to each other, and then everything gets better. A cynical friend of mine, Dr. Horseley, tells overeducated couples who are not getting along to stop communicating and start talking.

The trouble with all the words above is that they seem cold and dry and sterile even though they are not. Conjugation sounds like making a fire by rubbing two eggs together. Copulation sounds wet but slightly repulsive, while coitus just sounds sticky, like walking through molasses in a pair of sneakers. Sexual intercourse is an okay phrase to use in public or in writing, although it sounds too sensible to be much fun. For variety's sake, the sex act is a convenient synonym.

The words used for the results of all these activities are not much better. Sexual satisfaction is instead of a good steak for a man, or instead of a cheese soufflé for a woman. Sexual outlets are like the faucets on an aluminum coffee urn or the tap on the bottom of a boiler that you turn on once a month to drain out the sludge. Climax started off as a decent enough word, but it has been so overworked on the newsstands that it now sounds like the moment when two toasted marshmallows finally get stuck to each other. Orgasm, I think, is the best word to use in writing.

Lawyers have words of their own, but they don't help much. Their favorites are cohabitation, sexual relations, and adultery, all of which are charges or accusations. Lawyers have no interest whatsoever in whether sex is any fun. They are only interested in "establishing" it or "proving" it so that someone will have to pay for it. You pay just as much if it wasn't any fun as if it was the greatest thrill you ever had. There is no deduction for dreariness and no premium for ecstacy. Lawyers also have other words that are called crimes against nature, although nature has never filed any complaints. There is no such word in the legal vocabulary as decent exposure. All exposure is deemed indecent until proven otherwise. This seems contrary to the constitutional provision that says a man is innocent until proven guilty, or decent until proven indecent. Some of the biggest fights between lawyers are over the word *obscenity,* and we will talk about that later.

The real trouble with all these words and phrases is that they evade the issue, which is lust and pleasure and intoxication, and that is why they sound cold and dry and sterile.

C

SOME WARM DAMP WORDS

Mating sounds warm and fertile; it has a great future ahead of it, but it lacks presence. Perhaps the most human and least vulgar of all sexual terms is *making love*. It has a warm, damp, fertile ring to it, and also a promise of something more enduring than the act itself. Nobody knows what happens after sunrise to the people who copulate or have coitus or sexual intercourse. But people who make love are the most likely to have breakfast together, and that is why most young ladies prefer that term to all the others. Unfortunately, perhaps, it seems to be slightly less popular among men, even men who are willing to face their women at the breakfast table.

To *come* is another warm damp word. What it lacks in drama it makes up in coziness. Some people, oddly enough, say *go* instead.

D

OBSCENE WORDS

It is perfectly possible, and I think desirable, to talk about obscenities without being obscene. For example, we can write four of the commonest sexual obscenities backward or sideways as *cuff*, *swerk*, *kirp*, and *tunc*, without either misleading or offending anyone.

Cuff is the only word in the English language that gives the full feeling, excitement, slipperiness, and aroma of the sexual act. Its lascivious "f" sound also helps to give it a realistic punch. The synonyms mentioned in the previous section carefully avoid the idea of excitement and lust, and even more carefully avoid one of the most primitive and powerful elements in sex, which is smell. Cuff takes in all of these, just as a child does, because it starts off as a child's word.

Oddly enough, it is not, as is commonly supposed, an Anglo-Saxon word. It got into English from Scotland in the 1500's[1] and most probably came from an old Dutch or German word, *ficken,* which means to beat, very much like the Arabic *dok,* which means to pound like a pestle in a mortar. Thrusting or pounding is one of the most important elements in sexual intercourse, as we shall see. Equally important is what Arabic sexologists call *hez,* which means an exhilarating, lascivious, free-swinging movement of the female pelvis. It is just because cuff means *dok* and *hez* that it has such a thrust and swing.

Cuffing is something two people do together, where swerking is a more one-sided word. A very wise girl named Amaryllis once said to me, "I like cuffing, but I don't want a boy who will swerk me just for the glory of it." Balling is something people do together too.*

There is no need to discuss kirp and tunc and their numerous synonyms, since they are all mere vulgarities that add little to our understanding. Penis, to most people, brings up a picture of something skinny and not very imposing, or, for those who have little boys in the house, cute. It will do for the organ in its flaccid state. For the more noble state of erection, I think *phallus* comes closer to the truth, even

---

*EW: Balling is a post-pill phenomenon. There is no feeling of exploitation, it implies mutual consent, an act carried out together, not done to someone but with someone. It is the wet-word equivalent of "making love," used with pride and joy.

though it sounds artificial and lacking in juice. *Vagina* will serve for the female organ. It has the warmth, if not all the other qualities, of tunc. The main difficulty is with the external genitals of the female, called by anatomists the *vulva*. That is much too clinical a word for everyday use, but there is really no polite term for them, so we shall have to settle for the conventional *genitals*.

There are lots of other words that you can find in *Roget's Thesaurus*, in various dictionaries of slang,[2] and in the Criminal Codes of various jurisdictions, but the above list should be enough for everyday purposes.

E

THE NATURE OF OBSCENITY

I will now explain why I prefer to avoid the use of obscenity. The word obscene itself means sort of repulsive. Obscenity is usually divided into two types—pornography and scatology. Pornography means writing about harlots, and is properly applied to bedroom words, while scatology applies to bathroom vulgarities. Some people find both pornography and scatology offensive, while others find one obscene but not the other. This all makes it sound as though obscenity were a matter of artificial rules, but that is not quite so. It has a much deeper psychological meaning than that.

Any word worth saying arouses an image in the speaker —and also in the hearer. These images do not always present themselves clearly, but with a little care they can be fished up from the deeps of the mind. The images for most words are bland, poorly formed and shadowy, and fade into an unknown background unless they are very familiar. That

is why they are so seldom noticed when the speaker speaks. These may be called Adult or shadow images. Other words are accompanied by images which are more vivid and powerful. Those images are relics of childhood, and are called Child or primal images.[3] Because they are so detailed and colorful, primal images arouse emotional responses. Some of them are strikingly beautiful, like the images people often see when they smoke marijuana or take LSD. Others are repulsive, and these are the ones we are concerned with here, since they give us a psychological way of defining obscenity. A word becomes obscene when the accompanying image is primal and repulsive. It is so because the image and the reality it stood for became vivid and repulsive in childhood, as is commonly the case with odorous excretions during toilet training, and the image keeps that power in later years.[4] This definition of obscenity is not based on artificial rules made by oppressive and ignoble authorities to deprive the people of freedom of speech, but comes from the structure of the human nervous system and its profound psychology.

If obscenity is based on deep and universal psychological factors dating from childhood, then only childhood words should have such potency. If a language is learned later in life, say after the age of six, it can have no obscenities for the learner because he never heard its words in the primal years of life. Thus a proper Englishman may be able to say or read words like *merde, Scheiss, fourrer, vögeln, cul,* or *Schwanz* without embarrassment or diffidence because those words, although he may know very well what they mean, do not arouse any primal imagery, but maintain in his mind a more abstract quality. If the new language becomes deeply ingrained, however, and he starts thinking in it, certain of its words may gradually penetrate through to the primal layers, and thus become obscene.

Such observations indicate that the quality of obscenity is here to stay, but the particular words that arouse an obscene reaction are a matter of choice or chance. Basically it has to

do with smell and taste, and also slippery touch. Obscene words are ones that become connected with slippery sensations in primal imagery. In special cases, the most inoffensive words can become farfetched obscenities as a result of experiences during the childhood period when these images are formed.

Thus a new generation can knock down old obscenities, but their offspring will create new ones, perhaps by turning a common word into an obscene one ("pig") or by pulling a rare phrase into common usage ("mother-cuffer"). It is conceivable that children could be raised completely free of obscenity reactions, but it does not seem likely because of the way the human nervous system is constructed. I think it would be very difficult to train out the relief most people feel when they get outdoors from the community latrine.

The shock value of obscene words, or their relief value, if they are used for that purpose, or their erotic value, if they are used as stimulants, come from their aromatic quality as much as from their indecency. The strongest obscenities are those with the strongest fragrance—cuff, tunc, and tish; while the weakest are the scientific and literary words that are far removed from primal images and are completely deodorized. For the neurologist and psychologist, this is a fascinating phenomenon having to do with the whole structure of the brain and mind: the relationship between smell, visual imagery, words, social action, and emotional shock, relief, or stimulation.

Because of such psychological verities, a respect for the power of obscenity is not a quaint relic of an antique way of thinking. Rather it is one aspect of a way of life in which the most important quality is grace. Grace means graceful movements, and graceful moments of solitude or communion. This quality is well understood by dancers, rhetoricians, and students of Zen and other Oriental philosophies. It means speaking gracefully and making each hour a work of art. It requires an appearance and a demeanor that make

each year better than the last. And finally, it means that a whole lifetime of friendships and enmities, intimacies and confrontations, comedies and tragedies, will have at least the possibility of ending up with some strain of wholeness and nobility running through it. For me class = grace = reticence, the avoidance of overstatement and disharmony, in speech as in ballet as in painting.

To encounter ugliness and look it in the face is different from embracing it. Each person has his own idea of beauty, so there is no way to define it by saying what it is. But at least it can be split off by saying what it is not. There is one, and I think only one, universal rule of esthetics, universal because it became an inherited biological trait in the evolution of the human race. Beauty can be in spite of bad smells, but not because of them. And everybody knows what a bad smell is. It is the smell of a stranger's tish, his unwanted intrusion with every breath we draw. With a friend, it is the opposite. As Amaryllis once put it, "A friend is one whose tish and tarfs don't stink, and the sound of whose sipp is a song to your ears. If a stranger tries to give you that kind of park, you give him a kick in the tootches." (Amaryllis has a slightly vulgar turn of mind, as shown by her use of the word stink.)

In view of all this, I believe that obscenity should not be imposed on others without their consent. For some, it is part of their life plan and adds to their joy. For others, free speech stops not only at yelling "Fire!" in a crowded theater, but also at crying vulgarities before children. Poetry is always more appealing. Menstruation is not very attractive as "monthlies," but becomes charming (to men at least) as "blood on the face of the moon," or in the French term "I have my flowers."

Whatever you want to say, you should say it, provided you can still remain pure by your own standards. It is only that purity is very important when so many things are polluted.

—
F
—

THE TRASH CAN

It is true that you can find out an awful lot about your neighbors by looking in their trash cans. A philosophical scavenger could develop a whole philosophy of life from what he finds in people's garbage: he can see what they throw away, how economical or wasteful they are, and what they feed their kids. And there are a lot of people in the world who would see in him the purveyor of ultimate rock-bottom truth. Look in the trash can and that's the real scoop on the human race, man! But it isn't. Archaeologists often happen on kitchen-middens and very little else, and from this they try to reconstruct what a society was like. There are some writers who follow the same plan, trying to reconstruct and judge our way of living by its garbage. But archaeologists get much further by uncovering a city like Pompeii than by studying any number of kitchen-middens. By seeing the whole city, they can judge better what went on among its people, the noble as well as the ignoble. The office and the library, the nursery and the rumpus room, contain more of the universal truth about people than the junky's pad. The sweat and the humanity of a nunnery is more worthwhile than the sweat and humanity of a brothel, since the nunnery appeals, however narrowly, to the upward aspirations of the human race, while the brothel, at least as described by pornophiles and pimp-lovers, is static, or if it moves at all, goes sideways or downward. And there is, after all, more humanity in a baby than in a tumor of the womb, and an embryo has more truth in it than a fibroid.

All of which is to say that obscene books are no more enlightening and no nearer the nitty-gritty than proper ones. Only Tolstoi could see what he saw in *War and Peace,* but

any clever high school boy who was angry enough at his mother could have written de Sade's *Philosophy in a Bedroom,* including both the bedroom scenes and the philosophy.

G

THE MOTHER-CUFFERS

In the extreme case, obscenity becomes a way of living. The pornographer, sentenced to life in the bedroom, and eternally seeking the promise of an orgasm, will never see the forests and the oceans and the sunshine. The scatologist, closeted in his odorous little cubicle, must paw through every happening to find the tish that he is bound and indentured to prove that everything turns into. Both are losers, for the pornographer will never find the magic, all-satisfying vagina that he is looking for, nor will the scatologist, standing amid the piles of feces he has laboriously accumulated, ever succeed in transmuting them into gold. The pornographer is better off, for he at least wins some passing pleasures, while there is only one prize that can come out of a bathroom, and that is a crock of ungold. True, crying obscenities does give relief to some people, but this only confirms the fact that such terms have a special psychological primacy.

The childlike theory that if you only say enough dirty words everything will come out all right just doesn't work on a five- or ten-year follow-up. Right from the beginning it is a loser's approach. After such a person says "tish" or "mother-cuffer" 100,000 times in the course of ten years (at a modest thirty times a day) he nearly always (in my clinical experience) finds that things have gotten worse instead of better, and then he can only scream, "Look how hard I've tried! Why does this always happen to me?" Which only

proves that trying harder is not the answer, since things won't get any better if he says his favorite obscenity three hundred times a day.

It is not the theory itself that makes the loser, but the way it is practiced. A winner, working on the same assumption, would take two days off and run through the whole program, fifty thousand curses per day, and see if he got the desired result. If he didn't, he would find a new theory for success and move on to that, thereby saving ten years. That is the difference between a winner and a loser in life. Whether he is a winner or a loser is the most important thing for the course of a person's life as well as for its outcome, since that determines whether or not other people will trust him.

H

OBSCENITY FOR FUN

There are others who agree that uninvited obscenity is in most cases an assault and therefore reprehensible.[5] But there are two situations where it may be effective just because of its indecency, and those are in seduction and in fun.

In seduction, obscenity may be used as a sales talk. Then it is corrupt in the same way that the Boy Scouts of America (supposedly based on the outdoor idealism of Sir Robert Baden-Powell) are corrupt in having a merit badge of Salesman. It is the art of making a fast buck intruding on the beauties of nature.*

---

*Amaryllis tells about a male acquaintance who successfully uses obscenity as a method of seduction. As soon as possible after meeting a likely female, he makes a more than ordinarily indecent proposal to her in explicit language. In this way he wins the favors of some women and loses the respect of many others, thus demonstrating both positively and negatively the unusual corruptive powers of obscene words.

Obscenity for fun is a satire on corruption, and satire is the surgical laughter that opens the festers of the body politic and the corpus of human relations. Hence obscenity for fun makes life less obscene. Rabelais is more scatological than most writers because he was trying to enjoy his scatological times. The dedication to my favorite edition of his works (Sir Thomas Urquhart's translation) reads:

> One inch of joy surmounts of grief a span,
> Because to laugh is proper to the man.

But satire is different from the obscenity of revolt: "I'm going to say these dirty words so I can watch the expression on your face to see if you're a square or if you stop loving me as a result, you pig."

In the same way, the humorous poems of the Restoration Rakes about the clap and the great pox, syphilis, which were virtually unavoidable and incurable for a rake of those days, are different from the self-pitying word-spitting of some modern writers on the same subject. Obscenities are mostly obnoxious when they are taken seriously by the person who says them or by the one who hears them. If they are said in fun, and not thrown in the face like old grapefruit rinds, the reader or listener can either join in the fun or else withdraw and say, "I am not amused."

Puns, jokes and limericks are the favorite ways of having fun with obscenity. Unfortunately the number of possible puns that can be made on the six principal obscene words is limited, and they have all been made long, long ago. The number of possible obscene jokes is larger, but most of them come out of the attic too, since a hundred million college students have spent a hundred billion hours at a hundred thousand taverns in the past hundred years.[6] The principal field left open for originality nowadays is limericks.

One of the most amusing ways to make fun of obscenity and its censors is to use likely-sounding made-up words in place of the real thing, after the manner of the *Official Sex*

Manual,[7] which tells all about *erroneous zones,* the *vesuvious,* and the *plethora,* "a tiny football-shaped object located near the *frunella,* just above the *pomander* tubes." During *coginus,* of course, the male's *vector* has to break the *hyphen.* But *Billy and Betty,* a novel by Twiggs Jameson, has a made-up vocabulary that is even better because the Jameson words sound closer to the originals and are great fun for real lovers to use. For example, those who can't find partners for *clamming* can always *automate* instead, and Jameson illustrates by example how to go about finalizing that way, whether you have an empty *pudarkus* or a full *glander.*

—
I
—

OBSCENITY AND LOVE

Perhaps a proper place for obscenity is in making love.[8] This is the primal scene, and that is why primal imagery, at least of the sexual kind, may have its value here. This does not include seduction or exploitation. It means love-making in which both parties have already given their consent, and more than that, in which each is actively interested in increasing the other's enjoyment. The primal images aroused need no longer be repudiated, but for some people come into full flower. They reinforce, and are reinforced by, the multitude of sensations that set them free: sight, sound, touch, smell, taste, and the warmth which the flushed skins radiate to each other. This is quite the opposite of using obscenity as an insult and a blasphemy, as shown in the following verse:

THE DIFFERENCE

She said "Cuff you!" and then saw red
When he went out and found instead
A lady whom he took to tea,
Who later said, "Oh, yes, cuff me!"

J

SEX EDUCATION, JUNIOR TYPE

Our purpose here is a serious one: sex education, or even inspiration. We have agreed on a preferred vocabulary, including some anagrams, and we have agreed to avoid obscenity whenever possible. Let us also agree that there is no reason to avoid fun, and we can then move on to consider various approaches to the main subject.

The most bothersome question about "sex education" is "How do you explain sex to your children?" The reason this is bothersome is that it is a rather futile question, and makes no more sense than "How do you explain history (or geometry, or cooking) to your children?" It takes several years of concerted teaching and homework to "explain" history or geometry, and even then very few children, or for that matter not all teachers, really "understand" them. Many parents end up saying to themselves (or to each other): "So you don't know how to explain sex to your children, you nincompoop!" or even worse: "Ha! I'm one parent who knows how to explain sex to his children!" What is really wrong is not the parents, but the idea that there is really such a thing as "sex" that can be "explained." There isn't, any more than there is something called "cooking" which can be "explained." (*Larousse Gastronomique* doesn't even try—it just gives some history.) It might be helpful to talk about the heat and aroma of the pot, but you don't make a good cook by drawing a picture of the gas plumbing, or by warning against poisonous mushrooms. There is no such thing as taking your son or daughter aside and saying: "I will now explain sex to you. A B C + D E F = G. Any questions? Good night, then. Time for bed." Aside from what?

In the case of young children, the first thing they usually ask is where babies come from. Since nobody really knows the answer to *that*, most parents feel called upon to explain about cuffing. They either evade the issue by calling in the friendly neighborhood bird-watcher, or face it by saying, "The man puts his goodie into the lady's goodie and plants a seed, etc., and that's how babies are made." The parent in most cases either looks jolly or keeps a stiff upper lip as he says this, partly because he knows it isn't the right answer and wishes somebody would tell him what is. The child, instead of listening to the information, asks himself the really important question: Why is father looking so jolly or keeping his upper lip so stiff? The kids on the street are much more natural about it and really *explain* it. Even if they explain it wrong, or some of their pupils maintain that nothing like that happens between *their* parents, they all go away feeling that they have had a stimulating and instructive seminar. Everybody is serious, thoughtful, and argumentative, and nobody is jolly or keeping a stiff upper lip.

So much for junior sex education, age three to eleven. Intermediate sex education, age twelve to twenty, is not much better.

K

INTERMEDIATE SEX EDUCATION

Intermediate sex education is often offered in the form of books and lectures. You know that I think of every individual as being three different people: a Parent, who may be critical, sentimental, or nurturing; a rational, factual Adult; and a compliant, rebellious, or spontaneous Child.[9] Books and lectures about sex may be classified according to whether they come from the Parent (and even which Par-

ent), the Adult, or the Child (and even what kind of a Child). Each book or lecture has its basic attitude toward the subject, and these for the most part fall into one of five classes.

1. *Sex is a Giant Squid.* It's all right in its place, which is the marriage chamber, where it's kept chained under the bed. But if you ever run into it anywhere else, watch out, or you'll get dragged under. What you have to watch out for is the opposite sex, who are going to do you in if you give them the slightest leeway. These dangers have been best summarized in the limerick about a young lady named Wilde, and anyone who knows that limerick knows all that is necessary about this monster.

> There was a young lady named Wilde
> Who kept herself quite undefiled
> By thinking of Jesus,
> Contagious diseases,
> And having an unwanted child.

The Giant Squid was invented by Father Parent, as it is written, although Mother knows about it too.[10]

2. *Sex is a Gift of the Angels.* It is a beautiful and sacred thing which should not be blasphemed by earthly considerations nor sullied by lustful thoughts. The Angels were invented by Mother Parent. Father knows about them, too, but he is a little skeptical since he has never met them personally.[11]

3. *Sex is a Triumph of Mechanical Engineering,* a kind of assembly line in which natural products go in at one end and babies come out at the other. Or it may be miniaturized into an assembly kit, as described in the previous section: "Insert widget A into sprocket B and clamp down gudgeon C, and presto! there will be a baby on Christmas morning." This is a rational approach which states certain facts in cor-

rect Adult fashion, but it is not very inspiring. It may be true as far as it goes, but it is not the kind of truth that makes life better.[12]

4. *Sex is Naughty*. This is the approach taken when the rebellious Child gets the upper hand in a person of any age (most commonly in adolescence and over forty), and says: "You know, all these rules and prohibitions don't mean anything to me. I'm spilling my guts, using straight Anglo-Saxon words, and that proves I'm free." There are three things wrong with this. (a) The words aren't Anglo-Saxon. (b) It doesn't prove he's free. (c) It doesn't work. That is, ten years later, these people are no happier than most of the people around them. The Marquis de Sade is a good example.[13]

5. *Sex is Fun*. People who find that sex is fun don't usually talk about it very much. There is not much to say about fun except "That was fun," or "Wow!" This is a childlike approach like the one above, but certainly a more lovable and spontaneous Child.[14]

L

ADVANCED SEX EDUCATION

Advanced sex education is mainly slanted toward humorless collegians, wife-traders, Indian rajahs and maharajahs, and Arabian slaveholders, but many ordinary people can profit from it, too. It depends on whether you like to paint your own pictures or prefer the kind with numbered sections that tell you where to put each color.

The chief textbook for advanced sex education is the *Kama-Sutra* of Vatsayana, the founder of the Hindu, or Crafty, school of sex.[15] It dates from either 677 B.C. or

350 A.D. The companion volume is the *Ananga Ranga* of Kalyanamalla, written about 1500.[16] Both of these give subtle recipes for kissing, touching, skillful cuffing, leaving tooth and nail marks in the right places, conning your neighbor's wife, and salving your own conscience. They are undoubtedly instructive, but they are also predatory, and replace passion and creativity with technical virtuosity and sometimes crookedness.

As my friend Dr. Horseley says, "There may be a special thrill to learning the fine points of biting and scratching and whoring, but it's even more fun if you think of them yourself rather than getting them out of a book, just as it's more fun finding your own wife rather than getting her through a computer. On the other hand," he adds somewhat sourly, "if you want to know the methods used by prostitutes and paramours for extracting money from men, you're undoubtedly better off reading these books than trying to learn from your friendly neighborhood prostitute or paramour, since the methods are the same here and now as they were there and then."

"No point," agrees Amaryllis, "in ending up like the sailor with false teeth who visited one of the girls and lost them. That's the origin of the song 'The Gal That I Loved Stole the Palate I Loved.'"

These books do have the virtue, however, of recommending patience and gentleness, particularly with child brides.

Next to the *Kama-Sutra* in hoary patina is the *Perfumed Garden* of Shaykh Nefzawi, spokesman for the Arabian school of the 1400's.[17] This is a practical manual, giving many warnings against the deceits and treacheries of women, prescriptions for various sexual ailments (including some for making Small Members Splendid), and a set of reasonable positions for healthy couples. Beyond that, the sheik also describes special positions for special cases: fat couples, a small man and a tall woman, and people suffering from various deformities. He pays due deference to the superior

knowledge and acrobatic ability of the Indians, particularly the woman who can hold an oil lamp aloft on the sole of her foot and keep it burning during the whole procedure, but feels that many of their routines add more pain than pleasure to the act.

Nefzawi's long chapter on pederasty still remains to be translated, which is unfortunate, since this would no doubt throw some light on the fate of the slave boys and girls, ranging in age from four to ten, who are still imported by the planeload from the Sahara into the Arabian Peninsula.[18] (I myself have seen a two-year-old boy being trained in milder slavish arts in the Spanish Sahara.)

One more book deserves mention here, and that is Dr. Josef Weckerle's *Golden Book of Love*, which describes 531 positions—more than the *Kama-Sutra*, the *Ananga Ranga*, and *The Perfumed Garden* combined, in this respect making those works obsolete, and probably *The Beharistan*, *The Gulistan*, and the seven erotic manuals of Ibn Kamal Pasha as well. But even Weckerle is only a European empiricist. Legman, using modern American computer methods, calculates that there are 3,780 possible positions.[19] Such a sophisticated approach almost makes Vatsayana look primitive, sort of the Grandma Moses of sexuality, but it is not really so.

But enough of the sexual sinks of India, Arabia and Vienna. Before we go on to consider the sexual education of healthy, red-blooded, clean-thinking American grownups, a word about "sex education" in school. It will take about twenty years to judge the effects of that, until a whole generation that has been exposed to it has had a chance to grow up. The main thing is that it should not be taught by frigid people, with some dried-out members of the school board looking over their shoulders like kippered herring at a wake. In this situation, sex is like humor. Courses in humor, if they are given at all, should be given only by people who have laughed at least once in their lives—and enjoyed it.

——
M
——

ADULT SEX EDUCATION IN AMERICA

The United States has taken seriously the injunction "Make Love, Not War," and has evolved several indigenous schools of love-making, this by pure Yankee ingenuity, without any Federal or state funding, being one of the few fields in which research has proceeded independently of government support.

The first and most rigorous is the Sociology or Stopwatch School, whose slogan is "24-40 or fight," that is, twenty-four minutes and forty seconds for orgasm (or whatever figure the latest poll shows), the average time as determined by the sociologists quoted in the Sunday paper.[20] Although they pay lip service to variations, some disciples of this school imply that anyone who varies very much is either a failure, a kook, or a Communist—or all three.

Next comes the Woman's Journal of Standard Brands School, which gives the proper recipe for decorous middle-class lechery. You take your man out of the freezer and thaw him out, add a caress, place in a warm bed, and let simmer until a thin film forms over his eyeballs.[21] After that you are on your own and you can serve him or not, as you see fit. The recipes do not go into that part of it.

Then there is the Psychoanalytic or Bureau of Standards School. This is an officially recognized outfit that is the custodian of the International Standard Sex Life.[22] That is not the way Freud meant it to be,* but that is the way it has turned out. This school is the object of some fierce competition from the popular Communication Movement, founders of the School of Comparative Orgasms, whose members

———

*In fact one of Freud's most talented early followers expressly repudiates such judgments. (Karl Abraham, *Collected Papers*. Hogarth Press, London, 1948, p. 413.)

greet each other daily with: "How are you doing these days in interpersonal interaction in the area of orgasms?"[23] This is a polite way of asking, "Have you had one yet that matches the Standard Orgasm kept under glass in the U.S. Bureau of Standards next to the Standard Meter, the Standard Kilogram, and the now obsolete Standard Bowel Movement?" For these people, the Standard Orgasm has replaced the Holy Grail, and many a couple spend their lives chasing after it, crying "Tally ho! It slipped away from us again, dammit!"

N

A STANDARD SEXUAL VOCABULARY

Ideally, a complete sexual vocabulary should consist of four words. The Parental, or moral, aspect of the personality, acting as a kind of consultant, needs "Yes" and "No." The Adult, or rational and responsible organ, the one that sets up contracts and commitments with other people, also needs "Yes" and "No." The Child, or instinctual, aspect, the part that is actually going to take the trip, needs only one word to express his or her reaction: "Wow!" In rare cases, however, where the Parent or Adult aspect has made an error in judgment, the Child part may need "Ugh!" Anything beyond these four, Yes, No, Wow, and Ugh, means somebody is in trouble. Except for "Beautiful!" which may be kept in reserve. There are some who don't understand why and when people say "Wow!" and "Beautiful!" but for those who know the secret, there is nothing else to say.* So there are some for whom life is Yes and Wow, and others for whom it is No and Ow (or Ugh).

---

*Although "Wow!" has only recently come into common English usage as an expression of enthusiasm, the French have been using its equivalent for a long, long time in the form of "Ooh-la-la!"

Having thus surveyed a few of the problems which arise in talking about sex, and finding solutions for some of them, let us proceed to talk about it and see whether we will fare any better than our predecessors. And remember that not only is many a true word spoken in jest, but truth is simply jokes stated seriously.

NOTES AND REFERENCES

1. Stone, Leo: "On the Principal Obscene Word of the English Language." *International Journal of Psychoanalysis* 35:30-56, 1954.

2. E.g., Partridge, E.: *A Dictionary of the Underworld*. Bonanza Books, New York, 1961.

3. Berne, E.: "Primal Images and Primal Judgments." *Psychiatric Quarterly* 29:634-658, 1955.

4. Cf. Ferenczi, S.: "On Obscene Words." In *Sex in Psychoanalysis*. Richard G. Badger, Boston, 1916.

5. Freud, S.: *Wit and Its Relation to the Unconscious*. In *The Basic Writings of Sigmund Freud*. Modern Library, New York, 1938, pp. 692-696.

6. Legman, G.: *Rationale of the Dirty Joke*. Grove Press, New York, 1968.

7. Sussman, G.: *The Official Sex Manual*, op. cit.

8. Symposium: "What Is the Significance of Crude Language During Sex Relations?" *Human Sexuality* 3:8-14, August, 1969.

9. Berne, E.: *Transactional Analysis in Psychotherapy*. Grove Press, New York, 1961.

10. The most horrifying description of sex as a Giant Squid is the very scholarly and very morbid work of Dr. Julius Rosenbaum, *The Plague of Lust*. Frederick Publications, Dallas, 1955.

11. One of the most popular sex manuals is also one of the most sentimental. Van de Velde, T. H.: *Ideal Marriage* (revised edition). Random House, New York, 1965.

12. The latest addition to this approach is the serious and well-documented clinical study of W. H. Masters and V. E. Johnson, *Human Sexual Response*. Little, Brown and Company, Boston, 1966.

13. The Marquis de Sade is still the unsurpassed masthead of such literature. De Sade, D. A. F.: *Selected Works*. Grove Press, New York, 1966.

14. Legman's book, referred to above, is the most worthy example of the Sex Is Fun approach. It is interesting to contrast Legman's use of his broad and painstaking scholarship with Rosenbaum's misuse of his wide knowledge of the classics.

15. *Kama-Sutra of Vatsayana.* Translated by S. K. Mukherji, K.C. Acharya Oriental Agency, Calcutta, 1945.

16. *Ananga Ranga of Kalyanamalla.* Translated by T. Ray. Citadel Press, New York, 1964.

17. *Perfumed Garden of Shaykh Nefzawi.* Translated by Sir Richard Burton. G. P. Putnam's Sons, New York, 1964.

18. O'Callaghan, S.: *The Slave Trade Today.* Crown Publishers, New York, 1961. Includes the debate on this subject in the House of Lords (Hansard) Thursday, July 14, 1960. Burton has a long essay on the history of pederasty in Arabian countries and other regions of what he calls the Sotadic or pederastic zone (so called after Sotades, a scurrilous but rhythmic poet of ancient Greece). R. F. Burton: *Thousand Nights and a Night.* Privately printed for the Burton Club, n.d., Vol. 10 (probably 1886), pp. 205-254. There was even a hope among the debauched elements in Arabia that they would be supplied with "Wuldan" or beautiful boys in Paradise if they prayed regularly. In general, it appears from their literature and commerce that male Arabs regard their sexual partners as "supplies" rather than as people. For some more recent bloody examples, see *Musk, Hashish and Blood*, by Hector France (Printed for Subscribers Only, London & Paris, 1900).

19. Legman, G.: *Oragenitalism.* Julian Press, New York, 1969. It is hard to believe that anyone could write a monograph of 300 pages on this subject without being trivial, repetitive, or lubricious, but Legman has done it. For those who are interested, and are married, over 21, and live in a state where it is not a criminal offense (and have written permission from their parents?), this is probably the best book on the subject, although I should say it is the only one I have looked through (because the publisher sent me a copy), so I may be doing some other author an injustice.

    I have not seen Weckerle's book in German, and it has not yet been published in English.

20. Kinsey and his associates are the founders of the stopwatch school. (Kinsey, A. C., Pomeroy, W. B., and Martin, C. E.: *Sexual Behavior in the Human Male.* W. B. Saunders Company, Philadelphia, 1948, pp. 178-179.) This has been refined by Masters and Johnson by introducing tenths of a second in some of their measurements. Such measurements are useful to professionally trained people who can evaluate them properly,

but they are easy for laymen, and even for non-medical social scientists, to misapply and misconstrue.

21. Almost every woman's magazine gives recipes for sex in the same tone as it gives recipes for apple pudding, except that they are less explicit and are surrounded by a halo of hush instead of mush.

22. Masters and Johnson claim, and have movies purporting to support it, that there is no separation between clitoral and vaginal orgasms as psychoanalysts have maintained.

23. There are now in this country a large number of organizations which promote "encounter groups" and "marathons" where orgasms are freely discussed and compared in the vocabulary peculiar to such groups, a classical example of which I have given in the text. Compare Maizlish, I. L.: "The Orgasm Game." *Transactional Analysis Bulletin* 4:75, October, 1965. Also Hartogs, R., and Fantel, H.: *Four-Letter Word Games: The Psychology of Obscenity.* M. Evans & Company, New York, 1967. These authors give further bibliography on the subject.

PART I

Sex
And
Sex
Organs

1

WHY
SEX IS
NECESSARY

A

INTRODUCTION

Life is a union of complex chemicals formed into strings, rings and spirals. The first and most important job of any living thing is to survive—that is, to prevent the intrusion of destruction from outside, and to keep the strings, rings and spirals working together. Unfortunately, all living things are exposed to danger. If they live through that, it is only to grow old sooner or later. Then the strings, rings, and spirals lose their bounce, and the organism gradually dies. Thus no living things can live forever as individuals, and in order to survive they have to reproduce themselves. If they do not do so in sufficient numbers to live through all the

dangers, their kind will eventually become extinct, like the dinosaurs and dodos. So after ensuring its own survival, the most important thing an individual of any species can do is reproduce.*

It is well known that sex is one of the favorite ways of doing this, so next to staying alive, sex is the most important thing in the life of any sexy organism. In fact some animals, such as spiders, are even willing to sacrifice their lives for it.

Some humans do that, too, although it is something most people try to avoid. Thus sex is a means of survival. Protection is necessary for the survival of the individual's body, and sex is necessary for the survival of his genes. The body is mortal, but the genes can live forever if they are passed on from one body to another in the next generation. The genes are like a baton which is passed from one person to the next in a biological relay race which seems never-ending. But sometimes it ends in a whimper, as the poet said, and sometimes it threatens to explode.

B

WHAT IS SEX?

Sex is the result of evolution and the survival of the fittest, and human beings are at the top of the heap. People are more fun than anybody and human sex is the best (at least for humans), so as patriotic members of the human race we should all be proud of it. Anybody who isn't should go back where he came from, which is jellyfish.

Before sex, there were already two other methods of re-

---

*EW: Every individual? Not today, I don't believe.
EB: Even when it's undesirable, it's still important.

production in the animal kingdom, or what was to become the animal kingdom. The lowest organisms (or at least we think they are the lowest, and so far they haven't objected) reproduce by binary fission. These are one-celled animalcules who keep eating until they are too big for their skins. Then they burst asunder, and there are two of them where there was one before. This sounds like a drag: "Here we go again!" or even "Why does this always happen to me?" rather than "Wow!" And it is certainly monotonous, because the two daughter cells are made of the same rings and spirals as their mother, so there is not much chance for originality. Even worse, since all the cells are the same, any overall change in the outside surroundings which destroys one of them is likely to destroy them all.

Conjugation is a slight improvement. It takes two to conjugate, and both must be one-celled organisms of the same species. They cuddle up to each other and trade some rings and spirals before they split. The result is that the daughters are mixtures, each a little different from the parents. This helps them survive, because a change in their surroundings may kill some of them, but others, being different, may go right on living. There are no males and females among such organisms, or at least it is difficult to tell them apart.

More congenial to humans is copulation, where the animals concerned are divided into two sexes. The male, in one way or another, usually gets to put his sperm into the female and fertilize her eggs. Since the sperm contains many different genes, and so does the egg, the result is like a folk dance, and in the course of trading off partners, many different combinations are possible. Thus except in the case of identical twins, each offspring is different from the others, which increases the chance that some of them will survive any changes in the music of the earthly sphere. There are some animals, like fish, which are divided into two sexes but don't get to copulate because the female lays her eggs in the water and the male discharges his sperm on them instead of inside

her. Snails probably have more fun than anybody except people because they are hermaphrodites and both ends of them get to copulate at the same time.

Mating is the same as copulation but it sounds more romantic. Mating is a word used by bird-watchers, schoolteachers, and pet-lovers. It means that the animals that copulate are supposed to have chosen their mates very carefully and to love them dearly, but this is not necessarily true.

Human mating is called sexual union, which, as already noted, is a phrase used mainly by clergymen. It means that there is, or should be, a spiritual element present which makes it even more beautiful than animal mating; but this is not necessarily true either. Nevertheless, such unions are usually spoken of as blessed, especially if they produce offspring.

In all the above words, there is a feeling that the purpose of the whole procedure is reproduction, but that is not always or even usually true as far as human beings are concerned. Mankind has made a great leap by splitting off the pleasures of sex from its biological purpose, and man is the only known form of life which can deliberately arrange to have sex without reproduction and reproduction without sex.

What we can say so far then is that sexual reproduction is an improvement over binary fission and conjugation. It is a way of mixing genes so as to provide a larger variety of offspring, giving a greater chance for survival under changing conditions in the outside world. Organisms seeking sexual partners tend to venture farther afield and take greater risks than those that are content with less glamorous methods of reproduction. And the more magnetic sex is, the farther the organism will wander in search of it, and the greater the risks it will take. Hence from a biological point of view sex and its pleasures are an excellent means for the production of a large variety of organisms living in a large variety of circumstances and for the evolution of more adaptable and adventurous forms of life.

c

BUT WHAT IS IT ALL ABOUT?

The explanation I have given so far might satisfy an inquiring snail, so that he would shuffle off sadder but wiser, but it doesn't help much for understanding the vibrations that pass between men and women in everyday life. So here is a list of some of the things that sex is about in human living, what it may be at times for almost everyone, and what it can be for almost anyone.

First, it is about fertilization: the quivering dive of the sperm into the fecund pool of the egg, which blasts a new life into throbbing flowerhood. But that can be done without sex by artificial insemination. (Did you know that there is a whole profession that spends its days squirting turkeys in this manner, so that these miserable birds are not only plucked and eaten, but cuckolded, syringed, and swindled into the bargain?)

Second, it is about impregnation—which may or may not be sexy, but it satisfies the woman's need to be filled with growing new life, and the man's need to fill her and change her body and her life through the power of his instrument.

Third, it may be about duty, for people who talk about it that way, and this is what they say: the duty of a woman to bear children for her husband, and the duty of a man to give them to his wife; the duty of a wife to yield to her husband's desires, and the duty of a husband to offer her what she could not have as a maiden; and nowadays, the duty of a woman to give her man the orgasm she thinks he craves, and the duty of a man to give his woman the kind of orgasm she imagines is there.

Fourth, it may be about rituals: the ritual of sex in the morning, or the ritual of sex at night; and the ritual of sex on anniversaries, and the ritual of sex at Christmas.

Fifth, it may be about relief, which means deliverance of pent-up tensions which cause distractions, discomfort, and even pain. However reluctant the person may be to have such deliverance, and however much he regards it as unworthy self-indulgence, sooner or later he feels justified in getting it, or else he continues to struggle against it with a feeling of nobility and righteousness. For such people, relief is obtained through things called outlets. If the outlet is regarded as a person, then he feels guilty for using a person as an outlet; if she is not regarded as a person, then he feels shame for failing in humanity. If the relief does not require another person—"Every man his own wife, or a honeymoon in the hand," as they say—then he feels a secret triumph of self-sufficiency, along with loneliness and disappointment and separation from the human race, for this is one of the original sins forced on many by personality and circumstance.

Sixth, it may be physiological readjustment, a pact entered into to give a mutual feeling of well-being.

Seventh, it may be a pleasure to be sought assiduously, the eternal chase after the promise of an orgasm.

Eighth, it may be a mutual pastime, a way of spending the days while waiting for Santa Claus or death.

Ninth, it may be a play of seduction and retreat, of quarrels and reconciliations, with the bed as a playing field for all the psychological games that are known or that can be devised between a man and a woman.

Tenth, it can be a medium for union and understanding, for sealing other pacts and making new pacts, for approaching ever closer to a meeting of two souls, for two curves that slide along the carefully erected barriers between them.

Eleventh, it can be intimacy and attachment, the welding of two solids by the heat of passion in a union that may endure forever, if it does not crack under the hammer blows of life or waste away under the monotonous drip of ever-haunting trivia.

Twelfth, it can be the final and ever renewed expression

of love, culminating in its natural product, the fertilized egg, thus completing the circle.*

Often the question "What is sex all about, anyway?" is asked with a kind of desperation. Then it usually means two things. First, "Why do I want it so badly?" The answer is that we are built that way. Remember, we all started out as jellyfish, and it took millions of years of natural selection for us to evolve into people. The stronger and more energetic organisms that wanted it badly would on the whole leave more offspring, and so their kind survived better than the ones that didn't. So here we are striving to get it as hard as we can, except that we get mixed up about it, and all sorts of people are helping to keep us that way.

Which brings us to the second point that bothers a lot of people: "When am I going to get some?" The answer is that you will when you're ready. You can get some right now if you're willing to travel far enough and make the necessary sacrifices and take what comes along. But then you may have to face some consequences: possibly physical and mental and moral, perhaps the betrayal of yourself and your parents, so it may be better to wait until the time is ripe. In a way, waiting is a shabby way to live, and it goes against nature, but—each one can fill in his own but's, or throw them all away.

—
D
—

THE PURPOSE OF SEX

Sex best fulfills its purposes by being an end in itself. These purposes are of two kinds: those evolved through

---

*EW: Your idea is that humans absolutely have to need to must have children and if not they are denying their basic biological cravings. We can really only infer that it is biological to want children. Really all we can say is that the craving or need is for copulation.

EB: Ah, so!

a billion years by the workings of nature and those set up ten thousand years ago by the workings of men's minds.

From Nature's point of view our bodies are irrelevant except as they are productive. We are living on a very small planet—Jupiter is 1,300 times as large—and our chief distinction over other heavenly bodies is that we are inhabited by walking people. In order to stay inhabited, we must reproduce as fast as or faster than we die. If there is any purpose to sex, therefore, the greatest or cosmic purpose is the survival of our species, and beyond that its continual evolution through variation—that is, intermarriage—and improvement through natural selection. In this respect, therefore, our bodies are there only to carry the sperm and the eggs, and are themselves of no great consequence. Our only duty to the cosmos is to survive into puberty so that we can reproduce our kind. The only function of the sperm and the eggs, in turn, is to form a vehicle and an envelope for the genes they contain. In other words, the crux that makes the earth different from any other lump of rock that floats through space is a handful of human genes—and I say this literally, since all the genes for the whole human race could be held in the palm of your hand. So the sperm and the egg are there only for the sake of these genes, and our bodies are there for the sake of the sperm and the egg, and that is their holy mission. In the grand design of the universe, we are mail pouches for some great chain-letter scheme of our creator, whose end we will never know, any more than any other mail pouch knows what news and what propositions it carries in its belly. Sex is the fuel that drives this great project forward, and without sex it would come to a standstill and crumble away, leaving only dry bones to show that it ever existed.

All human life, then, may be seen as a preparation for our part in this production, followed by a nurturing of what we produce, and after that a fading away as we turn it over to the next generation. Fortunately, many can still enjoy sex

after they have played their parts. Those who fail to reproduce, through design or endowment, may still be driven around and into each other in a grand ecstasy which in part makes up for what they have missed.

For helping her to carry on this rare design, Nature offers us a strange and wondrous fee. The orgasm is her reward to us for making a new baby.* And with tremendous generosity, she allows us to take as many as we like from her great basket of pleasures, and does not even ask for them back if we fail to produce. She also pensions us off liberally when we are too old to produce. Nor does she punish us if we take steps to fool her with contraception. For religious people, all this must be an unparalleled example of God's inexhaustible charity. But there is, it is true, an exception: dread diseases, which strike seemingly at random. On the other hand, for those who refuse these gifts altogether, there is a slow eating of envy and turning to stone: the same thing that makes their sex frigid makes their brains rigid.

An offshoot of sex is the nesting drive, which makes men build houses and women decorate them, and thus provides children with a pleasant snuggery while they are waiting their turn. And men and women, fortunately, become attached to each other so they can keep these establishments going. At least that is the way it should be, and the sexual circuits are arranged in the chemistry of the body and the wiring of the nervous system so that this is what will happen if nothing interferes.

So much for Nature and what she has produced in the course of evolution from the first primitive genes that formed in the ocean to the human families that help each other survive by forming great societies. But we ourselves are not content to be mere seed carriers, and we elaborate sex and its possibilities into something more complex and finer.

---

*EW: This is a male's idea.
  E.B.: Some women have it too. Isn't that OK?

First, from sex comes our immortality. Our homes and businesses, our farms and factories, the books and paintings, and all those things that we put together and pass on to our children with the mark of our minds and hands upon them, will pass away, they tell us. Shelley told it to us, how all the monuments of Ozymandias crumbled into dust; and lean or ruddy ministers shout it from the pulpits every Sunday, and we see it in the dread phrase of our time when all things that have our personal mark are burned or taken away: "The tanks of the oppressors are coming, and they will destroy what we have built and what is dear to us." But our last hope is that our children, product of our sex, will survive, and that our grandchildren, product of their sex, will have some memory of us, and that our descendants far into the future will hear of us as legends, the Founder and the Foundress of the tribe.

Second are the more immediate gains we have already noted. As pure gratification, in every country it is a sport more popular even than football, bowling, or television: the ever-ready resort of the poor, and the sought-after delight of the rich. It makes pleasant hours that would otherwise be dull or even dreary; some cultivate it like a rare herb or grass to squeeze the last drop of dizzy delectation from it. It is an excuse to form attachments that we yearn anyhow to prolong; it cements us to the person who is the only hope in our cosmic core of solitude; and for those who find spiritual fulfillment in each other, it is a mystic form of primal communion.

And so in summary of what has been said above, sex is a matrix for all kinds of the most lively transactions: embraces and quarrels, seductions and retreats, construction and mischief. In addition, it is an aid to happiness and work, a substitute for all manner of drugs, and a healer of many sorts of sickness. It is for fun, pleasure, and ecstasy. It binds people together with cords of romance, gratitude, and love. And it produces children. For human living and human loving all that is what it is about, and all that is its purpose.

E

SEX AND SCIENCE

What have we given it in return? For the most part, up to now, fear, scorn, disgust, and repudiation. There have been many polls to tell us its varieties, and many journeys by anthropologists to study its regulation, which is too often only its negation. There is little of science, and that from many quarters met with cries of outrage or pretension. Most of what I have said comes from guesswork, intuition, and reports without stern statistical evaluation. The remedy is close at hand.

Let us take the statement that good sex means better health. This would be easy to test, and I would propose the following investigation.

It is well known that large numbers of college students have regular sex. Another large number have irregular sex. A third part has only masturbation, and a smaller number (probably) has no sex at all. There should be little difficulty in getting 4,000 volunteers, 2,000 men and 2,000 women, 500 of each in each of the four categories. (The only problem might be to find 1,000 who have no sex at all.) It would only be necessary to compare the sex records and the health records of each of these students during their four years at college in order to find out whether better sex means worse or better health, and that would be something well worth knowing, both for individuals and for the medical profession. It could be an inexpensive project, easily handled by one hard-working investigator (40 interviews a day for 100 days, and the rest of the time for sorting cards and making tables). For a lazy worker, it could be made into a more

expensive and impressive project with a few secretaries and a computer. In any case, it is quite practical and feasible. But no one has ever done it, as far as I can find out.

Incidentally, if Mr. Taxpayer paid $100,000 in taxes per year, his annual contribution to such a study would be only a small fraction of one cent. I don't think he should begrudge this small contribution to an important scientific undertaking; on the other hand, I don't think he should take advantage of it to interfere with the investigation.

—
F
—

SEX AND RELIGION

Nothing makes religious people as nervous as sex, or at least unregulated sex. Since each religion has its own regulations, people who go to different churches get nervous about different things. But their basic attitude is that sex *is* the concern of religion, and they leave it to the priests, elders, or medicine men to decide when it is sacred and when it is profane. Since these people are retained by the establishment, the rules they make usually favor older people rather than younger ones, and officers rather than enlisted men.

Religious or not, there are some people who regard all sex as sacred in some sense, and every man must have some secret place for sacred things; if he does not, his mind is dust and he is already on the road to death. On the other side are those who regard all sex as profane. This includes bigots, and men of principle such as the Russian Skoptzkies, who used to castrate themselves as a pledge of good faith. Somewhat different are the people who make it their business to profane everything that others hold sacred. These may be organized into cults like witches, or merely parade in pairs in public places in their Cuff You sweatshirts.

From a certain point of view,* sex is either straight or crooked. Which, depends on the "contract" or understanding between the two parties. If they have a clear understanding and stick with that, then it is straight. But if any corruption, exploitation, deception, or ulterior motive is involved, then to that extent it is crooked. Thus, even if there seems to be a clear understanding, taking advantage of a weakness is crooked because of its corruption. For example, getting sex from a child in return for candy is corrupt, because even if she agrees to it, she is being exploited; she doesn't know what she is getting into and what the consequences may be. This judgment follows the legal idea of a contract, where mere consent is not enough; it must be "informed" consent.

Clergymen who practice "transactional analysis" distinguish between sacred and profane sex as well as between straight and crooked. In trying to bring the two together, it is likely that all crooked sex would also be called profane. On the other hand, not all straight sex would be considered sacred, and that is where the two approaches differ.

There is a strong tendency to equate sacredness with solemnity: if it's fun, it can't be sacred, or if someone laughs, he is profaning it. I don't think either of these attitudes is correct. If sex is sacred, then fun and laughing, being equally happy and human feelings, are sacred too.

In civilized countries, as elsewhere, sex is often more sacred than human life. Thus in Texas people can be legally killed even for non-violent sexual transgressions. On a larger scale, in war it is all right to kill as many people as possible if the right person gives the word, but there is no one who can give the official word for an outbreak of sexual joy.

In civil life, the battlecry "Better death than sex" finds its most sinister application in the American prison system. There 200,000 inmates of state and Federal prisons are totally deprived of normal sexual relations. Hence these men

---

*This refers to transactional analysis.

and women, for the most part intense and energetic, take to homosexuality and murder for their emotional expression. But no one has so far dared give the word even for the married ones to relax with their legal wives, and thereby offer some chance for decency to prevail. (There are now some exceptions to this.)

2

THE
SEXUAL
ACT

A

MALE AND FEMALE SEX ORGANS

The sexual apparatus of men is less complicated than that of women, which is a source of pride to the biological female with her rounded hips and breasts and the four dimples on the lower part of her back which form the rhomboid of Michaelis that is so beloved of sculptors of the female form. Indeed, this rhomboid, when well outlined, is one of the most beautiful structures in nature, with its promise of all-embracing warmth and fecundity that stirs the deepest nature of protective and propagating biological man. If you have not previously looked at and admired this most promising and beautiful of all the valleys on this earth, I would recommend it to your attention. As an object for sheer es-

thetic pleasure, free of the more turgid passions aroused by the canyons found between the breasts, the buttocks, and the thighs, it is unsurpassed.

The sexual equipment of the male consists of two small crucibles, the testicles; each with its own still, the epididymis; and its own little tank, the seminal vesicle. These lead to a pump, the prostate, which delivers the product through a hydraulic ram, the penis. The female starts with the ovaries, which drop their ripened eggs like apples near the openings of the Fallopian tubes, whose gentle petals waft them down the tunnel toward the womb or uterus. The uterus is built to cradle the growing embryo and feed it into maturity. At the other end, the vagina is supplied with glands that lubricate to aid the brawny thrust of the penis as it slides down the ways ready to seed the new life with its seminal torpedoes. The vagina also has muscles that squeeze and pulsate and sweet-talk the semen toward its destination in the womb. Above its entrance is the clitoris, an organ especially designed and supplied with special nerves for exquisite titillation leading into ultimate ecstasy. In sum, then, the man has two exquisitely miniaturized cell factories and an aggressive delivery system. The woman is well equipped to encourage and handle his deliveries, which she pillows in the most beautifully constructed incubator in the universe. She also has the equipment to nurse its grateful product.

But psychological complications arise because the man sticks out while the woman is tucked in, or, as someone said, the man has outdoor plumbing and the woman has indoor plumbing. Thus the man has built-in advertising which he can light up at night when occasion calls for it, while the woman can only do promotional work behind the scenes. It is something like the difference between a roadside hamburger stand with neon lights, and an elegant inn with the most discreet façade concealing its single downy chamber.

B

HOW IT BEGINS

Sigmund Freud said seventy years ago that most dreams of adults treat of sexual material and give expression to erotic wishes.[1] He decided this by studying the psychology of dreams, but he had no concrete evidence. Many people, including medical men, found this idea unlikely, unpleasant, or even repulsive, but Freud stuck to his guns. Now the concrete evidence is here. Modern sleep research shows that nearly all dreams, in the male at least, are preceded or accompanied by an erection.[2] The same is probably true of females, although that is harder to establish. This means that there is a lot of sexual activity going on in both sexes while they are asleep, and that erections occur about every ninety minutes through the night. This can go on for years or even a lifetime without the person's ever being aware of it.

In waking life, the sex act for the male begins with an erection. No erection, no sex. The penis was designed by a careful engineer. All year round, the blood flows in and out smoothly and without hindrance, unless the inflow increases and the outflow is blocked. If these things happen, the blood collects in little caverns provided for that purpose. The organ soaks it up like a sponge and begins to hang a little bigger. As the blood continues to pile up, it fills all the spaces until they start to bulge. Pretty soon the whole penis is turgid and tight as a drum.

There are two theories as to what happens inside to bring the erection about. The blood is brought in by arteries and flows out through veins. One theory is that the arteries open wider so that the blood rushes in faster than the veins can carry it away. The other is that the largest vein is closed

off just before it leaves the penis to enter the body, so that the blood piles up in front of it.

Let us consider the second theory first, since it is more elegant. If the largest vein is blocked off, the blood cannot get out until the pressure is high enough to overcome the block or to force a passage roundabout through other smaller veins. This main vein is shaped like a thin-walled flexible rubber tube. Near its exit from the penis, there is a little band of muscle lying across it in such a way that if the muscle contracts, the tube is shut off. Then the blood cannot flow out as it usually does. It piles up behind the dam and the penis swells like a—like a—like a penis, and the more it swells the tougher it gets. The more excited the man is, the harder his phallus grows. It swells so much that if the cap on the end is flexible it may turn up a little. He may feel as though he is going to burst if he doesn't find a place to put it, but there is no fear of that. The blood can always force its way through the other little veins before things get out of hand. Nature has set it up so that no matter how hard the hydraulic battle, there is no chance of a blowout.

The little muscle that starts the ball rolling is known to anatomists as the *Compressor venae dorsalis penis,* compressor of the vein on the back of the penis (not the vein you can see there, although that may throb too, but one buried inside). It is called, for short, Houston's muscle. If it is true that erections depend on this muscle, then for the most part procreation depends on it, too. Houston's muscle will always contract if the right kind of electrical impulses go down the right nerves, but it will stay relaxed as long as they don't. Through natural selection in the course of evolution, this muscle and the nerves going to it have become one of the most reliable triggers known. It can function perfectly for as long as eighty-eight years without oiling or parts replacement, even under the hardest conditions of use.

Nearly all difficulties in erection originate with the operator and not with the mechanism—pilot's error, as they say in aircraft circles. The impulses to the penis are sent down from the brain, and there is a little man up there who is supposed to keep his finger on the button when the signal flashes green and all systems are Go. But if he gets tired, scared, distracted, or upset, he may relax the pressure or release the button, even when the light is green. Since it is a fail-safe button or dead-man's throttle, once it is released, the mechanism is disconnected and goes back into idle. The little man is of course the Child in the person, and if he chickens out there is no erection even though all the wiring is sound and even though there is lots of stimulation coming in from the outside.

It is interesting to note that the existence of Houston's muscle is unknown to many people, including medical men. It is not even mentioned by that name in Gray's *Anatomy,* so that most medical students go through medical school without ever hearing about it. Yet if this account is correct, the whole existence of the human race and its most ecstatic moments depend on this neglected strip of tissue, so beautifully set up to transform a short soft organ into a long hard one through the laws of physics.

There is no set of experiments in animals or humans to prove that this "rubber band" theory of erection is entirely wrong, but there are some that show that it is not entirely right.[3] In fact, any male can do his own experiment. If erection results simply from compression of the veins in the penis, so that blood can get in but cannot get out except under very high pressure, then anything that compresses the veins without shutting off the arteries should bring an erection about. It is easy to find an ordinary rubber band to fit tightly around the penis, and presumably compress the veins, without shutting the circulation off entirely. But even if it is left on for five or ten minutes, which is plenty time for blood to collect if it is going to, no erection will

follow.[4] Too bad, because if it did work, it would be an admirably simple cure for impotence, and a great deal of human frustration and unhappiness could be avoided. There are possible flaws in this do-it-yourself experiment, and it might not be completely convincing to an experienced researcher, but it does cast serious doubt on the "rubber band" theory in simplest form.

The second theory, that the arteries expand and pour in so much blood that the veins simply cannot carry it off, now seems more likely. But there is no way to expand these arteries artificially, so potency must be left in the hands of nature and psychiatry. There is a drug called yohimbine, that comes from the West African Yohimbéhé tree, which was once promoted as a true dilator of the penile arteries, but few people who tried it found that it really helped. Spanish fly, the most popular aphrodisiac in folklore, acts by causing an inflammation that may be dangerous or even fatal.*

We do not have to give up Houston's muscle and its elegant mechanism entirely, because it is likely that in man the best erections result from a combination of both effects. There is an increased flow of blood due to expansion of the arteries, and also some clamping down on the veins, and between the two of them the phallus attains its greatest degree of hardness.

With the woman, things are more complicated. Sexual excitement begins with lubrication of the vagina, which may take place a few seconds after she decides to go along. Some minutes after that, the clitoris becomes distended. No one knows quite how that happens, but there is no reason to suppose that there is not a Houston's muscle in the female as well as in the male, since anatomists agree that there are muscle fibers in the clitoris similar to those in the

---

*Dopa (dihydroxyphenylalanine), a substance now used in the trea ment of Parkinsonism or palsy, is said to be a true aphrodisiac and pe erector in people suffering from that disease, but it is considered too erful for normal use because of its many possible side effects.

penis. They may help by damming back the blood at the same time as the excited arteries pour it in, thus making the clitoris larger and firmer. But the clitoris is also pulled upward and may disappear from sight, which the penis does not. In a fully desirous woman, the cervix too swells and pulsates, "sending out urgent signals to the vagina to get filled up," as Amaryllis puts it.

C

MALE POWER

The sexual power of the male has three elements: potency, force, and drive. Potency is shown by the firmness of his erection, force by the ardor of his thrust, and drive by the muzzle velocity of his ejaculation.

There are several degrees of potency or erection. In the first, the penis is slightly enlarged and hangs a little away from the body. In a social situation, the bearer may hardly be aware that he is quickened. He will suffer no embarrassment, since the enlargement cannot usually be noticed by those around him. This condition may be called "social stir," as in the following news item: "Amaryllis caused a social stir among the men as she entered the room in her erectile miniskirt." At this point it should be mentioned that most women know the difference between "well-dressed" and "not well-dressed," but only a few know the difference between a "good-looking dress" or a "low-cut dress" and an "erectile dress." The same applies to other articles of female apparel.

In the second degree, the organ is long and stiff, but will still bend if it is hand-snapped or meets any opposition. Being so, unless the partner is open and well lubricated, it will not be able to penetrate, but will give way instead.

That was the predicament of the young Englishman in the famous limerick on this very subject.

> There was a young man of Kent
> Whose kirp in the middle was bent.
> To save himself trouble
> He put it in double,
> And instead of coming, he went.

In honor of this double-jointed Briton, such a state may be called the Kentish curse, although it should more properly be termed "cautious kirp," since it is usually due to the presence of some doubts as to whether to go ahead with the project. The man may be seduced by the woman or by his own desire to prove his potency, but "in peno* veritas," as Dr. Horseley puts it, his phallus remains unconvinced. It may be a question of making up after a quarrel, or of the immediate consequences of the act, or of what the future may hold, or of some lack of firmness in his attitude toward the opposite sex. In short, there may be some fear of or hesitation in committing himself at that time, which he (his Adult) may be willing to overlook. But his penis (under the control of his more sensitive Child) is not so easily inveigled as he is, and remains skeptical in spite of this license.

In the third degree, the phallus reaches its full size but not its full nobility. It is stuffed, rigid, and ready for action of a kind, but sometimes it falters too quickly and ejaculates before either partner has had a chance for full expression. This is colloquially known as "quick on the trigger." In the fourth stage, the man is like a charging unicorn, not only stiff and ready, but so turgid and eager that he feels he must start his thrust or burst with the fullness of his potency. It is in this state that the cap sometimes turns upward, as though pleading to the heavens for immediate fulfillment. That is the ultimate turn-on, when the

---

*I know "peno" is not the correct form, but it fits in better that way.

man will push ahead at almost any cost, and this is the carnal spindle around which all great courtship struggles are spun in literary romance. In general, this condition is called "raring to go." The special cases where the cap turns up (because some penises are constructed that way) may be called "Peyronie's pride," in honor of the physician who first made a formal study of that phenomenon.[5]

Once the stronghold is captured, in church or in the hay, the powerful urge of thrust takes over. The uncorrupted biological man feels an overwhelming desire to push into the vagina as hard as he can and deposit his semen there.* He will thrust again and again, reaching for the profoundest depths, and clinging to his partner with all his strength as though no earthly force could ever tear them apart through all of time, even though he senses that the end is not far away. Such ardor is most likely to occur if his phallus is in the fourth and most noble state of its erection, the genuine procreative instrument of human nature. But if there is any spurious element behind its force, the animal thrust will lose its power and must be consciously reinforced. This most commonly happens if the man is more interested in glory than in sex, is frightened of what he has got himself into, or is swindling the woman for his own pleasure. In those cases he may try to make it last as long as possible to hear her sighs, or as short as possible to get away quickly, or he may be aware of the time but callously indifferent. If a come too fast will hurt his pride, the thrusting scares him lest it throw the elixir out too soon; hence he may thrust but little, hoping thus to make it last at least until his mate is satisfied, after which he can proceed with a clear conscience and dignity unimpaired, at his own pace.

---

*This is the movement previously referred to, in the language of *The Perfumed Garden*, as *dok*, with the female response *hez*. In vulgar English, *dok* is bump and *hez* is grind. Kinematically, the man's pelvis pitches around a transverse axis, while the woman's yaws around a vertical or sagittal one.

The unhampered biological thruster is so intent on what he is doing, withal automatically, that he does not concern himself with time or very much with his partner's reaction, although it gives him the deepest satisfaction if she does react naturally at that great dynamic moment when he attains his goal and deposits his seed where it will do the most good. Such an intensive, almost insensible attitude is exactly the one most likely to bring the woman to the highest pitch of excitement and produce in her the most satisfying orgasm. The force of such thrusts is not brutality, it is biology. But if the woman, instead of responding from her deepest and most genuine nature, becomes interested in the thrust as an end in itself, she may regard it and crave it as brutality, and the same goes for the man.

But the description of unhampered biological activity is an ideal rather than a reality. There is no such thing as unhampered sex in the human race. All societies are organized around sexual prohibitions, which seep through even in moments of the highest excitement and corrupt the purity of these responses. At one end there is compliance and overconcern, and at the other rebellion, cruelty, and dishonesty. Somewhere in the middle is real intimacy, with free functioning of sexuality. At its best, sex can be a blast-off from earthbound to 30,000 feet, with an intoxicating slow descent. But less than that can still be more than plenty, and even a flight above the housetops is more invigorating than keeping both feet on the ground. No one can fairly demand more than going through the roof, and every foot above that is a bonus.

What we are talking about here is the third aspect of masculine power. Drive is the power with which the semen at the moment of ejaculation is hurled into the vagina by the piston-like contractions of the prostate. It is probable (although not certain) that the height of the orgasm, that is, the felt altitude of the orgastic trip in feet or meters, depends on the power of the drive.

Thus on the quiet side is the man with an incomplete erection, restrained thrust, and low drive, and at the other extreme the one with an overstuffed ramlike phallus, who thrusts with mighty abandon and propels the semen with great power into the place provided for it by nature. But anywhere along this spectrum, the man can impregnate the woman, and if she is properly prepared, also cause her to have an orgasm.*

Of these three elements, the one most under conscious control is thrust. The erection can be terminated by an act of will, which simply means saying Stop! (or, as it is told in the joke books, Down, Fido!), but there is no magic word which will bring it back or harden it again. Up, Fido! just doesn't work all by itself. There has to be some bait, either living or artificial, to make it rise. The most automatic is ejaculation, which cannot be consciously hastened and can be postponed for only a few seconds once it is triggered. The power of the drive depends mostly on physical factors, while the nobility of the erection and the force of the thrust depend on psychological ones.

The sexual power of a man is influenced chiefly by two women: his mother (or maybe his big sister), who encouraged or discouraged his masculinity and his sexuality while he was growing up; and his partner, who has it in her power to elevate and stimulate, or to depress and inhibit him, by the way she responds. The older man is particularly sensitive about his mate. If she turns him off too often, he may begin to lose his potency and go into middle-age droop, a condition which may become progressively more severe, but is nearly always reversible if put in the hands of an enthusiastic practitioner.

Often a man's sexual power is reflected in his daily life, as many wives maintain. He may be hard, aggressive, and

---

*EW: This "properly prepared" is an old idea in sex manuals, but what about her preparedness separate from his causing it?

full of drive; or he may bend easily in the face of opposition, lack force and thrust, and dribble off at the end or fail to finish what he begins.

D

FEMALE POWER

The female and the male complement each other, and her power has three corresponding elements: profusion, force, and grasp. Profusion is represented by lubrication, force is manifested in counterthrust, and grasp is shown by muscular contractions.

Lubrication of the vagina naturally makes it easy for the phallus to slide in. If there is no lubrication at all (analoiphia), someone is likely to get skinned. Some women get so turned on that the happy oil or joy juice, as they call it, overflows (hyperloiphia) while they swing into one orgasm after another. Sometimes a woman may get excited enough in a social situation to lubricate slightly or even profusely, much to her pride or embarrassment. As with the male, such an event may be called "social stir." Lubrication, however, does not always mean that the woman is going to respond; she may accept the penis, but refuse to be excited by it.* But if all goes well, lubrication is followed by a turgid clitoris. Vaginal lubrication, together with clitoral swelling, corresponds to potency in the male, so when it is convenient to do so, the word potency can be applied to both sexes.

Counterthrust may be biologically the woman's response

---

*EW: Women who do that can be called good sports.
EB: Why not sulks?

to the prospect of impregnation, or psychologically, to her drive for ultimate closeness. It may be demoted to a mere pleasure-seeking mechanism. True biological counterthrust is not self-conscious or calculating; it is not a question of trying to wring the greatest amount of pleasure out of the act; it is something the woman *has* to do because she wants so much to get the penis as deeply as possible inside her. Some women start off with counterthrust as pleasure-seeking, but are overtaken by its biological compulsiveness and begin to respond more naturally.

Grasping is the counterpart of drive. At the moment of orgasm, which may coincide with the man's ejaculation, the vagina grasps the penis again and again in waves of muscular contraction, as though trying to milk out the semen. This sends waves of reaction through her partner and may increase the driving force of his ejaculation. There may also be slower grasping motions that are equally pleasurable.

The woman's sexuality is reflected in her other characteristic responses to a man. She makes herself accessible to him and lubricates their actions together. When he comes toward her, she comes forward to meet him halfway. When he is driving toward some goal, she responds to him with exquisite emotional rhythm and helps to draw the best out of him, thus offering him inspiration. If she has been raised by her mother or father to avoid or despise such natural responses, she will be awkward or nasty, not only in her sexual transactions, but also in her other relations with men. She will be inaccessible or abrasive, unresponsive, and competitive or belittling, rather than receptive, responsive, and encouraging.*

At one end of the female spectrum is the woman who does not lubricate or get excited, lies still and unmoved, and

---

*EW: Why don't you put a list of similar not-OK words at the end of the section on male power?

receives the ejaculation passively.* At the other is the one who lubricates profusely, reaches a high level of excitement, responds to every thrust, giving as good as she gets, and grasps the penis tightly as though to help out the last lingering drop of ejaculation.

E

THE ORGASM

The human orgasm is one of the most intimately and admirably planned and synchronized events in all of nature. Both anatomically and physiologically, it shows the splendid selection of the course of evolution. Exactly what the man needs the woman has, and exactly what the women needs the man has. Their temperature, pressure, and precipitation match each other in just the right way to form Cloud 9 in an explosive discharge of creative energy that involves all of both of them: physical, chemical, muscular, electrical, and psychological. If it works right, each of them will emerge with a mind pure and free, brain washed clean of troubles and ready to start life anew. Or, as someone said, the only time human beings are sane is in the ten minutes after intercourse. Or, as someone else said, every night spent alone is wasted.

Each sex has two different ways of bringing this about. In the male, the glans or cap is the most sensitive part of the penis, and stimulation of that area at the right time can bring about a rapid and rather unsatisfactory ejaculation, which

---

*EW: Why blame her? Maybe he's a necrophile. And in the next sentence, you expect her to do everything.

EB: I'm thinking about natural selection, and picking out those items which seem to me to increase the chances of selection and fertilization, as well as the survival of the individual in a competitive world. Maybe it would have come out differently if Darwin had been a woman.

EW: That's an interesting thought.

justifies the Marquis de Sade's injunction to his partners: "Never touch the cap!" (This is one of the few things in his writings that come out right.) The shaft is less touchy and produces a more leisurely enjoyment. The most voluptuous area is where the shaft and the cap meet at the corona, which is a trigger area for the orgasm. Similarly in the woman, the clitoris is more touchy than the vaginal lining, and clitoral stimulation can bring about an orgasm which, according to many women, leaves much to be desired. Here again the most sensitive point may be where the tip of the clitoris and the vaginal lining lie close together.

There is a splendid synchronization between male and female orgasms. The man's loins move, his prostate contracts, and his semen hurls forward in exactly the same rhythm as the pulsations of the woman's vagina and clitoris. This is due to an automatic rebound of certain types of muscle fibers. This mutual rebound is repeated again and again until the reflexes of one partner wear out. The other may continue to contract and expand for a long time after that, often to the amazement and admiration of the satisfied one. Some partners even prefer to have their orgasms at different times so that they can get a kind of double enjoyment of one another in this way, but others would rather come together in one overwhelming wave of ecstasy.

This muscular rhythm of thrust and grasp feeds and reinforces the timing of the two clocks involved: one in the prostate, which determines the rhythm of the ejaculatory spasms, and the other in the clitoris, which has its own rhythm and regulates or coincides with the rhythm of the vaginal contractions. One of the wonders of evolution is that these two timers usually work at exactly the same speed: four-fifths of a second per pulse. The balance wheels of these alternating clocks are the ejaculatory centers in the spinal cord, so a nervous rhythm is at the bottom of it all, just as in a jellyfish or snail or an angel playing the harp.

F

THE PSYCHOLOGY OF SEX

The sexual responses in both sexes are determined partly by built-in, or biological, factors and partly by mind-cuffing, or psychological, factors. Once the orgasm is triggered, the built-in biological circuits take over and the mind gets uncuffed, but up to that moment, voices in the head and voices in the bed strongly influence what happens, how it happens, when it happens, and who happens. Even more important than those voices, however, are the hidden pictures in the back of the mind, the primal images of the two partners, which determine their potency and thrust if not their drive.

The psychological or mind-cuffing factors at work on the male, with a similar list for the female, are as follows:

1. Whether he is fearful or enthusiastic about sex. The most important single factor here is his mother's voice saying either "Watch out!" or "Go to it!"

2. Whether he is dishonest or honest about it. This is usually decided by his father's voice or example saying either "Snatch it!" "Listen to her holler!" or "Both of you enjoy yourselves."

3. Whether his partner is responsive, neutral, or discouraging. Her voice tells him which by being warm and soft, indifferent, or cold and threatening. Her muscles go along, being loving, dead, or uptight, while her glands can make it smooth and damp, or rough and dry.

4. The external situation, especially the possibility of being interrupted or stimulated by other people, including children, and mosquitoes and their ilk.

5. His primal image of the female sex organs.

If he succeeds in digging up his primal image, it may be quite different from what he expected. Thus an obstetrician, whose Adult was thoroughly familiar with the actual appearance of these organs under all sorts of conditions, was surprised to discover that his Child still pictured the vagina as an enormous dark bottomless cave in which his penis or even his whole body could get lost. In another example it was a narrow passage full of barbs that must be avoided by anyone who entered there. The power of such images to affect erection, thrust, and drive may depend partly on the actual physical condition of the vagina as seen and felt by the phallus. If it feels loose, that may turn it into a scary cave for the first man and relieve the second; if it feels tight, the cave man may feel safer, but the trap man may become alarmed and want to get out of there quickly.

Incredible as it may seem, sometimes the penis, or even the fingers, can see as well as feel. This is called synesthesia. Everybody's Adult knows that the vagina is really red and stays red, but to the phallus its color may change with the degree of lubrication. Dry, it may feel purple; slightly moist, it may seem brown; and when it is very slippery, it may feel bright blue. These are common synesthetic impressions, but each penis may have its own color card.[6]

The woman has her primal image of the phallus, which affects her responses in a similar way. To her Child, it may seem like a jutting mass of hardness which is going to penetrate too far, a sharp knife which is going to cut her, or a thin round which is too small for her to grasp and control before it slips away. Some women may also have color reactions depending on the slipperiness of the penis, which is really the result of their own lubrication.

There are also more favorable primal images. To the man, the vagina may look like a cozy resting place or a caressing hand, or the clitoris like a seductive nipple; while to the woman, his penis may look like a lollipop or a Tootsie-

roll or a mushroom. These images are not, as is commonly assumed, "unconscious." They can be easily seen by anyone who is alert enough to stop them as they float by. It is important to know this because primal images can have a decisive effect on male and female sexual power, and there is no need to lie around for a long time to uncover them. They are lurking stark naked in the background all along.

Many statements about the psychology of sex are based on personal preferences rather than on careful study. Some sex psychologists have their own kind of strict morality; for example: "The male is excited by what he does to the female, not by what the female does to him; while the female is excited by what the male does to her, not by what she does to him."[7] Like puritanical schoolmasters, they disapprove of energetic women and luxury-loving men. They set up a standard type of human being who can have all the different types of sex. This may work no better then the lawmakers' policy of setting up a standard type of sex for all the different kinds of human beings. And Amaryllis says that fashions change in sex. "Even the birth control movement has done a complete about-face," she remarks in her cryptic way. "It used to be a downward swing of the arm with the diaphragm, and now it's an upward swing with the pill."

G

THE BIOLOGY OF SEX

In the course of evolution, potency, thrust and drive in the male and profusion, counterthrust, and grasp in the female have probably all contributed to the efficient propagation of the human race. Animals raised a certain

way, for example, will lack these qualities and have a low reproduction rate.[8] Thus, by physiological selection, the sexier members would have an advantage over the less sexy ones in reproducing their kind, so we may assume that *Homo sapiens* has gotten sexier and sexier through the centuries and millenniums, and is far more lusty and lecherous and lewd than his ancestors who lived in caves. Or even than those who lived in the primeval monkey forests before there were any men, since man is the sexiest mammal there is, nearly always ready on any day of the week or at any phase of the moon.

The biological purpose of the male orgasm is to blast the semen at its target, which oddly enough is not the opening of the uterus, but a pocket at the back of the vagina. This puts the spermatozoa into orbit, after which they turn on their own little engines for the second stage, when they shoot for the moon, which is the little egg lying above them in the ovarian tube. This is a ruthless race, in which the winner takes all and the losers die. Whichever sperm hits the egg first captures it forever and excludes all the others; there is no vice president in this election, and no second place. The swimming distance, in man-size terms, is about two miles, all of it a steeplechase over curves and hurdles and rapids and dams, and much of it upstream. It is more exciting than ten million horse races, for there are several hundred million sperm in each race. It is certainly awesome to realize that that is what happens inside the woman every time the man fires his starting gun. And every man is a hero here. Whether he is tall or short, handsome or ugly, strong or weak, young or old makes no difference; as long as he can throw sperm, he can at his own will start a race which is the equivalent of the whole population of North and South America milling around in Lake Erie.

The intense pleasure attending the male orgasm probably serves mainly to make it attractive and sought after, and that goes for the female orgasm too. But the biological func-

tion of the female orgasm remains unknown.* Sexual excitement, especially lubrication, changes the chemistry of the woman's reproductive system to make it a more congenial summer resort for the sperm, but the orgasm itself does not seem to add much. At any rate, women seem to get pregnant just as easily if they do not have an orgasm as if they do, so the orgasm may be desirable, and possibly helpful, but it is not necessary.

It would appear that the male orgasm *is* necessary for impregnation, but there is no certainty even about that. Some men secrete "love-water" from the prostate long before they come, and that may have a few wandering sperm in it. This fact may be important for two reasons. First, it indicates that even if the man does not follow up the love-water with an ejaculation, or withdraws and ejaculates outside, he might still impregnate the woman. That would be particularly apt to happen if there were a few sperm swimming around in his spermatic system from a recent previous ejaculation, since that would increase the likelihood of some being washed out with the love-water. Secondly, any sperm that do leak into the vagina with the love-water have a headstart over those thrown in later, and might therefore have an advantage in the race to the ovum. Thus it may be that love-water sperm are more likely to start a baby than ejaculated sperm, and this might possibly have a bearing on various problems of fertility and development.

Let us review the biological events. Maximum erection and maximum lubrication ensure maximum penetration, aided by thrust and counterthrust. At the critical moment, maximum drive is reinforced by maximum grasp. All this ensures that the maximum amount of semen will get as far

---

*I believe that the real "purpose" of orgasm is psychological resuscitation. It acts like an electric shock treatment on the brain, redistributing its potentials so that the mind is cleared. This is similar to the sorting function of REM sleep noted in *Psychiatric News*, October, 1969, based on the work of R. Greenberg and E. M. Dewan.

back as it can go, and that is the best situation to ensure impregnation. As already noted, the contrast would be a little bit of semen dribbling down the outside of a dry vagina, which would give little chance for the egg to be fertilized; and there are many degrees in between. But one way is more likely to work than another, and in evolution a very slight increase in probability can expand into a large advantage over many generations, just like a thousand years of compound interest.

Something to remember, however, is that even with no erection, no lubrication, and no thrust, the probability of impregnation is greater than zero. It is possible for any ejaculation in the region of the female sex organs to produce, more or less rarely, a perfectly healthy offspring, or even twins. (It is possible to have twins, as the earnest clergyman learned to his surprise, even though you have only been naughty once.)

One of the most interesting biological features is the way the woman is set up to welcome the man. As her excitement increases, her vagina graciously widens and lengthens to accommodate him better, and as a final touch, her uterus politely lifts itself out of his way so that he can have an unobstructed channel. Only after he has permanently withdrawn does the uterus come down again to dip its mouth into the pool of womb-nourishing semen that he, responding to her open generosity, has lovingly and courteously and firmly presented her with.

On the other hand, in many ways sexual intercourse is a battle between the sexes. The harder he pushes down, the harder she pushes up; and the bigger his penis gets, the harder she clamps down on it; conversely, the harder she clamps down, the bigger his penis is likely to get. It is as though she is trying to make him smaller, and he is trying to make her bigger. But it is an interesting kind of battle, because if they bring it to a completely successful conclusion, they both win. He ends up smaller than he started out, and

she gets bigger and bigger and bigger. And on the average, there is a rough kind of arithmetic about it, too. His phallus gets a few ounces lighter ten or twenty or a hundred times to make her a few pounds heavier once.*

As long as this "battle" is equal, as it is supposed to be, it is actually a cooperative effort rather than a contest. But if it is unequal, it may really turn into a conflict, or even a running brawl, for then the stronger partner feels frustrated, disappointed and unappreciated, and the weaker one feeble, guilty and angry, or worse, gloating with perverse and unseemly triumph. These unhealthy feelings may be carried into the everyday living of the couple, deeply embedded in unpleasant games that cause their stomachs to churn, their muscles to tighten, and their blood pressure to rise, so that they may live for years in physical as well as mental discomfort. Not only do they wreak their vengeance on their children and the other people around them (sometimes with political force), but their bodies begin to give way under the strain until their troubles settle into the organ or system with the least resistance, starting with "psychosomatic" complaints.

People in such a situation are generally looking for ammunition to use against their partners, and I would certainly not want anything I have written here to be used for such a disreputable purpose. While in biology and evolution sex is the chief product of life (so that the first instructions of God to Adam and Eve, after saying hello, were: "Be fruitful, and multiply, and replenish the earth"), in the scale of human values it is, or should be, only second. That is why God said "Hello!" (or "Bless you!" *vyorech asom*, Gen. I:28) before he gave them any instructions, because "Hello" is the one thing more important than sex in human relations. It means, "We're in this together, so let's play it straight." The

---

*EW: I don't like that one at all.

EB: It's rough, but thought-provoking. Life is very strangely contrived.

moral is, don't put your man or woman down for not being an ideal sex partner. First listen to how he says "Hello"—and also to how you say it. A straight man with a crooked penis is better than a crooked man with a straight one, and the right woman with the wrong vagina is better than the wrong woman with the right one.

This brings us to the very human, but often unstraight, ways in which sex organs can be used for purposes other than fertilization.

NOTES AND REFERENCES

1. Freud, S.: *The Interpretation of Dreams* (fourth edition). The Macmillan Company, New York, 1915, p. 240.

2. Fisher, C., Gross, J., and Zuch, J.: "A Cycle of Penile Erections Synchronous with Dreaming (REM) Sleep." *Archives of General Psychiatry* 12:29-45, January, 1965. They found erections in 95 percent of 86 REM periods in 17 subjects.

3. The Ischiocavernosus is also called the Erector penis in men and the Erector clitoridis in women. Its action is thus described in Gray's *Anatomy* (28th edition, Lea & Febiger, Philadelphia, 1966): "The Ischiocavernosus compresses the crus penis, and retards the return of the blood through the veins, and thus serves to maintain the organ erect" in the male. For the female the same action is given, putting "clitoris" for "penis." Only one inconsequential word has been changed in this since the 23rd edition (1926), and that is what medical students have learned about the mechanism of erection for the last forty years. Houston's muscle would thus be a special band of Ischiocavernosus, functioning as the Compressor venae dorsalis penis (or clitoridis). The chief opponents of the Ischiocavernosus theory of erection nowadays are Masters and Johnson (*Human Sexual Response*, op. cit.). The lethargy in regard to this presumably important question is shown by the fact that the two pertinent citations given by these authors date from 1921 and 1933. They say that "little support is given now" to the Ischiocavernosus concept, but D. W. Fawcett, for example, who is Professor of Anatomy at Harvard, supports it in his article on the Reproductive System in the Encyclopaedia Britannica (1967). Masters and Johnson offer the alternative that "the veins of the penis are believed to possess valves that slow down the return of the

blood." If such an apparatus is found to exist, it does not necessarily mean that the Ischiocavernosus contractions *ipso facto* cease to exist. Dr. John Houston's valves work very well in the rectum (Houston's valves, plicae transversalis recti), and there is no reason why his muscle should not work equally well on the erectile tissues.

On the other hand, the 1933 reference mentioned above is an excellent piece of research done by two competent pharmacological physiologists from the University of Toronto ("On the Mechanism of Erection," V. E. Henderson and M. H. Roepke. *American Journal of Physiology* 106:441-448, 1933). These authors, working with dogs in the early days of acetylcholine research, conclude that "the vasodilatation on stimulating the dilator nerves to the penis is due to a local hormonal mechanism," and that "erection is not due to a compression of the efferent veins by skeletal muscle action," although "ischiocavernosus, muscular contractions may play some minor part." "There is a rapid rise of pressure . . . within the corpora cavernosa, which may well make the venous outflow inefficient." However, they did observe "sudden sharp increases in the volume of the penis . . . due to sudden short spontaneous contractions of the ischiocavernosus muscles, which, owing to their somewhat spiral arrangement . . . could produce some pressure on the parts of the corpora lying beneath them . . . after each [contraction] a gain in the amount of erection was noticed." There are a few other small ambiguities in their findings, and there the matter rests until someone figures out a definitive way of demonstrating the anatomical and physiological mechanism in human beings.

4. This simple method of verification was suggested by Dr. James Daly, of St. Mary's Hospital in San Francisco. It only remains for some courageous investigator to find out what happens if a rubber band exerting just the right amount of pressure is put on after erection is established. Will it maintain the erection indefinitely even if other stimuli are avoided? Or if it is put on after ejaculation, but with erection still present? Amateur researchers are cautioned *not* to have the rubber band on during ejaculations, as this will force the semen back into the bladder, a procedure once favored by Oriental and Arab voluptuaries, but one not recommended because the ultimate effects are doubtful and may be damaging.

5. François de la Peyronie (1678-1747). There is some question about the super-erection with the turned-up end. A lady who knows about such things informs me that in her opinion this is a normal manifestation of super-excitement. On the other hand, the same phenomenon occurs in Peyronie's disease (plastic induration of the penis), variously attributed to physical trauma,

vascular changes, prolonged abstinence, or lack of adequate gratification. Sometimes the curvature is so marked as to make intromission difficult or impossible. Peyronie's disease is usually accompanied by pain on erection. The plaques are palpable but may disappear spontaneously (*Human Sexuality* 2:56-57, September, 1968). Since a similar curvature occurs in many toy balloons when they are blown up as far as they can go, it may be a normal anatomico-physiological phenomenon due to differential elasticity in the dorsal and ventral anchorages of the glans. But cf. Glenn, J. F.: "Curvature of the penis," *Human Sexuality* 3:83, February, 1969.

6. Reports of sexual synesthesias are not easy to collect. I would be happy to hear from anyone who cares to send me details of his or her experiences in this regard.

7. Legman, G.: *Oragenitalism.* Op. cit.

8. See Chapter 6, section B.

3

THE
EXPLOITATION
OF THE
SEX ORGANS

A

INTRODUCTION

Strictly speaking, the only natural uses for sex organs are making true love and making babies. Any other purposes are to some extent improper. Sex for pure pleasure by mutual consent may be free of emotional counterfeiting, but it is a biological betrayal if contraceptives are used, as they should be in such cases. Beyond that, the human race has had so much time on its hands, and is so afraid of open intimacy, that it has devised many ways of using its organs for hidden purposes and for frivolous or false relationships. We shall now go on to consider some of these non-propagat-

ing uses, since they play such an important part in everyday living.*

B

THE EXPLOITATION OF THE PENIS

What use is a penis? Well, it is the best instrument for impregnating women and one of the best for sexual pleasure. Beyond that, it can throw a stream of water a reasonable distance and put out fires, but there is a catch there. Mr. and Mrs. Murgatroyd once agreed that whoever could urinate farther would be the boss of their home. Mungo, of course, thought that was a fine arrangement and stepped up to the starting line confident that from then on he would have his way. But just as he got started, Mysie cried, "Oh, oh, no hands!" With a rule like that, the crestfallen Mungo knew that he was done for.

But beyond these natural functions, man's ingenuity has found many ways of making the penis useful. In solitary enjoyment, it can be used as a plaything to pass the time on rainy afternoons and other boring hours. Children who are tired of lying in their cribs or sitting in a schoolroom find its reachability a great temptation. ("Their arms are made just long enough to reach it," as one mother said reproachfully to her clergyman.) In its erect state, it makes an admirable fertility symbol, and has been worshiped as such

---

*EW: There you go with propagation again. What is it with you?

EB: First of all, as a philosophical biologist, I really believe in what I am saying. Secondly, when I was an intern, one thing that got through to me was the beautiful faces of the women on the obstetrical ward. The pregnancies to cut out are the unwanted ones, not the wanted ones.

The people who demand the right to have babies and populate the world have to give equal rights to those who don't. In fairness and salvation, that means free access to every means of prevention.

privately from time to time, or even publicly with joyful ceremonies, at other times and other places. Sometimes it is used in simple social etiquette, aristocratic gestures of politeness or *noblesse oblige*, on the principle that no well-brought-up young man should leave a woman with any of her desires ungratified; her wish is his command. By men of lesser breeding, it can even be used in similar situations to earn money. Thus it becomes a tool of solace, ritual, courtesy, or employment.

In more informal society, it can be used in mutual pastimes, a ready instrument for exchanging pleasures with the fairer sex, although some dubious men make dubious jokes about preferring a good meal or a good bowel movement; such men should be left with their own kind stewing in the kitchen or the men's room. But beyond such frivolities, it is a great and versatile device for more serious games. Its mere phallic exhibition can seduce girls, frighten them, or excite their awe or admiration. As a poker, it can rouse them from lassitude and indifference. Proud men regard it as a trophy, which they bestow on the worthy as a gift or favor. The covetous man uses it as a branding iron, a sign that the woman has been possessed by him and in some measure is forever his, particularly if he has taken her virginity.

The clod may treat his phallus as a mere pleasure-stick, or as a pleasure-thief, entering under false pretenses, taking what it desires, and then silently shrinking away. The evil man shows his grudge against women, especially women far above him, by "spitting" in their wombs, or if he cannot win their favors, by battering through in criminal rape. The benevolent man will offer his phallus to the woman in distress as a comforter or even as a healing instrument that will surpass all medications, thus demonstrating to her and to himself its magic powers.*

Used thus in sexual games, the phallus has all the author-

---

*EW: A hot beef injection.

ity of a baseball bat to score foul balls, a grandstand play, or an away-from-home run.

As previously mentioned, the penis may be flaunted to advertise itself. Very often, a beach or a dance hall is like a supermarket for young girls, with all the goodies carefully packaged on open display. Tight swimming trunks or trouser pants may turn on the younger crowd or the hungry bar-fly girls, but more confident women may react differently. One of them put the question witheringly to a young man who sat across from her with his legs apart: "It's pretty, but what can it do?" In homosexual circles, where the main object may be to find someone who is "well hung" or has "a big basket," with little interest in the hanger or the man who is carrying the basket, such advertising may be more acceptable and pay off.

Finally, as an instrument of love, the phallus can be used to give pleasure to the woman, to caress and to stroke her most secret and sensitive part, and thus manifest and demonstrate that love. And this may end, with intent and mutual consent, in creating something that will be half his and half hers, with no exploitation and no charades.

C

THE EXPLOITATION OF THE VAGINA

The vagina too can be used by its owner to pass the time of day, being a responsive self-pacifier and comforter. As a fertility symbol to be worshiped by others (casually or in rituals and ceremonies), it gives dramatic promise of productivity and protection. And it is also the ultimate offering of the goddess of courtesy, either in sheer hospitality, or in order not to let someone down after having led him on. Its constant companion, the clitoris, can dance

attendance and add spice to all these sensuous jubilees. But the vagina has one advantage over both the clitoris and the penis: like a pet cat, it can be trained to do all manner of curious tricks, such as picking up a dollar bill (an old trick in "night clubs" of a certain type)—a stunt which no penis has yet learned to master. This is one of the ways in which the vagina can be rented out to make money, and in general, the more tricks it has learned, the better it will be at its trade.

In everyday life of relaxation and social intercourse, it can be used for a large variety of teasing games of less or more respectability. In the crudest of these, it may be half concealed behind layers of gauzy or gaudy embroidery, or let slip out for a peek, either at irregular intervals or rhythmically, like a stroboscopic mushroom flashing its sickly fluorescence through the movement of the dance. Or it may be conspicuously concealed behind a cache-sexe, like an enormous zircon, in the hope that the cash customers will think it is a diamond. This is the downstairs or saloon level of genital quackery, playing it for peanuts or drink money.

Upstairs the stakes are higher. It can be used as a come-on for financial, marital, or other entrapments, as a squeezer by women who want to swindle a man out of his semen for dishonest or desperate impregnation, and as an impotent constrictor by those who want to deprive a man of his virile organ by violence, instead of caressing it into humility as an honest trophy-thief would do. More modest and sensitive women may regard the vagina as a deserving reward for services rendered, a grateful comforter in time of need, a magic erector set for failing potency, or the great earth-healer for all male frailties.

The clitoris may serve as a pet, as a warm-up, and to demonstrate passion by its swelling up. For some who feel they are deprived by not having the grand prize of a penis, it is ruefully treasured as a token of what might have been. One of the most interesting aspects of the clitoris is its

"legal" value. A girl who has been forbidden to touch "herself" by her mother or father may put one over on them by legalistic mental quibbling: she refrains from touching her vagina, as instructed, but takes her pleasure from her clitoris instead, which she knows is naughty but convinces herself is not illegal.

As an instrument of enduring love, the vagina serves as a passionate grasper and caressing squeezer. It strives ever hopefully and ever vainly for total incorporation of not only the penis but the man behind it. But in the end, instead of taking, it may give forth the fruit of that love.

The woman, much more than the man, uses other parts of her body in a sexual way. She may use her breasts as advertising, either ethically and with pride, or subversively, or even competitively. She may use them in a false way to exploit men for other things besides sex: a form of petty theft most aptly called proplifting, making the wheels of her life turn smoothly by using them for what Amaryllis calls boobrication. Buttocks are used similarly, except that their motion is even more enticing than their form. Often a woman who puts her hands behind her head to thrust her breasts forward is not aware of what she is doing, and the same applies to women who squirm when they are seated in the presence of men. This kind of seductiveness was celebrated by Rabelais in his famous couplet *"Folle à la messe est molle à la fesse"*—girls who squirm in church have soft bottoms.

D

SEX ORGANS IN TIME-STRUCTURING

Before we go on to talk about the exploitation of the orgasm, we should understand why we have put things in a certain order in the last two sections.

Nearly every human being, as we shall see later, spends his life waiting for Santa Claus, and one of the great problems of living is how to fill in the time until he arrives. The exploitations of the sex organs discussed above are ways of doing that. Such methods of time-structuring can be divided into six different classes, which remain the same regardless of what instruments are used. Whether people concern themselves with sex, money, art, or religion, for example, there are only six types of transactions whereby they can express that concern, and these can be listed roughly in increasing order of emotional complexity.[1]

That was the plan followed earlier (see section title) in listing the uses of the sex organs, which explains some of the sequences which might otherwise seem peculiar: for example, putting phallic worship right after masturbation, and politeness right after that. The simplest things that people do are those they do alone, and the most complex are those involving the deepest intimacies, with their complicated interweavings of mutual feeling. For that reason, masturbation was put first, and intimacy last, with other types of transactions in between. In the same way, in talking about the psychological uses of money, the miser sitting in solitary splendor beside his adding machine, grubbing through his stack of annual company reports, would be put first, and the couple struggling to earn Christmas money for each other and their children would come last. In art, the solitary painter would be first, and the lover reading his poem to his mistress would be at the end; the religious sequence would start with solitary meditation and end with mystical personal union or a struggle against temptation from a loved one.

The six categories are named withdrawal, rituals, pastimes, activities, games, and intimacy. Returning to the subject of sex, withdrawal, which is a way of structuring time without being involved with other people, means using the sex organs as personal playthings. Here sex is instead of people; it is safer to sit alone and play with toys of whatever

kind than to risk becoming involved with others, especially in such an emotionally charged engagement as sex. Rituals and politeness are the safest ways of being with others: everyone knows what is expected of him, and as long as he sticks to the rules, nothing untoward will occur. The worship of sex organs and courteous service are both in this category.

An activity is work designed to accomplish something according to a previous agreement or contract, and the use of the sex organs to earn money or impregnation falls into this class. Personal involvement is kept at a minimum by the terms of the contract. Once that is fulfilled both parties can go their own ways with no further obligations.

The simplest level of individual emotional engagement is called pastimes, loose relationships that can be broken off at any time, like passing the time of day with an acquaintance. Mutual sexual stimulation just for fun is one of the more pleasant ways of passing idle hours. The next level of personal involvement is called games. These are more serious engagements, with an ulterior motive beneath the avowed purpose, giving many opportunities for emotional expression. The meaningful part of most people's lives is mostly made up of games, as we shall see in the chapter on that subject. The various forms of spurious love and seduction, or even outright swindling, are all examples of sexual games. And finally, a few fortunate people manage to find genuine intimacy in sex, particularly if they want to have babies.

Whether the person is waiting for Santa Claus to come in his red suit from the North Pole, or for his opposite number, Death, to come in his black suit from the South Pole, he can fill in the time in a variety of ways which will be stimulating and perhaps edifying. His sex organ is only one of many instruments provided by nature and society for this purpose. If he does use that, he tries to make matters as interesting as possible. The human race has been very imaginative in devising ways to structure time by the non-biological use of sex organs.

—
E
—

THE EXPLOITATION OF THE ORGASM

The orgasm is something that should just be allowed to happen, and enjoyed if and when it does. But many people, even people who can let music happen or not happen, cannot leave orgasms alone and have to exploit and meddle with them.[2] Most commonly they exploit them for reassurance of masculinity or femininity, or even beyond that, for competition, trying to be more masculine or more feminine by having more and better orgasms. Others try to turn it into an "experience," a trip, something to be reached for rather than something happening, or else into a production, a fancy embroidered orgasm with novel acrobatic thrusts, for example. It may also be regarded as a trophy or gift—"I had one with her" or "I gave her one"—and in many articles written by professionals it is treated as an attainment ("When her husband followed my instructions, she attained orgasm"). Some regard it as a comfort or a relief, carefully disregarding the pleasure; or as a mere reflex, a sort of accident that is irrelevant to the real sexual kick, which may lie in a fetish or a conquest. Even cynics of both sexes do better than that, taking it for a good squirt or a vaginal drink. But since having an orgasm is a healthy and exhilarating experience for most people, these counterfeit attitudes often become secondary after a while, or disappear altogether.

The more serious exploitations center around *not* having an orgasm. Many women and some men regard this as an accomplishment and a proof of superiority. Not having an orgasm may give a self-proclaimed "puritan" woman a feeling of righteousness that she prefers to the pleasure of having

one. This may go with teasing, tormenting, or lying to her husband or lover, often out of revenge or spite. In other cases the orgasm is avoided from fear or thrift. Some women have a fear that they will die if they let go. This may lead to complete frigidity, but sometimes they risk getting a little enjoyment, being careful not to let it go too far. Then they feel that they have cheated death, which adds a gruesome feeling of triumph to whatever pleasure they did get.

Thrift enters the picture on the strange but common theory that each person is only "allowed" a limited number of orgasms in his lifetime. That is, they are regarded as capital instead of interest, and are handled the way the person handles money when there is a limited amount. Some try to enjoy it as fast as possible, lest something go wrong before they can spend it all; others conserve it and ration it so that it will last as long as possible. This theory can be found in the most unlikely people, tucked away in the backs of their minds. Almost any layman, if asked how many orgasms a person can have in his lifetime, will come up with an answer ranging from 100 to 20,000. But even psychiatrists and sexologists, if they allow themselves to reply spontaneously, will often give some figure that takes them completely by surprise, since it shows that in spite of their Adult sophistication, the Child in them still believes that their orgasms are numbered.

In general, there are four ways in which people can handle their orgasms: frigidity, withholding, postponement, and release. Frigidity is usually justified on an "if only" basis: "Everything would be all right if only—you weren't a bum, you treated me better, you were a better lover, this were really true love."

Withholding is based on shady ethics: it's all right to have sex providing I don't enjoy it too much. This is the position in petting and making out. It was also the position of French prostitutes in the late nineteenth century: they would be forgiven at confession because they were having sex only

for business purposes.³ This attitude has also been forced on such girls by their pimps, probably ever since the profession came into existence. The girl gets beaten if she allows herself to enjoy it with anyone but him. This kind of "fidelity" is really the source of nearly all withholding. By not having an orgasm, the woman feels she is being "faithful" to either a real husband or absent lover, or to a phantom lover such as her father or a "celebrity" who has never heard of her. Half-virgins handle it another way: they will do anything except have an orgasm face to face; that they are saving for their real, phantom, or future lover.

In postponement, the woman allows the man to have his orgasm, but postpones hers until later. Either he has to induce it by following a certain procedure, or she waits until he leaves and then has it by masturbation, or in the worst case, she goes to another lover with a "wet deck" and comes with him.

A released orgasm is one which takes place during intercourse. It may be pure and intimate, or contaminated by ulterior motives and gamy feelings such as guilt, anger, inadequacy, hurt, or triumph. It may become a swindle if a phantom third party is involved: "I only have orgasms with my wife when I think of another woman." But in a released orgasm, there is at least honesty in action, if not always in thought.

F

SEXUAL DEVIATIONS

Sexual deviations, or perversions, as they used to be called, are hang-ups considered abnormal by people who think of themselves as normal, which they may very well be. Such deviations may be merely enjoyable when they are car-

ried on between consenting adults, but they become annoying, scary, harmful, or even vicious when they involve innocent victims. They range from esthetic preferences (enjoyable), through thefts of clothing (annoying), obscene telephone calls (scary), child molesting (harmful), to anal rape and murder (vicious). Some of the best-informed people, such as the staff members of state hospital-prisons for "sexual psychopaths," consider rape to be a crime against the person rather than a sexual deviation if the vagina is the point of attack.

There are three ways to define sexual deviations: legally, morally, and rationally. The virtue of legal definitions is that they are enforceable, or as the more salivating enforcers say, "You're damn right they are." Some of them are designed to protect the public from personal loss and verbal or physical assault, but others are mischievous and arrogant, and raise more questions about Them than about the people They are messing around with. Moral definitions may be more thoughtful, but they are often uninformed and based on dubious premises. Unfortunately, rational definitions also run into unforeseen difficulties. Deviation means literally something most people (more than 50 percent of people) would prefer not to do. But that doesn't make much sense, because it would make deviants of everyone who voted for the loser in a political election. Winners do sometimes take advantage of this to call their opponents perverts. As a sporting proposition, the winners would then have to admit that they were perverts the next time they lost.

The word "pervert" implies that there is a normal, natural course of development, and that the pervert is insulting nature. This can be and is easily twisted by some people into the proposition: "I'm normal and you're not." But that is a matter of opinion, and the man who writes his own certificate of sanity is not always an authority on the subject; his judgment may be coated with a vested interest as he pants after his prey, and the shoe may be on the other foot.

If sex is regarded as a reproductive function, then a perversion would be anything that interfered with natural reproduction. Thus a biological definition would state that nothing is a perversion which terminates with the deposit of the semen in the vagina. But this excludes the use of condoms and of coitus interruptus or withdrawal, although it allows for diaphragms, cervical devices, and pills. Certain technical difficulties also arise. For example, anal intercourse with vaginal ejaculation would then not be a perversion, but it is certainly biologically undesirable because it carries organisms from the rectum into the neighborhood of the urethra where they might end up causing a bladder infection.

The most practical and ethical definition is a humanistic one. Such a definition would recognize (1) that the participants are free agents, (2) that sex is an act of personal communion, and (3) that it must not damage the flesh beyond the perforation of the hymen. Then any sequence based on free, mutual, informed consent, which terminates in bodily contact and does not damage the tissues of either party is not a perversion. Hence there must be no force used, as in rape; there must be no exploitation of ignorance, as in child molesting; it must not culminate on an external object such as a shoe or a dildo; and there must be no violence, even with consent, as in sadism. This allows for innumerable forms of sexual excitement, but excludes rape, child molesting, the use of artificial instruments such as shoes or plastic penises, and physical abuse. Unfortunately it does not exclude crazy things like dressing in diapers or eating feces.

Perhaps it is simpler the other way around. Normal sex is any mutual enjoyment between two free and informed partners of each other's bodies and their usual decorations and trappings. While this is ethical in the best sense, it might be considered immoral by people with special interests. One difficulty is that it does not exclude incest, which no rational definition can do, since that is a moral problem, and indeed,

the incest taboo is the basis of nearly all morality and probably of all culture as well. Perhaps the best summary is to say if you don't want to do it, or it seems crazy, don't do it. If you only do it when you're drunk and hate yourself when you sober up, don't drink.

While sexual deviation may be damaging to its occasional victims, if any, much more serious is logical deviation, or perversions of thinking, which may affect large numbers of people. One of the most difficult of these deviations to understand is the prejudice against long hair, beards, and sandals, since George Washington wore his hair long, Abraham Lincoln had a beard, and Jesus Christ wore sandals(?), and in fact was guilty of all three. There is no reasonable way to explain the prejudice against long-haired men except on the basis that it arouses perverse desires in those who object to it so vehemently. Many other prejudices show perverted thinking. For example, if any Christian in the last 2,000 years were asked, "What would you do if you met Jesus Christ's cousin?" he would be unlikely to reply, "I'd kick hell out of him and his women and children." But that is exactly what large numbers of Christians have done. The inbred population of ancient Judea was small enough so that almost every Judean must have been some sort of cousin to Jesus, and so their descendants, the Jews, are nearly all related to him by blood and genes.

NOTES AND REFERENCES

1. Berne, E.: *Games People Play*. Grove Press, New York, 1964.
2. Maizlish, I. L.: "The Orgasm Game." *Transactional Analysis Bulletin* 4:75, October, 1965.
3. Philippe, C. L.: *Bubu of Montparnasse*. (With preface by T. S. Eliot). Berkley Publishing Corporation, New York, 1957.

PART II

Sex And People

4

FORMS OF
HUMAN
RELATIONSHIP

A

THE HUMAN PERSONALITY

It is most fruitful to think of the human personality as being divided into three parts, or even better, to realize that each individual is three different persons, all pulling in different directions . . . so that it is a wonder anything ever gets done. And of course in sex, if they are pulling very hard against each other, it doesn't get done, or at least it doesn't get done properly. We can represent this very simply by drawing three circles, one below the other, as in Figure 1. These represent the three people that everyone carries around in his or her head.

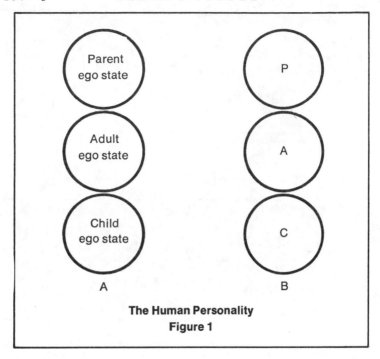

The Human Personality
Figure 1

At the top are his parents, who are really two different people, but in this diagram we show them as one circle, marked Parent, or P. This represents someone in his head telling him what he ought to do and how to behave and how good he is and how bad he is and how much better or worse other people are. In short, the Parent is a voice in his head making editorial comments, as parents often do, on everything he undertakes. You can tell when your Parent, or Parental ego state, is talking because it uses words like "ridiculous," "immature," "childish," and "wicked." Your Parent may talk to you that way in your head, and it may also talk out loud to other people in the same way. The Parent has another side, however. It can also be affectionate and sympathetic, just like a real parent, and say things like "You're the apple of my eye," "Let me take care of it," and "Poor girl."

The middle circle, marked Adult, or A, represents the voice of reason. It works like a computer, taking in information from the outside world, and deciding on the basis of reasonable probabilities what course of action to take and when to take it. It does not have anything to do with being "mature," since even babies can make such decisions, nor with being sincere, since many thieves and con men are very good at deciding what to do and when to do it. The Adult tells you when and how fast to cross the street, whether to raise or fold on two pair, when to take the cake out of the oven, and how to focus a telescope. In crossing the street, for example, it works like a very accurate and very complicated computer, estimating the speeds of all the cars for blocks on each side, and then picking the earliest possible moment for starting across without being killed, or rather without having to lose your dignity by running. The Adult ego state is careful whenever possible to preserve your dignity, unless it is your fate to be a clown. All good computers are like that: they choose the most elegant solutions, and try to avoid makeshift or sloppy ones whenever they can. You can tell when your Adult is talking because it uses expressions like "Ready?" "Now!" "Too much!" "Not enough!" and "Here, not there."

The bottom circle, marked Child, or C, indicates that every man has a little boy inside of him and every woman carries a little girl in her head. This is the Child part of the personality, the child he or she once was. But every child is different, and the Child ego state in each person is different, since it is the Child he once was at a definite time in his life. When the Child takes over, the person acts in a childlike way, like a child of a certain age: in one person it might be four years and three months old, in another two years and six months, and it is doubtful if it is ever older than six years. We do not call this Child ego state "childish"; we simply say it is like a child, or childlike. The age of the Child part of the personality in each person is determined by special fac-

tors which you can read about in another book if you want to take the trouble.[1] It is important to realize that the Child is not there to be squelched or reprimanded, since it is actually the best part of the personality, the part that is, or can be if properly approached, creative, spontaneous, clever, and loving, just as real children are. Unfortunately, children can also be sulky, demanding, and inconsiderate or even cruel, so this part of the personality is not always easy to deal with. Since your Child ego state is going to be with you for the rest of your life, it is best to acknowledge it and try to get along with it, and it will do more harm than good to pretend that if you ignore it or deal harshly with it, it will go away.

You will have noticed that I referred to these three parts of the personality—Parent, Adult, and Child—as ego states, and that is the scientific name for them.* These ego states determine what happens to people and what they do to and for each other. The best way, and so far the neatest and most scientific way, to analyze human social and sexual relationships is to find out which ego states are involved. Each ego state has to be looked at separately if the person wants to understand his feelings and behavior in such situations. Some people try to become "a whole person" by denying that there are different parts to the personality. A better way is to find out as much as possible about each aspect, since they are all there to stay, and then get them to work together in the best possible way.

*"Parent," "Adult," and "Child," capitalized, are used throughout to refer to ego states in the head; the same words in lowercase refer to actual people.

B

THE RELATIONSHIP DIAGRAM

There are in English, and in ancient Greek as well, hundreds of words describing different kinds of love and friendship between people.[2][3] It is interesting to discover that there are far fewer words describing hate and enmity. We are not concerned here, however, with finding as many different words as possible, but rather with picking out a few that refer to the commonest types of relations between men and women, and particularly those which involve different sets of ego states. One of the oldest classifications of personal relations, which attempts to boil them down to their barest essentials, is the legal one. For centuries, the law has dealt with them under four main headings: Husband and Wife, Parents and Children, Guardians and Wards, and Master and Servant (or Master and Apprentice). One difficulty here is that these are all one-up one-down relationships, with one person running the show and the other fighting for his rights, and that will never do for us.

A better way is to start off with a Relationship Diagram,[4] which tells us all the possible ways in which two people, each having three ego states, can relate to each other. This is shown in Figure 2. There are nine simple relationships possible, taking one ego state at a time in each person, and then of course various combinations of these. For example, there are 72 kinds of relationships involving two crossed arrows or vectors (the response going in a different direction from the stimulus), 432 involving three vectors, and so on. If we want to make it even more complicated, we can put in positive vectors for positive feelings and negative vectors for negative feelings, and then combine these in all sorts of dif-

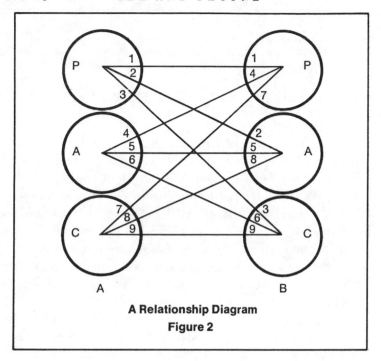

A Relationship Diagram
Figure 2

ferent ways. In this fashion, this simple diagram could be used to illustrate, I think, all of the hundreds of words used to describe positive, negative, and mixed relationships in English and ancient Greek.

But that is not what we are going to do. What we are going to do is take twelve common words that are familiar to everybody, which describe progressively more serious and longer-lasting emotional involvement between one man and one woman. Furthermore, we will try to choose words that have the same or a very similar meaning all over the world, regardless of local customs or local laws or any considerations outside of what happens between the two people themselves. We shall then see if we can fit these relationships into the relationship diagram. As we shall discover, some of them fit easily and others make complications, but never-

theless, I think this is one good way to find out how sex fits into people's lives all around the world.

C

ACQUAINTANCES

Acquaintances are full of potential. It is from among them that you will choose your more serious relationships, the ones that will continue and will give you something to remember them by. Every acquaintance is a possible friend or enemy, and you should choose both carefully. The more acquaintances you have, the more choices you have, so I would recommend that you say Hello to everybody. Acquaintanceship is a static relation, which can stay the same year after year. In order to go further, somebody has to make the first move, and the other person has to accept the overture.

Acquaintances are people who go through social rituals with each other. Such rituals have a value in themselves. They are one form of verbal stroking, and they have the same effect as patting has on a baby. When someone says Hello, or How are you? or What's new? or Warm enough for you? he tones up your muscles, clears your brain, soothes your heart, and relaxes your digestion. For this you should be grateful, and in return he expects you to do the same for him. If you are in a sulky mood and refuse to accept the benefits thus offered, then both of you will suffer. You will get even sulkier, and his stomach will churn and a film will form over his brain and stay there until he meets someone more courteous and appreciative of his presence.

The kind of things acquaintances say to each other, passing the time of day while carefully avoiding any intrusion on each other's privacy, do not come from either Parent, Adult,

or Child. They come from a mask or shield which the person places between himself and the people around him, called by some psychiatrists the *persona*. The persona is a way of presenting oneself, and is best described by an adjective: gruff, sociable, sweet, cute, busy, charming, contemptuous, or polite. With each of these words comes a different way of saying Hello or passing the time of day. The persona is formed during the years from six to twelve, when most children first go out on their own and are confronted with people in the outside world who are not of their own or their parents' choosing. Each child soon perceives that he needs a way to avoid unwanted entanglements or promote wanted ones in this world he never made, so he chooses his own way of presenting himself to that world. Usually he tries to be nice and polite and to appear considerate and compliant. He may keep this early persona for the rest of his life, or turn it in later, after more experience, for another one. Thus the persona is really a Child ego state influenced by Parental training and modified by Adult prudence toward the people around him. The main requirement for the persona is that it should work. If it doesn't work, the person is either in a continual state of anxiety when he is with people, for fear that his persona will break down, or else he takes to avoiding people and going off by himself.

The persona is really a special ego state: that of a ten-year-old Child trying to make his way among strangers, so it can be fitted into the structural diagram by saying that it is a special aspect of the Child ego state. Actually, it is a good example of adapting oneself to the situation and acting in an expected, predictable way, an ego state which is known as the Adapted Child.

D

CO-WORKERS

Almost as innocent and distant as the relationship between acquaintances is that between co-workers. Acquaintances keep each other at a distance by sticking to well-tried formulas of greeting and conversation, saying exactly the same thing time after time in the same situation, carefully choosing the most harmless and inoffensive clichés, or the most ingratiating ones. Co-workers accomplish the same end by talking at an angle instead of straight to the other person. They talk about something, so that their words are directed to that something, and bounce off it to the listener. Transactional analysts call occupational work an activity, and whatever is worked with is called the material of the activity. If the material is right in front of two co-workers, they will often look at it while they are talking, instead of at each other.

Helper (looking at frammis): "The frammis sure is decoruscated."

Mechanic (looking at frammis): "Yeah, that always happens in these mass-production Mercillacs. They're just parlayed Volkolets."

Helper (keeping his eyes on the frammis): "Yeah, you never see that in a Maserrari."

In this way, the mechanic and his helper may work all day together for months without ever looking directly at each other.

Paper-shufflers do exactly the same thing. In fact it is well known among boss paper-shufflers that if the clerical shufflers ever look you in the eye (or vice versa), something is going on. When they are talking to each other, they look at

the papers, not at each other. Business and professional men with new customers or clients also act like co-workers.

Thus co-workers are people who talk to each other through the material, and they talk about the material. This is an Adult-Adult relationship, which looks like Figure 3. If the boss breaks the Adult-Adult contract by coming on Parent, that entitles the worker to call him one free adjective: helpful or fussy or strict if he was nice about it, and mean, nervy or impossible if he wasn't. If the worker comes on Parent, the boss is likewise entitled to one free adjective: understanding, co-operative, impertinent, or out of line. If either of them comes on Child, the other feels entitled to call the offender ridiculous, undignified, unladylike, ungentlemanly, flirtatious, or groovy.

This means that the moment two co-workers look directly at each other or talk directly to each other instead of through the material, they are something else besides co-workers.

E

COMMITTEE MEMBERS

From Figure 2, you can see that there are three "straight-across" relationships, Parent-to-Parent, Adult-to-Adult, and Child-to-Child. Although co-workers talk at an angle to each other because they are discussing "the realities out there," that is precisely the definition of Adult-to-Adult transactions, so the vectors in the Co-worker Diagram of Figure 3 go straight across. Oddly enough, there is no simple English word which describes Parent-to-Parent relationships, although they are very common all over the world. In this country, the most likely place to hear one Parental ego state talking to another is on a "committee," so people in this relationship can be called committee members, for want of a better term.

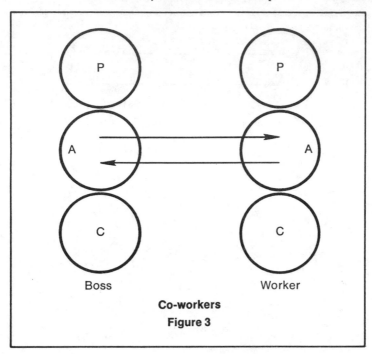

Co-workers

Figure 3

The kind of committee I am referring to is not the kind that gets something done, but the kind that gets together and talks about suppressing something Awful which either doesn't exist or which they don't really know much about, or whose existence is necessary for the well-being of society. Their discussions, in the guise of exchanges of information, are actually exchanges of indignation, based on Parental prejudices instead of facts. Here the contract is Parent-to-Parent, as illustrated in Figure 4. Again, just as in the case of co-workers, anyone who breaks the contract is subject to name-calling. For example, anyone at a Parental type of Suppression Society who gives an unbiased Adult view of the subject is likely to be called various kinds of nasty names. A playful Child makes Parental committee members even more nervous than a factual Adult does. Thus Pro-

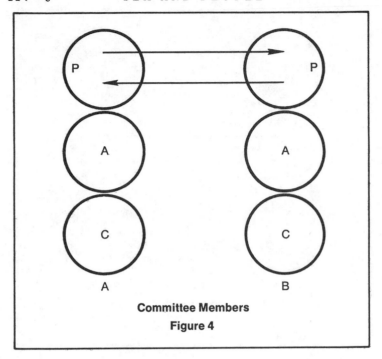

Committee Members

Figure 4

hibitionists of various persuasions become uneasy if someone tries to prove by Adult investigation that whatever they are prohibiting is not so bad after all, and they may place difficulties in the way of such investigations. But if someone tries to demonstrate the same thing in a playful Childlike way, they take much more drastic action to put a stop to it (put him in jail, maybe). Comedians understand this principle very well; they know that jokes upset Parental meddlers even more than facts do.

Besides formal committees where some or all of the members spend their time in Parent-to-Parent indignation without really knowing what they are talking about, there are many informal committees that work the same way. These are made up of people who get together socially and talk about their Awfuls in a Parental prejudiced way without

checking the other side of the question. Among the most interesting examples are the middle-aged landladies who get together for coffee or beer or a cocktail every morning, and are really an informal committee to fight juvenile delinquency, rising taxes, open housing, and the fiendishness of tenants, while promoting a better understanding of landladies and the need for higher rents. Similar informal indignation committees are popular among young married couples.

Actually, committee members, or committees, are of three types. We have discussed Parent-to-Parent committees above in order to demonstrate how this kind of relation works. Adult-to-Adult committees talk factually or "communicate" about their Awful if they are ineffective, or do something about it if they are effective. There are also Child-to-Child committees, both formal and informal, which are usually called grievance committees. Here it is the Child ego states of the members which talk to each other, as shown in Figure 5, and the Awfuls have to do with some form of Parental oppression. Adult grievance committees talk straight and negotiate fairly. Child grievance committees play games, sometimes distressing ones, since their real object is to discomfit the authorities they are complaining about, rather than to rectify the wrongs they bring up.

The alliances mentioned above are not always man to woman, but they are included in order to illustrate how relationships can be analyzed into ego states.

By this time it can be seen that there is an unspoken rule about relationships. They are not set up between people, but between ego states. Both parties understand, in some way or other, which ego states are allowed to express themselves in the situation. This understanding has the force of a contract. Anyone who breaks the contract by expressing an illegitimate ego state is therefore legitimately subject to being called names, or in flagrant cases, to being fired from the relationship.

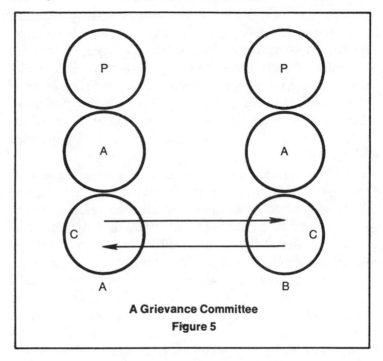

A Grievance Committee
Figure 5

In order to be clear on what we are talking about, we can define a relationship as a continuing set of transactions between two or more people, or rather between their various ego states, which can be represented by a drawing on the blackboard. If a person who uses the word "relationship" is unable to draw a convincing diagram, it is not worth pursuing the matter further, because there is no way of knowing exactly what he means.

F

RESPECT

The next kind of relationship to be considered is called respect. This is another Adult-to-Adult relation, and

is based on straight talk and the fulfillment of familial, occupational, and social contracts without alibis, quibbling, or private reservations. Talking straight comes from reliability, and fulfilling contracts comes from commitment. Reliability and commitment together add up to trustworthiness, and trust is what gives rise to respect. Trust is something that begins very early in childhood, if it begins at all.

The Child, as we have already said, is in many ways the best part of a person. It is the enthusiastic, creative, spontaneous part of the personality, the part that makes women charming and men witty and fun to be with. It is also the part that enjoys nature and people. Unfortunately, in order that he may live in the world it is necessary for the Child to be curbed and corrupted by Parent and Adult influences. For example, he must learn not to scatter his food enthusiastically around the table and not to urinate creatively in public; he must also learn not to cross the street spontaneously, but to look around before he does. If too many restrictions lead into confusion, then the Child is no longer able to enjoy himself at all.

One of the most valuable qualities of the Child is his shrewdness. The Adult's job is to learn facts about the environment, particularly the physical environment: how to drive a car, and why bills should be paid, and when to call a doctor—information which may be necessary for survival in a grownup world. The infant's survival, however, depends on people, so he is mainly concerned with them: which ones he can trust, which ones to watch out for, which ones are going to be good to him and which ones are going to hurt or neglect him. Children understand people much better than grownups do, including well-trained grownups who study human behavior. Such professionals are merely relearning something they once knew, but no matter how hard they study, they are never going to be as good psychiatrists or psychologists as they originally were when they were little children.

The reason for this is that most parents raise children not to be too intuitive and not to look at people directly to see what they are up to, because that is considered rude. They are supposed to figure people out with their Adults instead of feeling them out with the Child. Most children, including those who are going to be psychiatrists and psychologists, follow these instructions, and then spend five or ten years at college and sometimes another five years in therapeutic groups or psychoanalysis, all in order to get back 50 per cent of the people-judging capacity they had when they were four years old.

But the Child is still there, although he may not talk very loudly or clearly, and it is he who decides best whether or not someone can be trusted. Trust comes from the Child, respect from the Adult, with the Child's permission. Respect means that the Child looks someone over and decides that he is trustworthy. The Child then says to the Adult: "Go ahead. You can trust him. I'll keep an eye on the situation and review it from time to time." The Adult then translates this into an attitude of respect and acts accordingly. Sometimes, however, the Parent interferes. The Child and the Adult may be all ready to go ahead, and then the Parent brings up a prejudiced objection: "How can you trust a man with long hair?" or "How can you trust a fat woman?" To the Child, of course, long hair or fatness is quite irrelevant to trustworthiness, and he would much rather be with a long-haired man and a fat woman who love him than with a short-haired man and a thin woman who don't. Nothing interferes with Child intuition more than Parental prejudices.

The first situation of trust arises between the infant and his mother, where her reliability and commitment are put to the test in feeding him. His survival depends upon that, and his attitude toward life and people depends upon how it is carried out.

If he is being fed on demand, he gives the signal with his hunger cry. If she comes when he calls, she is reliable. If

she brings his milk shortly after, she is committed. But if she takes her time about coming, and also lets him down on the food, he never learns to trust her. This is not distrust, which is a broken trust; it is untrust, the absence of something that was never there.

If he is being fed on a schedule, say every four hours, the situation is different. Most babies seem to come equipped with a mental clock, perhaps the same clock some grownups use when they decide to wake up at 7:15 and wake up exactly at 7:15. The baby sets his clock for four hours, and expects his mother to be there when the alarm goes off, and to feed him soon after. If she does both, he trusts her. If she does neither, he doesn't.

In both cases, as he grows older, he is willing to accept longer and longer delays, and still later, even excuses, provided there are not too many of them. But if there are too many, either he never learns what trust means, or else he learns distrust. Basically, he expects her not only to be reliable and come on time, but also to be committed and bring the food when or soon after she comes. It is quite possible that his own trustworthiness will imitate hers: he may be reliable and committed, or one but not the other, or neither.

Trust is the basis of respect. To the baby, it means that his mother will be there (reliability) and will do what she is supposed to (commitment). Later he expects people to send a message if they are going to be late (reliability), and fulfill their contracts when they do come (commitment). He may excuse unreliability if commitment is there, and he may excuse lack of commitment if reliability is there, both under protest; but he is unlikely to respect anyone who is neither reliable nor committed.

Now for a homey example. A reliable husband is one who tells you without fail about every affair he has, no matter how *bad* it was. A committed husband is one who makes sure that every affair he has is a good one, even if he doesn't tell you about it. A trustworthy and respected husband is

one who doesn't have affairs, if he promised not to at the wedding ceremony, because if he did, he meant it.

The actual transactions that manifest respect between two people are Adult-to-Adult, as previously shown in Figure 3, but they have a different quality. They are not carried on through the material, as with co-workers, but eye to eye and man to woman, with full trust in each other's reliability and commitment unless and until it is proven to be misplaced.

G

ADMIRATION

All the relationships we have talked about so far are "straight across"—Parent-to-Parent, Adult-to-Adult, or Child-to-Child (Figures 2-5). Now we come to one which is "up and down," Child-to-Parent (Figure 6, going up). People use the word admiration in many ways, but in its true sense it means "wonder." Admiration comes about in the opposite way to respect. In respect it is the Child who looks the person over and tells the Adult to go ahead. In admiration it is the Adult who looks the person over and tells the Child to go ahead. The Adult says, "Boy! He really knows how to . . ." whatever it is—swim, or dance, or recite poetry, or whatever you may admire most and know how to judge—and the Child takes it from there.

Sex may come into this in the case of a schoolgirl crush on a boy or on a female teacher. The girl starts off admiring the teacher in an Adult way for something she does or is, and then her Child takes over and she may get hung up on the teacher and follow her around and perhaps begin to have sexual pictures about her. If the teacher keeps to her position, she will be like a good mother in dealing with the girl's attachment to her, but if she changes the "contract,"

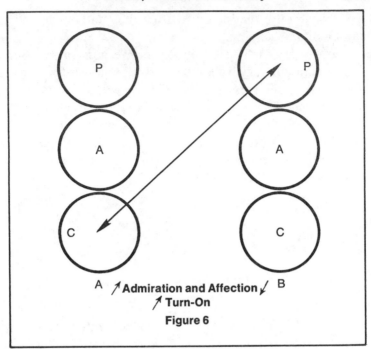

A ↗ **Admiration and Affection** ↙ B
↗ **Turn-On**
Figure 6

what might be an edifying relationship between a Parent and a Child is turned into a frolic between two uneasy Children.

I think that just as trust arises from the baby's relationship to his mother, so admiration has to do with his father, because father is the wonder-boy in the family. Mother is the one who is trusted because she is there when she is needed. Father may be there only irregularly, but his imposing voice and presence and his strength and power excite the baby's admiration. And it is true that genuine admiration is most often extended to men, although it may be shifted to women if they happen to be wonder-workers in their own right. That is what happens later, when children begin to admire their mother's accomplishments, such as cooking or painting, as well as respecting her as a person.

And conversely, they learn to trust their father as well as admire him.

People vary in their ability to receive admiration. Some don't tolerate it very well and avoid it or turn it away when it comes, sometimes angrily. Others exploit it, like the teacher who has an affair with an infatuated schoolgirl or schoolboy, or the gangster who takes on an admiring young punk to exploit him as much as he can. The best handle it gracefully and make it a worthwhile experience for themselves and the others concerned.

H

AFFECTION

Affection is another "slanted" relationship, this time Parent-to-Child (Figure 6, going down). In admiration, the Adult of one person excites the Child of the other.* In affection, the Child of one person excites the Parent of the other. A person who feels affection expresses it very much as a mother or father does toward a winsome child, and the object of the affection responds in a simple Childlike way. These are not roles. They are true feelings arising from specific ego states, and ego states are different from roles. Ego states are psychological realities; in fact they are the only psychological realities, although they can easily be adulterated into falsehoods. They are systems of feelings which are there for life quite independently of roles, although roles can be grafted onto them and corrupt them.

In an affectionate relationship, Adult-to-Adult transactions may also occur between times, but the affection itself

---

*But the Child responds as though it were a parent, so the actual transactions are Child-Parent as in the transactional diagram in Figure 6.

comes from a Parental ego state and evokes a response from a Child ego state. In many families the parents believe that it is necessary to look serious when giving affection, and many children follow these instructions and are firmly convinced that it is necessary. Such affection given with a serious mien is called concern. There is no reason, however, why one can't give affection while having a good time, and concern often seems a little oversincere rather than really helpful. That is the answer to one of life's—or death's—puzzling questions. Why is it that fatal cancer patients know they have cancer, even if the people taking care of them sincerely try to fool them? They may pretend they don't know, partly out of consideration for those around them, since cancer patients, like other patients, are usually good sports and go along with the scenario. But usually they do know.

How does the patient find out, and which part of him knows? He finds out, I think, because no matter how well the others succeed in acting naturally around him, there is always one exception: either they don't laugh when they should, or if they do, they stop too quickly. That's what's wrong when people make it a strong point to "demonstrate" concern, which is different from doing the most helpful thing. They are confused by something as grim as cancer, and their reluctance to laugh or their uneasiness about laughing gives the diagnosis away, even if their true concern makes them want to conceal it. The real concern they may have trips over their concern about looking concerned, thus spoiling the picture. It takes a lot of guts to give up *looking* concerned with a cancer patient, but it can be done, and it pays off, as experiments on cancer wards show.

Here is how the giveaway works. Let us say that Mrs. C has an operation on her abdomen to find out the cause of her pain, and the surgeon finds rampant cancer which will be fatal in a few months. In order to spare her anguish, everyone decides to pretend that it is something less serious,

although they keep her in the hospital. She is very worried and wants to know if she has a death sentence or not. But she is also afraid of it, so she may ask but not be too insistent on getting a straight answer. She may not be ready to face the problems it raises. Nevertheless, she would really like to know if she is going to survive.

While her Adult evades an open answer, her Child secretly bends every effort to finding out, and watches people's behavior very, very carefully to get some clues. Once she notices that people are laughing differently, she starts checking. People who were previously uproariously funny may continue to make little funnies to keep things going, but they hedge them so they won't be uproarious. The doctor's cheerfulness may be different from his pre-operative attitude or his demeanor with other patients. Concerned clergymen may stop telling even "officially permitted" jokes about the priest and the rabbi, St. Peter, etc. The result is that Mrs. C can pick up a dozen examples a day of laughs toned down and laughs cut off, and pretty soon she knows something is badly wrong with her, and she knows what it is.

In such cases, "showing concern" may feel satisfying to the person who does it, but because of its oversincerity, it does not work too well. In fact, "showing concern" as a way of handling cancer patients over a long period wears out both the staff and the patients and benefits neither of them. If the patients are regarded as dying people, then the cancer ward becomes that grim institution which used to be called a "Home for Incurables," with the unwritten motto above the door: "What do you expect of someone who is dying of cancer?" If, on the other hand, they are treated as "very much alive self-respecting adult human beings," then the motto turns into "What can we do for you today?" and the nurses and doctors come alive as well as the patients.[5] That is an extreme example of the difference between "showing concern" and feeling affectionate.

True affection is to find help or be helpful when it is

needed and to look concerned at critical moments. But when "acting concerned" takes precedence over thinking, it may do more harm than good, whether or not the concern is genuine. The firm statement "I am concerned" (said aloud or in writing, one time) is more effective than a determined effort to look serious. One reason for this careful discussion is that while the Parent and Adult may indeed be concerned, the Child usually has a different attitude unless he is in danger himself. Because of this ambiguity, "feeling concerned" should not be a matter for pride or self-righteousness, as it often is.

In milder situations, receiving affection allows people to laugh at their own troubles, but being an object of concern demands that they look serious in order to keep their helpers happy. Here a joke is often better than a frown.

I

THE TURN-ON

So far in our pursuit of relationships we have been in many different rooms: the workroom, the meeting room, the nursery, the schoolroom and the hospital room. Now we can follow our quarry into the bedroom. The turn-on is just what it sounds like: the right person pushes the switch and the whole body lights up, from the eyes into the brain and down through the chest and belly, and below that too. There is no social class or Parental prejudice cutting the wires, and no rationality or Adult prudence pulling the plug. It is the Child alone who lights up, and it either happens or it doesn't. It is very similar to what happens with imprinting in birds.[6] It is a sensory rather than a personal response, and it is mainly visual. Other senses may contribute, and it may be brightened by daydreams and glori-

fied by previous frustrations, but the flash of recognition nearly always comes from seeing.

In imprinting, the young bird will get turned on to a visual image of a certain form and color and respond to the object, which may be merely a piece of cardboard, as though it were its mother. It has no decision or free choice in the matter; it is torqued in by a certain stimulus and responds automatically. The stimulus may be only a silhouette, but the effect is full-bodied. In the same way, confronted with a turn-on, many people must give up the illusion that their feelings make sense and are proper to their being, because this is an automatic response which may go against Parental or Adult preference or logic, as the hero in *Of Human Bondage* learned the hard way. The ability to kindle this response is what movie talent scouts have always looked for, and in former days it was called many names from "It" to "Sex appeal," and sex appeal is what it is.

Fetishism is a special kind of turn-on, where the man gets the impact from a particular part of the female body or from some feminine personal possession: hair or scarves, hands or gloves, feet or shoes. These parts of the body or feminine objects are said by some to be "symbolic substitutes for the loved person." It is much more likely that they are imprintings from early childhood, due to events which happened just at the right time and under the right circumstances to make a permanent hookup. Fetishism is very difficult to cure, partly or mainly because few fetishists want to be cured. Many of them get the same bang from the sight or touch or smell of their fetish as a drug addict does from his heroin or Methedrine. The prospect of giving up these thrills for a square passion has little appeal for them unless their fetish is so far out that it gets them into serious trouble.

A fetish is not just a symbol, any more than a gun is. The fetish is the real thing to the fetishist, just as a gun is the real thing to a shootnik. The gun is not a symbol of the penis

but is used instead of it or in addition to it because it is more deadly than flesh and bone, and deadliness is something the gunki craves.* That is why he would rather go hunting than stay home with his wife. Even a toy water pistol is more than a phallic symbol. It works better than a phallus for its intended purpose of shooting a stream of water accurately from a distance. The idea may have come from nature, and the Child may enjoy the similarity, but there is a lot more to it than that.[7] One element is craftsmanship; the Adult appreciates the quality of the object, whether it is a rifle, a water pistol, an old slipper, or a glove.

Many mild fetishists have more fun than most "normal" people (at cocktail parties, for instance) if they are not hampered by their guilt feelings. Farther-out ones suffer from some confusion in their love relationships, if any, and may get distracted from more serious pursuits by their fancies. They may also get attached to degrading caterers, and suffer because of that. They are in fact enslaved by their imprinting to follow the fetish rather than the person, and so it is a matter of luck what kind of personalities they get mixed up with or attached to. A dedicated fetishist does not usually make a very good husband unless he happens to find exactly the right wife.

Since to some extent all men have their preferences, and a great many have at least mild fetishes, one of the easiest ways for a woman to please and hang on to a man is to find out covertly what his fetishes are and indulge or even cater to them secretly. This is certainly what makes (and has made throughout history) successful mistresses. Many a war has been fought and many a kingdom made or lost because of a bit of ribbon or lace worn in the proper fetching place. But the matter can be handled more honestly, and perhaps even more effectively, by asking him outright what

---

*This does not include honest marksmen. I have some of those in my own family. One of my sons, who works as a cowboy, can shoot a flea off the head of a flying rattlesnake at 100 yards with an elephant gun.

his fetishes are, and then indulging him. But because fetishes are fixed early in life, they are sometimes a generation behind the current styles, which the woman may find embarrassing. Even though a 1940 bathing suit turns her man on, she may understandably decline to wear one thirty years later.

Which brings us to a much neglected subject: the counterfetishist, what I would like to call the fetishera. Nearly all fetishists are men. But for every man who is hung up on shoes, there is a woman ready to cater to and groove with him, and for every man who gets his thrills from hair, there is a woman who gets hers from having her locks raped. Havelock Ellis has many cases of this meeting of the minds: the man who yearns to get pressed on by high heels sooner or later meets a woman who has daydreamed all her life of heel-pressing. These women are fetisheras, and very little is known about them because they do not come to professional attention very often. There are just as many women who specialize in hair, gloves, shoes, or underwear as there are men urgently searching for the delights they offer. This is borne out not only in the case histories collected by Havelock Ellis and other natural historians of sex, but also by the fetishists who put want ads in underground papers such as the *Berkeley Barb*.

Now back to the "normal" turn-on. There are men who are turned on by breasts and men who are turned on by legs—breast men and leg men, as they call themselves politely—and both are considered normal. Strictly speaking, however, and meaning no offense, such preferences are expeditions to the foothills of fetishism. A true fetishist is unable to get an erection in the absence of his fetish, no matter how desirable his partner is in other ways. Now if a leg man or a breast man were not allowed to look at or touch his favorite regions, he might suffer from the same difficulty. The normal turn-on, on the other hand, is based on the height, weight, conformation, carriage, gait, seat,

features, and skin texture of the woman: what is popularly called her "personality," that is, the general proportions of her body, the way she moves, her face and her skin. But the fetishes, the leg-breast preferences, and the "personality" turn-on, are all equally due to imprinting, and in most cases mother is the imprinter.

Thus the turn-on is actually a Child-Parent relationship, and fits Figure 6 (going up).

The turn-on is such a profound biological phenomenon that it has probably played a major role in evolution through sexual selection. Female birds are no doubt turned on by the brilliant plumage of male birds during mating season, and the brighter the plumage of the cock, the more birds he turns on. Similarly with rump colors in monkeys. The turn-on first occurs through distant senses: sight and sound, and in some cases smell. Male porcupines are strongly attracted by the urine of females in heat. Female moths give off an odor which can turn on male moths as far as a mile away.[8] The question is whether the male moth actually "smells" something, or whether there is just a chemical effect that pulls the switch without his being aware of an odor. The same question arises in the case of human beings. There are certain chemical turn-ons that people are aware of, and these are called perfumes, although sweat may serve the purpose too in many cases. But it is also possible that some women (and men also) give off chemicals that affect the nervous systems of other human beings without anyone smelling anything or being aware of what has turned them on.

As evidence for this, some people think that dogs can smell human odors that other humans can't—the smell of fear, for example. Now, people may not be aware of smelling fear, but they might still be affected in some other way by the same chemicals that the dog actually smells, whatever "actually smells" means for a dog. The same could easily apply to sex. In fact there is nothing, really, that

says men are any less sensitive than moths. It may very well
be that some men can sense the presence of a sexy woman,
and vice versa, at a distance of one mile in open country,
without being able to explain it. There is also the fact that
people of one race often say they can smell people of another: some Caucasians say they can smell Negroes, and
some Chinese say they can smell Caucasians, while people
of the same race don't seem to smell each other that way.
All this indicates that odorless smells may be important in
sexual turn-on.[9] Whether the smell is odorless because it
has no odor, or just because people don't notice the odor
if they have been around it for a long time, such smells or
chemical signals could still have a powerful effect on the
nervous systems of the opposite sex, or in some cases, of the
same sex.

There are tricks to every trade, but there are more tricks
to the turn-on trade than any other, since it involves all of
the senses and all of the man. Natural endowment of body
build, legs, breasts, hair, and buttocks is a good beginning.
Each man has his preferences, and some one of these elements just suiting him may be enough for a visual turn-on.
This usually depends on the way his mother looked to him
when he was a certain age: either four years old, when he
first began to be interested in the conformations of different
females, and decided at that time what kind of a girl he was
going to marry; or twelve to fourteen, when he felt the first
stirrings of adult sexuality. Usually he will look first at whatever features were emphasized in his family, which may be
hands or feet or ears rather than the larger proportions.
Some women go along with nature in the visual turn-on, or
enhance their appearance in socially acceptable ways, but
others do resort to tricks. One sits provocatively; another
stands with her legs apart, perhaps over a floor heater so
that her skirt balloons out a little. Some like to bend over
to pick things up, emphasize the roll of their buttocks when
they walk, or put their hands behind their heads. These are

things that well-brought-up young ladies are not supposed to do; hence they are an unfair form of competition and may arouse anger or contempt in other women.

Along with the visual turn-on, the groundwork may be laid for the fetish turn-on, which depends a great deal on dress. Here again, the man tends to be hooked by the things his family emphasized, particularly his mother. In fact the basic rule for fetishes is that the man's fetish is the same as the fetish of his mother's Child. If she took a childlike fascination in collecting a closet full of shoes, he may have a childlike fascination with women's shoes. And her daughter may, too. He becomes a shoe fetishist and his sister a fetishera, although it does not always work out that neatly. But in general, when a fetishist meets his fetishera and says, "My mother had a closet full of shoes," she is quite likely to reply, "So did mine." He means: "Mother loved her shoes and so did I; that's why I'm hung up on your shoes." She means: "Father loved mother's shoes, and that's why I'm hung up on shoes; so I'm glad you love mine." The same applies to large breasts or buttocks, long hair, tight slacks, ruffled skirts, petticoats, furs, or hiking boots. The combination of imprinting and sexy secrets in the family becomes irresistible.

Voice turn-on probably has the same background as fetishism. One overtone may hook a man for life. This extends as well to other sounds. Some men are turned on by women who cough or cry; in former days there were sighs. If a man's mother had asthma, his wife, by an odd coincidence, may have it, too. This type of sexual selection can obviously have an inherited effect on their offspring, thus passing on certain types of illnesses to the third generation.

Smell turn-ons also hark back to the early years of life. The commonest are cooking smells, just like mother used to make. Then come perfume and sweat, and finally other odors, more difficult for people to acknowledge even to themselves.

All of these are social turn-ons: sight, sound, smell, and

fetishes, which can happen anywhere during the most casual encounters. In the bedroom, they can be reinforced by powerful influences of mode and zone. Every man is to some extent a positionist, preferring a certain mode or position during intercourse, and every woman is a positura, ready to offer herself in a certain way. As noted in the introductory chapter, there are many manuals that list new positions for those who are tired of the old ones and are too tied up to discover others for themselves. Similarly, every man is an organist, preferring certain organs or body zones for his maximum excitement, and every woman an organa, with her own ideas of where she most likes to be touched or to receive. In some of the United States, intercourse other than in the vagina is illegal. But many religious authorities consider any kind of foresex permissible, as long as the ejaculation itself takes place in the vagina, so that even panorganas, women who enjoy all kinds of organic stimulation, can remain in good standing.

The ideal sexual mate for a man, then, is a woman with the right physical appearance, the right voice, and the right perfume, who dresses a certain way, and likes to have sex in a certain special position, freely using or making available certain parts of her body. The proper degree of initiative or activity, and compliance or passivity, is also very important. The turn-on is so powerful and so deeply ingrained that a marriage based on a complete turn-on, including all of the items given above, can stand all kinds of stresses and strains. But a marriage based on the turn-on alone can also turn out very badly, as men who marry call girls often discover when money problems arise. Nevertheless, it is very important to choose a mate from among the people who turn you on.

What has been discussed above may be called instant or primary turn-on. There are also two possible forms of delayed turn-on which can fortify a marriage mightily if the primary turn-on is weak. One is the conditioned delayed

turn-on. A man who likes good food and good care, for example, may get turned on every time he goes into the kitchen and sees his wife standing over the cookstove getting his dinner for him.[10] The more times he gets turned on by that, the more likely he is to carry the turn-on into bed. There are many other situations having nothing directly to do with sex in which a couple may turn each other on, and the more often that happens, the more likely they are to discover the buried sexual attractions in each other. This is something like what psychologists call conditioning, a relative of the conditioned reflexes that have to do with food.[11]

Secondary delayed turn-on occurs in couples who do not thrill each other sexually at first sight, sound, or touch, but who live together affectionately nonetheless. In the course of time, through accident, boldness, curiosity, or psychotherapy, they find certain things in each other that do turn them on, the buried sexual attractions referred to above. These may consist of certain kinds of naughty desires that they have kept hidden from each other, or even from themselves, and which turn out to be congenial to both of them. But the revelation of such a desire, when it is not congenial to the other party, may result in trouble, so there is a delicate balance here between boldness and discretion, Nevertheless, secondary turn-ons do often develop constructively in the course of time. They must be distinguished from phony turn-ons or one-sided lecheries, since both of those will end in turn-offs, which are worse than nothing.

The turn-on is what lends kicks and joy to a relationship and counteracts the drabness of living together with worry about finances and housekeeping, and petty job annoyances and drinking parties. Some people seek the turn-on by taking alcohol or drugs, but then it is the alcohol or drug that is doing the turning on and not the other person, and that can turn out badly in the long run. Certainly most women like to feel that they can turn on their husbands better than martinis or marijuana or a dose of LSD can.

If the turn-on is missing in a marriage, there is always the risk that some outside party will supply it. In a typical case, the wife does her duty and caters to her husband in some respects but is unable to go along with everything he asks for. On his side, he dare not ask for everything he wants, nor even admit some of his desires to himself. The wife tries hard and expects gratitude, and he in fairness to her tries to feel it. If he meets another woman who does more for him than he ever dreamed of, without "trying" and without expecting any gratitude, then the wife who has sacrificed so much pride in accommodating him feels that he is an ungrateful wretch. Or it may be the other way round, with the wife getting turned on by another man. In either case, the marriage is in deep trouble in this contest between upbringing and biology.

It is very difficult for a wife in her forties to face the fact that her husband's young mistress is giving him something she could give herself if she could cut loose from her early training. Most women in such situations would rather get a divorce than betray their parents by surrendering to their own and their husband's sexual desires, which after a lifetime of suppression seem strange, sinful, and scary, or just plain lecherous. So now let us turn our attention to the psychology of lechers.

J

LECHERY

Lechery is less spontaneous than a true turn-on, and more complicated. In fact, it is forced. An intelligent and alert lecher can actually hear the voices in his head which tell us the origin of his passion. It is the voice of a corrupt Parent saying that this is supposed to be exciting, and ordering the Child to get excited. (See Figure 17C).

The Child, of course, goes along with this because at first it is exciting. But the Parental voice keeps driving him beyond the limits of ordinary sexual endurance, so that he ends up exhausted and resentful.

This is openly declared in the Marquis de Sade's *Philosophy in a Bedroom*,[12] where the corrupt gang goads and prods the young girl again and again, and since it is her first experience, her ardor is almost, but not quite, inexhaustible. It then becomes clear that it is her father who is the source of her dogged persistence: it is not enough for him that his daughter is being thoroughly debauched by these experts, but he sends his wife along too and urges them to corrupt her as well. De Sade, of course, is fundamentally a coward in spite of his loud boastings, and he fails the crucial test: he does not allow incest with the mother, but calls in outside assistance to ravish and rot her. Nor does he explain this dereliction in the philosophy with which he fills in the time while waiting for the next erection.

Lechery, then, is a Child-to-Child relationship, in which neither party is interested in the other except as a technician, because they are really each following the instructions of the Parents in their heads: "More! More! Enjoy yourself, dammit! It's fun!" First the Child says, "It sure is," then he says, "I guess so," then, "I'm not so sure," and finally, "It isn't fun at all." Then like any red-blooded Child, he rebels, and rebellion in this case is repentance. That is why repentance is always more exciting than virtue; virtue is compliance, while repentance is rebellion against the corrupt Parent.

K

COMPANIONS

A companion literally is someone that you eat with. A comrade is someone that you share the same room

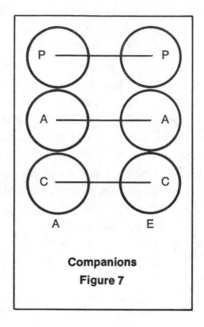

Companions
Figure 7

with (from the Spanish *cámara*, a room). A companion is someone whom you eat with, have fun with, talk with, and go out with. All the ego states of both parties are likely to be involved. Companions exchange Parental prejudices, give each other Adult advice, and have Child fun together (Figure 7). Companionship is a twosome and may or may not involve sex. Companions, however, are not necessarily concerned with each other's welfare, and the relationship may be temporary, as during a summer vacation, a ship's cruise, or a war. In these two respects it differs from friendship. Companions usually have a certain amount of respect and affection for each other. On the other hand, they may despise each other and go out together because they play the same psychological games.

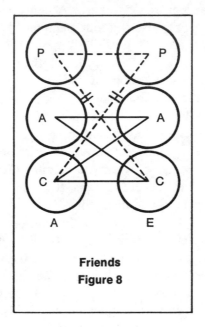

Friends
Figure 8

L

FRIENDS

The next step in relationship is friendship. The essence of friendship is that there is no active Parental ego state under ordinary conditions. That is, friends do not criticize each other in a Parent-to-Child way, although they may give each other advice. But this advice is not fingershaking, it is a rational, factual statement, Adult-to-Adult or Adult-to-Child, as in Figure 8. A friend does not say (Parentally), "Smoking marijuana is awful, and only degenerate people do it. I'm only telling you that as a friend." A real friend

says, "You know you can get a rap of up to twenty years for doing that openly. I'd miss you if you were away that long."

Friends "accept" each other. "Accept" is one of those words most people use without defining clearly, like "togetherness," "sharing," "hostility," "dependency," and "passive." If you ask them what they mean, they say, "You know what I mean," and get angry if you say you don't. The reason they get angry is that they don't know what they mean and they are relying on you to know. If you say you don't, you have left them stranded, and so they get angry. The only way to be sure you understand an abstract noun is to draw a diagram or picture of what you mean. I think Figure 8 is a diagram of what "accept" means. It means that the critical Parent is crossed out and decommissioned.

There are two exceptions to this, however, where two people can be friends even with active Parental ego states. The first occurs in any emergency where the caring Parent, but not the critical Parent, becomes active, so that if you really get hurt a friend might show you some sympathy and take care of you without damaging the friendship. But if the caring Parent is always there meddling around, trying to help you when you don't want to be helped, then that's not going to be a very good friendship. That is one way mothers keep from being friends with their children. Even if the critical Parent is restrained, they overcare and interfere, giving help when it is not wanted.

Another way in which friendship can survive an active Parent, even a critical one, is to criticize other people but not each other. Already given was the classical example of the "committee members," who can be good friends just because "nowadays everything is awful (except us)." What they are doing is repeating things their mothers and fathers taught them, and if their Parents agree, they will agree, even if nothing they say makes sense or has been critically evaluated. So you don't have to say anything sensible to have a friend, providing you both believe in the same nonsense.

A friend is basically a more solid form of companion. Friends may eat together, live together, talk together, have fun together, and go out together. But in addition they stay together for life and help each other in time of need.

To paraphrase Proust, a friend is one who has the same illusions you have, so he won't hurt your feelings when he finds out you have them, too.

—
M
—

INTIMACY

The closer together people get, the more independent and self-contained their relation becomes. Therefore the closest relationships are the ones that we know least about. People have been trying to define intimacy, for example, for 5,000 years, with little success up to the present. By using the idea of ego states, however, I think we can say more about it now than anybody has been able to say previously.

Intimacy is a candid Child-to-Child relationship with no games and no mutual exploitation. It is set up by the Adult ego states of the parties concerned, so that they understand very well their contracts and commitments with each other, sometimes without a word being spoken about such matters. As this understanding becomes clearer, the Adult gradually retires from the scene, and if the Parent does not interfere, the Child becomes more and more relaxed and freer and freer. The actual intimate transactions take place between the two Child ego states. The Adult, however, still remains in the background as an overseer to assure that the commitments and limitations are kept. The Adult also has the task of keeping the Parent from barging in and spoiling the situation. In fact the capacity for intimacy depends upon the ability of the Adult and the Child to keep the Parent at

bay if necessary; but it is even better if the Parent benevolently gives permission or, best of all, encouragement, for the relationship to proceed. Parental encouragement helps the Child lose his fear of intimacy, and assures that he will not be restrained by a burden or threat of guilt.

The reality of this dialogue between the three ego states can be checked by any alert person who is about to embark on an intimate relationship. If he listens carefully to the voices in his head, he will hear the Child exclaiming his desire to go ahead and get to know the person better, his Adult saying, "I think you have found the right one," and his Parent either grumbling about some aspect like social standing or religion, or throwing in some approving comment such as: "You deserve to enjoy yourself on your vacation, just so you work hard when you get back," at which the Child nods eagerly and promises that he will.

Once the Child is free of Adult caution and Parental criticism, he has a sense of elation and awareness. He begins to see and hear and feel the way he really wants to, the way he originally did before he was corrupted by his living parents. In this autonomous state, he no longer has to name things, as is usually required by his Adult, nor account for his behavior, as demanded by his Parent. He is free to respond directly and spontaneously to what he sees and hears and feels. Because the two parties trust one another, they freely open up their secret worlds of perception, experience, and behavior to each other, asking nothing in return except the delight of opening the gates without fear.

In order to have this kind of relation, the Child must cut loose from the inner Parent for the same reason that he must be away from his actual parents. Carefree sexual enjoyment and intimacy, for example, would be almost impossible if one of his actual parents were standing behind him, and the same difficulties arise if the inner Parent becomes active as a phantom in the bedroom. He must also cut loose from his Adult because his Adult expects him to make sense. Making

sense is one of the first ways in which parents corrupt their children. For instance, they do not for long allow them to listen with pure and spontaneous enjoyment. Sooner or later, when the baby is listening to a bird song, the father or mother will say "Birdie, birdie," and then the baby has to say "Birdie, birdie." Later, he may have to learn to tell the difference between a sparrow and a jay. This Adult activity distracts his Child from listening. Of course, such teaching is necessary and valuable, and the baby could not survive into grownup years without it. What goes wrong in most cases is that the person is never again able to suspend this Adult data processing, so that after early infancy, most people never again really hear a bird singing.

The same happens with looking. Parents teach children that they are not allowed to stare at people because that is rude, unless they are doing it for a specific purpose, perhaps in the course of a professional activity such as hairdressing, dermatology, or psychiatry.* The result is that most human beings never really see another person after they are five years old. In an intimate relationship, each party returns to the original naïve Child ego state, where he is free of such Parental prohibitions and Adult requirements, and can see, hear, and taste in its purest form what the world has to offer. This freedom of the Child is the essential part of intimacy, and it turns the whole universe, including the sun, moon, and stars, into a golden apple for both parties to enjoy.

There is also such a thing as one-sided intimacy, in which

---

*Professionals are allowed to stare because the client implicitly gives them permission to do so when he engages their services. In other words, certain professional contracts carry a built-in staring license. The Parent of the professional relaxes the anti-staring rule as long as the staring is part of the job, i.e., Adult. But sometimes the Child takes advantage of this relaxation to steal a look too. A crooked Parent may even go along with this abuse of the staring license, offering an interesting example of the lechery mechanism shown in Figure 17C. Therefore, whether or not the cheating Child feels guilty depends on whether the Parent (of the same or sometimes of the opposite sex) is or is not lecherous.

one party is ready for it and the other resists it. This is something like Balzac's typical situation in which one party is ready for love, and loves, while the other merely permits himself to be loved. Such a setup can be exploited by unscrupulous people for their own advantage. Many prostitutes and courtesans* know how to free the open and intimate Child in men without lowering their own guard, and pimps and predatory men can exploit women in the same way.

The "intimacy experiment," in which two people sit close to each other "eyeball to eyeball,"† and keep eye contact while talking straight to each other reveals many interesting things about intimacy.[13] First, it demonstrates that any two people of either sex, starting as strangers or mere acquaintances, can attain intimacy in fifteen minutes or so under proper conditions. Secondly, it shows that any two people who really look at each other, and really see each other, and talk straight to each other, always (as far as these and similar "encounters" go) end up liking each other.[14] This indicates that dislikes result from (1) people not really seeing each other and/or (2) people not talking straight to each other. The greatest preventive of intimacy seems to be a critical Parent, and next to that, a crooked Child. This is instructive as far as it goes, but further investigation is necessary before any firm conclusions can be drawn.

In fairness to parents, however, it should be said that there are many who successfully teach their children to see and hear more and better, to be open to intimacy, and to distinguish it from sexuality.

---

*Roughly speaking, at the going rates, a common prostitute is one whose fee is up to $100 in advance. A high-class prostitute is one whose fee is over $100 in money or goods, not in advance. A courtesan is one whose fee is high enough so that it takes a lawyer to draw up the papers.

†This procedure was first systematically studied at the San Francisco Transactional Analysis Seminar about ten years ago. Since then it has become a standard part of the repertoire of "encounter" groups. It was amusing recently to have it demonstrated to me by an "Encounterer" who was unaware of its history.

—
N
—

LOVE

Love is defined in many ways, and I will not review them here. In Greek there are *eros*, *philos*, and *agape*: desire, friendship, and affection. Since our subject is sex, I will talk about eros, the desire and intoxication of sexual love.

Sexual love, being sexual, will be full of lust, or better, lustiness; and being love, it will partake of that which sets true love apart from all other relations—and that is putting the welfare and happiness of the other person before one's own. Love is the most complete and noblest relationship of them all, and includes the best of all the others: respect, admiration, turn-on, friendship and intimacy, all in one, with its own grace or charisma added.

Such a relation can exist only if the Parent, with its watchful eyes and hearing aids, and the Adult, with its dreary prudence, are out of commission, and that is exactly the situation when people fall in love. At the moment they do so, they cease to regard each other with prosaic prejudice or to restrain their buxom behavior with more than a bare minimum of sweet reason. Love is Child-to-Child: an even more primitive Child than the intimate one, for the Child of intimacy sees things as they are, in all their pristine beauty, while the Child of love adds something to that and gilds the lily with a luminous halo invisible to everyone but the lover. This is a primal vision, the way the infant, I think, sees his mother: not only as the most beautiful object or person in this world, but with a shimmering radiance that outshines all other worlds.

This resembles the radiance that some people see with

LSD. The difference is that in mutual love there are two people involved, and they are involved with each other out there rather than with what is going on inside their own heads. Drugs are instead of people, and people are better than drugs. The person who takes LSD is intoxicated, while the person in love is in the purest state possible: he is detoxified of both Parental corruption and Adult misgivings, and his Child is free to embark on the greatest adventure open to the human race, next to the moon. In the intoxication of drugs, he is in the grip of an impersonal and inhuman force that will not listen and has no interest in his welfare. In the detoxication of love, he is in the grip of the most personal reality there is: someone whose greatest delight is to listen not only to his words but to the cadence of his voice, and whose greatest interest is precisely in his happiness and welfare. Love is a sweet trap from which no one departs without tears.

Some say one-sided love is better than none, but like half a loaf of bread, it is likely to grow hard and moldy sooner.

O

CLASSIFYING RELATIONSHIPS

Although some relationships are pure, a great many are mixed and not easy to classify. If they are looked at moment by moment, however, they fall into place. The following example will illustrate some of the difficulties and subtleties, and how they can be solved by means of relationship diagrams.

Susan, a young lady in her twenties who loved babies and had a strong nesting instinct, had always backed off from men because she feared them and their sexuality. She was progressing from acquaintances with whom she played games

so as to disrupt the relationship before it became threatening, toward intimacy and love. On the way, we had the following conversation:

Susan: I get along well with Roger, but it's not love, it's just cuffing. We're very good friends, but he might as well be my brother. He fixes things around the house and then we go to bed. I'm not afraid of sex any more, but there's not much more to it than that.

Doctor: Too bad there has to be a man at the other end of the penis.

Susan: Yes, it would be much simpler if there wasn't. If I could have a penis to play with and a man to take care of me, I'd be okay.

In the language of transactional analysis, Susan wants Roger to oscillate between being a nurturing Parent, a helpful Adult, and a sexy Child, while she remains in a Child ego state throughout. According to her description, the relation sounds like companionship or friendship, but there are certain differences from both. Companionship (Figure 7) is a "straight-across" relationship, Parent-to-Parent, Adult-to-Adult, and Child-to-Child, while this one has some oblique vectors. Companionship is symmetrical, in that both parties are equal, while the Susan-Roger relationship is not. Friendship (Figure 8) has oblique vectors, but these only rarely involve the Parent, whereas the Parent is a necessary part of the Susan-Roger relation. In addition, friendship is symmetrical and Susan-Roger is not.

We can break the S-R relationship into its three aspects as described by Susan, in which she remains always in the Child ego state (Figures 9, 10, and 11), while Roger switches from one to another. If we bring these three diagrams together, we get a picture of the overall relationship (Figure 12). This can be used to predict what the possibilities are. It does not look like a good diagram for co-workers (A-A) nor for marriage (which needs more than three vectors to work well), and we have already discussed the difficulties in

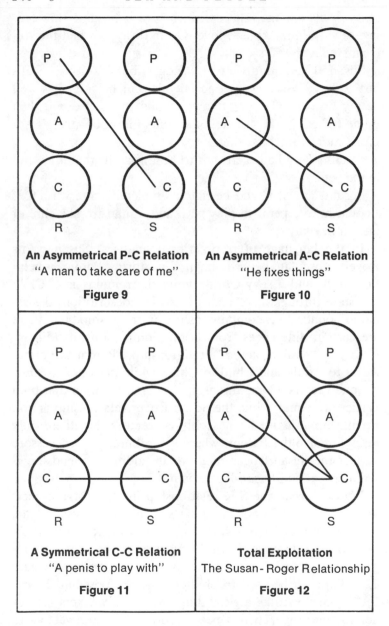

An Asymmetrical P-C Relation
"A man to take care of me"
Figure 9

An Asymmetrical A-C Relation
"He fixes things"
Figure 10

A Symmetrical C-C Relation
"A penis to play with"
Figure 11

Total Exploitation
The Susan-Roger Relationship
Figure 12

the way of true companionship or friendship. Intimacy and love are not likely either, because of its asymmetry. For those, Susan must change, either through psychotherapy or by meeting a different kind of man, so that she can overcome her Child's fear and meet him as an equal. Thus we can predict that the S-R relationship will be (and should be) only temporary, which it was. Although Roger got some satisfaction out of it, including sexual, from her side it was a relation of total exploitation in which she used all three of his ego states for her own needs without offering anything in return except what he could forage.

It is clear that sex can find a place in any of the relationships mentioned in this chapter, which gives us the following list, with a few comments about some of the items.

Acquaintance or casual sex. This may occur "by accident," on impulse, for money, to prove something, to "show somebody," or as a pastime in special situations of boredom.

Co-worker or office sex. This is common between workers in the same echelon. Most business men avoid it on the principle that it is easier to find another good mistress than another good secretary. Wise secretaries avoid it on the same principle that it is easier to find a good boy friend than a good boss. Aside from ethical considerations, therapists— and wise patients—avoid it for similar reasons. It is easier for a therapist to find a good girl friend than to find another good patient. And it is obviously easier for a patient to find a good boy friend than to find another good therapist, since there are millions of eligible bachelors in this country, but only a few thousand competent shrinks.

Committee sex. This is a matter of propinquity and individual preference. It may work in a working committee, but in an "Ain't It Awful" committee it is likely to be awful.

Respect sex. This is risky even if both parties are unmarried and sure of their potency. If it is not completely straight and completely satisfying, respect is soon cremated in the heat of ill-spent passion, and the ashes of respect are the

burning embers of scorn. Such an ill death of something so fine is seldom worth the hazard.

Admiration sex. This is a good way to get an autograph from an admired one.

Affectionate sex is groovy.

Companionable sex. A good way to share the room rent, some people think.

Friendly sex. Nothing interferes with friendship like sex, and nothing interferes with sex like friendship.

Intimate sex is wow.

Loving sex. Sexual fluids make a good cement, and they also produce babies.

—
P
—

MARRIAGE

Marriage may be based on or involve any of the situations previously discussed, and I will not attempt a formal analysis of this difficult relationship, which results in 500,000 divorces per year in this country alone. (The moral of this, obviously, is that the sovereign remedy for divorce is to abolish marriage.) But I would like to suggest a very artificial classification that has two advantages as far as it goes: it is not misleading, and it is easy to remember. It is based on letters of the alphabet: A H I O S V X and Y.

An A marriage starts off as a shotgun or makeshift one. The couple are far apart, but soon they find a single common bond, perhaps the new baby. This is represented by the crossbar of the A. As time goes on, they get closer and closer until they finally come together, and then they have a going concern. This is represented by the apex of the A.

An H marriage starts off the same way, but the couple never gets any closer, and the marriage is held together by

a single bond. Otherwise they each go where they were originally headed.

An I marriage starts off and ends with the couple forged into a single unit.

An O marriage goes round and round in a circle, never getting anywhere, and repeating the same patterns until it is terminated by death or separation.

An S marriage wanders around seeking happiness, and eventually ends up slightly above and to the right of where it started, but it never gets any farther than that, leaving both parties disappointed and bewildered, and good candidates for psychotherapy, since there is enough there so that they don't want a divorce.

A V marriage starts off with a close couple, but they immediately begin to diverge, perhaps after the honeymoon is over or even after the first night.

An X marriage starts off like an A. At one point there is a single period of bliss. They wait for it to happen again, but it never does, and soon they drift apart again, never to reunite.

A Y marriage starts off well, but difficulties multiply, and eventually each one finds his own separate interests and goes his own way.

There are undoubtedly many other types of marriages, but they do not fit into the alphabet we use, so they will have to be left for a more complicated system of classification.

Q

LEGAL RELATIONSHIPS

In contrast to the structural or ego state system of classifying relationships, let us briefly discuss the sexual aspects of the legal system of classification. Personal rela-

tions have been under continual scrutiny and definition by this profession ever since Roman times, and even before that to some extent. Besides the four main classes generally mentioned in law books,[15] we have included a fifth because, although it is not primarily a personal relationship, it easily becomes one.

HUSBAND AND WIFE

Sex is not only permitted between husband and wife, but it is more or less compulsory. If a marriage is not "consummated" that may be grounds for annulment. On the other hand, in many states there are strict limits to the kinds of sex which are permissible in marriage. Anything but face to face vaginal copulation may be called "a crime against nature" and constitute a felony with the penalty of imprisonment. Thus, legally speaking, one sexual act face to face makes a marriage, while any other form of intercourse turns both parties into criminals.

PARENT AND CHILD

Sexual intercourse between parent and child is forbidden because that constitutes incest, even after the child is grown up. The only sexual pleasures permitted by law are extreme perversions or far-out procedures justified as morality or hygiene. A father is allowed to spank his children, including his daughters, with or without their clothes on. A mother is allowed to give her son daily enemas (and a father his daughter) even without a doctor's orders. A father is legally permitted to lift up his daughter's dress when she returns from a date to see whether she has had intercourse. And both parents are allowed to do stripteases and go to the bathroom in the presence of their children.

GUARDIAN AND WARD

This includes many complex legal situations. Generally speaking, guardian and ward are not supposed to have sex with each other. In some cases it is expressly forbidden, in others it may be permissible and may be one of the pleasures of such a legal relationship. If the ward is a minor, the same perversions may be permitted as in the case of parent and child.

MASTER AND SERVANT

This may include master and apprentice, teacher and pupil. It is an established principle (or at least it happens frequently) that a master may have sex with his servants or a mistress with hers, and if the consequences are unfortunate the servant is then entitled to the redress provided by common law. Thus such relations are a form of manor house roulette. When the girl's number fails to come up, the master loses. In the old days when teachers kept their distance from their pupils, sex between them was regarded askance. But as the relationship becomes more intimate, sex becomes more and more common and accepted. Boss and secretary is a common sexual relationship, even in the face of good sense, but such double contracts are chancy. Many a woman can be either a good secretary or a good mistress, but it is not easy to be both to the same man, and often the two vocations interfere with each other.

SUPPLIER AND CLIENT

There are no laws specifically prohibiting a businessman from having sexual relationships with his customers, but there are certain professional relations of a "fiduciary" nature. There the client is in the hands of the supplier and

tends to rely on his judgment and take his advice, since that is the commodity being paid for. This is the case between lawyers or social workers and their clients, and between doctors or psychotherapists and their patients. It is considered unethical and sometimes illegal for the professional person to have affairs with his clients or patients. A few therapists do it on the principle that their patients will get better faster, but it rarely works that way. In the majority of cases it damages the therapeutic relationship and the patient gets worse.

What is wrong is that love is not included in the contract. The patient is paying for treatment and not for sex. Some therapists and lawyers get around the ethical problem by waiting until the case is "finished," and then have sex with their clients. This may be legal but it is certainly not ethical. Sometimes the supplier has sex with his clients and is also getting paid for his services, thus reducing himself to the level of a drug peddler or gigolo.

It can be seen that the legal classification of relations offers some possibilities for thought, but it is not as consistent nor as intellectually satisfying as the transactional approach. Nor does it offer any advantages for analysis, understanding, or prediction. It is actually more cynical than scientific. Much the same applies to other systems in common use. Psychoanalysis can analyze relationships but not meaningfully classify them, and the analyses are much more cumbersome than the transactional ones.

The Appendix to this book gives further information about classifying relationships in a more formal way.

NOTES AND REFERENCES

1. Berne, E.: *Transactional Analysis in Psychotherapy*, op. cit.
2. Dutch, R. A. (ed.): *Roget's Thesaurus*. St. Martin's Press, New York, 1963.
3. Liddell, H. G., and Scott, R.: *Greek-English Lexicon*. Clarendon Press, Oxford, 1883.

4. I try to avoid the word "relationship" as much as possible, along with several other words which have degenerated into shibboleths of psychosocial work jargon. An exception is made whenever one of these words can be represented reasonably rigorously in a diagram. The word "relationship" is used here specifically to mean that which is represented by its structural relationship diagram.

5. This is what actually happened when one cancer ward was transformed from a Home for Incurables (there actually was an institution by that name in Montreal, Canada, when I was a boy, and even then I knew there was something wrong with the idea) into a cooperative community where everybody had his job to do. Instead of lying in bed feeling miserable day after day as they waited for death, the patients actually began to have fun as they came back to life, even though death still awaited them, as it does every man. See: "Terminal Cancer Ward: Patients Build Atmosphere of Dignity." *Journal of the American Medical Association* 208:1289, May 26, 1969. Also Klagsbrun, S. C.: "Cancer, Emotions, and Nurses." *Summary of Scientific Proceedings*, 122nd Annual Meeting, American Psychiatric Association, Washington, 1969.

6. Lorenz, K. Z.: *King Solomon's Ring*. Translated by N. K. Wilson. Thomas Y. Crowell Company, New York, 1952.

7. This discussion of symbolism differs from the psychoanalytic view as expressed in the classical paper of Ernest Jones, "The Theory of Symbolism." In E. Jones, *Papers on Psycho-Analysis*. Beacon Press, Boston, 1961.

8. Ford, C. S. and Beach, F. A.: *Patterns of Sexual Behavior*. Harper & Brothers, New York, 1951.

9. The concept of "odorless smells," chemicals "broadcast" through the air by the body of one person, which can affect the behavior of other people without their being aware of what has happened, is not a metaphysical one. In the first place, such chemicals would work exactly the same as body odors, except that the recipient would not smell anything. Secondly, odorless gases such as carbon monoxide and certain military gases, and radioactivity, which is also odorless, can certainly affect behavior, although their effects are due to pathological changes. Thirdly, insects such as moths broadcast such substances, and these must be inhaled by moth and man alike, but man is not aware of their presence. In the case of insects, they are called pheromones, hormones which stimulate physiological or behavioral responses from another individual of the same species. The species' specificity depends on the presence of specific ketones.

Whether the male moth "smells" the pheromones given off

by the female there is no way of knowing. It is known, however, that the olfactory receptors are affected by them. This can
be established by taking electroantennograms. (Schneider, D.,
and Seibt, U.: "Sex Pheromone of the Queen Butterfly: Elec-
troantennogram Responses." *Science* 164:1173-1174, June 9,
1969.)

10. I have referred to the conditioned turn-on as "possible" because I do not have the clinical material to support it. What I
have said about it sounds plausible and is certainly hopeful.
Unfortunately, when I asked a recent divorcée about it, she
replied, "Emphatically no! It just doesn't work that way!" with
a clear implication that she knew because she had tried it in
her own kitchen. So it is just left as a possibility, for what it is
worth as a comfort to worried wives, experimental psychologists, and behavioral therapists.

11. Pavlov, I. P.: *Conditioned Reflexes and Psychiatry*. Translated
by W. H. Gantt. International Publishers, New York, 1941.

12. de Sade, D. A. F.: op. cit.

13. Berne, E.: "The Intimacy Experiment." *Transactional Analysis Bulletin* 3:113, 1964, and "More About Intimacy," ibid.
3:125, 1964.

14. While in these "experiments" the word used was "like," there
is something more to it because of the strange after-relation-
ship so often described in literature between torturers (official
or unofficial) and their victims if they really look at each other
and really talk straight to each other.

15. The California Civil Code is the basis for this discussion, although it has not been strictly followed.

5

SEXUAL
GAMES

A

INTRODUCTION: IT'S A CRAZY WORLD

Sex can be enjoyed in solitude or in groups, or in couples as an act of intimacy, a passion, a relief, a duty, or just a way to pass the time to ward off and postpone the evil day of boredom, that Boredom which is the pimp of Death and brings to him sooner or later all its victims, whether by disease, accident, or intent. For the truth of the matter is not that time is passing, but that we are passing through time. It is not what they said in olden days, a river on whose banks we stand and watch, but a sea we have to cross, either in solitary labor and watchfulness, like crossing the Atlantic in a rowboat, or crowded together over the engine oil and the automatic pilot with nothing to do but play some form of drunk or sober shuffleboard. Only a few glide in splendor

with sail unfurled in a lugger or a sloop or something grander, ahoy and belay there! up with the mizzen royal of our full-rigged five-master—the only one ever built to sail the Seven Seas! And it is still possible to fly nonstop, without being much bothered by what happens down below.

In the cities and in the country there are millions of birds, and how many of you with full awareness heard one of them sing today? In the cities and in the country there are thousands of trees, and how many of you with full awareness saw one today? Here is a nonstop story of my own. About five times a week, I walked from my office to the post office in the little village where I live. I walked by the same route for two years, about 500 trips, before one day I noticed two hairy palm trees with a cactus growing between them on a corner that I passed. I had gone by this rugged delight 499 times in a row without being aware that anything was growing there, because I was preoccupied with getting to the post office to pick up my mail so I could go back to my office and answer the letters so I could go to the post office and pick up the replies to my answers so I could answer the replies so I could go to the post office and pick up more mail to answer. My time was mortgaged to a self-imposed burden that I could never pay off but could at any moment, whenever I wished, tear up, and put the pieces carefully in one of the trash cans considerately provided by the village council so I would not litter the streets.

I thought of this one time lying in bed in a hotel in Vienna listening to the quiet of the night and then to the first rustles of life at dawn, the slow waltz of Vienna in the morning. First the six o'clock people danced out to prepare the way for the seven o'clock people, who got ready for the eight o'clock people who take care of the nine o'clock people.* These open their stores and offices so that shopping and business calls can begin at ten, so that the stores can be

---

*Six: bus-drivers, I guess. Seven: cooks, I guess. Eight: waitresses, some of them.

closed at twelve so that people can go home and get ready for lunch, so that they can re-open at two so they can close at five, so that they can get home by six to dress for dinner at seven so they can get to the theater by eight, so that they can get home by eleven to get a good night's sleep so they will be in good shape when they get up again in the morning at five, six, seven, or eight.

And there is a song about Sunday, when they are not bound by all this, and how on that day some of them jump into the Danube, which is a river and carries them in its flow as time does not. For time is not a river, but a sea that must be crossed, from the shore of bawling birth to the littered coast of death. And this is not a fancy of song writers, this fascination of the waters (Nepenthes en tw potamouth-anatw),* for in Vienna each year about 500 people kill themselves. Do you know which country has the highest suicide rate in the world? Hungary. That's Communism for you. Do you know which country has the second highest rate? Austria. That's democracy for you. Actually, since they're both on the same river, that's the Danube for you. Which Communist people have a lower suicide rate than white democratic Americans, but higher than nonwhite democratic Americans? The Poles, that's who.[2]

Since time does not pass, it must be passed through, and that means always scheduled or structured. Don't just sit there, do something! What shall we do this morning, this afternoon, tonight? Mom, there's nothing to do. He doesn't do anything. I've got lots to do. Get up, you lazy loafer. Awritechuguys, getcherasses outabed. Don't do anything, just sit there, and for one million dollars an hour I'll fill in

---

*Okay, here's what it means. Nepenthes, nowadays shortened to Ne-penthe, is a potion which brings forgetfulness of all pains, quarrels, griefs, and troubles.[1] Helen of Troy got some from an Egyptian's daughter and used it to spike wine. From that description in Book IV of the *Odyssey*, it sounds not unlike some form of hashish. The rest I made up myself. The root Potam- means a river, as in hippopotamus, and Thanat- means death. So it means that river-death is a drink to end all troubles.

your time on Channel 99. A million? He's worth it, man. Pay him two million if you can.

Sex may be an essential ingredient in structuring time, although eunuchs find plenty to do, don't they? Old Abdul the sick man of Europe and Asia sitting on Seraglio Point looking for excitement—you can't trust them, they've got hands and other ways, chop off their scrotums and what good does it do? Sex is in the head, it's not all in the scrotum by any means. You'll find that out the hard way, and then you'll have to tread slowly to satisfy your lust and have your bust. They say I'm Abdul the Cruel but I just have a sensual sense of humor, carry me back to old Istanbul and the randy life on the Golden Horn, get the girls out of the sordid honky-tonks and into the wholesome harems, I mean out of the sordid harems and into the wholesome honky-tonks. Have it your own way, Dad.

Meaning there's more to life than sex, you can't do it all the time, you can't even think of it all the time, animals do it only in the spring and fall, the rest of the time it's eat eat eat, who wants to be an animal? *Vive la différence!* The difference being that for people there is something more important than essential ingredients, eating and sex, and they think of it—the difference—between eating and between sex, and that is being me, I, myself. More than eating and more than sex (which are necessary, but not sufficient) I want to be a Self, and I am a Self. Unfortunately, for the most part, this is an illusion.

—
B
—

PARENTAL PROGRAMMING

From the beginning, man does what he is told. Most animals don't. That is really the difference, and as usual it is the opposite of what people usually say. Sexy men

are called (by some) animals, when men are by nature sexier than animals, and an unsexy animal would certainly not be called a man. Vicious men are also called animals, but animals are not vicious for the most part, just hungry. And man is called free, when actually he is the most compliant of all animals.

Some animals can be trained to perform a stunt here and there, but not tamed. Other animals can be tamed and also trained to perform a stunt here and there. But man is tamed from the beginning, and spends his whole life performing stunts for his masters: Mom and Pop first, and then teacher, and after that whoever can grab him and teach him feats of war and revolution or stunts of peace. Revolution, ha! Buzz off, Alex. Now I'm walking the wire in Joe's show instead. Foo, Manchu! It's Mao now for this brown kao.* Believe, work, and obey. I can't believe Manny so I'll obey Benny. I'm free to walk a mile to say Heil, hit the trail or go on trial, reach the goal or go to gaol. Man is programmed to obey, obey, obey, obey the obedient, or obey the civil or uncivil disobedients. Form a line on the right, left, don't straggle. Straggle, don't form a line. Which side shall I straggle on? Which side shall I struggle on? Don't struggle. Tune in, turn on, drop out. That's an order! Don't listen to those other pigs. Listen to your own pigs. Be anarchistic. Be independent, dammit. Be original, no no, not that way, this way. It's imperative that you enjoy yourself and be spontaneous.

Here's how it happens.

From earliest months, the child is taught not only what to do, but also what to see, hear, touch, think, and feel. And beyond that, he is also told whether to be a winner or a loser, and how his life will end. All these instructions are programmed into his mind and his brain just as firmly as though they were punch cards put into the bank of a computer. In

* I mean ☰, lamb.

later years, what he thinks of as his independence or his autonomy is merely his freedom to select certain cards, but for the most part the same old punch holes stay there that were put there at the beginning. Some people get an exhilarating sense of freedom by rebelling, which usually means one of two things: either they pull out a bunch of cards punched in early childhood which they have never used before, or they turn some of the cards inside out and do the opposite of what they say. Often this merely amounts to following the instructions on a special card which says: "When you are 18 (or 40) use this new bunch of cards, or turn the following cards inside out." Another kind of rebellion follows the instructions: "When you are 18 (or 40), throw away all cards in series A and leave a vacuum." This vacuum then has to be filled as quickly as possible with new instant programs, which are obtained from drugs or from a revolutionary leader. Thus in their efforts to avoid becoming fatheads or eggheads, these people end up being acid-heads or spite-heads.

In any case, each person obediently ends up at the age of five or six—yes, ends up at five or six—with a script or life plan largely dictated by his parents. It tells him how he's going to carry on his life, and how it's going to end, winner, non-winner, or loser. Will it be in the big room surrounded by his loved ones, or with his bed crowded out into the corridor of the City Hospital, or falling like a lead bird into the chilled choppy waters of the Golden Gate? At five or six he doesn't know all that, but he knows about victorious lions and lonely corridors and dead fish in cold water. And he also knows enough to come in first or second like his father or his dad, or to come in last like his old man, he sure can hold his liquor. This is a free country, but don't stare. We got free speech, so listen to me. If you don't watch out for yourself nobody else'll watch out for you, but (a) no, no, mussen-touchit, or (b) getcher cotton pickin' hans off my money, or (c) you gonna grow up to be a thief or something?

Well, hit him back. You hit him wrong. Say you're sorry. Watch out. I'll give you something to cry about, you little monster. Feel angry, inadequate, guilty, scared, hurt. I'll teach you how to think as well as how to feel. Don't think such thoughts. Think it over until you see it my way. I'll show you how to do it, too. Here's how to get away with it. You don't know what to be when you grow up? I'll tell you what to be. Be good. Do as you're told, Adolf, and don't ask questions. Be different. Why can't you be like other kids?

So, having learned what not to see, what not to hear, and what not to touch, and which feelings to have, and how not to think, and what not to be, the child sallies forth to school. There he meets teachers and his own kind. It is called a grade school, but it is really a law school. By the time he is ten (the age that lawyers are stuck at) he is an accomplished pettifogger in his own defense. He has to be, especially if he is mean or naughty. You said not to write over the stuff on the blackboard, but you didn't say don't erase it (or vice versa). You said not to take her candy, but you didn't say not to take her chewing gum. You told me not to say bad words to Cousin Mary, but you didn't say not to undress her. You told me not to lie on top of girls, but you didn't say anything about boys.

Later, in high school, come the real script setups. "Don't go to a drive-in. You'll get pregnant!" Up to that time she didn't know how to go about getting pregnant. Now she knows. But she is not ready yet. She has to wait for the signal. "Don't go to a drive-in, you'll get pregnant, until I give you the signal." She knows mother was sixteen when she was born, and pretty soon figures she must have been conceived out of wedlock. Naturally, mother gets very nervous when daughter passes her sixteenth birthday. One day mother says: "Summer is the worst time. That's when most high school girls get pregnant" (generalizing from her own experience). That's the signal. So daughter goes to a drive-in and gets pregnant.

"Don't go into a men's room because you'll meet a bad man there who'll do something nasty to you," father says to his eight-year-old son. He repeats it about once a year. So when the time comes, the boy wonders what the nasty thing is, and he knows where to go to find out. Another father packed not only the sex instructions but the whole life script into one pubertal sentence. "Don't let me catch you going to that house on Bourbon Street, where there are women who'll do anything you want for five dollars." Since the boy didn't have five dollars, he stole it out of his mother's purse, intending to go to Bourbon Street the following afternoon. But mother happened to count her money that same night and found it where the boy had hidden it, and he was caught and punished. He learned his lesson well. "If I'd gone down right after dinner instead of putting it off until the next day, everything would've been all right." He wouldn't have been caught with the five dollars. This is a good non-winner script. If you want women, get money. Spend it as quickly as possible, before you get caught. You can't win, but you can certainly keep from losing.

The loser's instructions generally read something like this: "If at first you don't succeed, try, try, try again. Even if you win a few, keep trying, and you're bound to lose in the end, because you can't win 'em all." The winner's read: "Why lose at all? If you lose, it means you played wrong. So do it again until you learn to do it right."

If it is not interfered with by some decisive force, the script will be carried through to the sweet or bitter end. There are three such forces. The greatest script-breakers are massive events which lumber inexorably down the path of history: wars, famines, epidemics, and oppression, which overtake and crush everyone before them like cosmic steamrollers, save for those who are licensed to clamber aboard and use them as bandwagons. The second is psychotherapy and other conversions, which break up scripts and make losers into non-winners ("Making progress") and

non-winners into winners ("Getting well," "Flipping in," and "Seeing the light").

In rare cases, a third force takes over, and the script is broken up by an autonomous decision or re-decision of the person himself. This happens with people whose script allows them to make an autonomous decision. The clearest example in recent times is Mao Tse-tung, head of the Chinese People's Republic, who started out as a middle-class person with a middle-class script, and by his own inner struggle became what he defines as a real proletarian, so that he felt comfortable in that role and uncomfortable in his middle-class script role, which due to the *force majeure* of Chinese history was a loser's role.[3] By flipping in with history, he became a winner in war and in politics, and in literature as well, since few if any authors in modern times are as widely read as he is in his own lifetime.

It is important to note that the script is not "unconscious" and can be easily unearthed by a skillful questioner or by careful self-questioning. It is only that most people are reluctant to admit the existence of such a life plan and prefer to demonstrate their independence by playing games— games that are themselves dictated by their scripts.

C
—

TYPES OF SCRIPTS

Scripts are designed to last a lifetime. They are based on firm childhood decisions and parental programming that is continually reinforced. The reinforcement may take the form of daily contact, as with men who work for their fathers or women who telephone their mothers every morning to gossip, or it may be applied less frequently and more subtly, but just as powerfully, through occasional cor-

respondence. After the parents die, their instructions may be remembered more vividly than ever.

In script language, a loser is called a frog[4] and a winner is called a prince or a princess. Parents want their children to be either winners or losers. They may want them to be "happy" in the role they have chosen for them, but do not want them to be transformed except in special cases. A mother who is raising a frog may want her daughter to be a happy frog, but will put down any attempts of the girl to become a princess ("Who do you think you are?"), because mother herself was programmed to raise her as a frog. A father who is raising a prince wants his son to be happy, but often he would rather see him unhappy than transformed into a frog ("We've given you the best of everything").

A winner is defined as a person who fulfills his contract with the world and with himself. That is, he sets out to do something, says that he is committed to doing it, and in the long run does it. His contract, or ambition, may be to have four children, become the president of a corporation, pole vault 17′, publish a good novel, make an artificial gene, or shoot down ten enemy bombers. If he accomplishes his goal, he is a winner. If he has no children, stays in the warehouse, sprains his back at 16′, stays with the newspaper, ends up with a lump of gristle, or gets shot down on his first mission, he is clearly a loser. If he has three children, becomes a vice president, hits 16′11″, publishes a mystery story, discovers a new amino acid, or shoots down nine bombers, he is an at-leaster, not a loser but a non-winner. The important thing is that he sets the goal himself, usually on the basis of Parental programming, but with his Adult making the final commitment. Note that the man who goes for two children, 16′, five bombers, etc., and makes it is still a winner, while the one who goes for four and only makes three, or goes for 17′ and only makes 16′11″, or goes for ten and only makes nine, is a non-winner, even though he outdoes the winner whose goals are lower. On a short-term basis, a winner is

one who becomes captain of the team, dates the Queen of the May, or wins at poker. A non-winner never gets near the ball, dates the runner-up, or comes out even. A loser doesn't make the team, doesn't get a date, or comes out broke.

And note that the captain of the second team is on the same level as the captain of the first team, since each person is entitled to choose his own league and should be judged by the standards which he himself sets up. As an extreme example, "living on less money than anyone else on the street without getting sick" is a league. Whoever does it is a winner. One who tries it and gets sick is a loser. The typical, classical, loser is the man who makes himself suffer sickness or damage for no good cause. If he has a good cause, then he may become a successful martyr, which is the best way to win by losing.

The first thing to be decided about a script is whether it is a winning one or a losing one. This can often be discovered very quickly by listening to the person talk. A winner says things like: "I made a mistake, but it won't happen again" or "Now I know the right way to do it." A loser says, "If only . . ." or "I should've . . ." and "Yes, but . . ." As for non-winners, they are people whose scripts require them to work very hard, not in hope of winning but just to stay even. These are "at-leasters," people who say, "Well, at least I didn't . . ." or "At least, I have this much to be thankful for." Non-winners make excellent members, employees, and serfs, since they are loyal, hard-working, and grateful, and not inclined to cause trouble. Socially they are pleasant people, and in the community, admirable. Winners make trouble for the rest of the world only indirectly, when they are fighting among themselves and involve innocent bystanders, sometimes by the million. Losers cause the most turbulence, which is unfortunate, because even if they come out on top they are still losers and drag other people down with them when the payoff comes.

The best way to tell a winner from a loser is this: A win-

ner is a person who knows what he'll do next if he loses, but doesn't talk about it; a loser is one who doesn't know what he'll do if he loses, but talks about what he'll do if he wins. Thus it takes only a few minutes of listening to pick out the winners and losers at a gambling table or a stockbroker's.

The next item is time structure. Over the life span of the individual, there are several types of scripts as to timing. The six main classes are the Never, the Always, the Until, the After, the Over and Over, and the Open End scripts. These are best understood by reference to Greek myths, since the Greeks had a strong feeling for such things.

The Never scripts are represented by Tantalus, who through all eternity was to suffer from hunger and thirst in sight of food and water, but never to eat or drink again. People with such scripts are forbidden by their parents to do the things they most want to, and so spend their lives being tantalized and surrounded by temptations. They go along with the Parental curse because the Child in them is afraid of the things they want the most, so they are really tantalizing themselves.

The Always scripts follow Arachne, who dared to challenge the Goddess Minerva in needlework, and as a punishment was turned into a spider and condemned to spend all her time spinning webs. Such scripts come from spiteful parents who say: "If that's what you want to do, then you can just spend the rest of your life doing it."

The Until scripts follow the story of Jason, who was told that he could not become a king until he had performed certain tasks. In due time he got his reward and lived for ten years in happiness. Hercules had a similar script: he could not become a god until he had first been a slave for twelve years.

The After scripts come from Damocles. Damocles was allowed to enjoy the happiness of being a king, until he noticed that a sword was hanging over his head, suspended by a single horse hair. The motto of After scripts is "You

can enjoy yourself for a while, but then your troubles begin." The fear of impending troubles, of course, makes enjoyment difficult. These are the people who say, "If things are too good, something bad is bound to happen."

The Over and Over scripts are Sisyphus. He was condemned to roll a heavy stone up a hill, and just as he was about to reach the top the stone rolled back and he had to start over again. This is the classical Almost Made It script, with one "If only" after another.

The Open End script is the non-winner or Pie in the Sky scenario, and follows the story of Philemon and Baucis, who were turned into laurel trees as a reward for their good deeds. Old people who have carried out their Parental instructions don't know what to do next after it is all over, and spend the rest of their lives like vegetables, or gossiping like leaves rustling in the wind. This is the fate of many a mother whose children have grown up and scattered, and of men who have put in their thirty years of work according to company regulations and their parents' instructions, and now live alone on pensions in obscure hotels and rooming houses. "Senior citizen" communities are filled with couples who have completed their scripts and don't know how to structure their time while waiting for the Promised Land where people who have treated their employees decently can drive their big black cars slowly down the left-hand lane without being honked at by a bunch of ill-bred teenagers in their hot rods. "Was pretty feisty myself as a teenager," says Dad, "but nowadays." And Mom adds: "You wouldn't believe what they. And we've always paid our."

All of these script types have their sexual aspects. The Never scripts may forbid either love or sex or both. If they forbid love but not sex, they are a license for promiscuity, a license which some sailors and soldiers and wanderers take full advantage of, and which prostitutes and courtesans use to make a living. If they forbid sex but not love, they produce priests, monks, nuns, and people who do good

deeds such as raising orphan children. The promiscuous people are tantalized by the sight of devoted lovers and happy families, while the scripty philanthropists are tormented by a desire to jump over the wall.

The Always scripts are typified by young people who are driven out of their homes for the sins that their parents have prompted them to. "If you're pregnant, go earn your living on the streets" and "If you want to take drugs, you're on your own" are examples of these. The father who turned his daughter out into the storm may have had lecherous thoughts about her since she was ten, and the one who threw his son out of the house for smoking pot may get drunk that night to ease his pain.

The parental programming in Until scripts is the loudest of all, since it usually consists of outright commands: "You can't have sex until you're married, and you can't get married as long as you have to take care of your mother (or until you finish college)." The Parental influence in After scripts is almost as outspoken, and the hanging sword gleams with visible threats: "After you get married and have children, your troubles will begin." Translated into action now, this means "Gather ye rosebuds while ye may, Old Time is still a-flying, And this same flower that smiles today, Tomorrow will be stultifying."[5] After marriage it shortens to "Once you have children your troubles will begin," so the young wife spends her days worrying about getting pregnant right from the first day of the honeymoon. But now chemists have provided a stout shield against the bilbo which would otherwise be her undoing, and so she can be queen of the household without having her happiness suspended by an heir until she is ready for one.

The Over and Over scripts produce always a bridesmaid and never a bride, as well as others who try hard again and again but never quite succeed in making it. The Open End scripts end with aging men and women who lose their vitality without much regret and are content with reminiscing about

past conquests. Women with such scripts wait eagerly for the menopause, with the mistaken idea that after that their "sexual problems" will be over, while the men wait until they have put in their time on the job with a similar hope of relief from sexual obligations.

At the more intimate level, each of these scripts has its own bearing on the actual orgasm. The Never script, of course, besides making spinsters and bachelors and prostitutes and pimps, also makes women who never have an orgasm, not a single one in their whole lives, and also produces impotent men who can have orgasms providing there is no love—the classical situation described by Freud of the man who is impotent with his wife but not with prostitutes. The Always script produces nymphomaniacs and Don Juans who spend their lives continually chasing after the promise of a conquest.

The Until script favors harried housewives and tired businessmen, neither of whom can get sexually aroused until every last detail of the household or the office has been put in order. Even after they are aroused, they may be interrupted at the most critical moments by games of Refrigerator Door and Note Book, little things they have to jump out of bed to take care of right now, such as checking the refrigerator door to make sure it is closed or jotting down a few things that have to be done first thing in the morning at the office. After scripts interfere with sex because of apprehension. Fear of pregnancy, for example, keeps the woman from having an enjoyable orgasm and may cause the man to have his too quickly. Coitus interruptus, where the man withdraws just before he comes, as a method of birth control, keeps both parties in a jumpy state right from the beginning, and usually leaves the woman stranded high and wet if the couple is too shy to use some way for her to get her satisfaction. In fact the word satisfaction, which is usually used in discussing this particular problem, is a giveaway that something is wrong, since a good orgasm should be far more

substantial than the pale ghost that is called satisfaction.

The Over and Over script is one that will ring a bell for many women losers, who get higher and higher during intercourse, until just as they are about to make it, the man comes, possibly with the woman's help, and she rolls all the way down again. This may happen night after night for years. The Open End script has its effect in older people who regard sex as an effort or an obligation. Once over the hill, they are "too old" to have sex, and their glands wither away from disuse along with their skins and often their muscles and brains as well. The man strongly programmed for punctuality has spent all his life waiting for Santa Claus to bring him his retirement pin—late to work only twice in the whole thirty years—while his wife has been waiting for Mrs. Santa Claus, whose maiden name was Minnie Menopause. And now they have nothing to do but fill in the time until their pipes rust away, taking their places in senior society according to what brand of car they drive, if any. If they are lucky, he may find a bleached divorcée at the trailer court who will give his plumbing a last fling, and as a result he may plumb his wife a few times in the afterglow, and after that, they've had it. The moral of this is that a script should not have a time limit on it, but should be designed to last a whole lifetime, no matter how long that lifetime may be. It may call for switching trades or sports, but retirement, no.

We have already seen that the sexual potency, force, and drive of a human being are to some extent determined by his inheritance and his chemistry. Incredible as it may seem, they are even more strongly influenced by the script decisions he makes in early childhood and by the parental programming that brings about those decisions. Thus not only the authority and frequency of his sexual activities throughout his whole lifetime, but also his ability and readiness to love are to a large extent already decided at the age of six. This seems to apply even more strongly to women. Some of them decide very early that they want to be mothers when

they grow up, while others resolve at the same period to remain virgins or virgin brides forever. In any case, sexual activity in both sexes is continually interfered with by parental opinions, adult precautions, childhood decisions, and social pressures and fears, so that natural urges and cycles are suppressed, exaggerated, distorted, disregarded, or contaminated. The result is that whatever is called "sex" becomes the instrument of gamy behavior.

D

NATURE'S TRICKS

In fact most human relationships (at least 51 per cent) are based on trickery and subterfuges, some lively and amusing, and others vicious and sinister. It is only a fortunate few, such as mothers and infants, or true friends and lovers, who are completely straight with each other. Lest you think that I am cynically distorting the situation, let me give you some examples of how Nature herself, through the process of evolution, has set up some gamy transactions. Some of these appear so cynical from the human point of view that it is hard to decide whether to laugh at them as practical jokes or weep over them as tragedies.[6] Yet their final outcome is to ensure the survival of the species. Indeed, human psychological games have a strong survival value also, else their players would soon have become extinct. It does not diminish that value, either for animals or for human beings, to see them as tricks and japes, nor does it increase the value to take them very seriously, as though to say, as some have said: "I am more solemn and indignant, and therefore more righteous than thou."

The simplest example of a biological trick is found in the barnyard hen. Sentimentally regarded, her story is this. After

laying her eggs, she sits on them with single-minded devotion. From time to time, with the foresight of a trained midwife, she turns them over so that the nurturing heat of her body will reach all parts of the calcified wombs wherein her brood is growing. Eventually, as a result of her constancy and care, they hatch into healthy chicks. In this way she offers the human race a sterling example of intelligent and resolute motherhood.

What actually happens is this. Due to certain glandular influences, after she has laid a clutch of eggs, her bosom gets overheated. Driven by discomfort, she looks around for some congenial object to cool her ardent breast. She sits on the eggs because they feel cool. But after a while, she begins to warm them up, so she turns them until the cool underside is uppermost, and then gratefully accepts the relief they offer once again.[7] After she has repeated this enough times, the eggs hatch and she finds herself, much to her surprise, faced with a brood of chicks. In effect, she has been tricked into sitting on the eggs, but it works just as well as though she knew what she was doing. In the same way, people who play sex games can be presented with babies who are just as bouncing as those whose parents plan them. It is a comforting illusion to think that the gland-driven hen knows why she is sitting on the eggs, and it is comforting to script-driven people to think that they know why they do things, too. In one case the script (and the deceptions that go with it) is supplied by the genes, in the other by Parental instructions.

Even more wondrous in its innocence is the behavior of a species of male stickleback. Sticklebacks are to fatherhood what hens are to motherhood. The male stickleback is just as devoted to his offspring as the mother hen is to hers. His first job, immediately after copulation, is to grab the fertilized eggs in his mouth, because if mother gets to them before he does, she will simply swallow them like caviar. But gentle father places them in a grassy nest of his own construction.

Once he has done that, he is afflicted with a kind of glandular lockjaw, which prevents him from opening his mouth again. He stands guard over the eggs until they hatch, swimming round and round the nest until the fry come out. He continues to protect them until they are old enough to strike out for themselves and venture forth into the seas. During all this time he goes hungry until his jaw loosens up again. This example of fatherly devotion, standing guard over his clutch while slowly starving, has not escaped the notice of our moralists. But the actual situation is probably different. As he gets hungrier and hungrier, the eggs in the nest look more and more appetizing. He stays around them, and also around the small fry when they first hatch, in the hope of making a meal of them, which he is prevented from doing by his locked jaws. So he stands guard over the nest, which has now become a food locker, waiting for his mouth to loosen up. Eventually it does loosen up—right after the newborn babies have swum away. In this case, what looks like fatherly devotion is really frustrated cannibalism.[8]

This particular stickleback comes closer to playing Tantalus than anyone else in real life except a hungry human. But hungry humans are the victims of mere human history, which they themselves can and have changed, while the stickleback is the helpless and unwitting butt of a more cosmic force which he can do nothing about. He is one of the Charlie Chaplins of evolution, funny and sad at the same time as he waits for his portion, only to have it vanish as he reaches out to grasp.

We should note that both the hen and the stickleback have been had. For the hen, the bait is a cool object that promises to soothe her heated breast. That promise is kept, but where did the chicks appear from so suddenly? "Now they tell me!" says the brooding fowl, but she does not learn from this experience and goes through it again and again. For the hungry stickleback, the bait is a promise of food, and that promise is not kept. Where did the fry disappear to

just as his mouth broke free? The disappointed daddy can only exclaim, "Why does this always happen to me?"

Higher up on the evolutionary scale, not too far from the human race, is another of Nature's jokes, this one set up partly by biology and glands, and partly by the players' own choosing. It is a musical comedy put on by seals at breeding season. First come the bulls, who congregate on their favorite rock or piece of shoreline. They stake out their claims with noisy huff and bluff or bloody battles, and the strongest gets the best piece of territory. A month later, the girls drift in—"cows," they are called, which does little justice to their fluency and grace. Each cow makes her choice of a daddy seal or is forced into his harem. Unfortunately, the result is that some of the strong and brave and handsome bulls get more than their fair share, and new fights break out as some of the stags try to kidnap a mermaid or two for themselves. In the end, the weaker bulls are repulsed and have to live as loveless bachelors.

The interesting thing is that the cows are all pregnant from the previous year, and they spend a month or two at the breeding ground watching the fights before they deliver. Soon after they have given birth, they take their babies into the water to teach them how to swim. While they are out there, the winning bulls have to stay home to guard their households and territories. But the bachelors don't have any territories to guard, so they just swim out and join the ladies who are running the nursery school.[9] In this way, in the long run, the bachelors have their fun while the old bulls have to stay home and take care of their real estate interests. So that's the way it is with seals, and many a human novel has been written on less material than that.

The great apes must have read some classics, too. The orangoutans come right out of the *Kama Sutra* and have their sex lives hanging from trees. They can think of more acrobatic positions than a whole regiment of Hindu philosophers. Baboons are more romantic—a cross between seals

and something out of Flaubert and Stendhal. Big daddy has the harem, leaving large numbers of young bucks without any chicks. These bachelors lurk on the outskirts of the seraglio, and when big daddy looks the other way, some Pappyo makes a pass at one of his concubines. She is perfectly willing to accommodate Paps, and if big daddy doesn't get wind of this, then nature takes its course and the lovers part in friendly cheer. But if dad comes to and catches them at it, the lady pulls a quick double cross. She splits and throws herself on the ground, making indignant noises and pointing at her Romeo—in effect screaming, "This big ape committed rape!" So big daddy says, "He did, did he?" and runs after the boy friend, who leads him a merry chase around the dell. This leaves the harem wide open, including the girl who started the game of Rapo, at which point the other bachelors, who have been watching and waiting in their lurks, close in and make out with whichever females are handy and willing.[10]

The biological effect of these harem scenes among the seals and baboons is to spread the genes. That makes for variety in evolution and thus serves a useful purpose. If each bull hung on to all his chicks like a rooster and nobody else got in, there would be a straight line of inbreeding and both species might go the way of the dinosaurs. But distributing the goodies by these merry bachelor pranks gives cross-breeding and variation. In fact the human race probably originated just because our simian ancestors played Rapo and Let's Make Hay While the Old Man Is on a Rampage, so we shouldn't put down these monkeyshines, because if they weren't there, we mightn't be here either.

Now, all this is probably not amusing to a big daddy baboon, or to a person who thinks baboons should have better morals, or maybe even wear muumuus,[11] but there is really no advantage in the rest of us treating it solemnly or indignantly. As a matter of fact, solemnity and indignation are what cause wars, and if everybody started laughing they

would soon stop shooting at each other. In fact, this is a well-established principle of chemical warfare. Each side knows that whoever can drug the other side into laughing will win the war. If the laughing side retaliates, the whole war will come to a stop, which from a military point of view is even worse than one side winning.* So someone who is more solemn and indignant than thou may be more righteous than thou, but he is also going to make more trouble than thou. The fact is that if the seals and baboons burst out laughing at their own gamy antics, the games would be broken up and things would settle down to a more equitable and peaceful way of life, where nobody got insulted or hurt. But until they do start laughing, the games will continue, and it is the same with human beings.

—
E
—

WHAT IS A GAME?

Human beings are, after all, just parlayed jellyfish, and many of their "voluntary" actions and responses are no more the result of free will than are those of the lowly animal from which they have ascended. In the lower orders, such as sticklebacks, "nature's games" are automatic responses programmed almost entirely by genes. As we go up the scale to seals and baboons, they are learned more and more by imitation and experience. Human psychological or transactional games are programmed to a large degree by the parents, but this programming is just as decisive as the automatic gene programming of the hen. Man is the freest of all animals, but the life script and the games that go with

---

*I believe this statement is historically defensible: that from a military or at least militant point of view, stopping a war is worse than losing.

it still make him the victim of a mighty joke played by the ineluctable forces of evolution. Despite our aspirations and our illusion of awareness, we are not much better off than a poet marching with upturned gaze and outstretched arms toward a rainbow, and slipping on an unseen banana peel or worse beneath his feet.

Let us now analyze the "Hen Game" and the "Stickleback Game." In each case there is a bait that looks to the player like one thing but is really "intended" for something else. The eggs are there to incubate chickens, but the hen is conned into sitting on them because they are cool. They hook right into what is bothering her, which is a feverish breast. Just as she cools off, nature pulls a switch, and the payoff is a brood of chicks. In the case of the stickleback, he is conned into staying there because the eggs and the fry need protection, but to him they look like caviar. This hooks into his need of the moment, which is hunger. Again nature pulls a switch, and just as his mouth loosens up, his lunch swims away, leaving him with disappointment for his payoff.

In the "Seal Game," the pasha's weakness is territory. The cow, rather than being grateful to him for guarding the ranch, has an affair at nursery school instead. In the "Baboon Game," the pasha's weakness is jealousy. The female plays into that, and then pulls a switch by doing the very thing he is trying to prevent.

Already a pattern for games emerges. There is a bait that has a handy attraction but really serves some other purpose. The bait hooks into a weakness, but after the victim responds there is a switch. The "real purpose" comes into the open and springs a surprise for the ending. For the hen, the fish, and the ape, Nature's joke follows the plan precisely; with the seal it is a little looser, but all the elements are there. It remained for human beings to refine this pattern into a way of life, and to plot out innumerable variations.

In transactional games, the bait, which seems like one thing but is really intended for something else, is called a

con. The weakness or need of the other player, which makes him respond to the con, is called a gimmick. The surprise ending is called the switch. The formula for all transactional games, then, is:

$$\text{Con} + \text{Gimmick} = \text{Response} \rightarrow \text{Switch} \rightarrow \text{Payoff}$$

As an example, consider the following set of transactions between a woman and her doctor, which is very similar to the game called Rapo.

Judith: Do you think I'll ever get better?

Dr. Q: Yes, I think so.

Judith: What makes you think you know everything?

It is clear that Judith's question was phony, and Dr. Q has been conned. In order to understand more clearly what really happened, we can translate it into game language, which is called Martian.

Judith (speaking as a helpless little Child): Help me, O Great One.

Dr. Q (speaking as a powerful Parent): I, powerful one, can help you.

Judith (speaking as a smart-aleck Child): Come off it, Buster.

This Martian translation shows that the con is "Help me, O Great One." Judith is apparently flattering the doctor and asking for help, but she really intends something else. Her con hooks into the doctor's gimmick, which is his humble feeling of power. He responds accordingly, whereupon Judith pulls the switch, and they both get their payoffs. Judith feels smart, which she enjoys, and the unwary doctor feels depressed, which he enjoys for reasons of his own. So Con + Gimmick = Response → Switch → Payoff. The nature of the payoff also makes it clear that Judith is playing Buzz Off, Buster, and the doctor is playing the complementary game of I'm Only Trying to Help You (ITHY).[12] Judith has led him into a trap, so that instead of being

thanked for his good intentions, he is put down, which is the standard payoff in the game of ITHY.

Before going further, let us consider what is a "not game." It is easier to understand what is a cat if we also understand what is not a cat. Some people think that any set of transactions which is repeated over and over is a game, but this is not so. There are many such sets which are not games, no matter how often they are repeated, because they will not fit into the formula. Take the following example:

Patient: Do you think I'll ever get better?

Therapist: Yes, I think so.

Patient: Thank you, it's good to hear that again today.

This is a set of straight transactions, with no con and no switch. The woman's question is exactly what it appears to be, and no matter how often she asks for reassurance, it is not a game, as long as there is no con and no switch.

Every game is a little drama, and Dr. Stephen Karpman has devised a very simple way to show this (Figure 13). It is called the Drama or Karpman Triangle.[13] It shows how the game switches each of the players from one role into another, which is the essence of drama in real life as in the theater. It is based on the game of Alcoholic, where the three main roles, victim, persecutor, and rescuer, are most clearly played out. The "victim of alcoholism" is persecuted by "bad" people, but there are "good" people who try to rescue him. The Alcoholic keeps the initiative at all times, since he can turn his nagging, persecuting wife into a victim by beating up on her, or he can start to defy his rescuers, thus turning them into persecutors. The triangles in Figure 14 show the switches (a) between the stickleback and his offspring (b) between the big daddy baboon and his errant wife and (c) between Judith and Dr. Q.

In Figure 14A, the stickleback starts out as a hungry cannibalistic protector or rescuer with his small fry as the potential victims. After the switch, they "persecute" him by swimming off, leaving him a hungry victim of their prank.

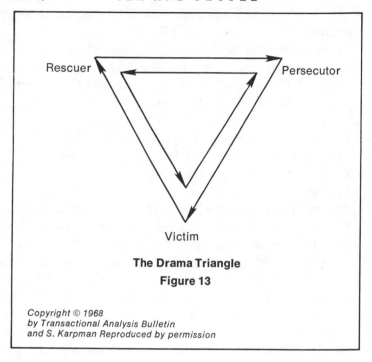

The Drama Triangle
Figure 13

Copyright © 1968
by Transactional Analysis Bulletin
and S. Karpman Reproduced by permission

In Figure 14B, the pasha baboon starts off as the rescuer of his "persecuted" wife, and ends up as the victim of her duplicity.

Figure 14C translates into Martian as follows:

Judith (speaking as a victim of emotional troubles): Rescue me.

Dr. Q (speaking as a rescuer): I'll rescue you.

Judith (switching into the role of a persecutor): Wise guy!

Judith now has the upper hand. She switches from victim into persecutor, and he is switched from being a rescuer into being a victim. She does to him just about what her namesake did to Holofernes 2,500 years ago: cuts his head off, figuratively at least.

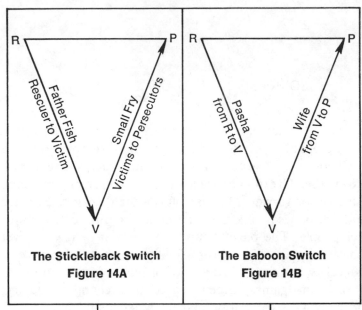

The Stickleback Switch
Figure 14A

The Baboon Switch
Figure 14B

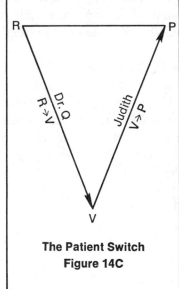

The Patient Switch
Figure 14C

—
F
—

SOME SEXUAL GAMES

Sexual games are exercises in sexual attraction, the exploitations of the organs and the orgasm described in Chapter 3. If we call the two gameplayers Green and Brown, then Green's con is either coming on strong by being seductive or forward, or else playing hard to get. Brown's gimmick or weakness is sexual desire or a need for power over people. The payoff may be either wet or dry. In wet games, the payoff is orgasm (finally), preceded by a lot of insincerity and followed by a lot of mixed feelings on both sides. In dry games, Green's payoff is a feeling of victory, and Brown's is frustration and the reactions to that.*

Nearly all two-handed games are variations of this game of Rapo, and most three-handed ones resemble Let's Make Mother Sorry.

Rapo is played most often by women. It follows the formula $C + G = R \rightarrow S \rightarrow P$. The Con, C, is a seductive attitude, and the Gimmick, G, is a desire for sex or power. The woman's Con hooks into the man's Gimmick, and he gives the Response, R, which is to come on strong. The woman then pulls the Switch, S, by saying "Yes, but," and after that they both get their Payoffs, P.

Rapo, like all games, is played in three degrees of hardness, each with its own type of Switch and Payoff. First-degree Rapo is a dry game, Flirtation, in which the Switch is "Yes, but we both know that's as far as it goes—for now, at least." The Payoff is mutual good feelings, and possibly hope on one or both sides.

---

*As it was said in *Don Quixote*, "She may guess what I would perform in the wet, if I do so much in the dry."

Second-degree Rapo is called Buzz Off, Buster. The Switch is "Yes, but I'm not that kind of a girl even though I led you on." The Payoff for the woman is to gratify her spite, and for the man it is to feel rejected and depressed. In this case the man is playing the complementary game of Kick Me. It is usually a dry game, but in the wet game the man pays for his fun by getting kicked harder.

Third-degree Rapo is a false cry of Rape. The Switch is "Yes, but I'm going to call it rape anyway." The woman's Payoff is justification as well as spite, and the man has his whole life and career on the line waiting to be kicked. It may be played either dry or wet, depending on how mean or sexy the woman is.

The payoffs in any game are not only enjoyed or suffered at the moment but are filed away for future use, very much like grocery store trading stamps. In this manner of speaking, every script has attached to it a trading-stamp book, and the script cannot be cashed in until the book is filled. For example, here is how it works in Second-degree Rapo.

The "existential" object of this game is to prove that men are no good. What the woman is really saying is "Buzz off, Buster (You're just like the rest of them—no good)." Her Payoff comes not only from seeing the man's discomfort but also from the fact that she can add the picture of another Nogoodnick to her collection. When her stamp book is full of such pictures, she can cash it in for a "Script Payoff." This may be a free suicide, a free homicide, or a license to be an alcoholic or a Lesbian—whatever her script calls for. The man, similarly, who is playing Kick Me, can add another Hurt to his book of Hurts. When he fills the book, he can cash it in for his Script Payoff. This may, for example, be suicide, in accordance with his mother's instructions: "I love you, but some day you'll come to a bad end," which means in effect: "I love you, but drop dead."

More friendly games of Rapo may be played as See What You Made Me Do ("You made me lose my virginity," "You

made me get pregnant," "I didn't want to, but you raped me"). These are useful in courtship or marriage for getting additional leverage over the man. Another form is Toy Gun, which is played by people who act grownup but are really precocious children. Some of the slogans in this game are: "I can't really go through with it," "I didn't really mean it," "I wasn't really ready," and "You shouldn't have taken advantage of me." Toy Gun is diagnosed when the player says "not really," which means it wasn't a real gun, or uses the subjunctive, as in "You shouldn't have," which means "You should have known it wasn't real." The original, non-sexual form of Toy Gun is played by amateur or crooked holdup men if they are captured. When they are confronted with the crime, they reply: "I'm not in the wrong, you're in the wrong for being stupid enough to think it was a real gun." This is a classical triangle switch: "I may look like the armed persecutor and you the victim, but it's really quite the opposite; I'm the victim of your stupidity." One of the greatest examples of sexual Toy Gun in literature is Thomas Hardy's *Jude the Obscure*, where the hero said, "I didn't really mean it," but the girl cried, "Rapo!" so he couldn't get away.

Rapo can also be played by men, with slogans such as: "You took me away from my work," "You've worn me out," "I only did it because I was drunk," and "Why didn't you tell me you forgot to take your pill?"

All the above are "Yes But" games, since each of the slogans really contains a Yes But, whether it is said aloud or not. There are also "If Only" types of Rapo. Yes But games are played by tightening up. There is either a refusal beforehand, an interruption during, or an argument afterward, in each case with the implication that the woman (or man) player is or was being unfairly seduced or raped and is uptight about it, which is usually literally true as far as the body muscles are concerned. If Only games are played by hanging loose, with the slogan "If rape is inevitable, you might as well let it happen, or even enjoy it." The player

still reserves the right to refuse, interrupt, or reproach, but in this case passively instead of actively. Thus Yes But games tend to be belligerent and argumentative, while If Onlys are merely wistful, whiny, or reproachful. Yes But Rapo says, "It's got to be different!" and in the extreme case ends with an abortion, while If Only says, "I wish it could be different," and ends in a whimper. ("If only you were more considerate [or careful] I wouldn't be pregnant.")

Yes But uses what in grammar are called the declarative or imperative moods, while If Only uses the subjunctive. On the West Coast, expressions like "Not really," "I (you) shouldn't, wouldn't, couldn't," "If only," and "I may look like the persecutor but I'm really the victim," are called the "Berkeley Subjunctive" by some. But there are people everywhere whose games are based on such end runs around reality, and they can often be picked out at social gatherings.

Refrigerator Door and Note Book, the games of interrupted intercourse, can be played either Yes But or If Only. "Yes but I have to interrupt this rape to check the refrigerator, gas stove, dryer," or "If only my notes were finished, I could rape you with a clear conscience." Telephone Call is a passive form. "There goes the telephone, thank God. Now I can interrupt this rape to answer it." Telephone Call may also be either Yes But or If Only. "Yes but there goes the telephone," or "If only mother would call right now." (He: "How come your mother invariably knows the exact time to call?" She: "How come you invariably start something at the time my mother usually calls?")

Games are played by people who are afraid of intimacy, either in general or with each other. They are a way of getting close to others and having meaningful transactions without the surrender that intimacy requires. Thus sexual games may be either a barrier against love or a step on the way to it— a sort of testing arena. With people who have abandoned hope of loving or being loved, they may become ends in themselves, for whatever advantages can be wrung out of

them. These advantages will be discussed in the next section.

Third Degree Rapo is played for the most part by such hopeless people. It is really a three-handed game in which the object is to make the man sorry by telling a third party: mother, father, lawyer, doctor, or police. It is the opposite of actual rape, which is meant to make the woman sorry, especially if she enjoys it in spite of herself—the most dreaded possibility. But the criminal rapist may not care much about the woman; she is just for fun, and once that is over, he is more interested in the chase and the game of Cops and Robbers. If she doesn't report him, he may send an anonymous letter or make an anonymous phone call to the police to stir them up and start the hunt. In extreme cases, he may even write a book about it, which is the best fun of all: playing Cops and Robbers with critics and philosophers, and raping their virgin minds. *How to Rape for Principle and Profit* will even outsell the Marquis de Sade when it comes on the market, because he was too proud to go commercial and hasn't even made it into the high school libraries yet.

One of the most interesting forms of Rape is called Sorry About That. It is also one of the most tragic, since it involves several people, often including broods of children. Here Right says to Left: "If you get a divorce, I'll marry you." So Left gets a divorce. Then Right says, "Sorry, I've changed my mind," leaving Left stranded with no spouse and no lover. The converse is Not Ready Yet: typically, "After the children are grown up I'll get a divorce. Meanwhile let's go ahead." Actually, both Sorry About That and Not Ready Yet are three- or four-handed games, since the spouses of the players know very well what is going on. Here is an example.

Mr. Right, who was divorced, told Mrs. Left that he would marry her if she got a divorce. She did, and then he said Sorry About That, and soon after remarried his former wife. Meanwhile Mr. Left was free to marry his girl friend

of many years' standing, which he did. Mrs. Left, who didn't really like men anyway, was thus left free to lead her own life. But all four parties exploited the situation as much as they could: Mr. Left and his former wife with great lamentations about being wronged by each other and by Mr. Right, and Mr. and Mrs. Right with great apologies, embarrassments, and guilt feeling concealing their pleasure at the fast one they pulled on the Lefts. (Thus the Rights were playing a variant of FOOJY—Let's Pull a Fast One on Joey, Joey in this case being Mr. Left.)

The spouses also come through, as reliable spouses do, in Not Ready Yet. Mr. White promised to get a divorce and marry Mrs. Black as soon as his children were grown. She said she was ready to divorce her husband any time White gave the word. But when their last child left for college, Mrs. White came down with arthritis. Then of course Mr. White could not leave her, so the affair with Mrs. Black continued on the old basis. Mrs. White knew which side her bread was buttered on. Eventually, however, she was killed in an automobile accident. Then Mr. White was ready to take advantage of his bargain with Mrs. Black. But the very next week, Mr. Black went for his first physical examination in five years and discovered that he had diabetes. So Mrs. Black could not conscientiously divorce him. She stayed with him and broke off the affair with White.

There is a grim and tragic humor about such games, with their almost unbelievable "coincidences," but as we have already seen, Nature herself has a sense of humor and sets up Hen Games, Stickleback Games, Seal Games, Baboon Games, and many more that are equally unbelievable in their exquisite design.

As we said at the beginning of this section, three-handed sex games usually follow the pattern of Let's Make Mother Sorry, which is described in its most gruesome form in de Sade's *Philosophy in a Bedroom*. There everyone gangs up on the unfortunate mother who values her daughter's vir-

ginity. The dissolute band first initiates the daughter into all the possible combinations of persons and orifices, so that her previously treasured virginity becomes a mere trinket in their frenzied orgy. The father then gives them permission to humiliate and torture the mother as they choose, which they proceed to do, with the daughter taking a principal part and disregarding her mother's shrieks and pleadings. And throughout they make it very clear to her why she must suffer: it is because she has tried to prevent her daughter from enjoying sex, and they are making sure that she will never again interfere with the girl's pleasure, and will be sorry beyond belief that she ever did.

In its more commonplace form, the daughter makes mother sorry by becoming promiscuous or getting pregnant, causing a neighborhood scandal and perhaps ending up in Juvenile Hall. The boy serves merely as an instrument, and the girl may never see him again once she has done the job on mother. If she cannot swing it on her own, the daughter may bring another party, called the Connection, into the game. He may simply pimp for her, or he may also get her hooked on drugs to make matters worse. Variations with increasing age are Let's Make Boy Friend (or Girl Friend) Sorry, Let's Make Husband (or Wife) Sorry, or Let's Make Aging Acres Sorry. Nowadays one of the most popular versions is Let's Make Welfare Department Sorry. Since Welfare Departments arc usually against sex, and also (I am reliably informed) against bubble gum, this is played by having lots of sex and many illegitimate children to be supported by State Funds; and spice can be added by chewing lots of bubble gum while all that is going on.

Making Someone Sorry (MSS) will only work if the Patsy, the one who is going to be sorry, is a person or organization that functions in a Parental ego state and plays I'm Only Trying to Help You, or at least After All I've Done for You. Then, the harder the MSS (or MS) players play, the madder the Patsy gets, which is just what the MS

players want. The Patsy, like most people in a Parental ego state, works under the illusion that the madder he gets, the more likely he is to break up the game, when exactly the opposite is usually true. The angrier he gets, the more fun it is for the MS players. If the Patsy gets angry enough, they may even feel entitled to shift into the third-degree game and call in a lawyer, which is more fun than a barrel of monkeys. Once the game gets legalized, however, much of the fun goes out of it, and the players settle down into dreary domesticity.

For those who are unable for various reasons to find other players, any of these games may be played as solitaire in the form of skull games or fantasies.

There are many three-handed games in which the third player remains under cover, so that the victim thinks he is in a two-handed game. Prostitution is often of this nature, where the man believes he is dealing with the woman, whereas the show is really being run by the pimp behind the scenes, who has taught the woman the rules and sees that she enforces them. How Was It is a similar game in which the husband is the hidden player. He sends his wife out to pick up a man and have intercourse with him on condition that she tell him all the details afterward for his edification and entertainment. In its most repulsive form, she is instructed to find a virgin. In That Was a Good One, the husband may actually watch from a place of concealment. Sometimes this is reversed, and it is the wife who sends her husband out or panders for him with her girl friends or by picking up a girl in a restaurant. In the third degree of these games, the hidden player suddenly appears on the scene. If he is a professional, he takes the Patsy's money by force or armed robbery, or in the guise of the Angry Husband, blackmails him. That is called the Badger Game. It is also played with homosexuals, when the third player may take the part of a Corrupt Cop. In the domestic form, too, there are many opportunities for surprises if the hidden spouse decides to

pull a switch. Then the game may end in murder, suicide, lawsuit, or divorce.

In Who Needs You? the wife takes a lover to make her husband jealous, or vice versa. Sometimes none of the three knows that that is the real reason, and sometimes all of them do, and the neighbors as well. Or the spouses may know and the lover may not, in which case he is the Patsy; but few lovers are that stupid. In Steal One, Mr. Right has an affair with Mrs. Left not to get back at his wife, but to make Mr. Left sorry; while Mrs. Left takes on Right not to get back at her husband, but to make Mrs. Right sorry. On the other hand, this may be a competitive game rather than a spiteful one, in which case it is called I Can Do Better Than the Other Guy, Didn't I? These three games—Who Needs You, Steal One, and I Can Do Better—make great combinations for plays, operas, novels, and short stories, especially since each of the players has it in his power to play counter-games if he wants to.

The Sandwich is a straight three-handed operation, not a game. Everybody is supposed to feel good and nobody is supposed to feel sorry. It may be operated with any assortment of sexes: three men, three women, two men and a woman ("*Ménage à trois*"), or two women and a man ("The Tourist Sandwich"). A has sex with B, then B with C, then C with A. Thus each party has sex twice and watches once. It is turned into a swindle in the Potato Sandwich. Here A and B have sex, with C watching and waiting expectantly for her turn, but her turn never comes and she is left holding the potato. Such swindles are very common in children's sex play. In You Show Me Yours and I'll Show You Mine, played two-handed, A shows his, but B doesn't show hers, or vice versa. Rat Fink Potato Sandwich is a three-handed game where C turns the tables. A shows his and B shows hers, but when C's turn comes she runs home and tells mother instead. Double Potato is a four-handed game. Mr. Green has sex with Mrs. Brown, his wife's best friend. Mrs.

Green and Mr. Brown would like to have sex too, but the others arrange it so they can't, and they are left holding the potatoes.

G

WHY PEOPLE PLAY GAMES

The advantages of playing games are nowhere shown more clearly than in sexual games.

(1) Straight sex keeps people happy in a straight way. Sexual games satisfy other needs besides or instead of sex: hate, spite, anger, fear, guilt, shame, and embarrassment, along with hurt and inadequacy, and all the other perverse feelings for which some people have to settle in place of love. By using their sexuality for bait as well as for pleasure, game players can satisfy both their hangups and their desires and thus keep themselves reasonably contented—on their way to lonely Loserville. This is called the internal psychological advantage of a game: it keeps the pressure down and prevents the person from flipping out. Sometimes, however, the pressure gets so great that no amount of such sports can relieve it. De Sade, for example, kept making his mother sorrier and sorrier, until he ended in the asylum at Charenton, leaving a trail of poisoned and beaten girls behind him, much to the admiration of Baudelaire, Swinburne, Dostoevsky, Kafka and others who are touting him even now.

(2) The second advantage, called the external psychological, is that games avoid confrontations, responsibilities, and commitments, a fact overlooked by de Sade's admirers of the existential school. Dry games avoid confrontation with the naked body and the call for action, as well as responsibility for defloration, impregnation, stimulation, affec-

tion, and other consequences of intercourse. Wet games end in orgasm, or at least penetration, but because they are games, avoid commitment to the partner.

(3) While games keep people from getting too close for comfort, they do bring the players together and keep them together, close enough to keep them from being bored with each other but not close enough to be seriously committed. This gives them the illusion of being part of the human race, or at least of heading that way. Actually, games are part of "until" programs. They are supposed to be preludes to the real thing, when the right person will come along. Too often, the right person is Santa Claus's son Prince Charming, or his daughter The Snow Maiden, who will never come, or in many cases, Death, who will. Games are something to do meanwhile, a way of structuring time while waiting in Destiny's bus station, and they have the same relation to real living as waiting in a bus station does to swimming over a tropical reef on a sunny day. They offer a framework for pseudo-intimate socializing indoors or in privacy, and this is called their internal social advantage.

(4) Since games are full of incidents and little dramas, sometimes real and sometimes phony, they give people something to gossip about on the outside, and this is called their external social advantage.

(5) Sexual games satisfy stimulus hunger and recognition hunger as well as structure hunger. For most people, they are more fun than sitting alone (withdrawal), being polite at cocktail parties (rituals), going to work in the morning (activities), or talking about golf (pastimes). They stir up the metabolism, stimulate the glands, make the juices flow, and keep the body, mind, and spirit from slowly shriveling up. Wet games do this better than dry games because in wet games odors, skin thrills, infrared rays, and fluids are exchanged. These invigorating effects are called the biological advantage of a game.

(6) There is something always interwoven with sex, and

that is Being or Self—the answer to the question "Who am I?" This, and the next question, "What am I doing here?" are existential questions. The existential advantage of sexual games is that they go a long way toward answering these two puzzles, although not as far as real intimacy does. They are particularly useful in answering the third question, which is "Who are all those others?"

Every script is based on these three questions, and the Parental programming usually tries to give ready-made answers. As long as the person follows his script, he will devote himself to proving that those answers are the right ones for him. In a winning script, the résumé may read: "You're a prince, you're here to give yourself to others, and the others are people who need you." Through sexual games, the person will try to confirm again and again that it really is like that: that he really is a prince (or at least a Derby winner), that he really can be generous, and that others (women) really appreciate him. Once he is satisfied that all those things are true, he may be ready to settle down to a more intimate relationship where he is not so concerned with trying to prove something. For a loser the answers might read: "You're a no-good whore, you're here to work your butt off, and the others are bums who will make you do it." In such a case the games will be designed to prove that she really is a whore (even if she struggles against it), that she has to grind her way through life with her pelvic muscles, and that all men will take advantage of her whenever possible. As long as she is in that script, the only intimate she can have is another whore or a pimp. It's a bum rap, but it works the same way a good script does.

Games keep people comfortably happy or familiarly miserable by proving that the Parental programming gives a true picture of their existence and the world around them, and sexual games are carefully planned to do that by picking the right players and setting them up to respond in the required way.

̄
H
̄

THE ILLUSION OF AUTONOMY

In a previous section, I tried to demonstrate that the road to freedom is through laughter, and until he learns that, man will be enslaved, either subservient to his masters or fighting to serve under a new master. The masters know this very well, and that is why they are masters. The last thing they will allow is unseemly laughter. In freer countries, every college has its humor magazine, but there are no such jokes in slave-holding nations like Nazi Germany or Arabia. Authority cannot be killed by force, for wherever one head is cut off, another springs up in its place. It can only be laughed away, as Sun Tzu knew when he founded the science of military discipline.[14] He first demonstrated this to the Emperor by using girls from the harem, but they giggled when he gave his orders. He knew that at long as they were laughing, discipline wouldn't work. So he stopped their laughing by executing two of them, and after that the rest did as they were told—solemnly and indignantly. Conversely, no comedian has ever been the head of a state for very long; the people might stand it, but he couldn't.

Man is born free, but one of the first things he learns is to do as he is told, and he spends the rest of his life doing that. Thus his first enslavement is to his parents. He follows their instructions forevermore, retaining only in some cases the right to choose his own methods and consoling himself with an illusion of autonomy. If they want to raise him to feel inadequate, they can start by requiring him to produce square bowel movements and refusing to be satisfied with anything less. Whatever conditions they impose on him he will spend the rest of his life trying to meet, and they can let

him know from the beginning that he is not supposed to succeed. In that way he will end up with a good collection of inadequacies to cash in according to their instructions. If he has a streak of independence, he may change the subject and geometry of his efforts, but seldom its essence. He may shift his striving from square bowel movements to pear-shaped orgasms, but he will still make sure that he ends up feeling inadequate. If, on the other hand, they raise him to succeed, then he will do that, using whatever methods he has to to hew his ends to the shape required by this destiny.

In order to break away from such script programs, he must stop and think. But he cannot think about his programming unless he first gives up the illusion of autonomy. He must realize that he has not been up to now the free agent he likes to imagine he is, but rather the puppet of some Destiny from generations ago. Few people have the courage or the elasticity to turn around and stare down the monkeys on their backs, and the older they get, the stiffer their necks become.

This programming starts at the very bottom, at the organs that lie below the mystically curled omphalos or belly button where the twisted silver cord was once attached from mother's womb. Consider the sergeant's classical greeting to the new recruits when they arrive at basic training. The true translation of this is even more anatomical than the anatomical sergeant dreams of. What he says is (and this is true of WAC sergeants too): "Your soul belongs to mother, but your ass belongs to me." This can be truly stated as "The inside of your pelvis belongs to mother, but the outside belongs to me." The pelvic organs of almost every human being belong to mother—and for the lucky ones it goes no further than that. In other cases she controls the stomach and the brain as well. Actually, the Army gets only the leftovers— the outside parts, for the external muscles are all that the Army really needs. As long as soldiers follow orders, the rest is of interest only to the Medical Corps.

The important instructions in the script remain unchanged; only the method and the object are permitted to vary. "Be devoted to your leader," says the Nazi father, and the son devotes himself either to his Fascist leader, or to his leader in Christianity or in Communism, with equal fervor. The clergyman saves souls in his Sunday sermons, and his daughter sallies forth to save them singing folksongs with her guitar. The father is a streetsweeper and the son becomes a medical parasitologist, each in his own way cleaning up the offal that causes disease. The daughter of the good-natured prostitute grows up to be a nurse, and comforts the afflicted in a more sanitary way.

These similarities and differences correspond to what biologists call genotype and phenotype. All dogs have doggy genes, and cannot undertake to be anything but dogs; but each dog can be a dog in his own way. The basic instructions of the parents are like genes: the offspring cannot undertake to do anything but follow them, but each can follow them in his or her own way. This does not mean that brothers and sisters will be alike, for each sibling may and usually does receive different instructions, since each may be raised to play a different role in the scripts of the parents. For example, Cinderella had instructions to be a winner, while her stepsisters were raised to lose, and they all followed their Parental programming. Cinderella with her sweet and winning nature found her own way of coming out on top. It was not the way her parents visualized it perhaps, or maybe it was, but she came through. Her stepsisters were taught to grump and sulk to make sure that nobody would want them except the two jerks who were ordered to marry them by Cinderella's prince.

This freedom to select methods for arriving at the predetermined goal helps to support the illusion of free choice or autonomy. That illusion is most clearly illustrated by the man who had his brain stimulated by an electrode during an operation. Since the stimulated area was the one which con-

trolled his right arm, he raised the arm. When the operator asked him why he moved it, he replied: "Because I wanted to." This is the same thing that goes on all the time in daily life. Each person follows the Parental instructions in important matters, but by choosing his own time and place, maintains the illusion that he is making his own decisions freely and that his behavior is the result of free will. Both of these aspects are built in. It is built in that the Parental instructions will work like an electrode, so that the person will end up following them almost automatically with little or no chance to decide for himself. It is also built in that he will think he is exercising free will. This can only be accomplished if he forgets the Parental instructions and does not remember hearing them. The moment he does remember, he may realize that it is they who have been deciding his feelings, behavior, and responses. Only by such a realization can he free himself to use his own decisions.

For some people, of course, and at some levels with everyone, there is no illusion of autonomy, and the person is quite aware that his behavior is determined by what his parents told him at an early age. This is the case, for example, with many virgins and frigid women who state quite openly that they are so because that is how their parents told them to be. In a way they are better off than those who pretend otherwise. And the study of parental injunctions was started by a gambler who wanted to be cured and who said to the therapist: "Don't tell me not to gamble. That won't work. What I need is permission not to lose." He had suddenly become aware that he lost because he was ordered to lose. What he needed was not more instructions, such as "Why don't you stop gambling?" but permission to disregard the instructions he had received in childhood.

Thus lechery, sadism, homosexuality, promiscuity, sexual games, and other biologically inappropriate forms of sexual activity are programmed in by the parents in most cases. But the person says, "I do it that way because I want to." This is

true in a roundabout way. He does it that way because he was so instructed, and he wants to obey the instructions because he is afraid not to. He turns this necessity into a virtue by claiming free will, which might fool Baudelaire, but it need not fool others. If and when he recalls the instructions, and finds out how the electrode was implanted in his brain, he may be ready to give up his parental programming and the illusions that go with it and perhaps become really free.

It is important to understand that what we are talking about here is biology and not youth movements, which in any case are carried on by programmed youths. Parental programming is not the "fault" of parents—since they are only passing on the programming they got from their parents—any more than the physical appearance of their offspring is their "fault," since they are only passing on the genes they got from their ancestors. But the brain chemicals involved in script programming are easier to change than the gene chemicals that determine physical appearance. Therefore a parent who wants to do the best for his children should find out what his own script is and then decide whether he wants to pass it on to them. If he decides not to, then he should find out how to change it, to grow princes where there were frogs before. This is not easy to do. It is even harder than trying to give oneself a haircut. It usually requires help of a script analyst, but that doesn't always work either. It is even more discouraging to think that if he does pass it on, it will probably be carried through to his grandchildren. This script transmission is the basis for the old saying "To make a lady, start with the grandmother," and it also explains why the Civil War is not over yet, and why it will take another hundred years for the angry scripts of nowadays to cool into a decent way of living. Now is the time to start programming the parents of the ladies and gentle-men of the next century. If we want things to be warm and straight later, we've got to stop being cold and crooked now.

NOTES AND REFERENCES

1. Liddell and Scott give *Odyssey* 4. 221 seq.; Theophrastus, H. P.
9.15.I; Plutarch 2. 614 C; Anthologia Palatina 9.525, 13; and
Protag. (presumably Protagoras) ap Plutarchus 2.118 E. Ne-
penthe is best known nowadays as the name of a restaurant in
Big Sur, California. Oxford gives *"Med.* A drink possessing
sedative properties (1681), and the plant supposed to supply
the drug (1623)." *Nepenthes* is used now only for a genus of
carnivorous pitcher plants, but these are not used as materia
medica; at least they are not listed in pharmacology texts, nor
in the U.S. Pharmacopoeia, nor in the U.S. Dispensatory as far
back as 1866, nor even in Culpeper's *Complete Herbal.* Nevertheless, they are of some interest from an evolutionary point of
view if we remember that *Homo sapiens* is very likely descended
from monkeylike tarsiers who fed on insects. *Tarsius spectrum*
likes to rob pitcher plants of their insect prey. Hence, according to the late Professor Francis E. Lloyd (Encyclopaedia Britannica), *Nepenthes bicalcarata* has developed sharp hooks "as
an adaptation for catching the tarsier if he tries this game" on
that species. This ancient battle between tarsiers and pitcher
plants no doubt played a modest part in the evolution of the
human race, as it did in the genetic selection of certain Nepenthes.

For those who like gossip, I might add that the owner of
Nepenthe, William Fasset, is a great and genial poker player,
and the father of several remarkable children. Professor Lloyd
taught botany at McGill and from him I learned what little I
know of the subject. I once extrapolated his personality into a
story I wrote under a pen name, which was published in the
old *Adelphi* for August, 1933 ("An Old Man," by Lennard
Gandalac). He fathered two sons, one celebrated for his re-
searches in neurology, and the other for the beauty of his children and the number and excellence of his grandchildren. As
for tarsiers, although I freely acknowledge them as my many-
greats grandparents, I have never had the pleasure of a personal acquaintance with one. Concerning pitcher plants, I do
not understand their ways at all. They have their ideas of what
a flower should be, and I have mine, but I bear them no ill will.

2. The following figures from the *World Almanac*, 1968, show
suicide rates for males per 100,000 for 1962–63 according to
the World Health Organization: Hungary, 35.5; Austria, 29.5;
U.S. White, 18.0; U.S. Nonwhite, 9.6; Poland, 16.6. The corresponding rates for females are 14.1, 11.1, 6.7, 2.7, and 3.5.
(In 1966–67, West Berlin was far, far ahead of the rest of the
world both in suicide rate [40.9] and in general mortality rate

[1798.8], exceeding in each even the most backward countries of Africa and Arabia. *United Nations Demographic Yearbook*, 1968.)

3. Mao Tse-tung: *On Art and Literature*. China Books & Periodicals, San Francisco, 1960.

4. Cf. Young, D.: "The Frog Game." *Transactional Analysis Bulletin* 5:156, July, 1966. Also Berne, E.: *Principles of Group Treatment*. Oxford University Press, New York, 1966, and Grove Press, New York, 1968.

5. That paraphrases Herrick's version (c. 1630). Other versions are: "Let us crown ourselves with rosebuds, before they be withered" (*Wisdom of Solomon*, 2:8). "Gather ye therefore roses with great glee, sweet girls, or ere their perfume pass away" (Angelo Polizeano, "A Ballata," c. 1490, trans. by J. A. Symonds). "Gather the Rose of love, whilst yet is time" (Spenser, *Faerie Queene*, I, 12, c. 1590).

   As for us passing through time, rather than vice versa, this idea was most neatly expressed by Ronsard in his poem "Le temps s'en va," later elaborated by Austin Dobson in *his* poem "The Paradox of Time."

6. Lorenz discusses this dilemma in *King Solomon's Ring* (op. cit.). He has one chapter on "Laughing at Animals" and another on "Pitying Animals."

7. This cynical interpretation of brooding behavior is adapted from Ruth Crosby Noble: *The Nature of the Beast* (Doubleday, Doran and Company, New York, 1945, pp. 161 f.), but it arouses considerable feeling among those who love poultry. In my efforts to verify it among textbooks and teachers of poultry science, I received categorical and sometimes heated denials. "That . . . is pure imagination. It is not to cool her breast." Poultrymen much prefer to hypostatize an anthropomorphic concept of gallinaceous brooding. "If the weather is hot, the hen may stand over the nest *to shade* the eggs. If the weather is cold, the bird nestles down *to keep* them warm. When a hen becomes 'broody,' you can't keep her from setting on eggs or potatoes or smooth stones" (teleological italics mine). But none of this is inconsistent with the view set forth by Noble. Thus, opinion is divided between an altruistic bird who wants to keep her eggs comfortable and a less estimable hen who merely wants to cool herself off. Noble cites in support of the icebag theory the fact that if the breast of an incubating bird is immersed in cold water, thus counteracting the abnormal heat, the bird will no longer be interested in brooding. But as she also notes, birds do recognize and prefer their own eggs to those of other birds. So there may be something more to it than mere poulticing.

8. I came across an account of this unusual stickleback behavior some years ago and made some notes, but neglected to record the source. Since then I have hunted for it assiduously but vainly. I have talked to and written to several fish men, but they were all skeptical, including Desmond Morris, who is a stickleback man of many years' standing. With the pride of a poultryman, he replied, "My sticklebacks never, to my knowledge, developed 'lockjaw.' "

9. Wendt, Herbert: *The Sex Life of Animals*. Simon and Schuster, New York, 1965; Chapter 7. See also Le Boeuf, B. J., and Peterson, R. S.: "Social Status and Mating Activity in Elephant Seals." *Science* 163:91-93, January 3, 1969.

10. Wendt, Herbert: *Ibid*. For the most careful study to date of baboon harems, see Hans Kummer: *The Social Organization of Hamadryas Baboons*. University of Chicago Press, Chicago, 1968.

11. The idea of putting muumuus on apes is no more original than the proposal of SINA, the Society for Indecency to Naked Animals, to put panties on pets, half-slips on cows, and Bermuda shorts on horses. Started as a hoax, with the slogan "Decency Today Means Morality Tomorrow," SINA hoped to expose some aspects of sexual hypocrisy through satire, but failed because millions of people took their crusade seriously. For an account of the barely credible results, see: *The Great American Hoax*, by Alan Abel. Trident Press, New York, 1966. For additional information about how violently some "pet-lovers" feel about "immorality" in animals, see: *Petishism*, by Kathleen Szasz. Holt, Rinehart and Winston, New York, 1969.

12. Berne, E.: *Games People Play*.

13. Karpman, S.: "Fairy Tales and Script Drama Analysis." *Transactional Analysis Bulletin* 7:39-43, April, 1968.

14. Sun Tzu: *The Art of War*, translated by Lionel Giles, *in* Phillips, T. R. (ed.): *Roots of Strategy*. Military Service Publishing Company, Harrisburg, Pa., 1940.

6

SEX AND WELL-BEING
OR
PREVENTIVE INTIMACY

A

INTRODUCTION

It is very difficult to decide on cause and effect in human behavior because most psychological theories are manufactured to explain what happened last time. But this does not prove anything unless the same explanation can be used to predict what will happen next time. If the explanation works for the future as well as it does for the past, then very likely it does say something worth saying about human nature. A theory that works for the future as well as for the past may be called a hard theory, while one that works for the past but not for the future is a soft theory. Thus the theories of psychoanalysis and transactional analysis, properly used by properly trained people, can not only explain

the previous behavior of a person, but can also foretell what he will do in the 'years to come; so these are hard theories. People who use soft theories, such as sociologists, generally say that they cannot predict the future because circumstances change, and that is very true. So a hard theory of human behavior is one that deals with hard facts, aspects that remain unchanging through the ages, while a soft theory deals with soft facts, those that are easily changed by external circumstances.

Soft theories are not as powerful as hard theories because there is no reliable way to check them and they do not indicate remedies. Usually they deal with Awfuls, items that can be traded like stamps between people who play Ain't It Awful, but don't know what to do with the Awfuls they collect except compare them with other collections. For example, comparing the frequency of sexual horsewhipping among college graduates versus grade school graduates does nothing to stop it, if it should be stopped, but it makes an interesting Awful to talk about, even though there is no reliable way to check the figures. Actually, such a study should be of interest mainly to manufacturers of horsewhips. Most people who want to read about such things are like the little old lady at the zoo who asked the guard whether the hippopotamus was a male or a female, to which the man replied: "Madam, that should be of interest only to another hippopotamus."*

Soft theories, which are usually based on the question "How many people do so and so?" are of value to administrators, politicians, economists, and businessmen. Hard theories, which say, "Human beings are so constructed that unless something special prevents it, they will invariably do such and such," are much more useful to scientists. Soft theories are made for the most part by dependent thinkers,

---

*EW: Do you know any jokes in which the woman doesn't end up looking stupid?
EB: Yes. See page 87 (Chapter 3, section B).

thinkers who are thinking for the benefit of someone else. Hard theories are made by independent thinkers, who like to discover things for the sake of discovery. In the long run, however, they prove more useful than soft theories do. So in the sections that follow, we will try to stick to hard facts and avoid soft facts whenever possible.

B

PHYSICAL CONTACT AND PHYSICAL HEALTH

If baby rats are not handled by their mothers or by human hands, they do not develop as well as they should, and many of them get sick and die. The same applies to human babies who are not picked up. They need to be held and patted.[1] In fact any human being who is not stroked with cheerful words or gentle hands will shrivel up and die inside. Dr. Harry Harlow and his friends studied baby monkeys who were taken from their mothers at birth and given a terry-cloth towel to rub up against instead.[2] They proved that monkey babies are designed by nature for physical contact with others of their kind. If they are deprived of that, when they grow up they cannot have sexual relations the way other monkeys do, and if one does get pregnant, her baby is likely to die because she will neglect or mistreat it. Some human parents do that too: ignore their babies or beat them up, even injure or kill them. Such parents were usually victims themselves as children, sons and daughters of non-touching shells of humanity, or of sad and angry sacks.[3] We can say all this briefly as follows: If any person is not stroked by his own kind, his mind shrivels and his humanity dries out.

There are two groups of people who suffer this way. In every city there are thousands of girls who go to work every

morning and travel home each night to spend nearly all of their spare time alone in their rooms or apartments, with nothing to do and no one to talk to or fight with. In a typical case, Sally has no dates; she may have a few friends who are not too enthusiastic about her; they invite her to dinner once every two months to meet a young lawyer from Kansas or Maine. In between, she may try going to movies or concerts, but she goes alone and lives the life of a loner. After a while she loses interest in cooking for herself, and eventually in eating. Then her skin begins to go bad and her legs start to shrink from lack of nourishment. Her muscles get weak and her stomach sags. It is not the lack of social activity that causes these bad effects, but it is the lack of social activity which leads to her loss of appetite, and that is what causes the body decay. Between her lack of social stimulation and her physical weakness, she gets depressed and loses her drive and energy. This may lead her to take drugs. Often these are amphetamines or pep pills, which further depress her appetite and make things worse.

In her case, as in most cases, drugs are instead of people, and the circle will spiral downhill and can only be turned up by social contacts. Thus she starts out living a lonely life, and through loss of appetite and other things that happen to loners, she ends up in bad physical shape. The end result may be just as bad if she overeats instead of losing her appetite. In one case she uses drugs instead of people, and in the other food instead of people. In both cases, she becomes less and less attractive and less likely to find someone who will supply the recognition and stroking she needs.

Another group that suffer in the same way are older men who lead lonely lives, such as night watchmen who live in cheap hotels. Many of them end up in an equally sad condition, which may be called night watchman's disease. They too, from lack of social life, lose interest in eating. There is no one to cook for them and no one for them to cook for. Their bodies shrivel from bad nutrition and lack

of vitamins, and their resistance to pneumonia and other infections is lowered. Their brains may shrivel, too, causing slow thinking, confusion, and sometimes delirium.

Lobar pneumonia itself is a good example of how important social contact is. Nowadays this ancient lung disease can usually be conquered with penicillin and similar medications. But before those remedies were devised, it had a very high death rate, something like 33 percent. City hospitals used to be full of lonely people suffering from pneumonia in the middle of winter. Often there were so many of them that they filled up all the beds on the wards and the overflow lay on mattresses in the corridors, and it was very difficult to save them all from dying. Many hospital internes in those days were convinced that patients who just lay there, with no one from the outside caring about them, had a higher death rate than those who had visitors.[4] Whether this lowered resistance was due simply to the lack of contact or to the loner's diseases (malnutrition and alcoholism) which result from that, the evidence is that people-hunger meant the difference between life and death, and a cool hand on the brow or a friendly squeeze was a powerful aid to the serum that was being injected. This is a specific example of something which also applies to many less common diseases as well, especially to the condition known as marasmus in infants.

Social and physical contacts, or lack of them, also affect the way people tread the world they live in. An experienced observer can pick out loners just by the way they walk down the street and look at other people and the things around them. Nor does this have to do with "extraverts" and "introverts." Many extraverts are really loners and many introverts can form lasting and intimate relationships. Sometimes a loner can be diagnosed by the way he talks on the telephone. My friend Dr. Horseley, for example, says that he can tell almost instantly, when a strange psychiatrist calls him, whether this colleague does group treatment or confines his

practice to individual therapy, sometimes just by the way the caller says Hello, or in other cases after the first two or three sentences.

The examples given above are meant to show that physical contact is necessary to produce healthy, vigorous and alert children, and that social contact is necessary in later life to sustain these qualities. Infection and malnutrition are the great killers of the world, and physical contact helps to prevent and conquer both if there is any choice in the matter. The friendly touch of a human hand can spread its benevolent influence to every part of the body and awaken the desire to fight and eat and live. Even where disease and starvation seem beyond help, everybody knows what help means. It means the friendly approach of another human being bearing balms and medication and boxes of food. Once recovery begins, baskets decorated with loving care are even better.

C

THE SIX HUNGERS

Just as the human body has a hunger for food and vitamins and will waste away without them, so the nervous system has a hunger for sensations and will fall apart if they are taken away. This is well known to the political police of many countries, and also to prisoners who have been put in solitary confinement. It was a great surprise when this fact first came to light during the Trotskyite trials in Russia in the 1930's. Most people thought that the Trotskyites who "confessed" to crimes must have been severely tortured to make them swear to falsehoods. But all that is necessary to make a person "confess" to almost anything is to keep him in solitary confinement long enough, either with a bright

light that is always lit or in complete darkness. Monotony is the key word: no human contact, no change in surroundings (not even sunrise and sunset), and the same food from the same dreary tubs in the same grim bowls every day. Under such conditions, the nervous system decays and the mind with it. The craving for sensations grows so great that the victim will do almost anything merely for a cigarette or a few words with another human being, no matter how evil.

A baby who is not picked up is in a similar plight. He lies in his prison crib hour after hour, day after day, with no change or stimulation except when he is fed, and this gradually leads to physical and mental breakdown. This happens because there is a special part of the brain, the "arousal system," that must be stimulated regularly to maintain good health.[5] If it is not stimulated, deterioration results. This can be seen in a mild degree in "sensory deprivation experiments," where people are hired merely to stay in a cell with their eyes covered to prevent looking, and their arms and hands covered to prevent touching. Few can stand more than forty-eight hours of this, and many of them begin to have hallucinations and delusions, very much as they might under the influence of a drug.[6]

Most people have a hunger for human contact, at least of sight and sound, and in most cases also for touch or stroking. Again we see that such contact may actually make the difference between physical and mental health or breakdown, and even between life and death.

Of all the forms of sensation, the one preferred by most human beings is contact with another human skin. This provides not only touch, but also warmth or heat of a special kind. The human skin is the best known emitter and absorber of infrared rays.[7] In fact people who study infrared rays use human skin as a standard, just as diamonds are used as a standard for hardness. Infrared rays are heat waves, and can easily be photographed with special film, or "seen" with special lenses such as snipers use to see enemy

soldiers in the dark. The infrared rays given off by the human body have a certain wavelength—just the right wavelength to have the best possible effect on other human skins. That is why babies respond so well to physical contact with their mothers, and why mothers in turn love to feel the warmth of their infants. There is something close to sexual pleasure in all this, and part of sexual pleasure is to receive infrared rays from another person. Actually, any living thing with a temperature of 98.6 degrees probably gives off the right infrared rays, and that is one reason why anything with a temperature of 98.6 degrees—an animal, a child, or a person of the same sex, as well as a person of the opposite sex—can become a sexual object under certain conditions.

The human nervous system is so constructed that verbal recognition can partly take the place of physical contact or stroking. That means that having people say Hello to you can keep your spinal cord from shriveling up almost as well as physical stroking, but it is never quite as satisfactory, and the hunger for physical stroking is still there, although it may be repressed. It is interesting to observe that in this country some bottle-fed babies never feel their mother's skin directly, but ever and always only through her clothes. The warmth does get through, but probably not as pleasantly as from the bare skin. Thus for the baby it is something like the old saying about "taking a bath with your socks on," only in this case he takes his infrared bath with his mother's blouse on.

There is even more specialization than that. The baby not only wants the warmth of another body next to his, but above all he wants his mouth stroked, and nursing mothers like to have their breasts stroked by the baby's mouth. When the nursing period is over, these desires may subside in the baby until after puberty, but then there is hunger again for closer contact of certain parts of the body, and these become grownup sexual cravings.

If we take all of these things together, we can call them

hungers, and sex is the most exciting way to satisfy all of them at once. (A) Stimulus hunger, for sensory stimulation of sight and sound and touch, with smell and taste as a bonus for gourmets. (B) Recognition hunger, for a special kind of warmth and contact in deeds or words. (C) Contact hunger, for physical stroking, although some people settle for pain, or even come to prefer it. (D) Sexual hunger, to penetrate and be penetrated, which gratifies the other hungers while it happens.

Thus sex hunger may start anywhere along the line. A sex-hungry girl who lives as a loner in a little room with not even a picture on the wall will get none of the gratifications. In large cities, there are a certain number who live this way by choice. They cannot afford the slightest luxury or relaxation because they are in therapy. They keep only enough of their earnings for low-grade food and gas and oil and give all the rest to their therapists while they slowly "make progress" year after year to a melancholy menopause. Others have hobbies that keep their senses awake (A), but recognition, contact and penetration with love are out of their reach. Still other men and women have sensory stimulation (A) and recognition (B) at work or at play, but veer away from contact or penetration, perhaps in favor of "causes" instead. These are the ones who surprise people when they commit sexual betrayals or crimes, nearly always of a cowardly nature. The half-virgins of both sexes like stimulation (A), recognition (B), and contact (C), but avoid penetration— from fear or on questionable principles which do not keep them from being crudely seductive and teasing until the last moment, when they cry "Rapo! I've scored again," and the crestfallen partner goes home to a lonely bed. People who find their proper mates can have all the hungers satisfied— (A), (B), (C), and (D).

One of the great problems in life is how to structure one's time, and this gives rise to a fifth kind of hunger. There are 24 hours each day, 168 hours a week, 52 weeks every year,

and 50 or 100 years to look forward to. All this time has to be filled or "structured." Structure-hunger is more widespread and almost as damaging as malnutrition or malaria. When it becomes acute, it turns into incident-hunger, which causes many people to get into trouble and make trouble just to relieve their boredom,[8] and that is one reason why they play hard and destructive games. (Another is so that they won't have time to stop and think.) This sixth hunger, incident-hunger, was far better understood by old-time poets, philosophers, and men of action than it is by modern social scientists, since it is poor fodder for either computers or government grants. Isaac Watts said it: "Satan finds some mischief still for idle hands to do." Military officers, sea captains, and others skilled in authority have not only always understood it as well as Watts and Kierkegaard[9] did, but they also know what to do about it: "Keep the troops busy (no matter how) or they'll lose their morale and their respect for you to boot."

Even people with the strongest drive occasionally feel acute structure-hunger, and it is chronic for most of the world with their over-and-over lives and repeating scripts. Long-term structuring is the least pressing and is taken care of by choosing a career. Shorter periods can be filled in by setting up something to look forward to: graduation, next vacation, good promotion, recreation. The most difficult problem for most people is what to do right now or today, if there is leisure or unstructured time. There must be somebody to do something with, or alternatively, some interesting way to pass the time by ignoring other people: meditation, masturbation, defecation, and intoxication are all good ways to loaf and invite your soul—to shrivel up, unless you are one of the great ones who can profit from such activities.

But if you stop to think, you yourself can create the very people who will keep you busy all the time without any initiative on your part, and manufacture incidents galore. They will see to it that you have enough to do today and to-

morrow, and 168 hours this week and 52 weeks next year, and you will feel in the long run, if you have any goodwill at all about it, that every minute of it was worthwhile. All you need to do to acquire these built-in time structurers is have sex once a year on the right day according to the calendar, with a willing mate. Babies are the greatest remedies for structure- and incident-hunger ever devised.

D

SEX AND ETHICS

I have tried to give some hard facts that should impress hardheaded as well as softhearted people. Physical contact is necessary for physical development and health, and is often life-saving. It is also necessary for mental development and health, and is often sanity-saving. And sexual contact is the simplest, pleasantest, most constructive, and most satisfying way of appeasing the six basic hungers of the human mind (or nervous system, if you wish). There is therefore no good reason (although there are several bad ones) why other people should meddle with sexual activities between consenting grownups, and such meddling is a poor basis for an ethical system. Its result in this country has been that sex is largely illegal, and violence is not. Sex is banned from the newsstands in most places where murder is freely sold, and from television where violence is freely seen: not only violence between consenting adults, as in Westerns, but unprovoked mayhem that sells cancer sticks and soap. An ardent teenager can learn from every corner store and in any living room new and better ways of charnel killing or wounding, but there is no one to tell him new and better ways of carnal love.

It is the other way round in places like Denmark, where

anyone over twelve, I am told, can watch a sexy movie, but
no one under sixteen can watch a violent one. So in this
country children are allowed to see hate but not love, while
in Denmark it is vice versa. Of course decent children with
decent parents in both countries will behave decently anyway, and I am only talking about where the official sanctions or sanctimonies lie.

Somewhere there has to be a simple and sensible system
of values, and I propose one that is not only simple, but also
I think makes some sort of sense. Furthermore, it can be
judged from one set of pretty reliable figures, so that different countries can be compared, and barroom arguments can
be settled with a wet thumb in the right book. It is based on
the single idea that if anything in life is significant and
worthwhile, it is the love between mother and child. It assumes that mothers (and fathers and uncles and grandparents too) want their babies to live. Although this is not
always so, it is as hard a fact as anything that can be said
about human desires. The proposed ethical system is therefore based on one item which comes out of that. Here is my
proposition. The goodness or badness of any society shall
henceforth be judged by its infant mortality rate. If that is
low, the society is good; if it is high, the society is bad. In
between there are gray areas for those who don't like black
and white. (The infant mortality rate is the number of deaths
of children under one year per 1,000 live births.)[10] This mortality rate is really a matter of national management and is
decided by the prejudices of each government and where it
puts its money (or as it is usually said in the words of the
people in charge and their donzels, by political and economic policy). We therefore say our ethic again to take account of that. We consider the total infant mortality rate
from all causes (disease, starvation, ignorance, and murder,
whether in peace or war), in all the territories controlled by
a government. If that rate is low, the system is a good one;
if it is high, it is bad. The reason I am down on India, for

example, is that while some of its people sit around sucking their psyches and kowtowing to their cows, babies are dying like flies around them. Therefore that system is a bad one.* By using this approach, all problems of sexual ethics can be solved by asking only one question: which decision will result in fewer deaths among babies born alive? It is not a question of making babies; almost anybody can do that. The real test is to keep them going after their first cry, and that takes careful thought, good governing, and decent concern for things that count. It is doubtful that it is going to be taken care of by what Amaryllis calls "smut-smellers" and "shootniks."

E

SEX AND ESTHETICS

It is also possible to set up a "one-item esthetic system" by proposing that nice pictures should have good frames and that art galleries should be clean and well built. This does away with the error that a beautiful inside excuses an ugly exterior, with its final challenge that Truth and Beauty should crouch in the garbage can and we should all go and look for them there. Picture frames can be disdained as merely gilded squares, and so can the people who build art galleries, but it takes both to set off Leonardo and Renoir to best advantage. True, the paintings can exist without them, but enjoyment goes beyond mere existence, and a good light is better than a dark alley to see how a man handles his palette. No painting can even exist in darkness,

---

*Note that this is a reductive system, which simply states that *for whatever reasons*, a system works well or badly. There may be *all kinds* of reasons, but the ailing infant and his mother are not likely to be impressed by them.

if existence means to live in the world of people. (This is Bishop Berkeley's paradox again.)

This principle can be applied to human behavior; for example, juvenile delinquency, whatever that includes. In some cases, delinquency is a matter of morality if it increases or threatens to increase the infant mortality rate. But in other cases it is merely unpretty, and reprehensible because of that. Evil is bad because it makes messes. This approach appeals to many of the "juveniles" themselves. They may be more willing to listen if you say that what they do is not pretty than if you say that it is wicked. The wickedness may not be visible, and may in fact be just a figment to the growing mind, while bloody litter on the sidewalk is very real, and is there for all to see.

Having now set up an ethical principle and an esthetic principle, both based on visible results, we are ready to consider whether sexual intimacy, which is good for the body beautiful, is less good for the body politic. Intimate couples usually love and care for children and respond to beauty in themselves and their surroundings. In this way they help decrease the infant mortality rate, which is moral (according to our proposed ethical system), and they also want to keep things beautiful, which is esthetic. Thus they contribute to both the health and the beauty of society at large. And beyond that, since they receive so much, they can give more. Being game free, they do not try to exploit anyone, prove anything, or make anybody sorry, and having each other in natural closeness, they do not need alcohol or other chemicals that may damage children's minds or bodies and leave unpretty sights for them to see. All this shows, I hope, that from both the moral and the esthetic points of view, sexual intimacy is the most desirable way for society as for the individual, for satisfying the yearnings of the human soul and mind. We have only to beware of pseudo-intimacy, which masks anger, fear, and hurt and guilt with sweet words, or drowns them in acids and alcohols, only to have them sur-

face the next morning or the next year to spread their fetid vapors through the house.

Thus marriage, in common or in canon law, can become a true sacrament if it is not bruised or abused by clumsy handling and phony dandling, or by the threats and exhortations of muddling fiddlers, moral meddlers, and venal peddlers.

F

SEX AND INTIMACY

I have talked above about sexual intimacy because intimacy without sex, outside the family, is rare. Every couple has sexual desires, which they will discover if they are intimate in any other way; if they do not reveal them, they are withholding that much of themselves, so that the intimacy is not complete. Some couples can have partial intimacy while looking forward to its fulfillment later; for example, engaged couples waiting for the marriage bed. Others seem unlikely candidates, such as a homosexual man and a homosexual woman; for a long time such a pair may confine themselves to talking about important intimate subjects, such as their hopes, their fears, and their telephone bills. But if they keep it up, they too are likely sooner or later to find themselves in bed with each other, trading infrared rays and exploring each others' bodies, even though they may not have actual intercourse.

Real intimacy takes place between real people, and usually progresses more or less quickly to sex. First comes the thrill of discovery: "Someone I can really talk to," "I've been waiting so long and I'm really excited I found you." The breathless talkies, which may go on for twenty-four hours at a stretch, as each one pours out his life's savings of opinions, feelings, and aspirations, sooner or later give way

to the smiling lookies as "really talking" is replaced by "really seeing" the other person. The lookies lead inevitably to the touchies, and after a period of entranced stroking, the feelies begin to take over and the hands move downward and inward. Unless the proceedings are postponed or terminated at this point, the desire to explore warmer places wells up as the warmies come to life, and after that there has to be a decision as to whether the cuffies will have their way.

At each of these stages there is the risk of Parental interference.

> You're not supposed to talk that way,
> You're not supposed to stare,
> You're not supposed to touch him so,
> You must not feel her there,
> And certainly, my dear young thing,
> Of *that* you must beware!
> Talking, looking, touching, feeling,
> What an evil pair!

These warnings have to be overcome gently and without rancor, since defiance or outright rebellion will be followed in due time by the guilties and the morning after, which will sully the joy and slash the canvas of intimacy. But in most cases, once two people "really talk" to each other or "really look" at each other, they are tempted to plunge into the great adventure of a candid, game-free relationship, in which orders from headquarters are likely to be reinforced by orders from hindquarters. Then one or the other is going to say: "Why spend our lives with an at least when we can have a wow?" If they are both levelheaded, read from right or read from left, both ways WoW spells WoW. But if things get topsy-turvy, it reads MoM from either side. If their venture is prudent and successful, however, at an appropriate time there will be a baby, who will show them all the valuables they had hidden in the pockets of their genes. And what could be more moral and esthetic than that?

G

SEX AND MARRIAGE

The marriage license is a service provided by society to take care of the Parental interference referred to above by replacing it with the Parental blessing, and it often succeeds at that. But a marriage license no more makes a good spouse than a driver's license makes a good driver. Good spouses and good drivers are both made by Parental instructions contained in the script. A winner will make a good spouse and a good driver, and a loser will be poor at both because he does not have permission to do well at either. There are, of course, many splits here, good spouses who are poor drivers, and vice versa. Most of these, I think, turn out to be non-winners, who either plod and shrink, or zoom and crash.

Since the license in favorable cases eliminates the guilties, married people have the best chance for continued intimacy, although informal ball and sockets often do better than welded ball and chains. Either way, if the intimacy works, the couple can be spotted by the way they walk down the street. Their eyes sparkle and their steps are springy, and their children, if they have any, will be laughing merrily much of the time. The lady should be congratulated on looking so well, and the gentleman on the good job he has done. My friend Dr. Horseley relates the case of a troubled marriage that improved to the point of real intimacy, as was easily apparent when the couple was together. He asked them: "Do I have your permission to say that intimacy such as yours makes people's eyes sparkle and their steps springy?" To which they replied: "You certainly may, and you can add that it makes the children happier too." The children may

not know what is happening when such a change occurs, but they know that something is different, and they react in a very favorable way.

While the physical and mental effects of sex and intimacy have a great deal to do with this happy condition, there is another element at work as well, and that is a sense of freedom. This is shown by the fact that some newly divorced people show the same spring and sparkle after they are released from the bonds of their matrimony. This is one manifestation of the age-old conflict between security and freedom. When a marriage is based on love and security, its restrictions are cheerfully accepted and even enjoyed. But when it is an obligation and a damper on the free spirit of humanity, its bondage is cheerfully given up in favor of something more important than sex and more invigorating than apathy, and that is liberty. There is a simple question to test the importance of sex vs liberty. How would a person choose between staying in a prison with conjugal visits and taking a sexless parole?

H

SEX AND RESEARCH

Very little research has been done on sex and well-being. The best known figures are those that show that married people can expect to live longer than single ones. The only systematic work on the subject was published in German in 1904, and is full of pre-Nazi exhortations to keep the race pure and forbid sexual intercourse (even with contraceptives) to anyone with any physical defect.[11] The antisexual attitudes of those times and places are still to be found in this country, although some research is permitted under protest, with many people hoping it will make the whole subject look even more Awful than it did before. Re-

search intended to find out whether sex is beneficial or harmful to the human race would arouse opposition in many quarters, but a determined investigator might be able to carry it through. I would propose the following studies as a beginning:

(1) I have already mentioned (Chapter 1, E) the project of keeping health and sex records on a large group of college students of both sexes. It would then be a simple matter to compare physical health with frequency, regularity, and quality of sexual activity, if any.

(2) Take 1,000 female teachers in a number of school systems. Half wear sexy clothes and half wear conservative clothes. Then compare the scholastic achievement scores and IQ's of all their classes. Since the teachers would be volunteers, we would really be comparing sexy teachers with conservatives ones. This study might show that sexy-looking teachers raised the IQ's of their pupils, while conservative ones lowered achievement scores. Or it might be the other way round. Or it might be that sexiness has no effect at all. Nobody knows until somebody tries it.* This is merely one of the more practical projects of the many that an agile mind could devise to test the connection between sex and well-being.

—
I
—

SEX AND WELL-BEING

At this point we are ready to consider the specific conditions that sexual intimacy can prevent, alleviate, or

---

*Some of the variables in such an experiment, besides Sexy-Conservative and IQ-Achievement, would be Over-achievers–Under-achievers, age and sex of pupils.

cure. We will rely for the most part on the clinical experience of Dr. Horseley, who cautions us that specialists in other fields than psychiatry might well disagree with him on many of the things he says. In fact the mere list of these conditions has caused many of his medical colleagues to raise their eyebrows, and some of them even to purse their lips. And no wonder, for here is what he includes: high back pain, low back pain, obesity, fluid retention, bladder trouble, stomach ulcer, stomach cancer, high blood pressure, hemorrhoids; palpitation, shakiness, sweating and nightmares; asthma, eczema and hives; alcoholism and drug addiction; insomnia; flat feet, dull eyes, and all manner of other afflictions.[12] It sounds like an ad for a patent medicine, but fortunately no one can get a patent on this mixture of nature's elixirs, which has more healing powers than all the mineral waters of Europe, all the trees of the tropics, and all the herbs of China.

(1) Back pains. First, says Dr. Horseley, while the saying "Stroking keeps the spinal cord from shriveling up"[13] is just a manner of speaking, in some ways it is literally true. For example, good sex keeps the spine lined up right, and vice versa; or as Amaryllis puts it, "Stiff necks, cold sex." There are a certain number of women who wear surgical collars as a splint against recurring neck pains. Such pains are notoriously unpredictable. Even if the X-rays show signs that there is something wrong with the cartilages between the vertebrae, the complaints come and go without much change in these abnormalities. In his experience, a permanent cure often follows a congenial marriage or a robust affair, and the collar is never worn again. The same applies to low back pain, which is one of the commonest complaints among people with unsatisfactory sex lives. This condition is seen in the greatest concentration in the U.S. Army, where it is frequently referred for psychiatric consultation, which is generally not the case outside. The sexual remedy in civil-

ian life should not be too vigorous, for on the other side there is the condition known as "bride's back," which comes from overindulgence. Nor should it be halfhearted or perfunctory, since an unsatisfactory orgasm may aggravate the discomfort or bring on a recurrence after it has gone away. For that reason, the local remedy may not work for the military, and they seem to do better if they can go home.

Now, love as a cure for pains in the back, from the neck down to the sacrum, is not available to everyone, and many would consider the suggestion unacceptable or even repugnant. In such cases the patient will search for some cause in his everyday activities. He and his doctor may decide, for example, that the pain is a result of mowing his lawn. It may be that he has mowed this same lawn every day for years, but it is always possible that the grass was especially long on the day he got the pain.

But the facts are that the sex organs in both men and women become so engorged if sexual excitement is not released by a well-developed orgasm that they may exceed the structural safety factor of the muscles and ligaments of the lower spine, just as an excessive load may exceed the safety factor of an automobile's suspension system and cause an awful racket when it goes over a bump. The excited uterus, for example, may triple its normal size and weight and stay that way for an hour or more, but after a satisfactory orgasm it will return to normal in five or ten minutes. If we add to the weight of the blood-laden uterus the congestion of all the other pelvic organs, it is not surprising that a small and normally harmless twist can throw the already strained back out of joint. The same applies to the male sex. It is advisable, therefore, for people who are not going to have physiologically effective orgasms to either shun sexual stimulation of mind or body altogether, or else get with it one way or another. In making up their minds, they should remember Amaryllis' epigram: "Sexually frigid is intellectually rigid." She explains it this way: "It doesn't mean that frigid people

can't learn, but that they're not flexible in applying what they learn."*

(2) Overweight. Most women in Western countries consider overweight repellent to the opposite sex, but in some Oriental harems, the fatter the better, and even in this country plump women can usually find mates who like them that way. Nevertheless, women in search of marriage, love, intimacy, or just plain sex try to stay slim, and medical men consider this healthy because thin people on the whole have lower blood pressure and live longer than fat ones. In this indirect way, sex, or sexual desire, can prevent high blood pressure and its unwholesome consequences, and possibly prolong life.

Overweight, when it does occur, is of two types, obesity and fluid retention. According to the Don't Look at Me Theory, which is well known among obese women, one object of overeating is to prevent men from making passes at them, or to repel their husbands. This means that when they are ready for intimacy, they are more likely to slim up, and in that roundabout way, sex can be regarded as a cure for obesity. Sometimes the relationship is more direct. A woman who loses a lover or husband will often begin to stuff herself, trading a man for a bag of groceries. On the other hand, a lonely woman who finds a mate may start to diet and take off weight.

Fluid retention is more variable than obesity and may cause quite large changes in weight from one day to the next. Some women who get angry at night find that they have gained the next morning, and this anger is closely related to their sexual activities. In these cases, a sweet-flowing sex life makes smooth-flowing kidneys, and the weight

---

*The word "frigid" is sometimes used in a general deprecatory rather than a specific physiological sense to mean "having an intolerant attitude toward sex." This would include people who are prudish and hypocritical (and withholding anorgasmic women) as well as those who are actually coldly repulsing or frigid.

changes are watered away.[14] The bladder is also toned up.[15]

(3) Stomach trouble. On the man's side, many a husband knows how sex can prevent cancer. He knows that it is his wife, or rather his choice of wife, and his responses to her, that make his stomach churn and the acid squirt. He also knows that if it churns often enough and fiercely enough, he may end up with an ulcer, and that it is not a very long churn from an ulcer to cancer in serious cases. So he pops executive mints to keep the acid down, and hopes for what script analysts call an At Least: for example, at least he might get high blood pressure before he gets cancer, and die a pleasanter death. But he will tell you that a good sex life would prevent the whole disaster: churning, acid, mints, and ulcer, and the cancer or stroke at the end of the line. And in many cases, all these things he says could be true.

(4) Hemorrhoids, oddly enough, can also result from sexual frustration. They are strongly encouraged by spending too much time in the bathroom. Now, people with a good sex life would rather spend an hour romping in the bedroom than reading in the bathroom, and in this way sex can be regarded as a preventive against piles. On the other hand, from this point of view, illiteracy might be a simpler solution.

(5) Anxiety symptoms. Freud's first theory about anxiety said that it was caused by simple sexual frustration.[16] He later made it more complicated, but his first equation seems to hold true in many cases. This means that palpitation, shakiness, sweating, and nightmares, if they are not caused by some physical or chemical disorder such as thyroid disease, may result from dammed-up sexual excitement. This may be simply due to lack of available partners, but it may also come from lack of real intimacy, so that sex, if it is indulged in at all, is not properly completed or is mere copulation, without the health-giving closeness and freedom that tones up the body and wards off such maladies.

In some cases, lack of opportunity, or lack of response to

sexual stimulation due to anger and other complications, may result in chronic, alarming, and sometimes disabling breathlessness, weakness, and tightness in the chest, giving the feeling of an impending "heart attack." This condition is known medically as neurocirculatory asthenia, and among soldiers and Australians as "the rare Hawaiian disease laka-nuki." It is often treated with large doses of tranquilizers and sleeping pills that reduce the person's efficiency and sociability, and this sets up a vicious circle.

(6) Allergic reactions. Good sex is good prevention for asthma, eczema, and hives. But bad sex may aggravate them. The same goes for arthritis and "rheumatiz" in older people, and for trichomonas infection, which often causes "the whites" in women. This condition is particularly common in those who are unresponsive (perhaps intuitively) to their husbands, who may be innocent carriers of the organism.

(7) Since alcohol and drugs are instead of people, good sex is a sovereign remedy for these addictions. They can cause death in many ways, ranging from cirrhosis of the liver to overshooting with heroin, setting fire to a mattress or sweating it out in the stinking hell of a badly run jail. Cigarette smoking belongs here too; sexual frustration and marital tension may lead to harder, faster, and deeper smoking and hasten the onset of lung cancer.

(8) Good sex is a cure for insomnia. On the mental side, it is something pleasant to think about in bed, and refreshing thoughts should bring refreshing sleep. Even if you don't fall asleep, blissful thoughts make lying awake more cozy, and more restful to boot. It should be more agreeable to think of rolling in the golden hay of sunrise with rosy-fingered Aurora as she colors the dawning sky than to toss and worry about all the people you hate, or why you can't make more money, or how guilty you should feel about something you've done or haven't done, or how scared to be of someone you have to deal with when the sun is really up. (Don't think you're going to shock Aurora with your lusty play.

Astraeus and Tithonus and Cephalus were there before you, and she is the reason Orion is always smiling in the sky.)

It is the four-year-old in a person that tosses around in bed, taking advantage of the enormous muscles at his disposal. And nothing soothes a tired or worried four-year-old like cuddling up to Mother, unless he is sulking or she pushes him away; the same goes for a little girl and her father. In this particular case, outcest is even more effective than incest.

Biologically, good sex is nature's sleeping pill, and should automatically lead into a healthy drowse that falls into a sound night's sleep. This may even be stated as a rule: If after bedtime sex enough a lover doesn't feel sleepy, then something is wrong with the sex. If he actually feels twitchy instead, then something is very wrong. But if it goes right, then in the morning it will be a cure for flat feet and dull eyes, if you remember the springy step and sparkling look of the well-cuffed couple.

(9) Beyond all the conditions mentioned above, there are probably hundreds of thousands of cases seen by doctors every year where physical symptoms in various parts of the body result directly or indirectly from sexual "problems." Tracking this down is an interesting field of medical detective work, but in most cases it would probably not help much in the immediate treatment of the symptoms. Every once in a while, though, it does pay off in the most surprising way. For example, consider the case of Mrs. Woble, who suffered from "tennis elbow," which is about as far away from sex as you can get. Since she did not play tennis, she was at a loss to account for her condition, which almost paralyzed her right arm. It was aggravated by the fact that she bumped her sore elbow several times a day passing through doorways or reaching for things. Her orthopedic surgeon treated it in the usual way by novocaine injections, ultrasound and rest. But every time she bumped it, she undid the effects of the treatment. He suggested that she keep it in a sling, which

she was reluctant to do because that kept her from taking care of her housework. Furthermore, when she did wear the sling on her right arm, she began to bump her left elbow.

One of her knowing friends told her it was all due to masochism, and another avid reader said it was hostility, but neither of them could explain why it settled where it did. Her housemaid, closer to the truth, said she thought it would go away if Mrs. Woble hit the right person real hard, but ventured no opinion as to who that person was. Then her psychiatrist noticed one day that she walked differently than she had before, that is, with her arms tensed up and her elbows slightly bent akimbo, as though she really was trying to keep from hitting somebody. They both knew who that somebody was: it was her husband, whom she was furious at and blamed for her sexual frustration. Her "tennis elbow" came about as follows. Since she had begun to stiffen up her arms and keep her elbows slightly bent, she was two or three inches wider than she was in her normal state with her arms relaxed. (Normal width, 20″. Angry width, 23″. Width of many doorways, 29″.) But when she walked through a doorway, she did not make allowance for the fact that she stuck out a little on each side, and therefore banged her elbow every so often. Only after the sexual problem was settled, and she went back to her normal diameter, could the orthopedic treatment start to take effect.

It should be clear from this list of conditions that sex is closely connected with well-being and is biologically healthy and desirable, and so we can speak of preventive intimacy as an important public health measure. Under certain conditions, however, it may do more harm than good, and a certain amount of caution has to be exercised, just as in swimming or riding a bicycle. There are always sharks and oil slicks to watch out for. These are similar to the dangers mentioned by Miss Wilde, the young lady in the limerick in Chapter I. She feared she might get an unwanted pregnancy, or venereal disease, or be denounced from the pulpit, or

forced to hide her cleavage under a big red A, and those are things that can always happen.

Sex may also interfere with other activities. Many athletes try to abstain during the playing season or when their big events are coming up. There used to be a legend that the members of the Oxford and Cambridge rowing teams would go to any lengths to prevent an ejaculation, even a wet dream, while they were in training for the big race, and inflicted all sorts of unpleasant prevention on themselves to avoid such accidents. Some movie producers try to prevent their stars from having affairs during a filming for fear that it might impair their acting ability in the love scenes. "If they're balling all night, how can they look as though they want to ball some more the next morning in front of the camera?" as one man put it plaintively. And some Old Masters felt that they did their best work in a state of temporary virginity.

Worst of all, it is a fact that sexual intercourse or even masturbation can occasionally be fatal for men with coronary heart disease or hardening of the arteries, by causing a heart attack or a stroke of apoplexy. This commonly occurs away from home, in a motel or the apartment of a lady friend, usually after a heavy meal and lots of drink. These tragic endings are much feared by madams of brothels, since they are almost sure to get busted, and badly, if there is a death in the house and the coroner is called in. The medical examiners who do the autopsies in such cases recommend that coronary patients limit their sexual attentions to their wives, in familiar surroundings, and on an empty stomach.[17]

On the other hand, there is the curious fact that Oriental potentates, who have unlimited opportunities for sexual gratification, often outlive their contemporaries (providing they are not assassinated), and there is no doubt that many older people are rejuvenated when they take a younger mate. Thus the Fountains of Youth, so ardently sought in Florida and other exotic places, may be right under our noses (ap-

proximately 2′ 6″ down). Since it is well established that married people, on the average, live far longer than single ones,[18] the prevention of aging may lie not in some rare drug or mineral but in an active sex life. Thus my young friend Amaryllis may be more philanthropic than saucy when she wishes her elders "Long life and good cuffing," for the two do seem to go together.

A more specific question for older men is whether sexual activity prevents prostate operations. There is no firm evidence that sexual frustration causes enlargement of the prostate, but it does make the symptoms worse by causing congestion.[19] Dog owners run into this during rutting season when their frustrated males get so uncomfortable that they have to be taken to the vet for injections at $35 a throw. Thus good sex may alleviate the symptoms and so avert a serious and very upsetting surgical procedure in humans. An allied question is whether it prevents cancer of the cervix in women, and the answer is no.[20] If it proves to be true, as some have said, that the viruses causing such conditions hide in the male's foreskin, then a small sacrifice on the part of the husband might be worthwhile, and he will be amply repaid by having an interesting conversation piece thereafter.

And now a practical hint about the dentist's chair. Novocaine injections are often requested by timorous people for simple fillings. The victim is then left for the rest of the day with a concrete jaw on one side, and sometimes when the novocaine wears off he suffers more pain than the original drilling would have caused. In order to avoid the injection, he should try Nature's anesthetic first, and that is sexual fantasies. In order for this to work, the more the drill hurts, the sexier his fantasies have to get. If his imagination is responsive enough, he may go through the whole procedure without feeling any pain at all, and in fact he may come to regard his dental work as a festive occasion. That is a right-now on-the-spot way in which sex can contribute to well-being. Unfortunately, this does not work as well for the

lower jaw as it does for the less sensitive uppers. But it may work for other pains besides dental, although that remains to be seen.

In closing this chapter, I would like to mention the key word that prevents intimacy and all the well-being it can bring. This is not a four-letter word; it has three: b-u-t. "But" prevents more loving than any other word in the English language, with "if only" running second. Intimacy is very much a matter of experiencing and enjoying what is here and now. "But" repudiates here and now, and "if only" moves it somewhere else or puts it off till later. "But" means apprehension for the future, and "if only" means regret for the past. Good sex contributes to well-being because it is right now. Living right now is seeing the trees and hearing the birds sing, and it is necessary to see the trees and hear the birds and know that the sun is out, in order to see people's faces and hear their spirits sing and know that the sun of their warmth is there; and that is the way to attain intimacy. That bright here and now of the open universe out there is what should be, before going indoors and living in the closed here and now of each other. For those things to happen, it is first necessary to have a clear mind and to forget for the time being all forms of tedious shuffle: shuffling papers and shuffling people and shuffling things in your head. That is why I asked you a long time ago whether you heard a bird sing today, and reminded you that it isn't time that is passing, but you who are passing through time—nonstop. And my last word is to repeat what I said there about that. Stop! And begin over again with the first word, which is Hi!

With this word, we bring these contemplations to a close. For those who want more, there follow some short discussions, some wise sayings, and a brief appendix for behavioral scientists. But for most people, it might be better to stop here.

NOTES AND REFERENCES

1. On rats see Levine, S.: "Stimulation in Infancy." *Scientific American* 202:80-86, May, 1960. Also "Infantile Experience and Resistance to Psychological Stress." *Science* 126:405, August 30, 1957. On babies, see Spitz, R.: "Hospitalism: Genesis of Psychiatric Conditions in Early Childhood." *Psychoanalytic Study of the Child* 1:53-74, 1945.

2. On monkeys, see Harlow, H. F., and Harlow, M. K.: "Social Deprivation in Monkeys." *Scientific American* 207:136-146, November, 1962.

3. Parents of "battered children" were often battered children themselves. (Personal communication, Ellen Berne, Bellevue Hospital, New York City.) Cf. Silver, L. B., Dublin, C. C., and Lourie, R. S.: "Does Violence Breed Violence? Contributions from a Study of the Child Abuse Syndrome." *American Journal of Psychiatry* 126:404-407, September, 1969.

4. The 1940 or "pre-penicillin" edition of Cecil's *Textbook of Medicine* (W. B. Saunders Company, Philadelphia) gives the fatality rate in large city hospitals of Europe and America as in the neighborhood of 30 percent, in Bellevue Hospital ranging from 30 to almost 50 percent, and states: "The fatality rate in private practice is distinctly lower than that in hospitals. This is due of course to the fact that mild cases are treated at home, while severe ones are sent to hospitals." It was Cecil himself who made this statement, but I think the differential mortality could also be interpreted according to the thesis offered in the text. Patients in private practice were obviously getting more personal attention than the patients in the corridors of Bellevue. The death rate of alcoholics was 56 percent. Cecil goes on to say that the patient's station in life is significant. "Patients in the higher walks of life, being well fed and clothed, and usually in good physical condition, are a better risk than those who are poor, underfed, and ill clothed." But the "well fed and clothed" patients are more likely to have and be allowed to receive visitors than the "underfed and ill clothed" patients lying in the corridors, so there is nothing here to challenge the internes' conviction that personal visitors increased the survival rate. But it was not fashionable in those days to make serious studies of such matters.

5. French, J. D.: "The Reticular Formation." *Scientific American* 196:54-60, May, 1957.

6. Brownfield, C. A.: *Isolation: Clinical and Experimental Approaches*. Random House, New York, 1965.

7. Barnes, R. B.: "Thermography of the Human Body." *Science* 140:870-877, May 24, 1963.

8. Heron, W.: "The Pathology of Boredom." *Scientific American* 196:52-56, January, 1957.

9. Kierkegaard, S.: *Fear and Trembling & Sickness Unto Death.* Anchor Books, New York, 1954.

10. According to the *United Nations Demographic Yearbook* for 1966, the infant mortality rate in Monaco and the Ryukyu Islands is 10 per 1,000 live births. In Canada and the United States, it is 23. In the Republic of South Africa, it is 29 for whites, and 136 for "colored," the highest in the "civilized" world except for India, where it is estimated at 146. For a further discussion of this ethical system, see my "manifesto" in *Transactional Analysis Bulletin* 8:7-8, January, 1969.

    (In 1967 the lowest rate in the world was—surprisingly—in Papua [4.3, non-indigenous population]. The figure for the Ryuku Islands excludes U.S. personnel stationed in the area, but is faulty because it also includes live-born infants dying before registration of birth. *U.N. Demographic Yearbook,* 1968.)

11. Senator, H., and Kaminer, S.: *Health and Disease in Relation to Marriage and the Married State.* Allied Book Company, New York, 1929. Two volumes, translated by J. Dulberg from the German original of 1904.

12. Kinsey et al. talk about health affecting sexual activity, but have little to say about the reverse. Senator and Kaminer have over 1,200 pages on the relationship between sex, marriage, and disease, but their conclusions, as noted, are prejudiced and unreliable. Most interesting are the statistics they give for mortality rates in Sweden, 1881-1890 (Vol. 1, p. 19). In almost every age group from 20 to 90, the death rate for single people of both sexes was significantly higher than for married people. At many levels it was almost double. The rate for widowed and divorced people was just about halfway between. In those days "single," especially for women, probably meant little or no sex, or at best, for a large population, infrequent and unsatisfactory sex; and widowed or divorced meant a period of regular sex, followed by infrequent or no sex. According to these assumptions, more sex meant more life, and less sex meant more death, sometimes twice as much, so that, broadly speaking, sexual abstinence was a fatal disease. (Just as a curiosity, the lowest death rate was 4.64/1000 for married men of 20, and the highest, 318.97/1000, was for bereft men of 90.)

    In the absence, then, of hard research, we must fall back on soft clinical impressions for the ensuing discussion.

13. Berne, E.: *Transactional Analysis in Psychotherapy.*

14. For psychiatric aspects of urological phenomena see: Smith, D. R., and Auerbach, A.: "Functional Diseases," in *Encyclopedia of Urology*, Springer Verlag, Berlin, 1960, Volume XII.
15. Smith, D. R.: "Psychosomatic 'Cystitis.' " *Transactions of American Association of Genito-Urinary Surgeons* 53:113-116, 1961. This paper gives 18 references on the subject, including some on water and electrolyte excretion.
16. Freud, S.: *Complete Introductory Lectures on Psychoanalysis.* W. W. Norton and Company, New York, 1966. Chapter 25.
17. Symposium: "Sudden Death During Coitus—Fact or Fiction?" *Human Sexuality* 3:22-26, June, 1969.
18. Senator, H., and Kaminer, S.: op. cit.
19. Finkle, A. L.: "The Relationship of Sexual Habits to Benign Prostatic Hypertrophy." *Human Sexuality* 2:24-25, October, 1967.
20. *Time*, November 11, 1969.

PART III

Afterplay

7

QUESTIONS

A

QUESTIONS AND ANSWERS

Although the lectures upon which this book is based were open to the public, the people who came were mostly connected with the University of California. They included (roughly in order of age and sophistication) students from Berkeley and Santa Cruz, younger technicians from the medical school, medical students, graduate students in the social and medical sciences, secretaries, and faculty members from Berkeley, Santa Cruz, and the Medical School in San Francisco. They asked many questions after each lecture, some of which may also have occurred to the readers of this book. The answers given here are not always quite the same as the ones originally given.

QUESTION: What is the basic meaning of what you have said? What have you really told us?

ANSWER: I don't think there is any basic meaning. I'm used to thinking with a question in mind, and if there was such a thing as "the sexual question," I would try to answer it. But there isn't. The question in my mind was: "Is it possible to give five lectures about sex without merely repeating all the trivial or solemn or acrobatic or statistical things that many people say on such occasions?" I hope I've succeeded to some extent. I may have repeated some of them, but I don't think I've been hemmed in by them. What I've really told you are my thoughts about the subject after fifty-odd years of living and thirty-five years of practicing psychiatry, during which I've listened to several thousand people talking in detail about their sexual joys and sorrows. The main advantages I've had were my training in anatomy, physiology, psychiatry, and psychoanalysis, and the privilege of asking them any hardheaded questions that occurred to me.

Perhaps I would settle for calling these lectures instructive and thought-provoking essays rather than basic messages. But I wouldn't be entirely happy about it, since I prefer being basic. I think the most basic thing I said was that the feeling of autonomy is largely an illusion, and that if we do want to live our own lives, free of corruption, we should stop, look, and listen, and think.

QUESTION: When you speak on this subject, do you always find a predominance of women in the audience, the way it is here?

ANSWER: I've never spoken on the subject before, so I don't know. The way to test it would be to see what happened with a female lecturer. Margaret Mead gave these lectures some years ago. Did she have a predominance of men in the audience?

DR. LUCIA: It is possible that women are more fearful. Their information on the subject is more "amateur," and they would like to know more about safety. The men seem to be scot-free, while the women have to bear the burden of this sublime relationship.

QUESTION: How can you account for so many laughs from all of us on such a serious subject?

ANSWER: I'm sure I could have been so dismal about it that nobody would have dared to laugh without my permission. But since sex is supposed to be fun, I don't see why a lecture about it shouldn't be fun too.

QUESTION: What about perversions?

ANSWER: I'm not sure they should be called that unless they're very nasty and hurt or humiliate people, because that's a nasty word as it is commonly used by righteous people. Freud suggested "displacements," and the dictionary defines a perversion as an aberration, and I would prefer those words in most cases. Animals are full of aberrations, from paramecia up through porcupines and man, and they seem to be ready for anything any time, although most of them prefer to fertilize a heterosexual mate according to the standard operating procedure of their kind. So we should not suppose that human beings are different because they don't have a stereotyped sex life.

QUESTION: You imply that the real purpose of sex is impregnation. If so, what about immediate gratification and the "Wow"?

ANSWER: It's reassuring to know that it's there for procreation, but most human sex is done for the Wow, and animal sex, too, since animals probably don't know about impregnation. If human beings didn't make it more complicated than fertilization requires, there wouldn't be much to talk about. People would just do it for the immediate gratification, and impregnation would follow naturally when circumstances were right.

QUESTION: But that's why we have a population explosion —because some people don't know that sex leads to impregnation. So isn't it necessary to discuss it with them?

ANSWER: I don't believe anybody is that stupid, really. Anthropologists used to say that some people didn't know the connection, but I've traveled in lots of countries, includ-

ing New Guinea, and I just don't believe it. There's something else going on. As some people say: "If we could only send our bright young people over there to explain to them that sex has something to do with babies, they would use their contraceptives." But it doesn't work. It's not ignorance that keeps people from using contraceptives, and I don't believe it's poverty either, because even if you give contraceptives away, people won't use them if they're not inclined to. So it's neither ignorance nor poverty, it's something else, something more deep-seated. Maybe poor benighted people want to be immortal, too.

QUESTION: Do you think talking about sex is exploiting it?

ANSWER: Maybe, but it doesn't work too well. It isn't true that sex sells more products than anything else does. There are an awful lot of cornflakes sold nowadays without sex, and there are lots of other products sold without it too. I'm sure that they outnumber the products that sex does sell. Phony sex ads sell phony products, like chromy cars and soap operas. I think the answer to the question is that you can exploit phony people but you can't exploit real ones.

QUESTION: How do you link economics with sex? Sex is closely tied up with the family, and the family is an economic unit. Is this a true relationship, this economic sex?

ANSWER: I don't believe the family is an economic unit, although it can be used as one. I don't believe real people get married for economic reasons, although they may include them or get married in spite of them. I have a prejudice against the idea of the family as an economic unit; it is used by Engels, for one, as a false premise to lead to false conclusions and false actions. It's like the idea of culture, which to me is an academic term that has little value except to administrators, moneymakers, and economists, and to those who want research grants, but not to any living people. As far as the individual is concerned, culture is for jerks. The majority, which is 51 percent of people, can do pretty much as they like within the law, and if they choose to do as every-

body else does, that's a good way to avoid responsibility, and that's what I mean by a jerk. And laws are not culture, because they can be made by politicians, or even by one politician, and reversed by politicians, or even by one politician. Culture in my estimation is just an old suit of clothes that can be changed overnight, as shown by Hitler and Stalin and Ataturk, and the people in Margaret Mead's village. I don't see any reason to take an old suit of clothes seriously just because most people look serious about it. Culture is the Emperor's old clothes, the perpetuated errors of previous generations.

QUESTION: Why are bedroom people winners and bathroom people losers?

ANSWER: Let's take the clearest possible situation, because what you see there can apply to other situations. The simplest way to study winners and losers is to play poker with them. There is no problem there in telling which is which, no questionnaires and no research and no doubts. You only have to know one thing: what they have in their pockets when they get outside the door. Now if you're an experienced poker player, you can tell within three hands usually whether a newcomer is a winner or a loser. He may win all three, but you still know he's a loser, or he may lose all three and you still know he's a winner. Here's how you tell a loser. First, he thinks poker is a game of luck. So if he gets bad cards he gets mad and says: "My luck's not with me tonight." Maybe he even slams his cards on the table. Secondly, he If Only's and I Shoulda's. "If only I had stayed in," "If only I had gone out," "I shoulda drawn three insteada two," and so forth. Thirdly, after the hand is finished he wants to do it over, and says: "Let me see the next card that I woulda got if only I'd got the next card insteada this card." The winners may say the same things to be good fellows, or to con the other players, but they don't really mean it. They know that if they lost the hand, they played it wrong or got bad cards, that's all there is to it, and cursing

won't help. They can wait for the next hand to do better.

A winner is a person who sets out to do something he decides to do and gets it done if it's possible; if he doesn't get it right the first time, he gets it right the next time. He knows that everybody makes mistakes—except winners. He doesn't let his Child or his Parent impair his judgment. That's why poker is a man's game. If there's a woman in the game, all the men are in trouble from their Child or their Parent—if they have a Parent. What would your father say if he saw you winning money from a woman? Even worse, what would your psychiatrist say if you came and told him you had won from a woman? You would have to spend your winnings analyzing why you did it before you could relax. So only scoundrels who are not going to psychiatrists can win in a poker game with women.

Another mark of a probable loser is that he uses a lot of bathroom talk. A winner may use it occasionally, but not in every hand. The biggest loser I ever knew, who wanted to throw everything into the pot, including his wife and daughters and the family ranch, talked that way all through the game, although he was very proper at other times.

So a loser cries: "My luck is out, if only and I shoulda." A winner says, "I won't let that happen again," and doesn't. Of course a loser wins occasionally, but he makes sure not to keep it, and a winner loses occasionally but he makes sure he gets it back.

QUESTION: What's the difference between ego states and roles?

ANSWER: An ego state is a natural phenomenon, and a role is put on. A person can play many roles without changing his ego state. For example, a person in a Child ego state can play the role of either a parent, an adult, or a child. Children do that when they play house. One plays mother, one plays doctor, and the other plays the little girl, but all of them are in the Child ego state. Grownups can do that too when they play charades.

QUESTION: Can transactional analysis shed any light on the occurrence of great love with great antipathy?

ANSWER: Only to analyze which ego states are involved and how the transactions got started. Thus the Parent may have a great affection and the Child a great antipathy based on jealousy. Or the Child may love the Child in another person and hate the Parent. Or the Child ego state itself may alternate between the two, just as real children do. Transactionally, it starts with Mother's ambivalence: giving food and taking it away, pushing for bowel movements and throwing them away, kissing the child and pushing him away. There's an enormous psychoanalytic literature which tries to explain the origins in early life of such ambivalence.

QUESTION: How aware do you think most people are of which ego state they are in at any particular moment?

ANSWER: Unless they've had training or therapy in transactional analysis, or thought a great deal about it, they aren't aware at all. So there are about three billion people in the world who have no awareness of which ego state they are in, and maybe a half a million who have. If the three billion became aware overnight, then everything would get better tomorrow morning. An easy way to do it is to listen to what's going on in your head, and then you'll hear your three ego states talking to each other. If everybody did stop to listen to their own heads, they would all become beautiful people and spread the goodies around, and that would solve a great many of the world's problems right there.

Parent, Adult, and Child ego states were first systematically studied by transactional analysis, and they're its foundation stones and its mark. Whatever deals with ego states is transactional analysis, and whatever overlooks them is not. So that's why an acquaintance with that particular discipline is necessary in order to be aware of one's own ego states.

QUESTION: What about people who realize that they're playing a role?

ANSWER: Realizing that you are playing a role is itself a role. I hate that kind of talk, a paradox that swallows itself until it disappears, but in this case it's true.

QUESTION: How do you get over playing games?

ANSWER: The first rule is to spend your time spotting your own games instead of other people's. The second rule is to try not playing long enough so your favorite players will realize you have stopped and they may stop, too. Then see what happens. If things go well, you'll get your reward in good payoffs instead of bad ones. For instance, a couple who play Uproar and get their payoffs through anger may discover that sex is more fun than anger, which may be hard for them to believe until it actually happens.

QUESTION: How can you say that kids know more about human relations than grownups do when we're learning more and more about it all the time?

ANSWER: What you're learning is more and more words about it all the time, but kids can still spot a faker faster than a grownup can. Grownups don't have permission to look at people or talk straight to them, but kids do have up to a certain age. So they look right at you and you can't hide from them. Grownups never look at each other for more than a few seconds, except under special conditions such as playing I Can Outstare You, or when they're in love, or in certain professional situations such as psychotherapy. If you follow your own eye movements at any social gathering, or watch other people's eyes, you'll see that's true. But if you want to know about people you've got to look at them, and kids are still allowed to do that. That's one answer.

QUESTION: What did you mean by preventive intimacy?

ANSWER: Intimacy properly handled may prevent cervical collars, low back pain, stomach cancer, hemorrhoids, and dull eyes. That's what I meant.

QUESTION: How long does it take a spinal cord to shrivel up?

ANSWER: Quite a long time. At first there is a hunger for

stroking, and that goes on and on: in a baby for weeks, in a grownup maybe for years. Then comes a point where the person gets irritable, and instead of receiving strokes gratefully, he tries to avoid them and won't receive them or "let them in." After that point is reached, he starts downhill, either naked on roller skates or fighting all the way.

QUESTION: What do you have to say about strong sexual mores and mental illness?

ANSWER: Let me tell you an anecdote about that. People go to Tahiti and say: "Isn't it nice, sexual freedom, and look how healthy they are." I know a very good reporter who went to Thailand and said the same thing. Well, if you want to know about mental health, you find out first about mental illness, and the mental hospital is the place to do that. Now, if you go down the street a mile from sexual freedom in Papeete, you'll find the mental hospital there. And in that hospital you'll find about the same percentage of mentally ill people and exactly the same mental illnesses as in any other place in the world, including New York and California. And if you stand in the dandy dance hall in Bangkok and look across the river, you'll see the mental hospital there. And in that hospital are the same percentage of mentally ill people suffering from exactly the same mental illnesses as anywhere else.

If you really want to be fooled, you can go to any small island in the Fijis, like Rotuma, and you'll find no mental illness there at all, and isn't that nice? But if you go to the mental hospital in Suva, you'll find all the mentally ill people from Rotuma, because that is where they were shipped. And the same goes for wild New Guinea and exuberant Africa and puritan Russia and China. So the answer to that question is that sexual mores in my experience have very little direct bearing on mental illness. Sexual conscience can get people upset, but that's an individual matter. As a matter of fact, the word "mores" I think only applies to very small societies such as villages, and is often misused, or at least

used to avoid finding out what's really going on, which is individual parental programming.

QUESTION: If your spinal cord is going to shrivel up without sensory stimulation, why not use hallucinogenic drugs?

ANSWER: Because then you may shrivel up your brain instead of your spinal cord. Ovid knew that 2,000 years ago. Also the stimulation should come from outside. Many people who come down from a heavy marijuana habit will agree to that. Drugs are instead of people.

QUESTION: You described the satisfied female. What manifestations do you see in the satisfied male?

ANSWER: His step is springy, his eyes sparkle, and his children laugh merrily.

QUESTION: How about going to a chiropractor to keep your spinal cord from shriveling up?

ANSWER: I don't like chiropractors. H. L. Mencken said they should be encouraged, because in a welfare state the only method of natural selection left is chiropractors, so he favored letting the people who want to go to them.

QUESTION: How do you explain the bounce and spring of a man who doesn't have a girl friend?

ANSWER: I don't know, but imagine what he would be like if he did have a girl friend.

QUESTION: In most of what you say you must be kidding. Are you ever serious?

ANSWER: All my kidding is serious if you can read it right.

QUESTION: Aren't you rather arrogant?

ANSWER: I act arrogant only when I feel humble because I'm not sure what I'm talking about. It's more fun to be that way. It's more fun for me to come on arrogant than humble, and it's more fun for the listener, because then he feels free to criticize. After all, you can't criticize a humble man. You either bow your head or crucify him, and I'm not ready for either of those.

QUESTION: You "put down" a lot of books. What books do you recommend?

ANSWER: See the following section.

B

A SELECTED LIST OF BOOKS

Interestingly enough, the best sex book, as valid for San Francisco and London as for ancient Rome, was written 2,000 years ago. It deals not with special titillations but with practical problems of everyday life: where to go to meet girls, how to start a conversation with them, how to keep them interested, and how to get by with limited funds. And beyond that, it deals with something that may be even more important: how to fall out of love with them if you're rejected. It also has a section on how to be sociable rather than athletic in bed, and one for women on how to improve their appearance.

The Art of Love, by Publius Ovidius Naso (43 B.C.E.–18 A.D.), called Ovid. Written 1 B.C.E. Translated by Rolfe Humphries. Indiana University Press, Bloomington, 1957. Paperback.

Regarding drugs, Ovid says:

"Philters are senseless, too, and dangerous; girls have gone crazy, given a dose in disguise; philters can damage the brain. Let unholy things be taboo. If you want her to love you, be a lovable man; a face and figure won't do. . . . That's not enough, you will find; add some distinction of mind." Which seems like very sound advice.

Next in line are the works of Havelock Ellis, which tell in a readable and poignant way the many variations of sexual behavior and the different factors that affect it. His case histories, many of them autobiographical, are as touching as

Victorian novels, and his comments are learned, fascinating, and reliable. He is human, not solemn or pedantic, and he has the added advantage of being educational and intellectually stimulating, since he cites many classical and medieval writers.

Studies in the Psychology of Sex, by Havelock Ellis. Written in 1898–1908. Seven volumes conveniently bound in two volumes by Random House, New York, 1940.

For those who are interested in the early development of the sexual instincts, Freud's book on this subject closely followed and drew from the work of Ellis, so that Freud's boldness set Europe in an uproar just as Ellis's had done to England. It is difficult reading, however, with words like "phylogenetic" and "ontogenetic," and the translations tend to be clumsy in their attempts to stick to the precise meaning and flavor of the original. But it is worth exploring to see what was going on in those days when sex and psychoanalysis were still unpopular subjects with most people.

Three Essays on the Theory of Sexuality, by Sigmund Freud. Written in 1905. Published as *Three Contributions to the Theory of Sex.* E. P. Dutton & Company, New York. Paperback.

In order to get a clearer idea of the psychoanalytic approach to sex, Ferenczi's essays are much easier reading.

Sex and Psycho-Analysis, by Sandor Ferenczi. Written 1906–1914. Dover Publications, New York, 1957. Paperback.

This book also contains papers on other psychoanalytic subjects, but the articles on impotence, masturbation, male homosexuality, and especially the one on obscene words, give a good view of psychoanalytic thinking on these matters.

So much for older works. Those who need reassurance or justification, or want to satisfy their curiosity about the habits of their betters or worsers, will want to look through the two chief works of Kinsey and his associates:

Sexual Behavior in the Human Male, by Alfred C. Kinsey, Wardell B. Pomeroy, and Clyde E. Martin. W. B. Saunders Company, Philadelphia and London, 1948, and *Sexual Behavior in the Human Female*, by the same authors plus Paul H. Gebhard, from the same publisher, 1953.

The most valuable and important parts of these books, however, are the first 153 pages (Part I) of the book on males, and the first 97 pages (Part I) of the book on females. These sections describe the methods and problems involved in this type of research, and show how unreliable most numerical studies of sexual matters are. Kinsey's group interviewed 12,000 people and plans eventually to interview 88,000 more. They show clearly why statistical studies of smaller numbers are of little value, and help to nourish a healthy attitude of skepticism in the reader so that he will hopefully lose confidence in statistics about fewer than 1,000 people. This will keep him from entertaining erroneous beliefs which he might get from reading other statistics about sex based on small numbers of people.

But it should disillusion him only about overeager statisticians and their computers, however, and not about serious thinkers, who can deal very ably with smaller numbers or draw valid conclusions from a single case. In order to get a broader understanding of what is going on with sex nowadays, he might want to know about sexual customs and practices in various parts of the world and among higher animals, as well as the physiological factors that influence sexual behavior. For that he should read:

Patterns of Sexual Behavior, by Clellan S. Ford and Frank A. Beach. From lectures delivered in 1949. Harper & Brothers, New York, 1951.

This book deals with sexual behavior in 190 human societies and a large number of primate and other mammalian groups.

A fascinating book about the sex lives of animals all the way up the scale from the simplest cells through worms, in-

sects, fish, birds, and us people, has been translated from the German.

The Sex Life of the Animals, by Herbert Wendt. Translated by Richard and Clara Winston. First published in 1962. Simon and Schuster, New York, 1965.

This is by far the most readable book on the subject, and here is where you will learn that although snails look dull, they have more fun than anybody because they are hermaphrodites and have simultaneous double sex (which may be called 138, 165, or 192, depending on how you look at it).

Then there is a book which summarizes a lot of the findings about human sex, together with a lot of other "scientifically established" facts about human social behavior and human behavior in general.

Human Behavior, an Inventory of Scientific Findings, by Bernard Berelson and Gary A. Steiner. Harcourt, Brace and World, New York, 1964.

Some of the findings are pretty dull, but there are a few surprises, and it is nice to have everything in one place.

The main thing about all these books is that they are reliable, and anyone who reads them can be as sure of his ground as it is possible to be in the present stage of our knowledge. They were all written by conscientious people of superior knowledge and intelligence, and some of them are quite lively.

The more clinical details of what happens during sexual intercourse should be of interest only to gynecologists, urologists, anatomists, physiologists, endocrinologists, zoologists, and psychiatrists, since they are the people best equipped to evaluate them. But a lot of other people would like to know about them too, for good or bad reasons. They are graphically described in:

Human Sexual Response, by William H. Masters and Virginia E. Johnson. Little, Brown & Company, Boston, 1966.

If you don't know what the origins and insertions of the Ischiocavernosus muscle are, or what a bilateral salpingo-oophorectomy is, you will not really understand what these authors are saying.

None of the above books, however, will really tell you what's happening to you sexually, or what you can or should do about it, if anything. What you need for that are some practical manuals. There are large numbers of these, many of them pretentious, sentimental, or sensational, and some of them inaccurate. The best plan is to choose books by reliable people, not all of whom may turn you on, but who will at least give you the correct answers where there are any.

Starting with the sexual interests and development of childhood and adolescence, there are two good books: one about just sex, the other about how early sexuality fits into the life course of the individual in his society.

The Normal Sex Interests of Children, by Frances Bruce Strain. Appleton-Century-Crofts, New York, 1948.

This is a rather elementary book, mainly slanted toward schoolteachers.

Childhood and Society, by Erik H. Erikson. Published 1950. Revised edition, W. W. Norton & Company, New York, 1964.

This gives a revised theory of infantile sexuality that is more understandable and useful than that of Freud, who was the pioneer in this field. But Erikson goes much farther than infancy and shows how sexuality, among other items, fits into the sense of identity and the eight stages of psychological development in man, with particular emphasis on youth.

For girls, there is a very sensitive book by an experienced psychoanalyst:

The Psychology of Women, by Helene Deutsch. Volume I. *Girlhood*. Grune & Stratton, New York, 1944. Volume II, *Motherhood*, is equally valuable.

Unfortunately, there are no books of equal caliber for

Boyhood and Fatherhood. Sorry about that. A book edited by Hanns Reich, *Children and Their Fathers* (Hill and Wang, New York, 1962), may be helpful, though.

Interestingly enough, there are more books about contract bridge than about contraception. Probably the best book on this subject is:

Birth Control and Love, by Alan Guttmacher. Revised edition. The Macmillan Company, New York, 1969.

Dr. Guttmacher is a man of impeccable qualifications in his specialty of obstetrics and gynecology (Johns Hopkins, Mount Sinai Hospital, Harvard), and from him you can be sure that you are getting the best and last word on the subject. He includes a section on impregnation and birth.

A marriage manual by a husband and wife who were concerned for many years about problems of fertility, contraception, and the enjoyment of marriage is called:

A Mariage Manual, by Hannah and Abraham Stone (revised edition). Simon and Schuster, New York, 1952.

This is recommended because the Stones are both reliable and experienced people of sound scientific background.

Square swingers can keep up with the latest developments in their fields through the girl's magazine, *Cosmopolitan*, and the boy's magazine, *Playboy*. Older people can find useful though slightly prissy information in:

Everything you always wanted to know about sex, by David Reuben, M.D. David McKay Company, New York, 1969.

If you have questions which are too far out to be answered by any of the titles given above, you may find what you want in Dr. Schoenfeld's interesting collection of questions and answers from the old *Berkeley Barb*.

Dr. Hip Pocrates, by Eugene Schoenfeld. Grove Press, New York, 1969.

Anyone who has read carefully this short list of fewer than 20 books can consider that he or she is exceptionally well informed in the field of sex—historically, theoretically, and practically.

And a final word, on the subject of pornography. This comes in three varieties.

(1) Literary realism (Joyce's *Ulysses*, Roth's *Portnoy's Complaint*). This includes books worth reading for themselves, which happen to contain sexual scenes.

(2) Erotica (found nowadays in reputable bookstores). These come as paperbacks with well-designed jackets and evocative titles. Their purpose is erotic stimulation of a reasonably healthy variety, buried with at least a pretense of style in some sort of plausible plot. *Evergreen* magazine belongs about halfway between (1) and (2).

(3) Filth (found in cigar stores that sell racing forms). This comes in paperbacks with plain covers and titles that are either common street slang or low-grade puns. They are often proctoscopic and are usually bummers.

8

A MAN
OF THE
WORLD

Both Cyprian St. Cyr, mentioned in the Foreword, and his friend Dr. Horseley pride themselves upon being men of the world. Some of their paragraphs and short sayings are worth recording here. But these are like after-dinner mints, to be taken a few at a time, and not all at once.

—
A
—

LOVE AND MARRIAGE

What happens is more interesting than how things are made, and how things grow is more interesting than what happens. Thus a mystery story tells how a plot is constructed, while a novel tells what really happened. But a Russian novel tells how people grow, and that is why Tolstoi and Dostoevski are the men to beat. In the same way, sexual intercourse is more interesting than sex organs, and the

growth of an orgasm more gripping than sexual intercourse.

Stendhal tells us of the crystallization of love in a French and romantic way, where men and women have no freedom from watchers, and deception is the order of the day. The Song of Solomon tells us how a king can love a slave. But in our times and places, where selection is the problem, and not deception or confinement, it goes differently. Let a man visit an art gallery every Sunday, and this is what will happen.

First, he sees her for the first time, standing and moving, and he thinks, "Maybe this is it." That feeling already makes life worthwhile, and if he has too many doubts he should go no farther than to glimpse her face, so that he can regret it sweetly for the rest of his life.

But if he dares the possible disappointment of talking to her, he may end up knowing, "This could be it."

After that, when he is alone, he starts to dream about seeing her again.

When he does see her again, he wants to be with her all the time.

He starts being with her all the time, and then he need no longer have dreams, for his life has become one.

Then come the first quarrels, the partings and reunions, for they cannot bear it long apart, and the only question is which will stop sulking first.

Then they move in with each other, married or unmarried, and between lovings they quarrel about money.

Twenty years later they are inseparable. Their love has been tamed into an affection that will unite them till the grave.

When at long last one goes to the grave, the other soon follows.

¶ These, then, are the stages of sexual bliss.

¶ First, looking and hoping sweet hopes.

¶ Then seeing and testing in delicious anticipation.

¶ Then the conquest with its glorious sighs.

¶ After that comes certainty and confidence, with its smug feelings of superiority when other men throw her admiring glances, or even more perceptive strangers bow to her or tip their hats in her direction.

The final stage of paradise, unknown even to Dante, is when there is not only certainty, but a guarantee from what has gone on previously, of the highest possible degree of sensuousness, response, and surrender, the attainment of the unattainable. This guarantee gives such an ineffable splendor of anticipation to whatever goes before, the dinner, the concert, or the starlight by the sea, that even the admiring glances of other men become irrelevant, and the whole evening is like a warm and gentle flight toward the interior of a golden magnet where you will be borne high over the earth on blue flames of pleasure.

Marriage is six days of excitement, and the world's record for sex.

Five more weeks of getting to know each other, fencing, lunging, and pulling back, finding each other's weaknesses, and then the games begin.

After six months, each one has made a decision. The honeymoon is over, and marriage or divorce begins—until further notice.

When a man meets a married couple, he too often thinks, "What could she do for me?" instead of "What is she doing for him?" If they have love, why look for beauty, brains, or sex, or the sordid pleasantries of money?

Middle-class husbands are like appliances. They come with a manual of instructions which you are supposed to read before you install them. They are guaranteed by the Church and Good Housekeeping, but the guarantee is void of you don't follow the instructions. There are maintenance manuals on every newsstand telling you how to keep them oiled properly. And when you have worn one out, madam, you can turn him in for a good price at the courthouse, after which you can stop worrying and send your clothes to the laundry. Then you will have plenty of free time on your hands, which you can use to sit around the house and bite your nails.

Middle-class wives are also like appliances. They come with a manual of instructions you are supposed to read before you install them. They are guaranteed by the Church and Good Housekeeping, but the guarantee is void if you don't follow the instructions. There are maintenance manuals on every newsstand, telling you how to keep them oiled properly. The difference is that instead of your wearing her out, sir, she wears you out, and instead of your turning her in and getting part of your money back, she turns you in and you have to keep up the payments. What kind of washing machine is that? No wonder some men prefer the laundromat.

The best age for a bachelor is thirty-nine. He is neither too old for the interesting young ones, nor too young for the interesting old ones. It may come as a surprise—an unwelcome or even a distasteful one—to people under thirty to learn that some of the sexiest women are fifty. As anyone who reads a novel by an under-thirty can see, sex between people over forty is considered improper and in bad taste. But the over-forties know that the young are too cocky and forget that a mile run covers more ground than four 220-yard sprints.

To every action there can be an equally happy reaction. Mr. Tolstoi had his roof built by Zenith Builders and his ceiling painted by Superior Paint Company, and used deodorants while listening to his hi-fi. Was he really happier than Mr. Shortstoi, who had his foundation laid by Nadir Concrete and his floor varnished by Inferior Paint Company, and used odorants while listening to his low-fi? Does a dwarf giant hamburger really taste better than a giant dwarf hamburger, as the industry would have us believe?

What you agree on is easy. Find out what you disagree on, what his demands will be, and what he will do if you don't meet them. You don't really know him until you've seen him angry.

In a divorce you are attending your own funeral with your lawyer officiating. There is really nothing you can do. Let him take charge, and play it cool like a good corpse should. It will be easier for you to come back to life after the wake is over.

A woman sitting in a short skirt must perpetually classify men out of the corner of her eye, and that is her hell. There are those who avert their gazes when they talk to her. These are scared or hard to get. There are those who look boldly at her thighs, the frankly sexual; and those who steal looks slyly, the dirty young men. There are those who look only at her face, the ones who don't need her. Then there are the ones who look first at her face and then at her thighs, and for them she is a person first and a sexual object after that.

Those who look away can be seduced, the bold used, the sly humiliated, the respectful respected, and the last loved. All this is noted by her and decided without a word or even

a glance in return, and she has known it all since childhood if she is a real woman. If she puts her coat over her knees, then she is waiting for something or somebody, or trying to make up her mind about some trouble; in that case she does not need nor want his glances, and the man has known this since childhood if he is a real man.

Women and their mysterious ways. Griping and nagging and then knitting you a sweater and cooking your favorite chicken. Saying they will not stay with you another day, and then if you say, "My, you look beautiful this morning!" they will stay with you forever. But once you are truly bound together by children, all this is less important, and then what?

The most common game played by women runs as follows:

"Do you promise not to kiss me?"

"I promise."

She wins either way. If he kisses her, he has broken his word and is no better than all the others. If he doesn't, she can say to herself: "That wishy-washy eunuch didn't even try to kiss me."

The man who is loved by a woman is lucky indeed, but the one to be envied is he who loves, however little he gets in return. How much greater is Dante gazing at Beatrice than Beatrice walking by him in apparent disdain.

If all else fails, here is a cantrap that will always work.

"The thrice multiplied panegyrics of all the lovers of eternity would but half describe your charms. The ten thousand joys of a thousand perfumed nights rolled into a doeskin bag would be but a mulberry compared to the Arcadian

pomegranate of pleasure which could be kissed in one fleeting moment from your lips."

If she doesn't appreciate that, she won't appreciate anything else you have to offer, and you are better off without her. If she laughs (appreciatively) you are at least halfway there. But then the other half is up to you, and you will have to come up with something better for an encore. That is the way it is with all cantraps.

An orgasm is like a rocket ride. First the ascent, then the blackout, and after that the burst of light as the golden apple turns into the golden sun and azure skies with the white clouds below. Then there is a glorious descent with a slow parachute until the earth appears below, streams and meadows or a city street. You slowly touch and bounce up again, invisible to the tranquil cattle by the stream or the busy passersby. Then you slowly touch once more, and then the afterglow and the deep refreshing sleep. It is Maireja the nectar of ecstasy that comes from Adhumbla or Sabala, the magic cow that gives you everything you want, which bursts into your mind like Tchintamani, the glowing jewel of all wishes. But, say the elders, all this is for us, since you might appreciate it too much.

—
B
—

SHORT SAYINGS

The sooner you make new friends, the sooner you'll have old ones.

The obstetricians say that menstruation is the weeping of a disappointed uterus.*

---

*EW: Garbage!

Knowing that Santa Claus is just Father is the beginning of wisdom. Knowing that your husband is just Santa Claus, so that you don't expect him to be real or there every night, is the end.

Real apples have worms, so you want golden ones. Well, do you like golden worms?

Your body is your friend. Don't treat it like an enemy.

If you can't see what's in front of your eyes, find out what's behind them, as Amaryllis used to say.

If you take away the big words and the solemn face, there is still plenty left, so there is no need to be scared.

Be willing to happen to somebody, and somebody will happen to you.

The trouble with a disagreeable wife is that she makes you angry. The trouble with an agreeable wife is that she makes you think instead.

With drugs you experience everything and understand nothing.

Some people look for anxiety like pigs look for truffles.

His mind was filled with hate and sex because he had no love.

There are no problems, only indecisions.

It is harder to give up failure than success.

The pube is the eternal triangle.

If you don't know which girl to choose, let someone else choose, and then choose the same one.

He tied a bunch of carrots to his head so he would have something to look forward to. He always did the right thing: he was even born on Labor Day.

According to the words of Bhagavant, women enchain men in eight ways: Dancing, Singing, Playing, Laughing, Weeping, and by their Appearance, their Touch, and their Questions.

Venereal disease is sordid because it is always second-hand. There is no such thing as a brand-new crab. Even if you acquire it in the highest quarters, and wear it like a badge of honor, its genealogy will soon disillusion you as it plunges to the most ignoble depths.

Whoever has had his soul turned to stone by Medusa's head will be Medusa's slave for life.

Women look at the trees, and men look at the forest. Men build, and women furnish.

Where there is a hare and a tortoise, it is best to be a winning hare.

The most disastrous attitude for a woman is: I need a man, but you're not good enough. Either don't be that anxious, or take what comes.

It is easy to tell the courting couple from the married one. The courting couple keep their faces taut while they listen to each other, and answer "You . . ." The married couple are relaxed, and answer "I . . ." not from ego but from uneasiness or ease.

Filial obedience. Her mother told her to be careful and wear her rubbers so she wouldn't get her feet wet. She also told her to drop dead. So like a good girl, she wore her rubbers when she dropped off the bridge.

Freud knew the answers. If you don't understand something about sex, don't say it's awful or mysterious. Look it up in Freud.

The reason so much is written about sex is that it was invented to happen and not to be described. Thus you can safely remember what went before, but in remembering an orgasm you spoil it. Those who want to remember don't really have one. A remembered orgasm is like a pie with a slice out of it, which someone has put aside to take home for a souvenir.

No man is a hero to his wife's psychiatrist.

Men like to be more masculine than the person they are
with. So do some women.

Dating bureaus offer dehydrated friendships. Add a little
moisture and you have plastic sex. Manufactured sex is not
as good as the home-made variety.

Here are some colors of different people's orgasms: cham-
pagne, all colors and white and gray afterward, red and
blue, green, beige and blue, red, blue and gold. Some people never make it because they are trying for plaid.

Some men are like snowmen. You build up an image of
them and then it melts away.

Since fighting and sex didn't mix too well, they gave up
sex.

Both are in trouble if she interrupts love-making to pull
some hairs out of his chest and tell him her troubles. She is
neurotic, and he has married one.

"I'd like to lay her" (with the implication that she wouldn't
let him) is blaming her for his own unattractiveness or impotence.

Uneasy women treat life like a boxing match. They lead
with their breasts, their bottoms, their vaginas, or their
brains, and always they feint.

A man's working effectiveness often depends on the phases of his wife's menstrual cycle.

In a car you remember incidents. On foot, you are part of them. A car is passing through; walking is being there. That is the difference between sex and loving.

Havelock Ellis confirmed: If you want to know next year's styles in women's clothes, look at this year's prostitutes.

Something not all women know about clothes and men. When a skirt conceals two or more different colors, such as stockings, legs, and other things, sex begins where the color changes, and grows where it changes again.

Unadorned spaghetti tastes pretty much the same all over. It's the sauce that makes the difference.

Romance is when a woman has woman-power over a man, and to the delight of both of them, becomes more important to him than other things.

Never return early, because goodbye is a promise that you won't.

Some men become impotent because they are overwhelmed by sheer overwork; others, because they are underwhelmed by sheer underwork.

One sign that a man's youth is going is hair growing out

of his ears. A more reliable one is when he talks about money instead of women at the lunch table.

Sex should be a treat for all the senses: sight, sound, smell, taste, temperature, and touch. Don't knock it until you try it. It's like money. If you don't have it, you're likely to be unhappy until you do. But once you have it, what you do with it is much more important than how much you have, and how you use it reveals what kind of person you are.

C

THE SAD ONES

Men drifted into her vagina and out again, without her getting to know them or them her.

After her trip to Kinseyland, she settled down on the Island of Monogamy.

Alive, millions claimed her every day. Dead, her body lay in the morgue unclaimed for many days.

Life is simple. All you have to do is figure out the most probable outcomes of various courses of conduct, and then pick the most attractive or the least troublesome. Only if you want certainty does it become difficult, because that you cannot have. Sometimes it amounts to deciding which of the things you don't want to do you should go ahead with. For example, each day a man may have to decide whether he would rather have his testicles cut off or his brain washed.

It is easier to sell people death than life, hence insurance salesmen can be more honest than those who sell encyclopedias.

What to do about death? Finish everything and then wait for it like a rotting log? Or leave some things unfinished and die with regrets? The art of living is to walk the earth like a prince, scattering apples wherever you go. The art of dying is to finish your own apple just at the right moment to say, "I am content, the rest are for you to enjoy at my wake."

D

FINAL RAP

Irresponsible love is an ego trip. If you love mankind but don't dig real cats and chicks, you're loving from your own container. Loving responsibility is real rapping. You've got to get out of the love bag and torque in to the real world of loving. There's plenty of balling on a violence trip, but it doesn't cancel out. If you're freaked out, a groovy smile is only a toothpaste ad. You've got to flip in to look and love what's really there, and that's what's beautiful. What you do after the ball is over is what counts.

A star is the glowing light inside the other person, distantly seen, brave soul's tiny flame, too bright to approach without great courage and integrity. Each person lives alone in inner space, and intimacy is out there. Intimacy is outer space, and if that's where you are, you don't say "Cuff you!" to a star.

APPENDIX: THE CLASSIFICATION OF HUMAN RELATIONSHIPS

A

INTRODUCTION

Structural analysis—the analysis of the human personality into Parent, Adult, and Child ego states—offers a consistent theoretical basis for classifying human relationships, both logically and empirically.

Psychoanalytic theory deals with mechanisms and drives and clarifies the nature of transference relationships, but it does not offer a systematic classification which can be applied outside of the treatment situation. Anthropological classifications deal with formal, contractual, and blood relations within the clan, gens, or tribe. The legal classification is a pragmatic one, designed to clarify matters of rights, injunctions, and sanctions. None of these offers a consistent, convincing, or comprehensive classification of informal relations as they occur in daily living, nor is any of them psychologically cogent and precise enough to have predictive value in

such situations. Prediction is one of the chief aims and values of the structural and transactional approach.

In the text of this book (Chapter 4), we have dealt reductively with observed phenomena, reducing complex sets of observations to simple diagrams. An *a priori* logical approach enables us to set up a consistent and systematic set of models with which living transactions can be compared. The discussion here will be confined to dyadic relationships, those between two people, although the theory is amply generous enough to include more if desired. When the number of individuals involved is great enough to form a party, group, or organization, new elements appear, and such social aggregations (strictly speaking, aggregations of more than two people) have been dealt with in a previous work.* The present classification, therefore, is intended to fill in the gap between individual psychology and the psychology of groups by dealing with two-handed relationships.

B

TYPES OF RELATIONSHIPS

I. *Simple Direct Relationships.* Simple direct relationships are those which involve only one active ego state in each person. An inspection of Figure 15 (which is the same as Figure 2) shows that there are nine such relationships possible, and that they are of two types: those in which the vectors go straight across, and those in which they are slanted.

A relationship in which the vectors go straight across is

---

*The Structure and Dynamics of Organizations and Groups. J. B. Lippincott Company, Philadelphia, 1963, and Grove Press, New York, 1966. This has also been published in German by Rowohlt Verlag, Hamburg, 1969.

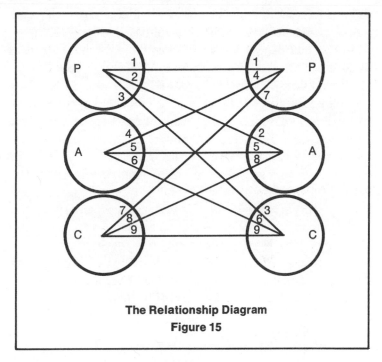

The Relationship Diagram
Figure 15

called a *Symmetrical Relationship.* Here each party exhibits the same ego state, so that they are on an equal basis, with a bilaterally reciprocal contract.

One in which the vectors are slanted is called an *Asymmetrical Relationship.* Here each party exhibits a different ego state, so that they are not on an equal basis, and the contract is skewed. It is evident from the diagram that there are three possible symmetrical relationships (1, 5, 9) and six possible asymmetrical ones (2, 3, 4, 6, 7, 8).

A family offers easily understood illustrations of both types. Schematically at least, the two parents are in a symmetrical relationship with each other, and in an asymmetrical relationship with their children. This statement offers an immediate yield in the hypothesis that if both clauses are not true in a given case, "something is wrong," and it sup-

plies a basic position from which to pursue investigation. Note that the equality is not a social or occupational one, but a psychological or transactional one. The same position can also be used to investigate secondary questions, such as: Under what conditions is it beneficial for a husband and wife to have an asymmetrical relationship? Under what conditions is it deleterious for parents and children to have a symmetrical relationship?

For a clearer understanding, let us now survey the diagrams in Figure 16, which represent the nine possible simple relationships between family members.

A. BETWEEN HUSBAND (H) AND WIFE (W)

SYMMETRICAL RELATIONSHIPS (S)

1. (P-P). This represents two parents functioning as parents. (Parents)
5. (A-A). This represents the same individuals as husband and wife, solving a practical problem. (Spouses)
9. (C-C). This represents them as lovers or playmates. (Lovers)

ASYMMETRICAL RELATIONSHIPS (A)

2. (P-A). This represents the husband encouraging the wife in a practical task. (Bolster-Worker)
3. (P-C). This represents the husband comforting the wife. (Comforter-Bothered)
6. (A-C). This represents the husband teaching the wife a new task which she is afraid of or resents. (Teacher-Pupil)
   The remaining three vectors (4, 7, 8) are the inverses of these.

B. BETWEEN PARENTS (P) AND OFFSPRING (O)

SYMMETRICAL RELATIONSHIPS (S)

5. (A-A). This represents a child and a parent working as equals. (Co-workers)

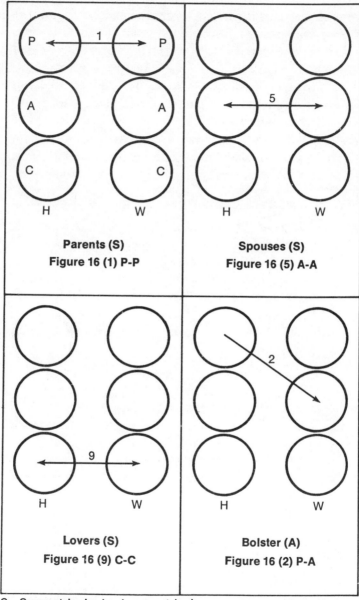

Parents (S)
Figure 16 (1) P-P

Spouses (S)
Figure 16 (5) A-A

Lovers (S)
Figure 16 (9) C-C

Bolster (A)
Figure 16 (2) P-A

S=Symmetrical A=Asymmetrical

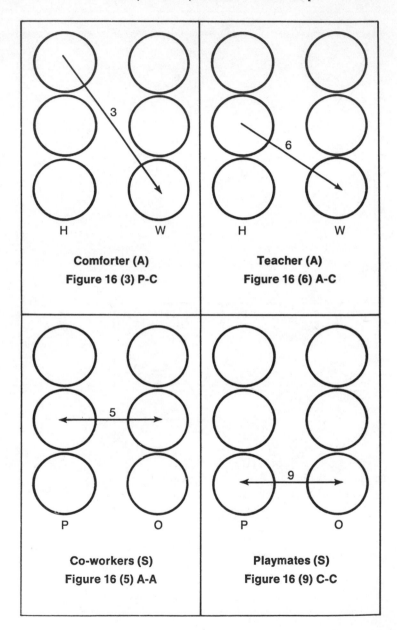

Comforter (A)
Figure 16 (3) P-C

Teacher (A)
Figure 16 (6) A-C

Co-workers (S)
Figure 16 (5) A-A

Playmates (S)
Figure 16 (9) C-C

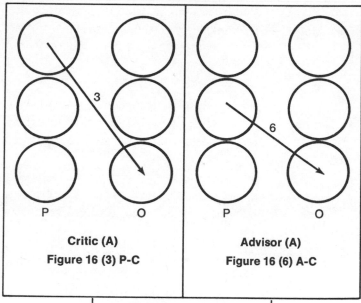

Critic (A)
Figure 16 (3) P-C

Advisor (A)
Figure 16 (6) A-C

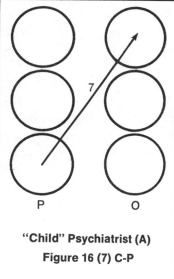

"Child" Psychiatrist (A)
Figure 16 (7) C-P

9. (C-C). This represents a parent playing with a child at the child's level. (Playmates)
1. (P-P). May also occur, as in families where the oldest child replaces an absent parent.

ASYMMETRICAL RELATIONSHIPS (A)

3. (P-C). This represents a parent encouraging, criticizing, or disciplining an offspring. (Parent-Child)
6. (A-C). This represents a parent advising or teaching a child. (Teacher-Pupil)
7. (C-P). This represents a troubled parent asking comfort from a child. (Bothered-Comforter)
2. (P-A). Is the same as between husband and wife.

The other two relationships (4, 8) are rare or anomalous.

Two children can have any of the nine possible relationships with each other, three symmetrical (which may in this case be called twin relationships) and six asymmetrical (which may in this case be called older-younger sibling relationships).

Thus, in all, the following sets of simple dyadic relationships are possible in a family with two children: 9 between husband and wife; 9 between father and each child; 9 between mother and each child; and 9 between the two children; a total of 36 possibilities, each easily recognizable, and each with a different implication. Triadic or three-handed relationships in such a family can be analyzed just as systematically and rigorously and profitably, the difficulties being purely schematic. The same applies to quadratic relationships.

This gives the complete array of simple relationships, which can be easily transferred to social relations outside the family.

II. *Simple Indirect Relationships.* A simple indirect relationship is one in which only a single active ego state is

exhibited by each party, but this exhibition is preceded by an internal dialogue involving another ego state. Examples of this have been given in the text under Respect, Admiration, and Lechery. In respect, there is first an internal dialogue between the Child and Adult before the Adult behavior is released; in admiration, there is a consultation between the Adult and the Child before the Child is released; and in lechery, a head transaction between Parent and Child, bypassing the Adult and urging the Child to go ahead. These are represented in the diagrams in Figure 17. Such situations are technically called "programming." Figure 17A represents a Child-programmed Adult, Figure 17B an Adult-programmed Child, and Figure 17C a Parent-programmed Child.

III. *Compound Relationships.* A compound relationship is one which requires more than two active ego states to sustain it. These are the more intimate and enduring relations of human living. Family relationships must be compound if they are to survive. In the family analysis given above, we have broken down what are actually, over any long period, compound relationships into a series of simple ones which might exist for brief periods.

Companionship, friendship, and intimacy are compound relationships which have been described in the text. The ego states of the two parties will shift under the impact of varying circumstances, so that in the long run all six of them will be exhibited at one time or another. Compound relationships may also be direct, or indirect with internal consultation.

C

DISCUSSION

To illustrate the value of this classification, two examples of predictive statements can be offered.

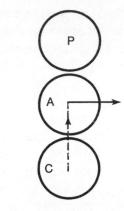

Child-programmed Adult

Respect

Figure 17A

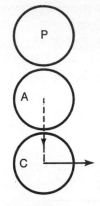

Adult-programmed Child

Admiration

Figure 17B

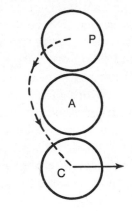

Parent-programmed Child

Lechery

Figure 17C

A. Simple relationships, both direct and indirect, tend to proceed smoothly until exhausted. People at parties can deplore together (P-P,1), compare together (A-A,5), flirt together (C-C,9), or console (P-C,3). They can do any of these smoothly and indefinitely until the active ego states are exhausted, and then the participants separate. Over a longer period, people can work together in an office (A-A, 5) smoothly and without incident, year after year, but they are usually glad each evening when quitting time comes. Incidents occur only when the relationship becomes compound by the intrusion of some ego state other than the contractual Adult-Adult ones.

The following example is instructive. A "leaderless group" met weekly for well-motivated intellectual discussion. Things went smoothly for about a year, but then the members began to get restive, although they wanted the meetings to continue. The transactional consultant they came to saw little possibility of the group surviving under the current simple Adult-to-Adult contract. He first recommended that they find a strong leader, but they didn't want to do that. He then suggested that they turn it into an "encounter" group, which meant changing the contract so as to permit exhibitions of Parental and Child ego states. This changed the relationships of the members from simple to compound, and the group survived for another year until new types of difficulties arose from the "encounters," as anticipated. These finally convinced the members that a strong leader was needed.

The basic transactional principle here may be stated as follows: In a simple relationship there is no possibility of crossed or ulterior transactions, since those require more than two active ego states. Hence communication will proceed smoothly and indefinitely unless and until exhaustion occurs. Exhaustion can be prevented by permitting the participation of fresh ego states to form a compound relationship. But that usually leads to games, which must then be dealt with.

B. Compound relationships tend to create misunderstandings, crossed transactions, and games, all resulting in "incidents," but they survive better because there are more gratifications than in simple relationships. The transactional principle is: In a compound relationship, communication may be disturbed repeatedly, but it is usually resumed because of the many payoffs available.

To recapitulate, a simple direct relationship involves only two active ego states. A simple indirect relationship involves in addition one or more latent ego states. Either of these may be either symmetrical or asymmetrical. A compound relationship involves more than two active ego states, and may also be symmetrical or asymmetrical. For example, companionship and friendship are compound symmetrical relationships, while the Roger-Susan relation described on page 145 was a compound asymmetrical relationship. The variables, then, are:

Simple	Symmetrical	Direct
Compound	Asymmetrical	Indirect

A simple, symmetrical, direct relationship is the simplest and straightest. A compound, asymmetrical, indirect relationship is the most complex and offers the most opportunities for games and other forms of ulterior transactions.

INDEX

HQ31 .B525   CU-Main

Berne, Eric. cn/Sex in human loving.

3 9371 00015 9434

HQ 31 .B525
Berne, Eric.
Sex in human loving

DATE DUE			
NOV 2 4 2000			
NOV 2 1 2000			
12/18			

CONCORDIA UNIVERSITY LIBRARY
2811 NE Holman St.
Portland, OR 97211